Other Books by Bruce Wilson

Death in the Black Patch

No Place That Far

Muckrakers 1917

Bruce Wilson

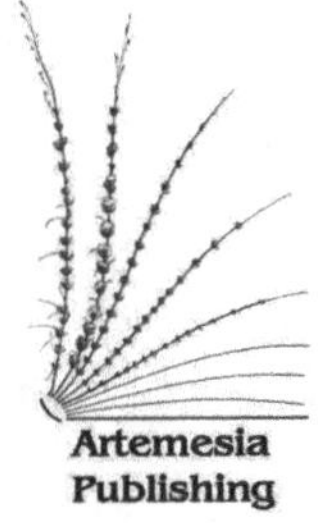

ISBN: 978-1-963832-17-4 (paperback)
ISBN: 978-1-963832-30-3 (ebook)
LCCN: 2025941024

Cover Design by Geoff Habiger

Printed in the United States of America.

This book was handcrafted by skilled artisans. No AI was used in the writing or cover illustration or design for this book.

Names, characters, and incidents depicted in this book are products of the author's imagination or are used fictitiously. Any resemblance to actual events, locales, organizations, or persons, living or dead, is entirely coincidental and beyond the intent of the author or the publisher. Some of the events in this story are true. Some of the characters are real and their thoughts and actions are the author's interpretation based on research into personal material. The story is a work of fiction created to fit the known facts.

Artemesia Publishing
9 Mockingbird Hill Rd
Tijeras, New Mexico 87059
www.apbooks.net
info@artemesiapublishing.com

First Edition

"Rather than love, than money, than fame, give me truth."

Henry David Thoreau
Walden

"A journalist is a person who is willing to report the truth regardless of consequences to herself or others… who is focused on reality rather than outcome."

Sebastian Junger
National Review

For Mary

Mary has always been my muse, my alpha-reader, my editor, my partner. Her insights and suggestions for change were always personal, but usually spot-on. Many of the changes she suggested made their way into this book. Unfortunately, she never got to read this final version, having lost her years-long battle with cancer. This book and my life are dedicated to her—Mary Wilson (1948-2025).

Prologue

LIGHT FROM THE RISING quarter moon cast a glow on the hillsides as the lonely wail of a single coyote drifted through the cloudless sky. The heat of the previous day was gone, replaced by the crisp, cool air of a southern Arizona summer night. The coyote, leading a small pack of females, crept into the sleeping town. The hackles on his neck rose when he stopped at the edge of a railroad track, his nose sniffing the darkness, sensing something ominous, unnatural. The pack shifted and growled as the rough ground trembled and the dust rose slowly like fog off a lake. Then, a bright golden eye, leading a snake-like ribbon of black train cars chugged through the darkness and slithered into the railyard, as if seeking to fill its belly with anything that breathed air. The behemoth's arrival drove the wild dogs out into the hills. The nearly silent clacking of the wheels across the seamed joints of the parallel rails seemed to hum and hiss. The sliding doors of the cars were ajar, and the odor of manure and decay trailed the slow-moving freight like a cloud, riding on the billows from the engine's stack.

In the deep shadow of a squat building next to the track, a dozen ghostly figures seemed to pulsate as the steam and smoke passed through their midst. The tips of their cigars glowed like red eyes, blinking, and shifting. The shadow-men's whispers and murmurs were barely discernible over the softly chugging engine as it rolled past them and then ceased altogether when the monster rolled to a stop.

As the engine noise faded, those same shadow-men walked swiftly to their cars and drove away from the railyard headed to Bisbee and the Copper Queen Mine offices. Within minutes, they walked into the large boardroom and joined the mine managers and city leaders.

"Well?" asked the general manager.

When none of the other men who had attended the train's arrival spoke up, the sheriff, Harry Wheeler, cleared his throat and said, "the train's here, sir, and it's long enough to carry most of the strikers."

"Excellent," said the manager, "now we can truly break the strike." He looked around the table and added, "At the same time, we can get rid of the foreigners and traitors and get back to making some money."

Exclamations of assent filled the room.

"Are you ready, Sheriff? Do you have enough deputies to gather up these traitors?"

"Yes sir, I do. Nearly two thousand of 'em."

Addressing the others, the manager said, "Alright then, let's go over the schedule and then get home for a few hours rest."

At two o'clock, Wheeler drove to his office and, rather than trying to sleep, drank a cup of bourbon enhanced coffee while he cleaned his pistol and made certain it was loaded.

"Come dawn," he said to the empty room, "Bisbee's gonna be a different town."

Chapter 1

The Bisbee Daily Review

ALL WOMEN AND CHILDREN KEEP OFF STREETS TODAY

Bisbee, July 12, 1917

I have formed a Sheriff's Posse of twelve hundred men in Bisbee and one thousand in Douglas, all loyal Americans, for the purpose of arresting on charges of vagrancy, treason and of being disturbers of the peace of Cochise County, all those strange men who have congregated here from other parts and sections for the purpose of harassing and intimidating all men who desire to pursue their daily toils. I am continually told of threats and insults heaped upon the working men of this district by so-called strikers, who are strange to these parts yet who presume to dictate the manner of life of the people of this district. All arrested persons shall be treated humanely and their cases examined with justice and care. I hope no resistance will be made for I desire no bloodshed. However, I am determined if resistance is made, it shall be quickly and effectively overcome.

HARRY C. WHEELER
Sheriff Cochise County, Ariz.

THE LIGHT FROM THE rising sun had not yet reached the streets of downtown Bisbee, but on top of the hills above Main Street and at the massive open-pit copper mine to the southeast, it flared brilliantly in the crystal blue sky. The day was going to be hot and the plans made by the Workman's Loyalty League would be equally as heated. Members of this Sheriff's posse had been awake for several hours and were spread throughout town, ready to follow their orders. By the time the newspapers had been delivered to the merchants and thrown onto the porches and yards of the city's residents, the roundup of striking miners and their sympathizers had begun.

Most of the miners lived in shacks scattered all over the terraced hills of the desert community. Some of the homes were substantial, but most were not. Thus, it was not difficult for the well-armed deputies to force their way through the doorways, grab the striking miners, and drag them out onto the paths and streets.

In a clean, two-room cabin far up Brewery Gulch, twenty-year-old Henry Carter finished his breakfast, rinsed out the cup and bowl, and got dressed for work, putting on his vest and newsboy cap. He sat on the edge of the bed, tied his shoes, and then reached for his coat as the door of the cabin burst inward and two men rushed into the room.

"Alright, Wobbly, hands up," yelled a hefty, red-faced man.

"What's going on? Get outta my house," Henry yelled, dropping his coat on the floor. Caught off guard by their sudden appearance, he fumbled for the hatchet by the woodpile.

The second man pointed a shotgun at Henry and said, "Don't do it! You heard the deputy, put your hands up and get outside."

When Henry hesitated, the red-faced deputy pointed a large pistol at his chest. "Let's go! Now!" Suddenly angry at Henry's defiance, he pushed him aside and barged across the room, knocking over the chair and sweeping the dishes off the counter and onto the floor.

"Stop that! What're you doing?"

"Shut up and get movin'. Your name's on the list, so get outside."

"What list?" Henry's voice was strong and, even amidst the confusion, he tried to reason with the two men. "What's this all about?" He struggled, pulling at their hands, trying to get himself out of their grasp.

Ignoring Carter's questions, the two men tugged him through the door, holding him up when he tripped over the rolled-up newspaper on the porch. They led him across the gravely yard to the rocky, rutted road and shoved him into a line of other men. Some were Henry's neighbors and most of them were miners. Several of the men had busted lips and black eyes. Henry saw one man spit out several teeth which landed on the dusty boots of a deputy. Henry looked around, hoping to find answers from his neighbors' lips, but none of them spoke. When he tried to ask another question, a third deputy, a much larger and surlier man than the other two, stood right in front of him, pushing him backward with the heavy gut that hung over his belt.

"Keep your mouth shut or I'll shut it for you," he said, thrusting the barrel of his gun under Henry's nose. "Now get movin' and no talkin'. That goes for the rest of you traitors."

Henry glanced up the hill and saw dozens of armed men with white armbands—the deputies—pushing their captives onto the road. When he turned his gaze down the hill he watched as a woman screaming for her man was pushed back into her cabin by a posse member. Her husband yelled at the outrage but was clubbed by an axe handle and went down on his knees. The deputies laughed and made two other strikers carry the unconscious man. Henry heard the woman continue to scream inside her home. *I'm going to remember this,* he thought.

"You can't do this," yelled an old man in the middle of the pack.

"This is illegal, we ain't done anything," said another.

"I ain't even a miner. I'm a painter!"

Underneath the comments and complaints, another sound seemed to push its way through to Henry's ears. There were moans and cries of pain that cut their way through the buzzing.

Angry wives and mothers yelled and screamed from their yards and porches. Others tried to comfort their small children as they cried out.

"Where are you taking my husband?"

"Don't let 'em take you, Hugo!"

One woman stood at the edge of her yard, her hands clenched into fists as she shouted, "Fight back boys! Hit someone! Make 'em bleed, too!"

Henry nearly stumbled over a man kneeling in the dust. Blood ran out of his mouth in a thin stream, forming clots in the dirt of the road. Reaching down to lift him up, Henry recognized the man who owned the small general store up the gulch.

"Are you alright?" he asked, then watched as the shopkeeper's eyes crossed and the man fainted. "Give me a hand with him," Henry said to a skinny fella on his right. "We can't leave him here."

The skinny man responded with words that Henry didn't understand, but he helped the reporter carry the old man to the edge of the road. A deputy ignored them as they gently lay the merchant down in front of two crying women.

"Can you watch him," asked Henry, "can you get him some water?"

But Henry never heard a response because another deputy pushed him back into the milling crowd of captives.

***

Across town, another group of deputies led by a mining shift boss named McRae, approached the home of a well-known union man, James Brew. Just as they reached his front porch, Brew yelled out through the screen door, "Stop where you are! I'll shoot anyone who tries to come in here and take me."

When one of the deputies grabbed the door handle, Brew fired his gun through the screen, killing McRae. Several of the deputies fired blindly into the house and when they rushed inside, they discovered Brew on the floor, blood pumping rapidly from the holes in his chest.

"We're in trouble now," one of them said. "We shoulda held our fire."

"Why? He shot first and killed McRae."

"I know, I know, but the Sheriff told us not to kill anybody, didn't he?"

"Well, I ain't gonna worry about that now. Let's keep goin', we got a lot more of these troublemakers to gather up."

Near the top of Chihuahua hill, a half dozen deputies approached the stout door of a cabin larger than most of the others scattered down the hill. According to their list, a half-dozen miners from Germany lived there. They'd been told by Sheriff Wheeler to make sure that the miners knew that Huns weren't welcome in Bisbee.

"C'mon outta there, you rotten traitors!" shouted one of the deputies as he pounded on the door. He signaled to two of the others to make sure no one snuck out the back of the building.

"There ain't no back door, Fred."

"Then watch them side windows. We gotta get all of 'em or the sheriff'll..."

The door opened and a large woman holding a cast iron skillet in her hand stepped out.

"Vat do you vant?" she asked, her accent strong.

The deputy aimed his rifle at the woman's chest and

said, "Get outta the way, we're comin' in." When she didn't move quickly enough, he shoved her away and she tumbled to the porch.

The deputy pointed his gun into the room, and followed by the rest of the deputies, he rushed in shouting, "Everybody outside, now! We're armed and we mean business. Get on out here!"

Almost at the same time, the deputies on the outside of the cabin broke the side windows and pointed their guns into the room.

"They must be in the back room, Fred, there ain't no windows or doors on that side."

"Both of you get in here with me, we're gonna have to roust 'em out."

The crowd of deputies aimed their weapons at the single door in the middle of the wall and Fred yelled again, "If you don't come out now, we're gonna open fire and anybody in that back room will be a dead German." He paused, waiting for a response and was about to pull the trigger on his rifle when the door opened inward.

"C'mon out with your hands over your head! Now! Do it!"

The first one out the door was a boy, maybe fifteen years old. He was followed by five men all of them mumbling in a language that the deputies didn't understand.

"Shut up. Nobody talks. Keep your hands up and move outside, now."

The captives moved slowly but didn't stop talking. One of the other deputies, Artie, swung his rifle butt and hit the oldest of the men on his nose, breaking it and generating a fountain of blood. The old man started to slide to the floor but was caught up by the miner behind him.

"I said no talkin', now get outside."

The miners kept their mouths shut, but their faces spoke anger. When the boy saw the unconscious woman crumpled on the porch, he reached down to help her and Fred jammed the rifle barrel into his ribs. One of the other captives started to turn on the deputy but was held back when Fred cocked the rifle and pointed it at the boy.

"All of you get goin'. This town don't want any German trash livin' here and we don't care if you get hurt on the way out of our city."

Artie pushed the group from the rear, while Fred and the other deputies prodded them to the road with their gun barrels. The boy held his arm to his bruised ribs while trying to hold back the tears in his eyes. From behind them the men heard the woman moan, but they couldn't help her. The old man cried out her name, but he was quickly shushed by the man holding him up.

As they reached the road, they were joined by two other groups of deputies pushing a small crowd of men down the hill. Some of their captives were limping, others covering bloody wounds on their heads and faces. Though no one dared to speak, their moans and coughs spoke volumes.

Sheriff Wheeler *had* warned the posse to avoid violence, but that didn't stop the deputies from manhandling the miners and beating some of them. At a number of the homes, they abused women and even stole property. The Sheriff, his backers, and the posse had just one thing in mind: gathering up the foreigners, the strikers, and their sympathizers, and getting them down to the train depot. By the time he'd reached the saloons on Brewery Gulch, Henry had seen dozens of men hauled from their homes. He'd watched deputies carrying things from the emptying cabins, and he'd heard several more crying and wailing women.

As the deputies herded their captives, Henry tried to keep track of what he heard and saw. Almost like a mantra, he repeated the phrases to himself, tried to picture in his mind what he'd observed—the strange dialects, the bruises, broken bones, and black eyes. He felt, more than saw, that the angrier men ended up in the middle of the mob and the frail and injured drifted to the edges. At the same time, the anger and encouragement from the supporters and families who trailed along behind and along the edges of the captives grew louder.

When they passed the Western Union office, Henry watched as Rosa McKay, a state representative was knocked down by a deputy as she tried to enter the building.

"Building's closed," he growled.

"Not to me it isn't, she shouted. "Do you know who I am?"

"No, I don't. I don't care if you're the president's mother, you're not going in."

"I'm the Arizona State Representative for Cochise County, so you'd better get that gun out of my face and let me in or I'll have you arrested." The man seemed to consider her point just long enough for her to push him out of the way. She marched up to the counter and began to scribble a message to the Governor's office.

As representative of state from Cochise County I am asking protection for the women and children...

Henry Carter pushed his way toward the edge of the crowd hoping to recognize someone beyond the circle of deputies. But so far, he'd been unsuccessful. As he waited to find out what was going to happen, he noticed that most of the men around him weren't speaking. Even those who dared to do so spoke Spanish or one of the many unrecognizable European dialects. *I need to get out of here and let the boss know what's going on,* he thought.

Some of the men, including Carter, had been standing in the plaza for a long time. The sun was beating down on the detainees and the deputies still hadn't done anything other than add more hot, tired, and confused men to the crowd. Most of the men were miners—union miners—and most of *them* were foreigners. As they sweated in the street, the murmuring grew, and they began to protest.

Their supporters in the crowd outside the ring of deputies yelled encouragement, but the posse made no effort to quiet them.

Then, seemingly without notice, movement started on the east side of the plaza. The deputies prodded the men with their rifles into lines and started marching them out of the city.

"Where are they taking us?" Henry asked, but the men around him remained silent as they walked away from Bisbee on the southeast road.

As he passed the depot platform, Henry heard the Sheriff say to some of the deputies, "Push 'em hard all the way. We need to wear 'em out, take the fight out, so don't let 'em stop or rest."

The captive miners and storekeepers continued marching east. They stumbled down Slag Dump Hill, past Sacramento Hill and Jiggerville through Lowell in the direction of Warren. Although it was still early, the sun was afternoon-hot and baked the long line of men. The dirt they kicked up from the road stuck to their skin and clothes, almost like the rock dust in the mine. Henry took off his cap, then wiped his face with a handkerchief. He couldn't even gather up enough saliva to spit the dust from his mouth, but he did manage to roll up his shirt sleeves and unbutton his vest.

When they turned north into the town of Warren, Henry figured that they were headed to the baseball park. But he still didn't know why. Even though they weren't allowed to speak, it didn't stop Henry from thinking. *It looks like the mine owners and the city decided to end the strike without negotiating. It also seems like they're getting rid of anyone who's not American.* He paused in his thinking. *So why am I here?*

As they passed the Douglas mansion, Henry looked up and saw several children leaning out of a window, watching the lines of tired, sweaty men. They pointed and laughed until someone, their mother or a nanny, pulled them back in and shut the window. One small boy kept his face pressed to the glass. Henry had a quick thought that perhaps the boy was trying to remember what he saw, but the thought drifted away into the growing box of memories in Henry's head.

The detainees were marched past a long line of boxcars on the track and through the northwest gate out onto the playing field. The deputies continued to surround them, but by now the miners' families and supporters had followed, yelling and screaming at the deputies. They rushed into the stands, hoping to find a spot to look out over the crowd and find their husband, brother, or father. Henry also noted that not all of the men around him were miners. He saw more shopkeepers and even some businessmen in the crowd and realized that something more than breaking the strike was going on.

Henry watched as an old, one-legged woman on crutches hobbled past the ring of deputies into the crowd.

"Where are my boys?" she cried out. "Anybody seen the Payne boys?"

A tall deputy kicked at one of her crutches and she fell to her side on the ground. One of the striking miners reached down to help her up and was clubbed on the back of his head by the deputy. Mrs. Payne groaned as she tried to pull herself up. Not even considering what happened to the miner on the ground, Henry rushed to the woman's side and gently lifted her up. The miner standing next to Henry picked up the crutches and held them until she was steady on her single foot.

"You alright, ma'am?" Henry asked.

"No, I ain't," she cried, turning her face to Henry as he wiped the blood off her cheek with his handkerchief. She looked at him and nodded her thanks, then got her crutches settled under her arms.

In the meantime, several of the nearby striking miners surrounded the deputy and forced him away from the woman, but he quickly drew his pistol, pointing it at them. The men began to yell and move toward the deputy, so he turned and ran away stumbling and nearly falling down.

"I just wanna find my boys," the lady cried out as she continued to push her way through the miners. She called out for her sons and stopped only when the Sheriff stepped in front of her and told her to leave.

"You're a dirty coward, Sheriff," she said, her hand reaching up to the still bleeding wound on her cheek. "Your deputies are brutes, and you know that my boys ain't strikers and they sure ain't union. Now get out of my way."

Even though they were being held back by the deputies, many of the miners began yelling in support of the old woman. The Sheriff, a short pugnacious man, frowned and looked around. Then he told one of his men to find the Payne boys and get them and their mother out of the park.

"We don't need this kind of thing going on" he said, casting an evil glance at the woman. Then he turned away from the angry, snarling men and strode off in the direction of the grandstand.

Once all of the marchers were inside the park, several of the mine managers rode horses around the perimeter of the detainees. On a raised platform, the mine foreman yelled through a large megaphone, "If any of you will renounce the strike, we'll let you go home and get back to work."

A lot of them took the opportunity and walked away, but they still had to face the displeasure of the union loyalists, who immediately began calling them cowards and scabs.

Henry made his way toward the line of deputies and spotted Mr. Greenway, the president of Calumet mining company, on a tall roan. He pushed his way forward and called out to the man.

"Mr. Greenway, sir!"

The man looked down at Henry from the back of his horse. "Do I know you?"

"Yes, sir. I'm Henry Carter of the *Daily Review*. I work for Calvin Langley." Greenway looked confused, so Henry added, "We met a while back when Cal wrote the article about the government's need for copper to fight the war."

"Yes, yes, Mr. Carter, I remember you."

"Sir, I'm trying to get out of here and back to work." Henry gently nudged his way through the last row of strikers. "Could you tell these deputies to let me out?"

Greenway looked around and spotted one of the deputies, recognizing the white armband they all wore. "You there, deputy, get this reporter out of here now!"

The deputy, a man about Henry's age, started to object but recognized the president, so he nodded and moved quickly toward Henry. With as much authority as he could muster, the deputy said, "You, sir," pointing at Carter, "step this way."

Henry walked past the deputy and up the steps into the stands and stared at the corralled miners. Beyond them, across the left field wall, he saw that there were machine guns mounted on top of two of the twenty or so cattle cars. The slide doors were open on all of the cars and the pungent odor of manure wafted across the field on the breeze. The urgency he'd felt to hurry back into town disappeared as he rushed out of the stands, through the gate toward the tracks.

When the train engine's whistle blew two short blasts, Henry watched as the deputies herded the miners like cattle through the gate and prodded them onto the cars. Carter watched as a dozen deputies pushed fifty of the strikers up the ramp of the first car, while others began to load the next car.

Henry ran toward the front of the train and stepped up onto the platform of the engine.

"My name's Carter. I'm a reporter for the *Daily Re-*

view," he yelled to the engineer. "Can you tell me where you're taking these men?"

The engineer leaned out the window and looked back along the side of the cars. He turned back to Henry and said, "I ain't supposed to say, but we're headin' east and leavin' the state."

Henry thought quickly and asked, "You're going to New Mexico?"

Again, the engineer looked back down the track, then he nodded his head, and said, "I can't say."

Henry ran around the perimeter of the ballpark to the road. He took one more look at the train and the herd of men being loaded on the cars, then walked as quickly as he could back toward Bisbee and the newspaper office.

Chapter 2

"Cal!" Henry said as he rushed into the editor's office.

"Hold on a minute, Henry." The older man continued to move his pencil across the page.

Folding the sheet in half and slipping the pencil behind his ear, Cal looked up at Henry and said, "Now what's got you all excited?"

"I got arrested this morning before I could get to work. I was in the crowd that got marched all the way to Warren."

"What? You were arrested?"

"I was. They came into my house and forced me onto the road with the miners."

"But why? You're not one of them."

"That's what I kept telling them, but I ended up in the crowd at the plaza and walked with them all the way to Warren."

"Listen, Henry, let me fill you in on what happened last night. I got a call at home from Mr. Brook, one of the mine executives. He told me to get to my office as soon as I could, that we had an emergency at the paper. When I got here, he and Bert were standing by my desk and he said that we needed to rerun the whole paper."

"Why?"

"I'm getting to that, Henry. Mr. Brook handed me a notice issued by the Sheriff and said it had to be on the front page of the paper, the one that Bert was already running."

"What was the notice?"

Cal handed him a copy of the paper, the same one that had been delivered all over town that morning.

While Henry read the article, Cal stood and walked to the window that overlooked Bisbee's Main Street. The foot traffic was anything but normal after the morning's event. There was an energy, an electric feeling about what had happened. He returned to his chair and sat down.

Henry read it again and looked at Cal.

"That's right, I was given no choice. If I refused to run it I'd lose my job, so, I worked all night with Bert to reset page one and we started over. We finished in time to start deliveries only a half-hour behind schedule."

"I didn't even see this before I was pulled from my house," said Henry.

"I don't imagine many of the other folks did either. I thought the Sheriff's plan would lead to a few specific arrests, not a wholesale sweep of the town."

Henry set the paper on Cal's desk and turned to his boss."

"Cal, I want to write a story about what happened to me this morning. You have to let me do this. You have to let me write *my* story about what happened!"

"This certainly is big news."

"But..."

"Let me finish. Henry, you don't have enough experience yet," he said, hoping to mollify his friend. "Now sit down before you wear a hole in my floor."

Henry wiped the sweat from his forehead and slumped into the high-backed wooden chair across from Langley. He knew better than to argue with the man.

"What I'd like to do Henry, is to let you write your story and then I'll review it. I'm not saying that we'll publish it, but I'll consider it." He paused, making sure that Henry was listening. "But remember this, we've got to be careful what we say about the town leaders and the mine management. Get started, take your time, do your research and make it a good one."

He looked at his protégé, making sure he had the young man's attention. "Henry, this isn't a story about a baseball game or a new store opening up in town. This is an important issue, a serious event. You're going to be writing about more than just Bisbee. What happened here today is about mines and money, about workers and families and about power, especially power." He paused, then said, "Are you sure you want to do this?"

Henry started to answer Cal, then stopped. He ran his fingers through his thick hair, looked at his boss and spoke firmly. "Yes, sir. I do."

"Alright, then listen to me. Some of this I've said before and a lot of it you already know.

"You need to find out who was involved in the decision to round up the strikers. That means asking people questions they won't want to answer. It means finding out details about the mining companies, the IWW—the Wobblies—and the copper market. A strike was declared last week. Was it the reason for the roundup or was there something else?"

Cal removed the pencil from behind his ear and pointed it at Henry. "I want you to be certain that you don't put anything in the story that you can't ensure is true. Don't write anything that *you* did not see or hear *yourself*. Even if someone tells you what they saw, it's just hearsay unless you qualify *who* told you, *who* they are, and then ask yourself if they are credible."

"Look, Cal, I know what I have to do, and I know that you'll edit it anyway. But I need to tell what I saw and heard and experienced."

"Go ahead, write it, but remember who your audience is. It's not just the people who buy our paper. It's not just the people who advertise in it. Your audience is going to include the Sheriff, important people in town including the mine managers, their suppliers and employees." Noticing that he was still pointing his pencil at Henry, he put it down. "Learn what you can, especially about the IWW. What do they believe, what is their objective here in Bisbee and elsewhere?"

The afternoon breeze coming through the window was hot and it ruffled the papers on Cal's desk. He put a rock on the top of the notes and walked to a filing cabinet against the wall. Pulling the top drawer open, he leafed through some files. Finding the clippings he sought, he slipped them into his coat pocket.

"Tell you what, Henry, let's go down to the St. Elmo. I want to give you a few ideas about how to write this..." he paused and then finished, "this epic tale of power and greed."

Ten minutes later, as they stood at the counter, Cal said. "I want you to look at something." He pulled the sheaf of clippings from his pocket and handed them to Henry.

"The world's changing, Henry. There're things happening now that even your Pa wouldn't have understood." He watched the young man and continued. "If I was you, I'd choose to do something no one else is doing, to be different, to be... I don't know... be bold, be a rebel, tell the truth. You can be anything you want, but you've got to work hard." He paused for a moment. "Do something only *you* can do, Henry. Write something only you can write."

The two newsmen spent the next hour discussing the day's events. Cal gave Henry a few more ideas but insisted that he not begin writing his story until he'd done his homework.

In the clippings cut from *McClure's Magazine* and various newspapers, Henry had read Lincoln Steffens' story about corruption in St. Louis. Ida Tarbell had written a lengthy and powerful exposé on Standard Oil. Others were about the meat-packing industry, the railroads and even iron and steel. Henry had, at first, wondered why Cal wanted him to read the older journalists' works. But Langley's reason finally dawned on him just after midnight. These reporters were thorough—they covered all aspects of the issues at the core of their topics. They wrote, it seemed to Henry, without fear of the trouble that would come to them from very powerful men. They didn't hold back when writing about corruption or greed. Then, just before he fell asleep, he recognized Cal's warning to him in the assignment. *It's like he's telling me to be careful, to tell the full story only if I'm willing to face the consequences my words may generate.*

Henry didn't sleep well that night. His experience in the roundup continued to replay itself in his many waking moments. He spent the dark hours in the cabin thinking about what he'd seen and heard. Several times he'd scratched a match and lit a candle, then scribbled notes on paper, hoping they made sense when it came time to write. He was glad he'd managed to escape the crowded stadium but felt bad about what had happened to the men in the boxcars. Being hauled away like cattle was bad enough, but that they'd been beaten and ripped from their homes bothered him.

Henry woke early the next morning, unrested and groggy. He thought about the story he had to write. He knew it would take a clear head to do the work, so he'd left his house and the noise of the mining town and walked to the crest of a hill at the far end of Brewery Gulch. For as long as he could remember, Henry had visited this remote part of Bisbee when he had serious thinking to do. But after spending the previous afternoon and long into the night reading the clippings Cal had given him, Henry's mind was full. The story of his arrest, the march, and his release was important and interesting. But he still wished his own writing had the style and power of the articles that the journalists—the muckrakers—of the previous decade had written. If he wrote articles like they had, he knew, or at least suspected that the powerful and wealthy men in Bisbee would not be pleased and would likely bring trouble to the *Review* and to Calvin Langley himself. *So,* he thought, *is Cal warning me not to write the story or to write it even knowing he can't publish it since the paper is owned by the mining company?* The sound of the wind as it pushed its way through the canyons was as soothing and mind-cleansing as a mountain stream in a land where streams were never permanent. Henry rose from the flat rock and started down the hill toward home. *What is he telling me?*

Even as he considered the potential consequences of writing the story, he began to craft his opening paragraph.

Back in his cabin, Henry Carter was surrounded by the good memories of his parents, his friendship with Cal, and the lessons, and losses that come with growing up. Sitting on a chair his pa had built at a table upon which his ma had served him thousands of simple meals, Henry stared at a blank sheet of newsprint. He'd sharpened three pencils and set them next to the paper. He closed his eyes for a moment, took a deep breath, and picked up a pencil.

By midday, the sun had warmed up the cabin and Henry wiped sweat from his forehead as he stared at the still-blank paper in front of him. The dozens of attempts to start his article lay tossed about the floor, some merely crumpled into balls and others ripped into tiny shreds. Henry's head pounded like a mill-hammer. The opening paragraph for his story, the one he'd pondered that morning, seemed childish and boring, yet nothing else he had written seemed any better.

Henry rose and went to the wood stove across the room. From a pitcher on the counter, he filled a coffee pot with water, dumped in some fresh grounds and set the pot on the stove. He opened the grated door and tossed in a chunk of wood, watching until it caught fire. Henry shut the grate and looked out the cabin's single glass window at the road and the hills that seemed to crawl, one after the other all the way to the eastern horizon. When the churning water pushed steam out the spout, he poured the dark bitter coffee into his cup. After he'd stared through the window for a while, he mumbled to himself,

"Damn it, Henry, if you're a writer, then write." He glanced across the small room at the table and saw what remained—the pencil stubs, and the snow-like mess of paper on the floor. "Writers write," he said as he kicked the scraps out of his way and sat down. Blowing the steam off the top of the cup, he took a quick sip and began to write.

By early evening, he'd run out of paper and decided to take a break. Even though the day had been hot, as the sun set, the oncoming night was cool, so he pulled on his coat, set his cap on his head and walked down the hill toward the *Review* office. On the porches of most of the cabins and small homes along the gulch, Henry saw women, some with children, sitting on the steps. They appeared forlorn, devastated, alone. He heard sobs from one cabin and angry shouts from another. The women who created the sounds were hurting in different ways from the events of yesterday that had separated their families. Some of them even called out to him, asking if he'd seen their husband or son. Others asked if he knew where they'd been taken. Henry wanted to give them answers and maybe even some comfort, but he didn't really know any more than they did. When he passed the empty cribs and whorehouses, he tipped his cap at the one which had been owned by Helen McHenry—a kind woman who'd once hired his ma as a laundress. At the bottom of Brewery Gulch he passed the St. Elmo bar, Cal's favorite place. Even though Henry had asked him why he liked it so much, Langley would never tell him more than that he'd once had a beer with a fella who'd been important to him.

He walked the few blocks to the office, opened the tall front door and walked up to the office, feeling the rumble of the press as it printed out parts of the next day's paper. The press foreman was standing behind Cal's desk shuffling sheets of newsprint around, seemingly looking for something.

"What's up, Bert?" asked Henry.

"Huh? Oh, evenin' Henry. I'm lookin' for somethin' Mr. Langley was supposed to leave for me before he went to Columbus this mornin'."

"Cal went to New Mexico?"

"Yeah, that's where they took them damn strikin' foreigners."

"When's he coming back?"

"He said tomorrow unless he learned somethin' new." Bert continued to move the papers.

Henry was frustrated. He wanted to talk to Cal.

"Tell you what, Bert, I'll go through all of this stuff, get it in some kind of order and then see if I can find what you're looking for."

"Thanks, Henry. It's supposed to be the advertising copy for the Copper Queen Hotel and I need to get the type set so it don't miss the final run of the mornin' paper."

"I'll find it and get it to you right away," Henry said to Bert's back as the ink-covered man left the office.

It took Henry about ten minutes to organize the paperwork on Cal's desk. He picked up the advertising copy and grabbed a ream of paper and a few more pencils, left the office and stopped to see Bert in the pressroom. By the time he walked out of the *Review* building, he was ready to go home. Back in his house, now fully restocked with the tools of a writer, Henry Carter once again sat down at the table and this time he truly began to write.

Throughout the evening, Henry had caught himself drifting off topic as he wrote about his experience. He felt, at times, that he needed to accuse the sheriff or the mine owners of the crimes he'd observed. He'd find himself making statements that would most surely create problems for himself and for Cal. But he realized each time that he'd not done the research, he had no proof of their involvement, and these passages would likely be cut out of the story by Cal. So, he kept going back to his story, his personal experience at the hands of brutal men. He wrote about what he saw and heard, and his words were rich with descriptions of beatings and strong-arm tactics by unreasonable authorities. Henry wanted his story to be as thorough and damning as those of the *muckrakers*, but he had heard Cal's admonition. He *did* write about what he felt—pain, anger, humiliation, and outrage—and made sure that he considered his audience. He knew that no one could disprove what he'd written because he knew that it was true.

The next afternoon, just two days after the round-up, Henry delivered his story to Calvin Langley at the *Daily Review* office and paced in front of the editor's desk.

"Give me some time to read this, Henry. Go get a cup of coffee and be back in an hour."

Exactly sixty minutes later, Henry once again stood in front of his boss.

"Have a seat, Henry." When the young man sat, Cal said, "Most of this is just your opinion, Henry."

"No, Cal, it isn't just my *opinion*. It's my own personal experience. I saw everything in that story. I *heard* every shout, cry, scream, gunshot, and crushed bone. I *saw* men with white armbands beating other men and assaulting women. I lifted a one-legged woman from the ground and wiped the blood from her face with my own handkerchief." He reached into his pocket and pulled out the cloth. "This one, Cal. This bloody piece of cotton."

Cal took the handkerchief from Henry's hand and set it on the desk. The deep red stain had soaked through several folds of the cloth, but there was no doubt in his mind that it was blood. Langley picked up his ever-present pencil and rolled it between his palms, pondering the evidence on his desk and the fire in Henry's eyes.

"You know, don't you Henry, that this is only part of the story."

"Of course, I do." Henry tried to quell his anger. "Damn it, Cal, I wrote a hell… a whole lot more about that fiasco, but I couldn't prove any of it, so I didn't include it."

"The story needs a little polishing," Cal said, "but it's good, Henry, really good." He watched the boy, thinking *he's already writing like a reporter*. "Here's what I'm going to do. I'll edit it and think about putting it in the paper."

"Thanks, Cal. I think I hear a 'but' coming next."

"You're right. *But* I'll have to clear it with the owners first. If I owned the paper and I was officially the publisher, I'd put it on the front page. If I was like McClure was in the nineties, I'd put it in my magazine. But I'm not McClure, or the publisher or the owner of the *Review*, and that means I have to get permission." Cal stood up, walked around the desk and stopped in front of Henry. Hooking his thumbs in the armholes of his vest, Cal looked directly into Henry's face.

"Here's another but," he said. "But we both know that this story isn't complete. We need to find out who planned and set up the roundup. We need to know who stands to benefit most from the deportation of the strikers. What do we know about the IWW and its objectives here or at other mines? Is the union really interested in the workers, or are they spies for the Germans like so many folks say?" He stepped back from Henry and returned to his chair. "We need to dig into this and find out so much more before your story ends up in print."

"So?" asked Henry.

"So, unless you get drafted and have to go to France with a million of your fellow citizens, this will be your new job. You do the research, you find the people involved, you ask the questions and compile the answers. Then, you will write the definitive story of this event, not the stories that lazy reporters will probably tell, nor the watered-down version that I suspect will come from the Sheriff's office. Your personal account of the event will be the glue that holds the facts together."

"Where do I start?" This was just the first of dozens of questions that began to fill Henry's brain, piling up on one another, pushing and shoving themselves, trying to get his attention.

"I suggest, Mr. Muckraker Carter, that you start at the beginning. Turn that empty closet over near the window into your office," he said, "and start making notes of all your questions, ideas, suppositions, and plans."

Henry stared at his boss, his lips moving, his eyes darting between the desk and his new office.

A tiny smile crept onto Cal's face. "*Now*, Henry. Now is a good time to get to work." Langley pulled some papers from his in-basket, sorted through them and began writing notes.

Henry turned slowly around and walked away from Cal's desk. His mind clicking like a telegraph key. When he opened the door to the small room, he saw that he had a lot of boxes, brooms and buckets to move. *My first office.* He looked back toward Cal. *He trusts me.*

Several blocks away from the *Review* building, in an upstairs office, the sheriff leaned across his desk and looked sternly at each of his half-dozen official deputies as they stood in a semi-circle in front of his desk. He had gathered them together to discuss what he'd learned in yesterday's follow-up meeting after the roundup. At that meeting, he had listened to the concerns of those powerful men about how the arrest and deportation of the traitors, strikers, and disruptors of the peace had gone. They had heard plenty of complaints from some of the more liberal citizens about the lack of compassion and restraint shown by the deputies, as well as their failure to deal with some of the offenses against individuals—especially women—who were neither miners nor suspected troublemakers.

The sheriff had listened to these reports but knew that the mine executives were unconcerned and had likely approved of the offenses, since they wanted to end the strike and prevent the foreign traitors from disrupting the war efforts of the federal government.

The general manager had reminded the sheriff that since the young sports reporter of the *Daily Review* had been gathered up in the arrests, he *might* be a threat to the mines' business and to the peace of the community if he should try to publish anything about the roundup in the paper.

"We don't want to have to publicly advise the young man or Cal Langley, the editor, to avoid any such anti-American information showing up in the paper," he'd said.

"We'll keep an eye on them, sir," the sheriff had replied, "and make sure they understand."

The gathered deputies weren't sure why they'd been called together. Some were likely concerned about losing their jobs or worse for what they'd done, but the sheriff quickly set their minds at rest.

"Some of the special deputies let things get out of control—people got killed, women got molested—so, I'll expect each of you to personally deal with those few men who had a role in any of that." He paused and added, "If you saw any illegal activity being carried out, make sure that the special deputies keep quiet about their involvement. Find out who it was who offended the state representative and bring *him* to me."

He then gestured to his newest official deputy and said, "I have a special assignment for you, Stiller, so stick around. The rest of you get to work." When the others had gone, Wheeler said, "I want you to follow that young reporter, Henry Carter. Keep track of where he goes, what he does, and who he sees."

"Yes, sir," the deputy replied. "You want I should stay out of sight?"

"Obviously." Wheeler stood erect, shaking his head. "And try to act like a real deputy. I want you to keep me informed, so give me a report every night before you go home. Got it?"

"Yes, sir, Sheriff. I'll get right on it." The deputy started to salute Wheeler, thought better of it, and left the office quickly.

Sheriff Wheeler walked over to the window that looked down onto the street. *What's this fella Carter up to*? he wondered. *He could be trouble.*

Chapter 3

For the rest of the day, Henry used up a lot of pencil lead and several dozen sheets of paper, none of which ended up balled or shredded. The reporter kept them all. He tried to remember all of the ideas he'd had while working on the personal story, but many of them seemed lost. At first, Henry was angry at himself for not making notes earlier but pushed the disappointment aside when he realized that those ideas crept back into his head while he worked. Henry wrote down each of the points Cal had made while they discussed his story. He even set aside several pages just for questions. The first lesson on journalism that Cal ever gave him was that reporters ask questions. So, on his "questions" page, Henry listed the ones he developed under six headings: Who, what, when, where, why, and how. He had learned that each category was important, but that not all of them were *equally* important.

He needed to find out more about the International Workers of the World union—the IWW, the Wobblies, its beliefs and principles and who the national and local leaders were. He thought he knew a lot about the Phelps-Dodge mining company but realized that his knowledge was limited to what he'd heard from miners in town or what he read in the paper. He'd forgotten most of what his pa would have told him before he died, but the accident that took his life was never far from Henry's thoughts.

The miners themselves were another topic entirely. Why, he asked himself, did some of them join the strike while others didn't, and why did some of those who *did* strike go back to work? What were their issues? Pay?

Safety? Not enough work or too much work? Henry also wondered if the strikers were rounded up because of their work demands or, as he suspected, it happened because they were foreigners.

He continued to make notes.

Several hours later, Henry stretched at the table in his small office. He looked at the last several sheets he'd written in this long and curious day. He believed that it was still a good start. Placing his palms on the tabletop, he pushed himself up and out of the chair. He took his cap from the hook on the wall, slipped into his coat and left the office. Outside, the air was clear and the stars were bright against the dark sky as Henry headed home to get some much-needed sleep.

The next morning, just two days after the roundup, Henry started some coffee and sat at the table to review his notes from the day before. It was early and the sky was crystalline blue. He felt good about what the day held for him and pulled on a pair of pants, poured a cup of coffee, and walked out onto the porch carrying his papers and his personal story. Henry looked up toward the top of the gulch and felt the breeze ruffle his hair, then stepped barefoot onto the hard ground and sat down on the wooden steps to reread what he had written.

When he got to the paragraphs about the one-legged woman, he thought of his ma and recalled something she had told him often while he was growing up. It had to do with the accident that killed his pa and how afterward many of the miners and their wives came by the cabin. The women had put their arms around his ma, and the men, the tough hardened miners patted him on the head. He'd not understood what his ma felt until she shared it with him several years later.

Henry turned his face toward the cabin door and remembered what she had said. "Henry, in a time of trouble, you can help heal someone's pain and their broken heart with kindness. Maybe not forever, but for just that moment, they'll not hurt so bad."

Standing on the hard-packed lot, he unrolled the story and read the passage about Mrs. Payne again. Then he knew what he had to do. He had to honor his ma and pay a visit to the woman who thought she'd lost her sons. He poured the dregs from his cup on the ground and walked back into the cabin.

Summers in Bisbee were always hot, especially in July. By the time Henry had walked half a block down Brewery Gulch, he'd removed his coat, hooked his finger in the collar and slung it over his shoulder. As he made his way down the rutted, rocky street, he was reminded of being in the crowd of miners as they'd been herded by the deputies. The street and cabins were the same ones from before, but they looked different, felt different. Henry sensed that *he* was different as well. Maybe not on the outside, but the experience in the march and the reminiscing he'd done this morning had changed him on the inside.

He didn't think anyone would be at the *Review* building on their day off, but when he reached the top of the stairs, he saw Cal at his desk.

"Morning, Cal," he said as the editor looked up from his work.

"What are you doing here, Henry?"

"I'm working on the story, boss, and came by to get something I left in my office." He stopped at Cal's desk. "Why are *you* here on a Sunday morning?"

"Getting caught up on my editorial," Cal responded. "What I saw in New Mexico was just as bad as what happened in Warren." He stopped for a moment, remembering. "Maybe even worse. The train got all the way to Columbus, but the sheriff there wouldn't let the miners out of the cattle cars. He said they weren't going to let any strikers into their town. Sheriff Wheeler's deputies couldn't convince the Columbus sheriff. They were forced to back the train up all the way to a place called Hermanas. That's where they were when I came home the other night. Those men were treated like cattle, and when they finally let them out of the boxcars, they were thirsty, hungry, and beat down. Those who hadn't taken off for the border just wandered around trying to decide what to do."

Hearing no more from Cal, Henry walked over to the file cabinet and took the city directory out of the top drawer. He carried it into his office and flipped through the pages. He found the entry on Mrs. Payne, wrote down the address on a slip of paper and put it in his pocket. "See you tomorrow," he called out.

Henry walked out of the newspaper building and headed up Tombstone canyon. He strode along confidently, with a natural grace. Usually, he was focused on his mission and keenly aware of his surroundings. But on this occasion Henry's natural vigilance was absent as the task before him took his attention. He didn't notice the man following him at a distance. With very few people on the street, the man tried to keep out of sight and Henry's lack of caution made things easier.

While he searched for the address, Henry thought about the approach he wanted to use when he arrived at the woman's house. Heavily influenced by the memory of his ma's words, he was going to visit Mrs. Payne because he was concerned about her well-being, not because he was a reporter.

When he arrived at her home, Henry put on his suit coat, took off his cap and stepped onto the porch. He tapped on the screen door and stepped back.

The heavy wooden door opened inward and a man about Henry's age looked through the screen. "Who're you," he growled. He stood rigid, tense, as if ready to attack.

"My name's Henry Carter, and I'm here to see Mrs. Payne," he said, his voice strong, but the tone soft, relaxed.

"Go away, haven't you done enough?" The young man

was tall, lanky, and, Henry noted by his clenched fists, seemed ready for a fight.

Mrs. Payne called out from the back of the house, "Who is it, son?"

"Just a second, Ma," the tall man yelled over his shoulder, then turned back to the visitor. "What'd you say your name was?"

"Carter, Henry Carter."

"He says his name's Henry Carter," his voice loud again.

"Is he wearin' a badge? Does he look like a deputy?" she yelled.

"Can't see no badge, Ma."

"Well quit yellin' then, and invite him in. What's happened to your manners?"

Henry heard the clumping of the woman's crutch approach the door and watched as the man stepped back to make room for his mother.

"Please forgive my son's rudeness, Mr. Carter. Come in and have a seat."

She pushed open the screen door and then allowed her son to help her get seated on a small, worn-out sofa. Henry entered the room, excusing himself as he brushed by the young man, and stood with his back to the wide window that looked out over the porch.

Comfortably resting on the sofa, Mrs. Payne directed Henry with a stiffly pointed finger to a seat across the room. "Please, Mr. Carter, sit down so I don't have to keep lookin' up and get a sore neck."

Henry sat, his face silhouetted by the sunlight coming in the window. He started to answer the woman, but another man, a few years older rushed into the room from the back of the house. He was sweating and held a chunk of firewood in his hand.

"Who're you?" he growled.

"Will you two quit actin' so tough and let this man speak. Be quiet and mind your manners." She looked across at Henry and said, “Please, Mr. Carter, tell me why you’ve come to my house.”

Henry lightly cleared his throat and said, “Ma’am, you may not recall, but we met the other day at the ballpark…”

Before Henry could continue, the woman exclaimed, “Oh I remember you now. You’re the young man who picked me up off the ground.”

“Yes, ma’am.”

“Boys, this is the fella who cleaned the blood off my cheek.” She looked at her sons, chastening them with her eyes. “He didn’t know me, and he helped me anyway.” Turning to Henry, she said, “Thank you for your kindness, Mr. Carter.”

“You’re welcome, Mrs. Payne. I didn’t want to bother you or your sons on a Sunday, but I did want to see if you were okay.”

“I am, thanks to you.”

“It’s clear that you found your sons as well,” he said, looking directly at them. “I’m glad they didn’t get herded onto the train.”

“No, they didn’t, no thanks to that crooked sheriff and his damned deputies.” She paused and looked directly at Henry. “What I’d like to know is what you were doin’ in that crowd. You ain’t a miner.”

“No, ma’am, I’m not a miner. My pa was though. He died in a cave-in a dozen years ago.”

“I’m sorry about your pa, son.” Mrs. Payne seemed pensive for a moment. “If you ain’t a miner, why were you there with them strikers?”

“I don’t know. I’ve been trying to find out, but so far, I’m out of ideas.”

“Excuse me, ma,” interrupted the older son. He looked down at Henry. “You ain’t a miner, and you don’t know our family, so why’d you come all the way here? Can’t be to check on my ma. There’s some other reason you’re here.”

Henry stood up; his cap held lightly in his hand. He looked at the man and then down at Mrs. Payne. “Ma’am, I was concerned about your injury and I just wanted to see if you were alright. I didn't want to intrude on your day or upset your family. If I've done that, I apologize." He looked at her two sons and added, "Sometimes I can't help but do what my ma taught me when I was a boy."

Henry stepped toward the door, nodded at the Paynes and walked out into the bright sunlight.

Hiding behind a tree across the street, the deputy pulled a small notebook from his pocket, made a note of the address where Carter had visited, and then followed him down the street into town.

On Monday morning, Cal and Henry met for breakfast at the Copper Queen Hotel. The large, open room was nice, the food good, and the atmosphere quiet. The paintings on the walls, the velvet-cushioned seats, and the tuxedo-clad waiters were in stark contrast to the cafés on Main Street. While they ate, they avoided talking about the roundup of the previous week.

"Did you get any writing done yesterday?" Cal asked after they'd finished eating.

"I did. Some at least, but there's so much more I need to find out."

"Were the articles I gave you helpful?"

"They were, boss. But instead of finding answers I ended up with more questions."

"You know, Henry, you could find yourself doing so much research that you never get around to writing the story."

"On the other hand, boss," he said with a wide grin, "we've read some pretty poor stories written by reporters who didn't do *enough* research."

Henry sipped at his hot coffee for a moment, then asked, "When will I know that I have enough background information?"

"What usually happens for me is that I'll write until I get stumped and then realize I need to do more research."

For just a moment, Henry stared down at his empty plate, then looked up at Cal.

"I've got some other things on my mind, boss. Are we in a hurry to get back to the office?"

"Of course not. What do you want to talk about?"

Henry cleared his throat and said, "What's more important about my story, getting it on the front page and in front of the people here in Bisbee *or* making sure that I can say why I was grabbed up in the roundup?"

"Well, Henry, writing the truth is risky. Reporters have to take risks."

"I guess I know that, Cal. But if I do write the whole story, the one that states names, my chances of getting it published in the *Review* or any other paper are pretty slim. It just doesn't seem fair or right to not be able to say what really happened."

"What kind of reporter do you want to be, Henry?"

The young man sat back in his chair and placed his hands palm down on the table. "I guess I'd better figure that out before I do any more writing."

Cal nodded and stood up from the table, left enough money to cover the bill and a tip, then they headed back to the office.

An hour later, Cal called Henry over to his desk.

"Henry, before we go see the banker, I want to talk to you about something."

"Sure, boss, what is it?" Henry watched as Cal picked up his pencil and rolled it between his palms. *This must be serious*, the young man thought.

Cal took a deep breath and exhaled slowly, continuing to roll the pencil. "Okay, let me ask you a question first." He looked at Henry and saw the boy he'd been when Cal had first met him. "Tell me what you remember about John Dawson."

Henry sat back in his chair and looked at Cal, trying to read his face, his eyes. He would always remember *some* things about Dawson, but over time he'd probably forgotten far more.

"Why, Cal?"

"Henry, this is important. What do you recall about John Dawson?"

"I'll never forget that I got caught in a flash flood right out there on Main Street and Mr. Dawson pulled..." he stopped and reached up to touch the still vivid scar above his eyebrow. "He pulled me out of the water after I'd bumped my head on something." Shaking his head as if surprised at the memory, he said, "I see this scar every time I look in a mirror, and yet I'd nearly forgotten where it came from."

Henry was quiet for a moment then added, "I remember once that Mr. Dawson came up to our cabin to have dinner with us." He glanced at Cal, "and he and my ma both seemed nervous and drank whiskey at the table. Ma thought he was special because he'd saved my life."

Cal remained silent, wanting to ask if there were more memories, but with the patience of a seasoned reporter, he simply nodded his head.

"I also remember the big fire, the one that burned down so many of the buildings and homes. I'd been up the gulch looking for my ma and I couldn't find her. I knew Mr. Dawson was staying at the Grand, so I ran down the hill through the mob of people and he was..."

"Where was he, Henry?"

Henry rose from his chair and walked over to the window. "He was right there, Cal," pointing down into the street. "And he said he'd help me find her, but he had something to do first." Henry reached into the pocket of his vest and pulled something out. "He gave me a gold coin, this one, and then walked me over to the corner and asked Helen McHenry to watch me."

"You still have a twenty-dollar gold piece after nearly

ten years?"

Henry chuckled, "Yeah, my ma said that if I hung onto it, the good luck from a good man would always be close by and I'd never be poor."

"So, here's the one thing I want you to know about before we go to the bank," Cal said, "I first met Mr. Dawson at the St. Elmo, back before they passed the law against serving beer and whiskey. We'd connected through a friend I had down in Naco. I owed this friend a favor and he asked me to do something for someone here in Bisbee. There's a whole lot more to the story, but what it boils down to is that Mr. Dawson helped save the man's daughter from getting into big trouble with a fella here in town. If he hadn't taken care of the problem, the girl might have ruined her life and destroyed the rest of her family."

"Mr. Dawson didn't just help my ma and me, he also helped the banker?"

"And me too, Henry. Don't forget that. He helped me find *you*, my best friend," Cal said as he looked into Henry's young face.

Henry and Cal were ushered into the office of the president of the Bank of Bisbee.

The banker, Mr. Thaddaeus Samson, was seated in a high-back, padded leather chair behind a desk almost as large as Henry's office. Behind him, on a credenza was a portrait photograph of the man with two women. His wife and daughter, Henry presumed. As they walked in, Samson stood and greeted them cordially.

"Mr. Langley, it's so good to see you."

"You, as well, sir," Cal said. "We work in adjacent buildings and still only see one another infrequently. May I introduce Mr. Henry Carter, my best reporter."

"Good morning, sir, I'm pleased to meet you," Henry said, his grace apparent to the banker. The flutter of nervousness in his gut was brief.

"Young Mr. Carter, good morning to you as well. Please

sit, gentlemen."

Cal and Henry sat down in the soft chairs across from the man's desk.

"Would you like coffee?"

Speaking for both of them, Cal said they'd already had some and that they didn't want to take up a lot of his time.

"Oh, I may be a busy man—we bankers are always busy with something—but I've been waiting a long time to meet this young man." Samson sat back in his chair his hands resting on his rather large belly. "You certainly have grown into a fine example of young American manhood."

A faint tinge of pink brushed Henry's cheeks. "Thank you, sir."

Cal spoke quickly, hoping to steer the conversation away from Henry's embarrassment. "Mr. Samson, I asked to meet with you this morning because I find myself in sort of a dilemma."

"Oh, well certainly Mr. Langley, but please call me Thad."

"Alright, Thad, I wanted to meet with you to introduce Henry and to see if you could help me with a problem."

Samson held up his hand and palm outward. "We'll get to your situation in a moment, Calvin. I want to speak to Henry first." He turned to Carter and said, "When I first saw you, what was it, perhaps eight or ten years ago, you were just a boy. It was just a few days after the big fire, and you and a woman, your mother I suppose, were part of a large crowd that had gathered in the plaza opposite the train station."

"Yes, sir. I was there with my ma."

"On that day a detective for the Southern Pacific Railroad, carried out an atrocious act, one so vile that it still rattles me to this day. He presented the dead body of a man in an open casket leaning against the front of the depot. There were women and children present, and this detective seemed unconcerned about the horror of his actions and how such an awful display might upset them. He claimed that the man was a known criminal, an arsonist. The detective bragged about his long pursuit of the man and the successful conclusion to his case." At this, the banker sat up straight in his chair. "You knew John Dawson, didn't you, Cal?"

"Yes, Thad, I did. I knew him quite well."

"Henry, I knew Dawson as a man of honor and decisiveness. He was driven, focused, and able to accomplish things that others couldn't." He paused, looking at his two visitors. "I became his friend when he resolved a situation that saved my daughter from making a serious mistake. I'll share this with you, but please keep it to yourself, since it's an issue that haunts her even today."

Both men nodded.

"A man with a bad reputation had been courting my daughter. Her mother and I knew little of his background at the time, but I learned of his habits and turned to Mr. Dawson to see if he could encourage the man to leave town. Mr. Dawson discovered the depths of this man's evil practices and, with the help of Cal, drove him out of town. John Dawson saved my daughter from a life of trouble and her mother and me from endless grief." He paused and looked directly at Henry. "You, young man, may have been just a boy, but that morning at the depot you acted like the man I always wanted to be. You stood up to that detective, told him he was wrong about Dawson. You climbed up on that platform and pummeled the detective with your fists. When he pushed you away, you threw a rock at him. You, among all of us on the plaza, had the fearlessness to oppose the man's lies. The dead man was not a criminal. He was John Dawson, a fine man known to many people in Bisbee."

Henry remained speechless for a second or two.

"Mr. Samson, Thad, Cal reminded me this morning about that day, and I had to confess that I couldn't remember much of it.

"But, I remembered, Henry, and that's why it's such an

honor to meet you and have you here in my office." He stood and reached across the broad desk, extending his hand to shake Henry's.

The banker sat down, turned to Cal and said, "Now, Cal, tell me about your dilemma."

Over the next half-hour, Cal told Samson about how much Henry was needed as a reporter for the *Review*. He pointed out that as acting publisher, he was unable to do the bulk of the reporting required to keep the citizens of Bisbee informed. Cal acknowledged that Samson was the head of the local draft board and that Henry had already registered and was prepared to join the army when he was called up.

"But frankly, Thad, I need Henry here. Some of my contacts in the New York press are considering offering him a position as a war correspondent," he said, "and Phelps-Dodge, the owner of the *Review*, has agreed to support the wire services if they hire him."

"That's certainly interesting, Cal. But what can I do?"

Cal paused, not wanting to offend the banker, or put Henry in jeopardy.

"I was hoping that in your position with the Draft Board, you could delay Henry's induction into the Army. Henry has told me that he won't do anything to defy the government—he's a loyal American—but if you could recognize his value to the community and be willing to endorse him to the wire services, should they ask for it, he and I would be grateful."

"Of course, I'm willing to provide a reference for Henry. In fact, I will do all I can to influence the rest of the local board to delay his induction." He turned to the young man. "But, Henry, if your country calls you, Cal and I and all of Bisbee know you would do your duty."

"Yes, sir, I will do my duty. Thank you for considering our request."

The two newspaper men stood, thanked Samson for his time, and left the bank.

Once they reached the street, Henry looked at Cal and said, "The New York papers are interested in me?"

"Don't get excited, Henry They mentioned it, but had to consider a number of candidates."

Since it was nearly noon, instead of going into the *Review* building, they walked a few blocks to Brewery Gulch and went into the St. Elmo to reminisce more about John Dawson.

Chapter 4

In downtown Phoenix, Henrietta Pearce sat at her desk in the busy newsroom and wrote another good article about a boring subject for the *Arizona Republican*.

Although grateful for her job as a reporter, Etta hated her assignments. *I want to write real news,* she thought, *exciting news, like the roundups of workers and unionizers in Jerome and Bisbee. Why won't they let me report on politics or crime instead of dances, theater, and fashion*?

Etta was a Progressive, both politically—believing strongly in women's suffrage and against political corruption—while she was also socially progressive. She had been educated at the Normal School in Tempe. Her parents, wealthy and conservative, were convinced that she would make a fine teacher. They also hoped that such an education would steer her away from her growing political interests. Interests that they believed would be the downfall of society and ruin her chances for a good marriage.

Etta looked up from her tiny desk and acknowledged the young man standing before her with a loud sigh.

"Please, Etta, say you'll come out with me tonight." Her suitor, a junior editor and favorite of the publisher wasn't actually begging, but to Etta that's what his whining sounded like.

"I'm busy right now, Clyde." She shook her head, liking the way her curly bobbed hair brushed against her cheeks.

"Yes, I see, but what about tonight?"

Etta put her pencil down and looked up at the tall man. She stared directly into his face, her deep blue eyes not wavering, her expression was serious. She spoke firmly and directly.

"Clyde, I'm not interested in going with you anywhere. I work here as a writer. I know you're the junior editor and I have to work with you, but I don't have to spend my hours away from the newspaper with *you*."

"Perhaps another time, Miss Pearce." The disappointed man walked briskly away.

Although the paper's publisher liked Etta's work and had praised her efforts, he clearly saw her as a society writer. He'd told her on more than one occasion that serious news was for men, not blue-eyed young women. Even most of her female friends thought she was crazy to want to be a reporter and they tried to discourage her, saying such banal things like she wouldn't find a decent husband or people would say she's loose and immoral. As a result, Etta's list of close female friends was short—very short.

Etta looked at the large clock on the wall above the office door. It was half past five and it was Friday, so she slipped on a light coat, settled a cloche hat on her head and walked out of the room and into an oven-like Phoenix evening. She strode briskly down the two blocks to the streetcar station and caught a car leaving for her neighborhood. She'd gotten used to people staring at her; men, because they ogled her legs, short hair, and brash openness; and women, who stared, aghast and disapproving for the same reasons. But she truly didn't care what they thought or believed. She knew who she was and what she was capable of doing and becoming.

As the streetcar approached her stop, she reached into her small clutch bag, removed a cigarette and placed it in her mouth. As the women around her gasped, she struck a match on the ceiling of the car and lit the cigarette. Etta inhaled briefly and blew out a stream of smoke as she stepped onto the sidewalk and strolled down the street, her hips swaying naturally and the smoke from her cigarette disappearing into the growing dusk.

* * *

In Bisbee, Cal looked across the desk at his reporter. "Henry, I want you to find out if any of the miners who left on the train last week have snuck back into town." Cal watched Henry's face as the young reporter considered the assignment.

"Considering that the Sheriff set up roadblocks everywhere," Henry said, "what do you think the chances are that anyone got through them?"

"You're probably right, Henry, but *if* one or two did make it back, and *if* you can find them, what they experienced on the cattle cars and in the desert would fill in a lot of blank spots in your story."

"There's a third and very important *if*, Cal. What if they won't talk to me? They don't know me, and they'll probably be afraid to talk to me. Everyone in town knows the mine owns the paper and if I work for the paper, don't I also work for the mine?"

Cal sat back in his chair and, as usual, picked up his pencil. "Then you'll have to convince them that you aren't a spy, that you intend to tell the truth. Even then, they may not want to say anything. How *might* you get them to open up?"

"Hmm," mused Henry. "If I could promise them I wouldn't use their names, or any names at all they might. Also, if I explain that their experience will make the story believable and probably lead to some of the original demands of the union being met."

"See, Henry, I knew you were smart." Cal smiled and set the pencil down.

"But I would keep my promise, Cal. I wouldn't even give *you* their names."

"And *I* wouldn't ask for them." He paused and added, "So why don't you get out there and see if anyone made it back? It's not going to be easy, you know. They won't be carrying a sign."

Henry walked back to his office and put on his cap

and coat. Before he left, he grabbed his notebook and put two freshly sharpened pencils in his shirt pocket. "See you later, boss," he said as he left the building.

The large front door swung closed behind him and Henry smiled. He already had a plan to seek out the "Deportation Survivors"—a title that he'd just created—and knew where his first stop would be. Henry was pleased that his own plans were consistent with Cal's.

As he walked up Main Street toward the Payne house, he mulled over the questions he'd ask and even how he'd ask them. It seemed important that Mrs. Payne be treated with respect and concern. When he knocked on the door, he heard the familiar thumping pace of the crutches.

"Well, if it isn't Mister Carter," she said with a smile. "What are you doin' all the way up here?"

Henry relaxed a bit and returned her smile with one of his own. "Good afternoon, Mrs. Payne," he said, removing his cap. "It's been a few days since I saw you last, and I wanted to see if you were okay."

"I am, thank you."

"To be frank, ma'am, I also hoped I could visit with your sons." Henry paused, knowing that what he said next might ruin his plan. "Mrs. Payne, I'm a reporter for the *Review*."

The wrinkle-faced woman didn't seem surprised, and the look on her face told Henry a lot about her character.

"I already knew that, Mr. Carter, and I knew that you'd tell me when the time was right." She pushed open the screen door and invited him in. "My boys are workin' at the mine and won't be back 'til this evenin'."

Henry hesitated. "I could come back later."

"No, sir, you come in. Perhaps if you tell me what it is you're lookin' for I can discuss it with the boys first."

Henry stepped into the room, watched Mrs. Payne as she sat down then took a seat opposite her.

"So, what is it you want to talk to my sons about?"

"I've written a story, whether it's for the *Review* or

not, I don't yet know. It's about my experience in the roundup, what I saw and felt. But I also want to know what the others experienced."

He had opened his notebook, looked at it, then put it down. "Mrs. Payne, my story won't be finished until I can fill in some blanks, such as what it was like in those cattle cars and how the men felt when they were abandoned in the New Mexico desert, and why they felt they had to strike."

"My boys weren't on the train, so how can they help you?"

"I know they weren't, ma'am, and I'm glad for them and you. But, maybe they know someone who was, someone who *did* ride the train and maybe even snuck back into Bisbee."

"Mr. Carter, my boys just go to work and keep to themselves. They don't want any trouble. They don't know about anyone sneaking into town."

"I know what you're thinking, ma'am. I'm not asking them to betray anyone and risk losing their jobs. That's why I want to sit down with them and see if we can just talk about what they know and what they've learned. If they can grow to trust me—to believe I'll keep my promise of anonymity—then maybe we can get the… returnees to tell me their side of things."

"I hear what you're sayin', Henry, I do. But what you're askin', my boys will have to decide. I won't try to influence 'em. They have good jobs, and we depend on their money to live."

Henry nodded and rose from his seat. "I think that's the best approach. But, I want you to know, Mrs. Payne that before I talk to your sons, even though I work for the *Review*—and everyone in town knows that the mine owns the paper—I am writing this story myself, for my own reasons, and do not intend to be a… a *mouthpiece* for the mine. Instead, I want people to know the truth. But if they choose for themselves to help me, then I stand a good chance of telling the real story, and by doing that maybe helping these other fellas out."

"*If* anyone's come back," she said.

"Right, ma'am. *If* anyone's come back. You can trust me, Mrs. Payne, and so can your sons." He paused and looked directly at her. "A good reporter never betrays the trust of his sources, and I am going to be a good reporter."

Henry knew that the information he might get from deputized miners, mine managers, or any of Sheriff Wheeler's deputies would be tainted and likely come at a high cost, either in expected bribes, or, worse yet, in the form of pressure on him or Cal to squelch the story. As he made his way down Main Street, past the Grand Hotel, Henry once again pondered the risk of publishing his story; the risks to him, Cal, and the paper had to be considered. He wasn't afraid. He'd learned early that telling the truth, regardless of the cost, was far better than holding back to avoid any consequences.

He walked into a café to get some dinner. Not yet dark, the place wasn't busy. He found a small table in the back of the room and sat down with his back to the wall. He asked the waitress for the special and a glass of water. Watching people pass by the large glass window going about their daily business reminded him of something he'd learned a few years before his ma died.

He'd been twelve or thirteen years old and was still helping her with the laundry business, washing sheets and blankets for the brothel. On that day, he'd delivered a large bundle of dried and folded bedding to the back door of Mrs. McHenry's building. Andy, the madam's houseboy, had met him on the steps and asked Henry to carry the load upstairs to the linen closet.

"I gotta get the parlor swept real quick, or Mrs. McHenry'll get mad," Andy said.

Henry and Andy were good friends, but because Andy couldn't go to the school with the white kids, and because he lived in a brothel, they had to keep their friendship a secret. So, Henry lugged the bundle up to the second floor, found the linen closet, and stacked the sheets on the empty shelves.

As he turned back toward the stairway, the madam came out of one of the rooms.

"Why, Henry Carter, what *are* you doing up here?"

"I was putting the sheets in the closet for Andy."

"And why wasn't Andy doing his own work?" she frowned.

Henry hesitated, wondering if he should cover for his friend or tell the truth. Strangely, it was the hesitation he showed that became the lesson. He told her the truth, that Andy was doing another chore that needed to be done so she, Mrs. McHenry, wouldn't be mad. When she smiled at him and thanked him for his help, he realized that always telling the truth was a good thing.

Sitting in the café, he sensed that the memory of the event on the second floor of a brothel was resurrected because of his talk with Mrs. Payne. *If I stay truthful with her sons*, he thought, *that's what I'll get from them—the truth*.

He finished his meal, stopped at the end of the counter and paid. He smiled at the waitress, pulled his newsboy cap on and hurried back to the office.

Just inside the narrow alley across from the café, the deputy watched as Henry walked toward the *Review* building.

Chapter 5

Etta Pearce wore what she called her business suit—a gray tweed skirt that reached mid-calf with a matching tailored coat over a starched white shirt. The black tie, knotted like a man's, was pulled tightly up to her collar. She glared at her image in the restroom mirror and put on a fresh coat of lipstick as she considered what she wanted to ask her boss and how she knew he'd respond. She tried to relax the frown wrinkles that stretched across her forehead and to convince her lips to make at least the semblance of a smile. Taking a deep breath, she whispered to the empty room, "I will ask him for the assignment, but if he says no, I will go anyway." She let the pent-up air drift past her now barely smiling lips and strode out the door.

"Agnes, I need to see him right away," she said to the publisher's secretary.

"I'm sorry, Miss Pearce, but he doesn't want to be disturbed." Agnes cared little for Etta's attitude, style, and sinful way of life and made no effort to hide it. She turned back to the letter she was typing without formally dismissing the reporter.

Etta looked down at the top of Agnes's head, noting the ruler-straight part in the secretary's graying hair, all the while feeling the woman's disdain. Etta didn't care what the woman thought of her. She also wasn't so easily brushed off.

"I'm sure he won't mind, Mrs. Jorgenson, this is very important." Etta stepped around the woman's desk, marched straight to the door, opened it and walked into the spacious office.

The publisher, Mr. Sidney, looked up expecting to see Agnes.

"Miss Pearce," he said, looking past her to see the older woman rush into the room.

"I'm sorry, Mr. Sidney. I told her you were busy." Agnes gasped, clearly upset that protocol *and* her instructions had been ignored.

"I *am* busy, Miss Pearce. Make an appointment with Agnes and we'll talk later." He looked at his secretary and signaled her to lead Etta out.

"Sir, this really won't take much of your time. I just need a minute to ask you something important."

Sidney looked up at Etta, sighed loudly and shooed Agnes away with a flip of his hand. He put the cap on his fountain pen and set it on the leather blotter that covered his desk. "Alright, Miss Pearce, you have one minute to tell me what it is that you want." He stood up from the desk and walked over to the credenza. Glancing out of the large window that overlooked the busy Phoenix avenue, he asked, "Well?" Keeping his back to her, he poured two fingers of bourbon into a cut-crystal glass.

"Mr. Sidney, I want to go to Jerome and write a story about those Wobblies, the ones who were shipped to California." Etta spoke confidently, without fear, her voice strong and businesslike.

"Oh, you do, Miss Pearce?" He turned toward her. "Now why would I send *you* there? The story has already been told. The unionizers and strikers were gathered up, put in boxcars and shipped to Needles. What more is there to be said?"

"There is a lot more to be said, sir, and a lot more to be learned." Etta didn't even take time to breathe before she went on. "Why were they picked up? Why were they driven from the state? What did they experience in the boxcars and what does this mean for us, here in Phoenix?"

"Slow down, Miss Pearce." He raised his hand and glared into her eyes. "Most of our readers do not care about those traitors and are glad they no longer live in Arizona." He turned back toward his desk, ready to return to his work, even yet knowing that Etta had more to say.

"Miss Pearce, why can't you see that all that needs to be said about that incident has already *been* said? More to the point, what could you, a metropolitan society reporter, add to the fine work of our best reporters?"

Holding back her trouble-making tongue, Etta replied, her voice calm, even. "Sir, I believe that the women of Phoenix and the rest of the state would like to know how such an event affected the wives, mothers, and children of the men taken out of their homes. The women readers may not care or understand about *why* this happened, but they will want to know how the other women dealt with the pain of their husband's absence and not knowing about their son's experience." She paused briefly. "Mr. Sidney, please let me write their story. If it's necessary, I'll cover my own expenses. I just think the story needs to be told."

"Is that all, Miss Pearce?"

Etta didn't hesitate. "Yes sir, that's all."

Sidney turned once again toward the window, then looked back over his shoulder at his reporter. "Okay, Etta, you have one week to cover this story. Make sure you have everything ready for this Sunday's edition before you go. You are responsible for *all* expenses, and I will decide whether or not your story will ever be printed in the *Republican*." He looked directly into Etta's blue eyes. "Any questions?"

"No, sir. Thank you, sir." A confident Etta turned and marched out of the office and smiled sweetly at Agnes. The young reporter was excited that she finally had a meaningful assignment, one that she'd have to dig deep to write about.

Not wanting to do anything that would cause Mr. Sidney to change his mind, Etta spent the rest of the day finishing up her stories for the Sunday edition. Two weddings, three engagements (she knew all five girls) and a review of the latest motion picture something called, "Poor Little Rich Girl," generated enough words to fill her weekly target. Before gathering her things and leaving the office, she decided to call her parents and let them know that she'd be out of town for a few days. Setting her briefcase and clutch on the desktop, she lifted the phone by its long neck and took the earpiece out of its cradle.

"Switchboard!"

"Hi, Elsie, it's Etta." Elsie was one of Etta's few friends working for the paper. "Could you dial my parents' number please?"

"Sure, Etta." A moment passed, then, "Here you go."

The telephone rang twice before it was picked up by the family's maid.

"Pearce residence, may I help you?"

"Good evening, Marisol, this is Etta. I need to speak to my father."

"Mr. Pearce is in his study. If you hold on a moment, I'll let him know you wish to speak with him."

Etta thanked the woman, then, carrying the phone by its long neck, she began pacing back and forth behind her desk. Two minutes passed before her father finally picked up the phone.

"I was wondering if you'd call me, Henrietta."

By his formal tone and the use of her given name, Etta suspected that he already knew why she was calling.

"Hello, father, how are you this evening?" She hoped her own formality would throw him off, maybe change his mood.

"Before you leave town, I'd like you to drop by the house."

"How...?"

"Never mind how I know you're off on a wild goose chase," he said. "Just be here first thing in the morning. I've got some things I want to discuss with you, and I won't do it on the telephone. Be here at eight sharp, young lady." Then the line went dead.

He hung up on me. My own father hung up on me. Her thoughts started racing. *And how did he find out I was leaving... unless, Agnes decided to send a little bird to whisper in his ear.* She hung the earpiece in the telephone's cradle and put it on the desk. Gathering her things, she walked out of the office and headed to her apartment.

At eight o'clock the next morning, Etta opened the huge front door of her parents' home and marched straight to the back of the house and into her father's study. She knew that's where he'd be. He always had his breakfast at half past seven and read the papers until he headed to his office at the Merchant's Exchange. Etta had grown up a rich girl. Her father was a broker in all sorts of commodities, and he'd made a lot of money in the years since Arizona had become a state. As she expected, he was sitting behind his desk.

"Well, at least you learned something from me before finding so many ways to drive your mother crazy."

"What do you mean?"

"I mean, thank you for being on time. I'm a busy man and you know I don't like tardiness."

"No, father, what do you mean about driving mother crazy?"

"Sit down, Etta." She remained on her feet until his brow creased and his lips tightened into razor-thin line, then took a seat. "You know," he continued, "that your mother is worried about you. She doesn't understand why you can't, or won't, dress properly like a lady. She is still upset about your hair, of course, and the idea that you smoke in public causes her to tumble into one of her spells."

Etta didn't respond verbally, since she'd learned long ago that discussions about her habits and her mother's response to them created endless dialogue.

"Nevertheless," her father said, "I have heard that you plan to go to Jerome to, how did Mr. Sidney put it... oh yes, to write a story about how the women of that town responded to the departure of so many striking mine workers."

"When did he call you?"

"That's not important. What is important, however, is that your desire to do such a daring thing will do nothing to calm your mother's fears."

"Daddy..."

"Hold on. Etta, you are an intelligent—although not necessarily smart—woman. You are educated, diligent, and aggressive. All things that most people admire in a *man*. Why do you insist on being that way?"

"I want to do these things because they are important. I want to show Mother and you that you didn't raise a limp-wristed, flower-sniffing, society debutante. I want to do things that matter, things that can change the world."

Mr. Pearce sighed and sat in his chair. "I know, Etta. I've done everything I know how to convince your mother that you'd grow out of this, this phase." He looked at his daughter again, only this time the stern brow had softened, and his jaw unclenched. "Tell me, if you will, what were the most important things I ever taught you to do?"

"Well, you taught me to think for myself..."

"Not those things, but the physical things. What kinds of *things* did I teach you to do?"

Etta relaxed in her seat and said, "You taught me how to climb a tree and to shoot a gun. You taught me to drive... in that Packard we used to have. You even taught me how to change a tire."

"That's right, Etta. I'm the one who taught you things that other fathers only taught their sons. I truly believe that *I'm* the one to blame for your mother's grief, not you." His shoulders slumped a little, but a smile began to grow on his lips. "I think I did a damned good job, maybe too good a job raising you to take care of yourself."

Through silver-edged eyes, Etta saw her father in a different light.

"So, young lady, let's not worry too much about your mother's spells. Instead, you and I are going outside. There are a few things I want to show you before you take off for that strange town built on the side of a mountain."

He got up and walked up to his daughter. Etta stood as well. Nearly as tall as her father, she looked directly into his eyes and said, "Thanks, Daddy."

When they walked into the garage that housed her father's very long, very shiny Cadillac sedan, she saw another car parked beyond it.

"Whose car is that?" she asked.

"That, Henrietta Pearce, is your brand new, Ford Model T Runabout." He smiled at the shocked look that spread across her face. "If you think I am going to let you take off and walk to Jerome, you are mistaken. Now before you get all mushy, I want you to look in the front seat." She couldn't move. "Go one, girl. Look in the front seat."

Etta approached the shiny black, two-seat roadster as if it were a panther ready to strike at her. Ducking through the open side, she reached in and grasped a heavy gift-wrapped box. "What is it?"

"Why don't you open it?"

Tearing the ribbon loose and ripping the paper off the box, she nearly dropped the gift. Catching it before it crashed to the ground, she pulled the top off the box and gasped. "It's a pistol!"

"It is a pistol, and it's yours. I don't want you wandering off into the wilderness of the old west without a good horse, or in this case, a good car. Neither do I want you to go out unarmed."

"But..."

"But nothing, Etta. You want to change the world, but the world may not be ready to be changed, at least not for the next twenty years or so. But if anyone *can* change it, especially for women, it's probably going to be you."

Etta put the gun back on the car seat and turned to her father. Her eyes once again silver-lined, she hugged the man who had held her as an infant and had beamed when she graduated from college. "Daddy, I don't know what to say."

"If you are the reporter you purport to be, you better find the words," he whispered in her ear. "Now, why don't you get this baby car out of my garage and let me go to work."

By six the next morning, Etta was on the hard-packed road heading north out of Phoenix. Her pistol was cleaned and loaded and rested on the passenger seat at her side. The capabilities of her new car—which she'd spent the previous evening memorizing—were running through her brain. Four cylinders; ten-gallon fuel tank; forty miles an hour; pneumatic tires. Every block she drove when she was leaving the city caused pedestrians to stare. The few policemen she encountered at the busy intersections watched her, their mouths hanging slack jawed. But she didn't care what anyone thought. *I'm doing this, she thought. I'm doing this for myself. I'll show Mr. Sidney and ugly Mrs. Jorgenson and those annoying men that I can write as well as they can.*

The flat road ran through the flat desert landscape. Mile after mile of sand and scrub brush flew past the open windows of her car. The saguaro cactus which rose out of the sand like fictional giants, seemed to wave at her as she sped by them. Several times she had to swerve as jackrabbits and roadrunners raced across the road. The sun was hot, but most of the time the wind racing into the car cooled her off. Etta was having the time of her life. The smile on her face felt permanent.

Etta had figured that it would take her two hours to get to Prescott and maybe another to reach Jerome. All of her figuring changed when she hit a sharp rock in the road and one of her back tires went flat. She maintained control of the vehicle and coasted to a stop on the narrow shoulder of the road.

"Damn it," she whispered. "I'm glad this new car comes with a spare tire," she mumbled to herself. She got out of the car, rolled up her sleeves and loosened her tie. Walking around to the back of the car, she opened the lid to the trunk and pulled out the jack. Remembering what her father had taught her about changing a tire, she looked around for a rock flat enough to set the jack on. That important task took a few minutes, but she soon found what she needed.

Etta spent the next hour changing the tire. When she climbed back into the driver's seat, her sweat-soaked skirt and blouse clung to her like a second skin. Her hands were dirty, her make-up smudged, and her hair—so beautiful at the beginning of the day—hung about her cheeks like limp rags. Once she got going again, however, the breeze through the side windows cooled her off. When she arrived in Prescott just before noon, she decided to leave the flat tire at a garage, then find a room and put off the trip to Jerome until the next day.

In her room, just off the town square, Etta, stripped out of her dirty clothes and took a bath. That evening, she enjoyed a nice dinner at a local café and went to bed early. Just as she drifted off to sleep, a thought entered her mind and carried on into her dream. *I'm a reporter for the Arizona Republican.*

As she rose from the small bed the next morning, Etta felt ready to do her job. She called her father at home but had to leave a message with the maid. "Tell him I'm in Prescott." She also called her office and left a message for Mr. Sidney, even though she didn't think Agnes would pass it along to him. By nine o'clock she was on the road again. At first, the terrain was still relatively flat, but soon the road began to climb higher and higher into the mountains. Her car had ridden quite nicely at nearly forty miles an hour on the flat land. But in the mountains, she felt happy when she was driving at twenty. At times, the road was barely as wide as her car, or so it seemed to her. Fortunately, she didn't encounter any vehicles coming down the mountain and no one was following her either. At times she was so enchanted by the grand vistas of the desert as it spread out and away from her that she got a little dizzy. After the sensation occurred a second time she pulled over in a wide spot. She sipped water from a Mason jar and rested for ten minutes before resuming the trip. This time, though, she kept her eyes straight ahead on the road.

When she pulled to a stop in front of the brand-new Cottonwood Hotel in Jerome, she stepped out of her car and put the pistol in her purse. Standing in front of the hotel, she took a moment to feel the breeze blowing across the vast openness. It seemed that she could see forever. The floating clouds cast shadows on the valley below and she was struck by how different Jerome was than Phoenix. That night, after a satisfying dinner, Etta slept well.

While drinking her first cup of coffee the next morning, Etta laid out a plan, listing places she thought might have information on the events several weeks past. She hoped that people would be willing to talk about the strikers and their issues. Etta was convinced that she could gather sufficient information to write a great story about this historic event.

Etta started her investigation at the Mayor's Office, believing that, if nothing else, the authorities there would have the most information about why and how the strikers were gathered up. The mayor, J.J. Cain refused to speak with her. One of his secretaries, a stern looking bald man told her, "Mayor Cain wants the press to know that the reign of the IWW in Jerome is over."

"I suppose it is," replied Etta, "since they were all shipped out of town. But why? Why did this happen? There has to be a more to the story." She looked at the man again. "Since the mayor won't meet with me, can you suggest someone else in the administration who will?" Etta was annoyed by the secretary's haughtiness.

"Listen, young woman, we have nothing to add to what has already been written by real newspapermen." With that, he turned and walked away, leaving Etta stunned.

Etta wanted to respond that she had plenty more to say, but, instead, gritted her teeth and walked briskly out of city hall.

Her next stop was the Sheriff's office, but the only person who would listen to her was the desk sergeant, a surly, near mute individual who seemed to struggle through a memorized speech.

"We loaded up sixty-seven Wobblies into two cattle cars and shipped 'em to Needles over in California, but they didn't want 'em. They got left in Kingman. If you wanna talk to the Wobblies, you'll have to go there."

"That's it? That's all you know about why they got shipped out of the state?"

"Everyone knows them foreigners are troublemakers. They're traitors and anarchists and they're gone. Ain't that enough?"

"No, it's not. How do you know they are traitors?"

"I know because they're foreigners...Germans, Mexicans, all of them and they don't belong in our town." He paused for a moment and stared at Etta. "You need to get something clear in your head *Miss* Reporter."

"And what great wisdom is it you wish to share with me *Deputy* Desk Sergeant?"

When puffing out his chest and frowning didn't seem to affect Etta, he shouted. "You'd better watch yourself in our town. Just because you're from a big city don't mean you have any authority or say-so here. Make sure that you don't go stirrin' up any trouble or you'll find yourself staying in one of my cells. Now get out of here and leave me to my work."

Etta walked out of the office and found a bench in front of the general store. She sat down, discouraged by the brush-off she'd received from the town officials. Convinced that the city leaders and the lawmen likely led the drive, she decided to speak with some of the merchants in the mining town. That effort also provided nothing. Etta wanted a drink but knew that she'd have to find something illegal since Arizona was a dry state. But as a stranger in town, she'd probably be unsuccessful with that as well.

She rose from the bench and wandered down the street until she found a soda shop. For some reason, the clean white walls and shiny counter were refreshing. The girl behind the counter wore a white pinafore over a light blue dress and was actually smiling at Etta.

"Can I help you ma'am," she said through her sweet grin.

"You sure can. Could you make me a chocolate soda?" replied Etta as she sat on one of the revolving stools. "Could you also direct me to the nearest place in town where I can get a *real* drink?"

Without losing her smile, the girl pretended not to hear Etta and turned toward the long mirror against the wall. She stared at Etta's reflection while she constructed the cold drink. She seemed fascinated by the woman's appearance. When she'd finished the concoction, she stuck a paper straw in the glass and placed it in front of Etta.

"Excuse me, ma'am, can I ask you a question?"

Etta sipped some of the chocolate soda through the straw and looked up at the girl.

"Of course, but would you stop calling me ma'am?"

"Yes, ma'am, I mean yes." A bit flustered, the girl seemed to be rethinking her question. "I know that you're not from around here. I can tell by the way you're dressed." She swallowed, as if trying to wet her dry throat. "You look beautiful, and I was just wondering if that's the way women dress in the city. My father would whop me with his razor strap if he caught me wearing a skirt that short."

"What's your name?"

"It's Mary Elizabeth, but my friends call me Mary Beth."

"Well, Mary Beth, I don't know any other women who dress this way. To tell the truth, my father wanted to… how did you say it? He wanted to whop me too the first time I dressed like this."

"But he didn't? He lets you dress how you want to?"

"Since I'm grown up and live on my own, he does." Etta paused to shift the conversation to her reason for being in Jerome. "I'm a reporter for the Phoenix newspaper and I'm trying to find out more about the event from last week, the deportation." She looked at the girl, noticing the disappearance of her smile.

"We're not supposed to talk about that," she said. "My father got really mad at some reporters right after the train left and that night he told me that nobody in this town is supposed to talk to any more newspaper men, uh, people."

Trying to build some camaraderie with the girl, Etta leaned over the counter and gestured to Mary Beth to move closer. When their faces were just inches apart, Etta said softly, "Do you always do everything your father says?"

"Not always," she gulped, "but even if I did know something, I'd still be afraid of the whopping."

"That's too bad, Mary Beth, because when you finally do get out on your own, you may not know how to think for yourself." The girl's lower lip started to quiver, but she still wanted to hear what the reporter had to say.

Etta said, "But you're still young, and you'll have a far easier time than I ever did of convincing your father that you are capable of doing anything a man can do." She left a dollar on the counter, spun the stool around and started to walk out of the shop.

"Miss Pearce," Mary Beth whispered loudly, "there is a small place down the block where my daddy goes..."

"Thanks, Mary Elizabeth." Etta returned to the counter, reached into her purse and pulled out one of her favorite tubes of lipstick. "This is for you," she said. "Be careful when and where you use it."

The girl let the tube rest in her palm. She held it like something precious. Lifting her eyes to Etta, she whispered, "Thank you." Mary Beth wrote the name of the place that sold whiskey on a piece of paper and slipped it across the counter. The two young women smiled knowingly to one another as Etta left the soda shop.

It was barely mid-morning and Etta was already convinced that she wouldn't find out anything in this small, closed-mouth town worth writing about. She found the bootlegger and purchased a bottle of bourbon. At least that's what was handwritten on the paper label. Slipping it into her bag, she headed toward her car. Etta saw a group of women standing on the steps of a church and decided to speak with them.

"Excuse me, ladies," she said, her voice on the pleasant side of neutral.

The women, a mixture of sizes and hairstyles and attire looked in her direction. Their expressions also varied—some judging, some cautious, and three or four who responded much as Mary Beth had—with smiles.

"My name is Etta Pearce. I'm a reporter for the Arizona Republican."

Almost immediately, the unsmiling women turned away and left the group. The oldest of the remainder said, "A real reporter?"

"Yes, I am. I'm here to write a story about women. Especially what they think about the recent deportation and its effects on families and the community."

The women glanced at one another; their expressions blank.

"I understand the local authorities have suggested that talking to reporters could lead to trouble." She paused, wondering how to get a response. "Most men, especially powerful men—bosses, policemen, politicians—don't believe we can think for ourselves."

The two younger women quickly nodded.

"I think they're wrong," said Etta. "For instance, I believe you probably knew other women whose husbands or brothers were forced to leave."

The rest of the ladies looked shyly at the oldest woman in the group.

"We do know, miss, and we do think about them."

"My cousin was one of them, one loaded in a boxcar," said a young blonde.

"Have you seen or heard from him? Have any of the women who were left here alone or with their children been in touch with you?"

The older woman said, "They all disappeared right away, trying to find their men, feeling unwanted here in Jerome."

Turning to the blonde, Etta asked, "What about your cousin?"

"We haven't heard anything. My aunt thinks he won't ever come back home."

Etta took a chance and asked one more question. "Do you think any of your women friends would be willing to talk to me, maybe as a group?"

The fourth woman, the quiet one, said, "Maybe."

"Is there someplace, someplace more private that we can use? That way you and any of your friends who're willing to talk about the roundup won't have to worry about getting into trouble with your husbands or fathers."

The older woman said, "My husband was forced onto a boxcar, so my home is available. When do you want to hold this meeting?"

Trying to hold her excitement in check, Etta said, "As soon as we can do so without putting anyone at risk."

The older woman extended her hand toward Etta. "My name is Martha."

Just after noon, Etta, Martha, and the younger women from the church were gathered in Martha's living room. A few of them were seated on a small sofa and the available chairs. The rest stood wherever they could find room. Etta's heart was pounding so hard she wondered if the ladies could hear it. Taking a calming breath, she said, "I want to thank you ladies, all of you, for risking yourselves to speak with me. So many men, especially those in authority, simply do not believe that women can think for themselves. They are convinced that we should stay in the kitchen and keep our minds closed and our mouths shut."

Etta heard the affirmative words and saw the heads nod.

"But, we all know better. Some of you are still wondering when or if your husband, son, or brother will be coming back. You all have friends or neighbors who are faced with the unknown. You are frightened and anxious. These feelings are natural as well as personal."

Etta had their attention and wanted to keep it, so she said, "I'm a reporter with the *Republican*. I believe that you and others who have experienced the stress of this deportation are filled with questions and worried about your families. I believe that your concerns and experiences need to be told. There are women across the state who'll be deeply interested in what you have to say, and the only way that can happen is if we can put the story on the front page. Women in Phoenix or Tucson can't hear what you say across the fence to your friend in Jerome."

What followed over the next two-plus hours was an open, emotional, energized discussion about the fears, sadness, loneliness, and anger the women felt. Etta took copious notes and watched the women wipe tears from their eyes and hug their neighbors.

* * *

As she drove down the mountain, Etta crafted her story from the anecdotes shared at Martha's house. Without editing, she considered the tales of passion and compassion, the fears, tears, and anxiety that had overcome the innocent mates and mothers of the deportees. Every once in a while, despite her desire to get home in order to actually write, Etta would stop on the side of the road. Sitting quietly behind the steering wheel, she remembered the faces and the sound of women's voices. At one point, about halfway to Phoenix, she got out of her car and walked into the desert. Hugging herself, she wept for these women, tears flowed from her eyes, and she didn't care what they did to her makeup.

When she finished typing the article at her tiny desk, Etta believed it was the best she'd ever done. Confident that it met all of the criteria of news, she delivered it to Mr. Sidney, again by-passing Mrs. Jorgenson.

"What's this?"

"It's my story on the Jerome Deportation from a woman's point of view."

The publisher looked at the neatly stacked pages on his desk and frowned. "I'll read it later. Now, if you please, why don't you get back to your job and write your assigned stories."

Etta evidently didn't move quickly enough for him. "Now, Miss Pearce. I'm busy."

Chapter 6

Henry Carter opened the door of his Brewery Gulch cabin and invited Mrs. Payne's sons, William and John, into his home. As they'd requested, he'd turned off the lanterns on the porch and in his kitchen. A single candle rested on the table in the far corner of the room.

"Thank you for agreeing to talk to me," Henry said. "Please, have a seat." He indicated the two chairs that straddled the small table with the candle.

"That won't be necessary, Mr. Carter. We won't be stayin' long," said William. "We talked to our ma, and she told us what you wanted to know. She said you'd keep our names out of this." He looked at his brother, who nodded, then continued. "Before I say any more, you should know that we don't know about anyone who was on the train that might be back in town. That don't mean there ain't any, just that we don't know."

Henry nodded, felt like asking the man to go on, but remained quiet.

"Our ma seems to trust you, but she told us to make up our own minds about whether we would talk to you."

John spoke up before his brother could go on. "How do we know that you'll keep us out of the paper? How do we know that you won't turn us over to the union or the sheriff?"

"You can't really know unless you believe what I have to say." Once again, Henry asked them to sit, and they each took a chair. "I need to tell you about myself, about why I became a reporter, and why it's important to me to tell the story of what happened to those fellas who ended up out in the desert." The brothers glanced at each other, and

William nodded.

Henry spent the next twenty minutes talking about his parents, especially how he felt when his pa had died in the mine. He talked about Calvin and what the reporter had taught him about the need for the truth to be told. He told them about his own experience during the roundup, what he'd seen and heard and felt. When he'd finished with what he'd planned to say, he added one more thing.

"I promise you this: I will *never* reveal your names, your ma's name, or the name of anyone who actually got dumped in the desert; not to anyone; not my boss, not the sheriff, not the IWW or anyone at Phelps-Dodge." He looked at each of them, hoping they could see or feel his sincerity. "That's all I can say. I do appreciate you coming up here and if you do encounter a returnee and are willing to get him to meet with me, I'll always be grateful. I think everyone needs to know what those fellas experienced, and if I don't tell the story, I believe that no one ever will."

The brothers stood up, shook Henry's hand and walked out into the night. Henry stepped out behind them and stood on his porch. He watched the two men sneak quietly down the street, then looked up at the star-filled sky. *All I can do is wait,* he thought.

Rereading his story for what seemed the hundredth time. Henry kept finding places where he could improve the narrative by changing a word here and there, but he was at the point where the only truly valuable changes had to come from someone who rode the train to New Mexico. He'd hoped that by now the Payne brothers would contact him and give him a name, or names, of someone willing to talk about their experience.

For the next few days, Henry worked on his regular assignments, yet the deportation was never far from his thoughts. But this day was different. When Henry walked up the stairs to his office, Cal looked over at him and said, "Henry, there's a young fellow here to see you."

A boy, perhaps ten or twelve, spun around in the seat facing Cal. He rose and approached Henry.

"Are you Mr. Carter?" he said, his high-pitched voice on the cusp of manhood.

"I am. How can I help you?"

The short, gangly youngster reached deep in the pocket of his overalls and pulled out a folded piece of paper. "I'm supposed to give you this message," he said, "and to, uhh, to tell the man who sent it that you got it."

Henry took the square of paper and opened it, quickly reading the penciled words. He glanced at Cal then turned again to the boy. "You can tell them that you delivered it to me and that I truly appreciate their information." The boy stood still, waiting, so Henry said, "Just tell them I got it."

"I will, Mr. Carter, but uhh, they said that you'd give me a quarter."

"They told you that?" asked Henry.

The boy stuck out his hand, palm up.

Henry smiled and reached into his vest pocket. "I'm sorry, young man, I don't have a quarter."

The boy looked deeply disappointed, his brow creased and his hand dropped to his side.

"So, I guess you'll just have to take this instead." Henry reached down for the boy's hand, lifted it up and put a silver dollar in the center of his palm. "I hope this is okay."

"Mr. Carter," he squeaked, when he looked up from the treasure in his hand, the smile on his face looked like it spread from ear to ear. "Mr. Carter, this is a dollar, a whole dollar!"

"It is, and you can keep it on one condition."

"Huh?"

"You can keep it if you tell me your name."

"It's Timmy, Mr. Carter, Timmy Cree."

Seeing the grin on Cal's face, Henry said, "Well, Mr. Cree, thank you for bringing the message. I hope that you will spend your wages wisely."

"I don't know what that means," Timmy said as he

turned toward the stairs. "But I ain't gonna spend it right away. I'm gonna save it."

The two journalists laughed out loud as the boy flew down the stairs and ran wildly up Main Street, his laughter echoing off the buildings.

Catching his breath, Cal asked Henry what was in the message.

"It says, 'You can meet our friend tonight at ten at the rock pile on the hill directly across the Tombstone road from the Grand Hotel. Come alone.'"

"Do you know the place they're talking about?"

"Sure, it's that ledge with a cliff back and some stacked rocks in front."

"Might be treacherous going up that trail in the dark," Cal said.

"It could be, but it'll be worth it if the fella has some good information."

"Do you think you'll need some protection, a gun maybe?"

Henry thought about that for a moment. "I think it'll be alright, I guess they believed me when I said I would keep them out of it."

"So, you're going?"

"I am, Cal. This could be exactly what I need to finish my story." He looked once again at the note and then over at Cal. "I sure hope it is."

Henry stayed in his office all afternoon and skipped dinner as well. Even as anxious as he was, Henry managed to be productive in the vacant office. The rumbling presses calmed him as he thought about the questions he'd ask. He contemplated getting to the meeting place early but thought that maybe the miner would want to see him coming up the trail.

From about half past nine on, Henry checked the time frequently, and when the minute hand reached the eight on the face of his pocket watch, he slipped on his coat and hat and walked out of the building. As he walked away from the *Review* building, Henry thought a lot about what he'd said to Mrs. Payne, particularly the part about his link to the newspaper and the paper's link to the mine. *What would the management think I'm up to by talking to their employees at odd times and in strange places. Guess I should pay attention in case they follow me.* He looked back over his shoulder as he crossed the road toward the meeting place. He didn't see anyone, but that didn't mean much in the dark.

The trail on the other side of the canyon was barely visible in the scant moonlight, but the glow from the streetlights on Main Street gave Henry a good point of reference. He'd calculated his time accurately and when he reached the stacked rocks, he smelled the aroma of a cigar before he looked up from the trail to see the glowing tip flare as the man inhaled.

"Are you Carter?" The man's voice wasn't exactly calm, but it was measured, grown up, older.

"I am," Henry said, catching his breath after the uphill climb. "Please don't tell me your name, sir. I don't want to know it, and I don't need it for the story."

The man drew on his cigar again, then tossed it to the ground, burying it under his boot in the soft sand.

"The fellas who told me about you said that you want to write about the train last week. They said that they trust you and that you want to tell people what really happened."

Henry said, "Maybe they told you that I got pulled out of my house and rounded up with the rest of you. Fortunately, I got out of the ballpark before the train cars were loaded." He waited for a comment. "I've already written about what I saw and heard, but I need to know what happened on the train if my story is going to have any effect. I need to know what happened to *you*."

"You said you were in the ballpark?" the man asked.

"I was," replied Henry, "and I even talked to the engineer on the train. He's the one who told me all of you were leaving Arizona."

The man nodded, cleared his throat and said, "They put us on cattle cars, and them cars hadn't been cleaned out either. There was hay and dirt and manure all over the floor. They packed us in there so tightly we couldn't sit down even if we wanted to. Most of us hadn't eaten since the night before. Do you think they gave us anything to eat? Well, they didn't. And there was only one barrel of water and it was in the back corner where most of us couldn't get to it." He took a pint bottle of whiskey and tipped it to his lips, draining half of it at once.

"It was hot that day, too," Henry added, hoping to encourage the man to continue.

"Hot ain't the right word, son. Hell-hot is better. Fellas were faintin' and some were pukin'. By the time the train pulled out there'd already been a couple of scuffles just in our car." He paused, "Lord knows what they were fightin' about. The other thing I remember is that it was dark. The walls didn't let much light in and we were crowded together just like the cows they carry to the slaughterhouse. I can't say it any better than that." The man's voice had changed. He choked out his next words. "We were human cattle on the way to be butchered."

As Henry looked toward the man's face, he noticed the city lights reflecting in his eyes. Even in the dark, Henry could sense the deadness, the despair.

"Not a one of us wore a watch, so we couldn't tell how long we were on the train. Every time it stopped we thought the trip was over, but it turned out that the engine got more water than we did. By the time we finally got to Deming, at least half of us were sick, and most had pissed our pants."

Henry tried to imagine the smell and the terrible feeling that would come to men reduced to such shame.

"When we finally got to Columbus, the sheriff there wouldn't let us off the train."

The man was quiet for several minutes, but Henry remained still.

"We sat there a long time, then they backed the train toward the west for another couple hours. We didn't know what was goin' on and by that time the water barrel was empty and we were hungry. Some of the men were passed out from the heat, I guess."

Henry wanted to ask more, but the man's huge intake of breath stopped him from speaking.

"We finally stopped near some little town. Hermanas, I think it's called. They let us off the train, but then they disconnected the cars and the engine pulled away." The man sighed. "We didn't know what to do. A couple of fellas said they'd go hunting for food and water, but I never saw them again. The rest of us just looked for a cool place to rest."

The miner looked around and finally slumped down on the ground. He sighed and continued. "That town was too small to handle all of us. It was already past moon rise but at least it was cooler sittin' outside on the ground. I don't remember ever seein' anyone from that little town. They sure didn't bring us any food. The next morning another engine came and hooked up to the cars. There were enough armed deputies to push us back on them, but we weren't as crowded this time."

"Why not?" asked Henry.

"Because a bunch of the fellas took off during the night. Best I can figure, they walked to Mexico or back to Deming. Could've gone north into New Mexico toward Lordsburg or Silver City, I guess. The rest of us got back into the cattle cars and they took us back to Columbus, to the army base there. They kept us there one night and then just kicked us out."

Henry waited for several long minutes, but it seemed the man was finished. He wanted more information so he asked, "What happened when you tried to get back into Bisbee? Everyone here knows that the sheriff has blocked all of the roads coming into town."

Even as tired as he likely was and emotionally drained by his memories, the man chuckled. "The sheriff don't know *all* the ways back into this town and he don't know what everyone of us looks like either. If you don't mind, I ain't gonna tell you how I made it back in. I don't want any of my friends to get in trouble."

"It's not really important *how* you got back, and I don't need to know. I'm just glad you did and that you agreed to talk to me." Henry glanced across the canyon toward town. The streetlights were still on, but most of the shops were dark. "Sir, I'd like to thank you for your time and especially for your story. You've given me enough good, rich information to finish my article." Henry was brought up short by a quick thought. "No, I mean *your* story."

"I just hope that when people read what you write they'll think about what the sheriff and the men who own the mines did to the workers who make them rich. We ain't all traitors or anarchists. Most of us don't care about the Wobblies. We just wanna work and feed our families. Make sure you tell people that."

The man stood and brushed past Henry, slowly walking out of sight down the trail. Henry felt around for a flat rock and sat down. He was tired physically, but his brain wouldn't shut down. He wanted to go home and sleep but instead decided to go back to the office. *If I don't empty all of this onto paper, I may forget something important,* he thought. *I probably couldn't sleep anyway*. He pushed himself up off the rock and followed the trail back down to the road.

Chapter 7

Back at her desk and disappointed about not getting her Jerome article published, Etta casually leafed through the office copy of the current *New York Monthly*. She liked the well-written magazine, especially its coverage of serious current events and the broad range of topics. She spent little time on the society stories and advertisements—for books, automobiles, and week-end retreats—and focused, instead, on the political articles. There were several of them about the war in Europe, one concerning the freshly arrived American troops and the other, an analysis of the Allies' military leadership. When she turned to the next page, she stopped short and picked up the magazine. She looked around at her co-workers, but none of them seemed to be paying attention to her. Turning back to the magazine and the article that caught her attention, she read it quickly and then again critically. Once more, she read with real interest the bold title and by-line:

Inhumane Treatment of American Mineworkers; My Personal Experience in the Bisbee Deportation
By Henry Carter

All afternoon, in between her regular assignments, Etta kept returning to the article. Carter's style was refreshing, almost youthful. His descriptions were vivid, as if he were drawing pictures for readers unfamiliar with this part of the American desert. The characters were, of course, real people, and Carter didn't hold back on showing their pain and anguish. Etta noticed how he qualified almost every assertion, reporting only what he saw or heard. *This man Carter must have gone to journalism school,* she thought. *He's just too thorough, too insistent on reporting the facts.* Etta knew she was capable of producing the same kind of *reporting,* but this man's *story-telling* skills held her in awe. What gave her some satisfaction was the similarity in his narrative about the men and their fears and her own report of the women left behind. Other than the difference in the number of people loaded into boxcars, the two deportations were very much the same.

Etta closed the magazine and slipped it into her bag, left the office and went down the hall to the archives. The clerk behind the counter, Ed Greene, was busy making check marks on a list of some sort. He looked up when Etta spoke his name.

"Good afternoon, Miss Pearce," he said.

"Good afternoon to you, too, Ed." Etta smiled at the elderly man. She always felt comfortable around him because he was never bothered by how she dressed or acted, and he never tried to take her out for dinner.

"What can I do for you today, dear lady?"

"What is the name of the local paper in Bisbee?"

"Umm, let me look." He pulled a bound book from the corner of his desk, opened it and flipped through a few pages. "Here it is, it's called the *Bisbee Daily Review.*" Looking up at Etta he asked, "do you want the telephone number?"

"That would be nice, Ed. Thank you." Etta waited while he wrote the information on a slip of paper and handed it to her. "See you later, Mr. Green."

"I certainly hope so, Miss Pearce."

Their friendly laughter drifted across the counter as she left the room.

Just before five o'clock, Mr. Sidney stopped by her desk.

"Miss Pearce," he said gruffly, "I haven't seen your column for tomorrow's edition."

"I'm sorry, sir. There are a few last-minute changes I need to make." She looked up at him, forced a smile on her face and added, "I'll have them ready for Clyde in a few minutes. It shouldn't take long for him to approve."

"I'm sure he would like to leave the office in time for his dinner. Don't make him wait." He set a derby onto his small head and walked out through the door.

Etta picked up the already perfect article on what new brides would be wearing for fall weddings and carried it over to the editor's office. She handed it to the man's secretary and went back to gather up her things. *I need to get out of here,* she thought and headed home.

Etta stopped her roadster at the curb in front of The Emporium, a combination café and soda shop. She set the brake and got out of the car, then took her handbag and briefcase and walked into the bright interior of the shop.

"Miss Pearce," said the man behind the counter, "it's so good to see you."

"Good evening, Mr. Scott."

"My wife, Lizzy sure liked your article in last Sunday's paper. She told me that she wishes there were more women reporters. Of course, I told her that even if there were, none of 'em would be as nice a person as you are."

"You'd say that about anyone who was a member of your secret club, wouldn't you George?" Etta leaned across the counter and said, "You be sure to thank her for me." She paused and asked, "Did that special order from Kentucky arrive yet?"

"Ahh, yes, Kentucky." George smiled and walked through the door into his kitchen. "It arrived just this morning. The supplier sent two bottles. I hope that's alright."

Etta reached into her handbag and drew out a five-dollar bill and set it on the counter.

George returned with a box wrapped in butcher paper and gave it to Etta. He picked up the money and put it in his pocket.

"You can keep the change, Mr. Scott. I sincerely appreciate the good service."

"You don't have to tip me, Miss Pearce."

"Oh, but I do. You see, I think you could buy your wife a nice bunch of flowers on your way home this evening."

George chuckled as Etta turned and walked out the door, waving goodbye over her shoulder. She drove off down the street, the package of Kentucky bourbon on the seat next to her.

Etta's apartment was small, nothing like the large house where she'd grown up. It had a small parlor and an even smaller kitchen. The bedroom and the bathroom each had a door off the parlor. They were furnished with items her mother no longer wanted, but they were just fine for Etta's needs. Other than a small sofa and a single padded wooden chair, her parlor was lined with bookshelves. On the shelves were her college books and others she'd either purchased for herself or borrowed from her father's library. On the walls of the room, she had hung a portrait of her parents and a few of her early *Arizona Republican* articles. She opened the package from The Emporium and set the two bottles of bourbon on the counter, turning them to look at the labels. They weren't fancy, by any means, and the spelling, she knew for certain, would not have been approved by the copy editors at the paper.

"But, in this case," she whispered to herself, "I don't care about the label, just the contents."

Etta tossed her jacket onto the sofa and slipped out of her shoes. She opened the smaller of the two bottles and poured an inch of the golden liquid into a crystal glass—borrowed from her father's study, since bourbon tasted better in fine glassware—and took the drink over to the small window that looked out onto the street. Etta had not yet learned to enjoy swallowing the liquor in one gulp. She preferred to sip it, to let it burn her lips and take her breath away. She pulled the curtain aside with her empty hand and brought the glass to her lips. "This one's for you, Mr. Henry Carter of Bisbee, Arizona," she whispered and let the curtain drop, then sat down on the sofa. That evening, with the copy of the *New York Monthly* on her lap, Etta Pearce began planning a trip to Bisbee.

"Henry, we need to talk." Cal walked into the young man's office and shut the door behind him. He placed the *New York Monthly* magazine in the center of the desk and said, "Look at page 37."

Henry glanced at the heavy pale blue paper cover and turned to the page. He seemed stunned by seeing his name in print and looked back up at Cal, a huge smile spread across his face. "How did my story get to New York?" He looked down at the open magazine. "They actually printed my story, Cal."

"Yes, they did. I'm proud of you, Henry. It's a good story and deserves to be read." His words were positive, yet Henry could tell that Cal had more to say. "It's great news, but I think it's going to make us some trouble."

"What kind of trouble?"

Shaking his head slightly, Cal leaned back against the closed door and took off his wire-rimmed glasses. He started to speak, then halted while he wiped the lenses with his handkerchief. When he finally started talking, his voice was softer.

"I know that a copy of this magazine goes to the library, but I'm not sure if any of the mine managers get copies. I can probably get hold of the library's copy—check it out and then lose it—but if anyone in town has one, it won't be long before the rest of the people who'd be concerned will know what you've written."

Henry slumped a bit in his chair and ran his fingers

through his hair.

"Has anyone from the mine office talked to you? Are we in trouble?" He closed the magazine and stared at the cover for a moment.

Cal looked at his young reporter and said, "I've been thinking it might be a good idea to send you out of town."

"But how can you do that without getting in trouble yourself?"

"Listen, Henry, sometimes things like this flare up for a while and then die down after a week or so. Sometimes they stay hot for months and turn into trouble for anyone involved. There's just no way to know in advance." Cal reached over and patted Henry on the shoulder. "I'm not worried about my job. I might get scolded, but they won't fire me... there's not a long line of fellas who want this job. I'm going to make you a stringer. I can handle the local news for quite a while. I did it that way before I hired you and I can do it again. If you're out of town, working on things like the war, for instance, your absence will cool off some of the hotheads." He cleared his throat and added, "I think I can also get Mr. Samson, next door, to support us. He may be a little reluctant, but if he knows that you're out there reporting on the war, he'll back me up."

"But how'll I report on the war? I can't run off to France."

"No, you can't, but you *can* go to Fort Huachuca, or over to Camp Cody in Deming. Most of the army officers like to talk to reporters, maybe get their names in the paper and let the folks at home know that they're doing their duty." He waited for Henry's response.

"How long do you think I'd have to be gone?"

"I don't know for sure, maybe a few weeks or a month. But if you send me some good stories focused on the soldiers and the war effort, your byline will have a positive impact on the community *and* likely squelch some of the trouble from your deportation story." Cal went on to say that Henry should pack a bag and get out of Bisbee by nightfall if he can but certainly by early morning. He handed the young man an envelope containing several hundred dollars and told him to keep in touch. "Don't tell me where you're going, just send me a story and move on to someplace else. If you run out of money or get in trouble some place, then call me."

Henry stood and shook Cal's hand. "I thought I'd be happy when my story got printed, but somehow it doesn't feel good. I guess that there's a cost for telling the truth, isn't there, Cal?"

Two days after Henry left Bisbee, Cal sat at his desk working on his budget when the phone rang.

"*Bisbee Daily Review*, Langley," he said gruffly.

"Mr. Langley, this is Etta Pearce," the voice soft, but direct. "I'm a reporter for the *Arizona Republican*."

"How can I help you, Miss Pearce was it?"

"Yes, Etta Pearce. I'm wondering if you'd be willing to help a fellow journalist. I'm looking for a person from Bisbee and thought that you might know how I could locate him."

"I suppose I could help. Who are you trying to find?"

"The gentleman's name is Henry Carter."

Cal didn't immediately respond, instantly wondering if the woman really was a reporter or snooping for the mine management.

"Mr. Langley, are you there?"

"Yes, sorry. Can you hold for just a moment?"

Cal took a deep breath, unsure how to handle the woman's inquiry.

"Sorry about that, Miss Pearce, you said, Henry Carter?"

"Yes, sir, I read his story in the *New York Monthly* and decided that I needed to talk to him about his experience. Do you know Mr. Carter or how I can find him?"

"Well, yes, I do know him, but it may take some time to locate him. Is there something *I* can help you with?"

"I see," said the young-sounding woman, "but are you willing to help me contact him?"

"If I can find him and if he's willing to speak with you, then I will have him contact you at your office in Phoenix."

"Thank you, Mr. Langley. If it's not a bother, I'd like to follow up in a few days to see if you've had any success. This is important to me, sir. As a journalist yourself, I suspect that you support writers from any source who are able to report the news as capably as Mr. Carter has." She paused, then said, "I'm sorry, I suppose you *have* read the article, haven't you?"

"Yes, I've read it and yes, it is a fine piece of work." He paused for a moment, considering what he'd tell Miss Pearce when she called back. "I need to go now, Miss Pearce," he said, wondering if she was interested in something other than Henry's writing skills.

Cal hung up the phone and sighed deeply. He wrote the reporter's name on a slip of paper and set it in the center of his desk.

In Phoenix, Etta made a few notes on a pad and then walked down to the archives. She asked Ed Greene if he had any copies of the *Bisbee Daily Review* on the shelves.

"Maybe some from last year," he said and walked back into his storage area.

Etta paced in front of the counter, her mind ruminating on the conversation with the *Review* editor. *He seemed reluctant or cautious,* she thought.

"Here you go, Miss Pearce. I'm not sure why we'd have these on the shelf, but there are two editions from a few months back." He handed them across the counter. "When you're finished with them, you can put them in the rubbish. I don't think we'll have anyone else looking for news from Bisbee."

Well maybe we should *have someone looking into Bisbee,* she thought.

Smiling, Etta thanked Ed and walked back to her desk.

She spent the rest of the day looking at the combined dozen or so pages, combing through stories, advertisements, letters to the editor, and theater reviews looking for the name of Henry Carter. Although he may have had other assignments, his by-line only appeared on sports stories and movie reviews. Not finding his name on any of the general news stories, she re-read every page looking for anything that reflected the man's style. The sports stories about baseball were clearly Carter's work. There is little to compare between the game and the deportation of a thousand striking miners even if style and tone are the same.

Two days after getting the call from Miss Pearce a telegram was delivered to Cal's desk an hour after dinner. He gave the delivery boy a nickel and tore open the envelope. Henry promised to call him at nine o'clock that night.

When the phone rang at 9:02, Cal answered.

"Henry?"

"Yeah, boss, it's me. I wanted to tell you that I sent an article by mail this afternoon."

"Great. You want to give me a brief summary?"

"Sure. I got a chance to meet with the camp commander at Huachuca and he had one of his Lieutenants give me a tour. I got to talk to officers and sergeants, watched not just marching, but combat practice. What was most interesting was getting to spend so much time with the recruits from different parts of the country. I learned when and why they joined up, what they thought of their training and mission, and mostly discovered that they all believe that having Americans in the war will lead to a quick end... a surrender by the Germans."

"Sounds good, Henry. Where are you headed next?"

"My plans are to head to Camp Cody in Deming tomorrow to write about the training and also to talk to some of the town's citizens about their relationship with the army. You can reach me at the Commercial Hotel until

Sunday. I'll have another story to send to you then." Henry knew not to ask about his published story, since they'd decided not to trust anyone but themselves with the information.

"Okay, Henry. Keep up the good work and stay in touch."

By late Sunday night, Cal hadn't heard from Henry, so he placed a call to the hotel.

"Is Mr. Carter staying with us, sir?" said the man, his voice deep, reminding Cal of a bullfrog.

"He should have arrived two days ago from El Paso."

"Well, that would explain why he's not registered. We were sold out that night, so if Mr. Carter did arrive late we'd have referred him to another establishment."

"Do you recall where he might have been sent?"

"Sorry, sir, but we wouldn't have kept a record of that. There are a number of hotels in this part of town, perhaps you could call them and inquire of their management."

It took Cal less than ten minutes to discover the phone numbers of the other Deming hotels, and fewer than two more to hear the phone ringing in Henry's room.

"Hello?" Henry must have been sleeping, thought Cal.

"Wake up sleepyhead, this is your boss."

"Cal... what?"

"Henry, you were supposed to call me tonight."

"Sorry, Cal, I was out on a training patrol with an infantry company this afternoon and I'm beat." He paused a moment to rub his eyes. "Has there been any trouble about my story?"

"Henry, no one is talking about your story. It's been out more than a week and I've not heard anything about it. I guess it helps that I lost the copy from the library."

"That's good news," said Henry.

"It is and I hope that it stays quiet. But there's been another interesting development and I'm not sure how we should deal with it."

Henry asked, "So what's this new development?"

"I got a telephone call the other day from a reporter in Phoenix. She works for the *Republican*—"

"She? It was a *woman* reporter?"

"Yes, Henry, she's a woman and she's a reporter."

"Well, what did she want?"

"If you'll be quiet for a minute I'll tell you." He took a sip of his now cold coffee. "She asked me if I knew anyone by the name of Henry Carter."

"She asked about me? What did she want? What—?"

"Will you hold on a minute?" Cal interrupted. "She said she'd read your story and wanted to talk to you about your experience. I didn't let on that you worked for the paper or that I knew you personally."

"How'd she read the story?"

"Henry, I know this may sound odd, but the people in Phoenix do know how to read and I would expect the *Republican* gets a copy of the same magazines we do."

"I suppose," said Henry, a bit chagrined. "So, what am I supposed to do?"

"Well, that's up to you. If you want to talk to her, then I'll arrange a meeting. If you don't want to talk, I'll tell her that you enjoy your privacy and won't meet with her."

"Why would a reporter for the state's biggest newspaper want to talk to me?"

"I'm not sure, Henry. She seemed to think that you were a capable writer of news."

"Really?" said Henry." He thought about it for a moment then said, "I suppose, as a stringer, that I could travel to Phoenix and meet this woman reporter. It might be interesting, but do you think she's got another motive?"

"No, I don't. I checked her out and she's just a society reporter for the *Republican*."

Cal waited patiently while Henry pondered the news. "Since you still work for me, and since I'm trying to protect you from certain powerful people in our town, I'm going to suggest that you meet her in Tucson two days from now. I want you to finish your Camp Cody story before you move on to anything else."

"I'll put it in the mail in the morning."

"Then here's what I'll do. I'll call her in the morning and set up a time and place for you to meet her in Tucson the day after tomorrow in the evening. You stay put in Deming and I'll send you a telegram with the details." He paused in thought and said, "If the schedule doesn't work for her, then I guess she isn't *that* interested in your story."

"I guess that's the best way to handle it. I'll make sure I have a ticket on the early train."

"I hope that all of this stays quiet, Henry, because I want you back to work in Bisbee. In the meantime, give me one or two stories a week until things blow over."

"I'll do that, Cal."

"And let me know what happens between you and Miss Etta Pearce as soon as you can."

Chapter 8

CAL PICKED UP THE phone and asked the operator to connect with Miss Henrietta Pearce at the *Arizona Republican* in Phoenix. He made sure he had the address of the Santa Rita Hotel in Tucson at the ready. He also made a note to call Henry as soon as he confirmed the day and time for the young reporter's meeting.

After just a few minutes, the telephone on his desk rang and he picked up the long-necked device, lifted the earpiece off the hook and said, "Calvin Langley."

"Mr. Langley, this is Sally at the phone company. I have your party in Phoenix on the line."

"Thanks, Sally." Cal waited through a few buzzes and clicks and then heard the familiar voice of the female reporter.

"Good morning, Mr. Langley, this is Etta Pearce." Cal could almost feel the excitement in her voice.

"Good morning to you as well. I promised that once I'd spoken with Mr. Carter I'd get back to you. Is this a good time to talk?"

"Yes, it is."

"I managed to contact Mr. Carter late yesterday, and he has indicated to me that he'd be willing to meet with you." Cal waited for a response.

"That's wonderful, Mr. Langley."

"Mr. Carter is presently out of the state but believes that he would be available for a meeting in Tucson tomorrow evening."

The surprise in the woman's voice was interesting. "Tomorrow evening? That quickly? Why Mr. Langley I'd be *delighted* to meet with Mr. Carter in Tucson tomorrow."

"I'll let Mr. Carter know that you'll meet with him at the Santa Rita Hotel tomorrow night at six o'clock. I believe that you can arrange public transportation from Phoenix to Tucson that will meet the schedule."

"Of course, Mr. Langley, I *could* use the train. The schedule is very convenient, but I think, instead, that I'll drive my own car."

Hmmm, Cal thought, *she's got her* own *car.* "I see. Alright, then. I'll let Mr. Carter know that you will meet him tomorrow evening at six o'clock at the Santa Rita Hotel in Tucson."

"Mr. Langley, I sincerely appreciate your assistance in setting up the meeting. Thank you so much."

"You're quite welcome, ma'am. I hope the conversation meets your expectations."

Cal returned the earpiece to its cradle and whispered to himself, "Although I still don't know what those expectations are."

Langley penciled the meeting details on a blank telegraph form, addressed it to Henry at the hotel in Deming. He had Bert send up one of the newsboys to run the wire over to the telegraph office.

"I want you to wait for a reply. Tell them to bill me for the charges."

The boy ran down the stairs and out of the building. Cal sat back in his chair and breathed a sigh of... relief? Or was it concern? He couldn't tell at the moment, but he hoped that the meeting between the metropolitan female reporter and his rookie reporter would go well, since he had no idea what Etta was seeking. Then he pulled a letter out of his inbox and got back to work. Rather quickly, a familiar voice interrupted him.

"Good morning, Langley."

"Oh, good morning, Mr. Brook." Cal was very surprised to see the mine executive in his office. He wondered why Brook was there, but he suspected it wasn't a personal visit. Shuffling around a few papers, he finally asked, "Is there something I can do for you?"

"Perhaps, but that remains to be seen."

Cal sat back in his chair, trying to look relaxed and calm.

"It's about your young reporter, Carter I think his name is." Brook paused, waiting for some kind of response from the editor. There was none, so he continued. "Mr. Greenway wanted to make sure that Carter's experience in Warren didn't affect him negatively."

"Negatively?" Cal responded, "How do you mean, Mr. Brook? You do know that he should never have been arrested in the first place."

"Yes, but rumor has it that he's still talking to people in town about the incident. We just hope that the young man's loyalty hasn't changed because of how he was treated, and that he's not become aligned with the union or the strikers. We wouldn't want his youthful exuberance to lead him to support the strikers or their allies."

"I can tell you absolutely, that he is not aligned with the union or the strikers, Henry Carter is a good reporter and a loyal citizen, sir. Mr. Greenway and the other mining executives have nothing to fear from him. In fact, I've sent him out of town to do some stories about army training."

"Wonderful, Langley, that's good. I'm sure he'll do a fine job." He reached out to shake Cal's hand and added, "You will keep an eye on him, won't you?"

In Deming, Henry was checking out. He'd paid his bill and was lifting up his single suitcase when the messenger arrived.

"Mr. Carter, hold on a moment. This wire is for you," said the hotel clerk.

Henry took the proffered telegram from the bespectacled man. He read it, turned to the messenger and asked him if he had a blank form.

"Yes sir. Would you like me to wait?"

"Please," said Henry as he grabbed a pencil from the

counter, wrote a response and handed the form to the boy. "Please send this as soon as you return to the telegraph office. Here's a quarter for you and have them bill the charges to the *Bisbee Daily Review*."

The messenger ran out of the hotel lobby and Henry quickly followed him. He had just enough time to make the train to Tucson. If Cal was confused about his *own* feelings regarding the meeting, Henry's thoughts were much more intense. After a restless night, he'd been unable to decide what the woman might want to know or why she wanted to talk to him. Regardless of how the meeting might turn out, he realized that he was taking the train to Tucson.

As Henry Carter took his seat in the passenger car of the Southern Pacific train, Etta Pearce sat at her desk in the news office of the *Arizona Republican* in Phoenix. She had hoped that the editor of the *Review* could locate Carter and then convince him to meet with her. Langley had done that... and more. He'd arranged a place and time in a location that was convenient for her. *Well, it's sort of convenient*, she thought. *I can get there early enough tomorrow if I drive, but I still have to finish my column today and then convince Mr. Sidney that I need to take the day off tomorrow.*

Determined to meet with Carter regardless of the consequences that missing a day of work at the paper might create, Etta spent the next six hours writing and rewriting her theater and society columns. Although she was convinced that they didn't measure up to her typical work, she still believed they were better written than most of the work done by the men in the office. At seven o'clock that night, she clipped the two articles together and took them to Mr. Sidney's office. She hand wrote a note and placed it on top of the manuscripts. In her direct style and clearly legible writing, she'd written, *Mr. Sidney, I have submitted my two columns a full forty-eight hours early, since I must be absent from the office all day tomorrow. If you have any concerns, we can discuss them when I return. Etta Pearce.*

Back at her own desk, Etta picked up her clutch bag, turned off the desk lamp and left the office. Outside, she took a deep breath of the warm summer night air and walked briskly toward the lot where she'd parked her car, paid the attendant and fifteen minutes later, walked into her apartment. Calculating the time she'd need to drive from Phoenix to Tucson, Etta decided she could sleep in late the next morning and still have time to visit her parents at home before leaving for her meeting with Carter. She poured two fingers of bourbon into her purloined crystal glass and carried it into her bedroom. She changed her office clothes for a silky nightgown, brushed her teeth at the sink and sat down on the edge of her bed. She gazed out the window through the chintz curtain and wondered what tomorrow might bring. Etta quickly swallowed the whiskey, feeling the liquid burn its way down her throat. She punched her pillow and lay down on the bed. Convinced that Carter was older than she was, Etta feared that he'd try to get personal with her, to distract her from her agenda. *I can't let that happen,* she thought. *I don't want him to take me for a drink or to the theater. I won't put up with that. All I want to talk about is where he learned to write, how he builds his stories, what he's working on now.* Sleep didn't come quickly for her that night.

At six o'clock the next evening, Henry walked into the dining room of the hotel. He stopped a waiter and told him he had a reservation and was expecting a guest. The waiter asked his name and said, "Your guest has already arrived, Mr. Carter. She's sitting at the table next to the window."

Henry turned in the direction the man had pointed and realized that the woman sitting by the window was not how he'd imagined her. In his hours in the Pullman yesterday, Henry had decided that Miss Etta Pearce was likely an older woman, forty or fifty at least. She would be unattractive, of course, not nearly as nice looking as his ma had been. She'd probably expect him to pay for the dinner and she would probably talk down to him as if he were still in school. Instead, the woman he saw sitting at the table was young and modern. He had not expected to see such a lovely woman. He certainly hadn't anticipated her short hair or short skirt. He clutched his cap in his left hand and walked toward the table.

"Miss Pearce?"

Turning up from her copy of the *New York Monthly*, she said, "Mr. Carter?" Henry clearly wasn't the only person in the dining room who was surprised. Etta's own vision of what Carter would look like was also wrong. The young, clean-cut man standing in front of her was nothing like the one who'd filled her thoughts last night.

Henry broke the brief silence. "I hope you haven't been waiting long," he said. His throat was suddenly dry. "May I sit down?"

Etta smiled and said, "Please do, Mr. Carter. I'm so glad that you agreed to meet with me." Her own mouth dry, she asked, "Would you like something to drink?"

Henry pulled the chair away from the table and sat down. He didn't know what to do with his cap, so he dropped it on the floor next to his feet. "If you'll join me," he said, "I'd like something cold." What he really wanted was a cold beer.

Etta wanted a double shot of bourbon, but she'd have to settle for something legal instead. "I'll have iced tea."

The waiter arrived and took their order—iced tea for both of them.

As the waiter walked away, the two young reporters both spoke at once.

"How was your trip?"

"Did you have a nice trip?"

The fumbling overlap of their words caused both of

them to chuckle, then neither of them spoke for a few seconds and the sudden silence generated more laughter.

Henry said, "You first, Miss Pearce." The smile on his lips was evident in his eyes as well.

Etta smiled in return and asked, "Did you have a nice ride to Tucson?"

For the next fifteen minutes or so they discussed how they got to Tucson, the weather, and a number of other topics that had no connection with why they were sitting together. The waiter brought their drinks and each of them took quick sips of the cold tea.

"Mr. Carter, I suppose that you are wondering why I wanted to meet with you." Henry nodded. "It's just that, as a journalist, I so appreciated your story." She tapped the cover of the *New York Monthly*. "Its accuracy, thoroughness, and compliance with the principles of journalism not only caught my attention but fascinated me."

"Thank you, Miss Pearce..."

"Please let me finish," she said, her smile genuine. "But more than the journalistic quality of the piece, I was enthralled by the quality of your story-telling ability. Your article showed me what you saw, made me feel what you felt." She shook her head from side to side. "You must have had some wonderful professors. Where did you go to school?"

"School?"

"Yes, what university?"

"Miss Pearce, I truly appreciate your comments on my story. You make it sound far better than it probably is." Henry didn't want to talk about where he went to school but finally relented. "I didn't go to college or to journalism school. I graduated from high school in Bisbee."

"Mr. Carter, I'm sorry, I just assumed that..."

"Please, Miss Pearce, it's okay. Don't worry about it. I had made some assumptions about you that were totally wrong as well."

"You did?"

"I did, and I will *never* tell you what they were." Henry smiled.

Etta sipped her tea and returned the smile.

The conversation was interrupted when the waiter delivered their dinner. While they ate, Etta described her job at the *Republican*—how boring it was, the ridiculous assignments—and how she'd always wanted to do something important with her life. She quickly decided not to tell him about her Jerome article.

"My father is a very successful businessman," she said. "He's a commodities broker and makes money off of the things that other people want."

"It sounds important, but not very exciting." Henry just wanted to keep her talking, because he enjoyed listening to the sound of her voice.

"It is boring. Both he and my mother wanted me to be a teacher. In fact, they insisted that I had to go to the Normal School in Phoenix so I could become a teacher and find a good husband." Etta started chasing peas around her plate with a fork. "I never wanted to be one, and I'm certainly not looking for a husband, at least one who'd be willing to marry a teacher."

Etta set the fork down and looked across the table at Henry. For a moment, he was uncomfortable, her eyes seemed to be drilling into him. "If you never went to college, how did you learn to write like this?" She pointed her finger at the article in the magazine.

Henry wanted to answer her question because he could sense her sincerity. He'd never thought much about education, especially his own. As a boy, he hated school and grew weary of his ma's prodding. Now, sitting across the table from an educated, experienced reporter—who was also an incredibly beautiful woman—he didn't know how to start. So, he simply took a swallow of his tea and began telling her about his pa's death, his ma's insistence on learning, and about the man who taught him the things a boy needed to know.

"When I was ten, a friend of mine was murdered. He was a man who'd once saved my life." Etta watched his face, saw the silver shimmer at the edge of his eyes. "For a while afterward, I was sad. Then another man, the one who helped me grow up, became my friend, my *best* friend."

Etta almost reached across the table to touch his hand, but hesitated, not wanting to interrupt Henry's tale.

"He took me, a ten-year-old delinquent and taught me to read and to *want* to read. He taught me to write and showed me how important the two skills are." Henry had forgotten the meal in front of him, his memories filling him in a different way.

Etta asked with tenderness, "Was the man a teacher or a preacher?"

Henry smiled, his eyes sparkling. "No, he isn't a teacher, but he taught me more than I'd ever have learned on my own. He's not a preacher either, but he does preach *at* me sometimes."

"Who is he?"

Henry looked at Etta's face, her soft skin, the way her bobbed hair draped around her cheeks, her entrancing eyes. Somehow, he knew he could tell her anything.

"His name is Calvin Langley."

"The editor of the *Review*?"

Henry nodded his head. "Yes, my boss, my teacher, and my best friend all in one."

Etta sat back in her chair and looked at Henry. "I have to meet the man who taught a bright young man how to be a great reporter. There are a lot of men I work with who've had a formal education, and combined, they don't have the skills, the talent, or the voice you have." She shook her head and smiled.

"Well," Henry said, "maybe someday you'll come to Bisbee and meet him."

"Yes, Mr. Carter, maybe someday I will."

Each of the young reporters had learned a great deal

during their dinner meeting in Tucson. There were a number of differences in their experiences, both professional and personal. Not the least of these was the difference in education. Henry felt a little awkward during their conversations, not because of any weakness in his conversational skills, but by the mere fact that Etta was a college graduate and he had only a high school diploma. His background—living in a cabin on a dirt road and helping his ma wash sheets for a brothel—couldn't compare with Etta's wealthy upbringing. Yet, he was comfortable with her. Their discussions felt natural, like they'd known each other for a while. One thing Henry knew was that he wanted to see her again.

Etta left the dining room mostly amazed. She was deeply impressed by Henry's commitment to telling the truth, whatever the cost, and with his maturity. She knew that he was more grown up at twenty than any of the journalists she'd encountered at the *Republican*, including her boss. Before she fell asleep that night, she wondered how long she could continue writing about plays, weddings, and women's fashions. *I really do need to visit Bisbee*, she thought as she closed her eyes and drifted into a dream.

The next morning as Etta drove north out of Tucson, the hot desert air rushed through the open side windows and ruffled her hair. She had removed her cloche hat and jacket and even undid the top two buttons of her blouse, hoping to stay cool. She also took off her shoes in order to feel the rumble of the road. She had purchased a pair of dark-tinted sunglasses which now perched on her nose. Tan sand and dust billowed behind her Ford as she reflected on her meeting with Henry Carter. They had spoken about their backgrounds, their interests, and their work, but what stuck with her, the thing that filled her head on the north-bound highway, was how similar their long-term plans were.

Etta stopped in Casa Grande to buy some gas and stood on the shaded porch of a filling station, drinking a

Coca-Cola, staring across the vast openness and wondering if her life would be as empty as the wasteland that spread all around her. The night before, watching Henry Carter talk about his own dreams, she had seen in his eyes something that reached deeply into her consciousness. Even now, while setting the empty bottle in a box next to the ice chest, that same *something* clicked like a light switch in her mind. *We want the same thing. We want to tell the truth about... what?* She looked back toward Tucson, wondering if similar thoughts had occurred to Mr. Carter... *Henry*. After paying for the fuel, Etta climbed into her roadster and sped away, her mind wrestling with an idea. Nodding ever so slightly, she told herself, *Yes, I want to work with Henry Carter on something exciting, to dig deep into the truth. But will he want to work with me*?

Chapter 9

When Henry got to Benson, he telephoned Cal. The editor answered casually.

"Langley."

"Cal, it's Henry."

"Where are you?" he asked as he set down his pencil and took off his glasses.

Henry looked around the depot, wiped the sweat from his forehead, and said, "I'm in Benson. Did you get my telegram?" Before leaving Tucson, Henry had sent Cal a telegram about his meeting with Etta. He left out the personal items and focused on Etta's comments about the story. In the last line of the wire he'd said, "She's smart and wants to be the kind of reporter you taught me to be."

"I did. It sounds like you have an admirer." The editor chuckled to himself.

"Well, I guess." Henry's brow wrinkled a bit, "I liked her. I'm not sure what she thought about me, but we got along well. Anyway, I'm headed to Fort Huachuca to follow up on my earlier story. After that, I'm off to Kelly Field in San Antonio. There's an aerodrome that may be more interesting to the folks in Bisbee than the troops at Huachuca."

"Wait a second, Henry." Cal set the phone down, got up and looked down the stairwell to see if he was alone. "Hold off on the army camps. I want you to take the late train back here tonight, then wait at the depot until I come to you." He paused, thinking, and added, "We need to talk face to face. After the depot clears out, move around back to the platform and I'll meet you there."

"Okay, Cal, but what's up?"

"Just meet me on the platform. I'll tell you then." Cal said goodbye and put the earpiece back in its cradle. He picked up a pad and started making some notes.

Henry stared at the telephone for a moment, then returned to the ticket booth and swapped his two tickets for one to Bisbee. He walked across the street from the depot to a café, ordered a cup of coffee and sat wondering what the mystery was. He had a difficult time focusing on Cal's mystery, since thoughts about Etta kept interrupting.

The sun had been long set when Henry arrived back in Bisbee. A faint glow still rode the western sky, but it was dark on the plaza in front of the depot. The streetlights of the town were on as was the single shaded bulb hanging over the door, but they cast little, if any light on the open space in front of the depot. Henry waited until the passenger car emptied before he stepped onto the platform. He found a dark spot at the western end of the building and stood where he could see in the direction of the *Review* office. Cal was already rounding the corner in front of the bank. Henry saw him cast a glance over his shoulder and then hurry to the backside of the depot.

Cal whispered loud enough for Henry to hear. "Stay in the dark, Henry. I want to make sure no one is following me." The editor put his foot up on the platform, took out his kerchief and wiped the dust off his shoe.

"I'm glad you made it, Henry. I know we're taking a chance here, but I wanted to see you in person, to make sure you're alright."

"It's good to see you, too. The sneaking around must mean that I'm in some kind of trouble." Henry kept his back against the building and his voice low.

"Grab your bag and let's go up the back stairs. Bert and his crew are busy printing tomorrow's edition, so they won't see us. We've got a lot to talk about tonight."

When they walked into Cal's office, the editor switched on the small lamp on his desk. Henry set his bag down and took the empty chair.

Cal took out his notebook, set it on the desk and said, "Here's what's going on, Henry. Apparently, the mine management was following you around town before you left last week. They must know that you visited the Payne house, but I don't think they are aware of your meeting with the fella who came back to town." Henry started to ask a question, but Cal held up his hand, wanting to finish his point. "Mr. Brook came to the office the other day and made it clear that they were concerned about your business in town. They wondered if you might be siding with the union. I told him that you were a good reporter and a loyal citizen. I think I convinced him that they had nothing to worry about."

"But?" Henry said, knowing that Cal wouldn't have called him back to town if things were going well.

"Right again, Henry. *But*, I think that one or more of the mine's stockholders in New York might have sent a copy of your story to Greenway."

"I guess we knew this could happen."

"We did, and it probably has happened. Your being out of town has helped keep their interest in you subdued, but I don't know how long that'll last."

"So, what do you want to do?"

"I think that you'll need to keep working out of town for a while, probably keep up with the war reporting. Your idea about Kelly Field is a good one. If your story gets some good comments here in town, it'll be good for the paper and maybe management will overlook your youthful exuberance."

"Exuberance? That's not fair, Cal. That was good reporting, that..."

"I know, I know. That was Brook's word, not mine. If that's all they think it was, you probably still have a job."

"Do you think that if I keep up with the military reports that their concerns about the roundup will go away?"

"Yes, but there's another thing going on that'll keep their attention and, perhaps, take it off of you." Cal glanced at his notebook and continued. "There are rumors going around town that the IWW is going to sue the mine owners and some of the city officials. They seem to have the governor's ear on this, and he is an acquaintance of President Wilson."

"Lawsuits take a long time to happen, don't they?"

"They do, son, but they also absorb the attention of the very same people who have an interest in what you are doing, at least as it applies to the company."

They spent another half hour talking about the story, the lawsuit, and the short-term impact on Henry's life.

"Now let me fix you a cup of coffee and you can tell me about Miss Etta Pearce." Cal withheld the smile that was trying to find its way to his lips. "Tell me, young man, what was she like?"

"When I tell you about Etta you'll think I'm exaggerating about her." Henry seemed to gather his thoughts before he continued. "Okay, she's young, maybe a couple years older than me. She went to college, she's from a wealthy family, she's smart," he paused, took a deep breath, and said, "and she's beautiful."

"How is she beautiful?"

"She's not like any of the women you've ever seen, certainly not like anyone in Bisbee. Cal, she has short brown hair. She wore a short skirt that barely covered her knees and she even smokes cigarettes. I wouldn't be surprised if she also drinks." Even in the subdued light of the desk lamp, Cal noticed a rosy glow started to creep up Henry's cheeks.

"So, I take it that you didn't get along with this young, beautiful, smart, rich girl?" Cal smiled.

"We got along *just fine*. It was so easy to talk to her, Cal, and she was actually interested in what I had to say. She really liked the story. Etta asked me where I went to journalism school. When I told her that *you* taught me, she said that she wanted to meet you some time."

Cal watched and listened as Henry continued with a description of the dinner meeting. The young man didn't leave anything out and drew a vivid picture of the scene, the characters, and the results.

"I think that we'll be seeing each other again, Cal. I just hope it's sooner rather than later."

"You know, Henry, that gives me an idea." He was still for a second or two and then said, "If you think that Etta," Cal smiled as he used her first name, "is interested in meeting me and if you believe that she's the type of girl who can take being observed wherever she goes, maybe we should invite her to visit Bisbee."

"She's tough, Cal. I think she could get the Germans to quit over in France."

"Her presence in Bisbee might be enough of a distraction that would make the management forget about your story. That is if you can get her to stop complimenting your work."

"You're serious, aren't you Cal?"

"I am." He sat back in his chair, picked up his pencil and pointed it at the reporter. "You spend the night here in the office and get over to the depot before the town wakes up. Get a ticket to San Antonio and write your aviator story. While you're gone, I will send Miss Pearce an invitation to visit our fair city and try to coordinate her arrival with your return from Texas."

"What reason will you give her? What if she doesn't want to come?"

Cal stood up, turned off the desk lamp. "You leave that to me, Henry. Now get some sleep and don't miss the morning train." The editor picked up his briefcase and walked down the stairs and out of the building.

Henry went to the window and looked down onto Main Street, then took off his coat and shoes and sat on the bench. Using his rolled-up coat as a pillow, he lay down and tried to sleep.

Chapter 10

Henry spent ten days in San Antonio talking to people in the town and at the new aerodrome. He wanted to find out how the new pilots were trained, what kind of aircraft they used, and even how the planes worked. His press-pass gave him clearance through the heavily guarded gate and proved to be an effective calling card when talking to the officers in the headquarters building. His youthful appearance also made it easy to interview the student pilots and the ground crews, the soldiers who kept the planes operating. In San Antonio, he talked to merchants, politicians and people on the street, seeking their opinions on the airbase. Henry thought that this would give his story a balance of sorts—civilian and military, good and bad. Throughout his efforts, Henry kept meticulous notes, wanting to stick with his and Cal's standards of reporting.

One afternoon near the end of his stay, he was having lunch with the student pilots at the mess hall. They spent most of the time talking about all they'd learned in the last six months. But today, they said, was their last flight before graduation. Their reverie was interrupted when the chief instructor stopped by the long table.

"Mr. Carter?"

"Yes sir, Major. How can I help you?"

"I was wondering if you would be interested in riding in my aircraft this afternoon. We'll be putting some of your table guests through their final flight exams, and your observations from up there," he pointed right through the ceiling of the mess hall, "might enhance your story."

"Yes, sir, Major. I'd appreciate the opportunity. I've never been in a plane before."

"Then let this be your first time. I'll expect you on the airfield at fourteen hundred, dressed and ready to fly." He turned to the young man seated across from Henry. "Cadet Larson, you will see to it that Mr. Carter is provided with the proper clothing and equipment and is given a brief training session in the use of a parachute."

"Yes, sir." Larson stood and saluted the Major.

"Parachute?" Henry hadn't thought about that aspect of flying. He gulped as a knot formed in his stomach and thanked the Major as the senior officer marched out of the mess hall.

"Well, Henry," Larson said, "let's go get you ready to fly."

At precisely two o'clock, the Major revved up his engine and started the plane down the runway. Henry was excited and maybe a little frightened, but before he knew it, the aircraft lifted off the ground and soared into the air. He laughed out loud when he felt the wind in his face. The student pilots, all six of them, followed directly behind the Major's plane. At one point, Henry saw that they'd formed into a V, like a flight of geese. He watched as the Major signaled to the students with his hands and they spread out across the sky.

Over the next hour, Henry collected a lifetime of memories. Barrel rolls, spins, steep climbs and screaming dives didn't seem to bother him. He watched as the pilots mirrored the Major's actions. He'd been told that their efforts would be evaluated by the Major and by the other instructors on the ground.

Henry looked down onto the airfield he'd only recently seen from ground level and then stared out in amazement over the vast landscape that was wider than any he'd seen from the mountains around Bisbee.

When the major pounded him on the shoulder, Henry turned to see him point down toward the airfield. A bit disappointed, he assumed that the show was over, but now had something that would make his story not only interesting to the readers but provide them with an exciting personal experience.

Henry watched through the spinning propellers as each of the six students landed their planes on the dirt runway. The Major followed them down and smoothly landed his aircraft, then taxied toward the side of the airfield. As they rolled up to the other planes, Henry saw that each of the pilots was standing at attention near the front of his plane.

Before the propeller on the Major's plane had stopped spinning, the officer had jumped out of the cockpit and helped Henry down to the ground.

"Come along with me, Carter," he shouted, and marched toward the students. Stopping at each of the young men, the Major made a point to first address the few weaknesses that the students had shown and then to praise them for the good work they'd done. Each of the young pilots saluted him and much to his surprise, shook hands with Henry.

The morning after Henry's great airplane adventure, Cal sat at his desk in the *Review* building. He'd received a wire from Henry advising him that he expected to return to Bisbee by the weekend with a story about Kelly Field. He'd added a line that said, "You'll not believe what happened." Cal wondered what that was about for a moment.

He placed a telephone call to Etta Pearce in Phoenix. She hadn't been in the office, so he'd left a message for her to contact him. He had worked out a plan which he thought would get her to Bisbee where her presence would distract the paper's owners from the concerns about the young reporter and give Henry a chance to settle back down at home. Cal was also curious and wanted to meet his new reporter. It all depended on whether or not Miss Pearce was willing and able to take time off.

When Cal returned from lunch, he found a note on his desk that Etta had called. He took off his coat, sat down, picked up his pencil and called the *Arizona Republican*.

"This is Etta Pearce." With Henry's description of the young woman in his mind, Cal knew that the boy wasn't lying since her voice was strong and definitely feminine.

"Miss Pearce, this is Calvin Langley from Bisbee."

"Good morning. Mr. Langley. I'm sorry I missed your call. I was just away from my desk. How are things in Bisbee?"

Cal liked this girl already. "Things are fine in Bisbee, Miss Pearce. If you have a moment I'd like to discuss something with you. I have an idea that may seem strange and because of some assumptions I've made, it might also be offensive to you."

"Hmmm. Strange or offensive. This sounds interesting." Etta asked him to tell her more about his idea.

Cal leaned back in his chair, holding the long stem base of the phone in one hand and the earpiece in the other. *Here goes*, he thought.

"Miss Pearce, Henry filled me in on your meeting when he got back from Tucson. Henry was impressed with you. These are not exactly his words, but my interpretation of them. He suggested to me that you were smart, not just because of your formal education, but common-sense smart. He said that the two of you seemed to share the same principles, at least as they relate to journalism."

"I'm pleased with his assessment," she said. "I'd like to add that for a young man with just a high school diploma, Henry Carter is smarter than most people might expect. He gave you most of the credit for his education."

"We've known each other for over ten years and have had a lot of time together." Cal moved back to the topic. "Henry also said that you were dissatisfied with your assignments at the *Republican*, that you wanted to be writing on more important, more interesting topics."

"Mr. Langley, how should I address you?"

"Call me Cal."

"Thank you. Please call me Etta. I may be a woman, and I may even have a college degree, but to most men, especially those I work with at this newspaper, think that women aren't designed and built to handle anything other than society news. But I'm not like their mothers or wives or sisters. I want to do something important with my life."

"Etta, I can see that Henry's opinion of you, that you're smart *and* tough, is correct. That's why I'd like you to hear my idea. If it doesn't work for you, then we three can each move on with our careers. If, by chance, it is something you want to try, then I believe that you two young reporters can actually do something important with your lives."

Failing to keep the excitement out of her voice, Etta said, "Please, Cal, what is your idea?"

"In simple terms, I would like to think about a possible future for all three of us. I believe that you and Henry would make a very effective reporting team. He mentioned that you and he share an interest in the Muckrakers and the work they did a few decades ago. Maybe you two could become modern-day muckrakers." Cal paused briefly. "I would like to discuss this idea in person."

"I don't have to think about your suggestion, Cal. What you have described is what I want to do. What does Henry think?"

"I haven't talked to him about it. I didn't want to distract him on his current assignment. But, frankly, young lady, I think he'll be as interested as you seem to be."

They spoke for a little while longer, and Cal concluded the conversation with, "So, Etta, if you can get to Bisbee by the end of the week, we'll find a place for you to stay and then the three of us will talk this out." Then Cal mentioned his one concern. "I won't be able to pay you very much if this plan goes forward. Our small newspaper doesn't have the budget for two reporters."

"Cal, if this works out, you won't have to pay me anything."

"Pardon?"

"My father has given me a trust fund. I'm independent in more ways than my attitudes. I'll pay my own way."

This just keeps getting better, he thought. "Will you be arriving by train? If so I'll be sure to meet you at the depot here in Bisbee."

"That won't be necessary, Cal. I'll pack a few things, load them in my car and see you on Saturday."

The huge dust plume that billowed behind Etta's roadster as she roared down the road toward Bisbee might have been a sign for the residents if they had seen it and if they'd known it followed a very non-traditional driver. In her trip from Phoenix with a stopover in Tucson, Etta had discovered that she liked driving fast. She'd also learned that she could control the automobile enough to dodge potholes and the frequent critters that raced across the desert. Turning left at the train depot, she spotted Main Street and pulled in at the curb across from the *Bisbee Daily Review*.

As Etta exited the low-slung vehicle with her long, slender legs leading the way, she crossed over to the tall stone building. Keenly aware that she was being watched by nearly every pedestrian on the street, she ignored them and walked into the newspaper building following the sign that read "Office Upstairs."

Cal heard the unmistakable sound of high heels coming up the stairs and, as Etta reached the top of the stairwell, he looked up from his desk and then back down at his work. Immediately his head popped back up and he stared in wonder at the young woman striding across the floor toward his desk.

"Good afternoon, Cal." Etta stood tall and the grin that spread across her face was genuine. She was glad to be in

Bisbee and equally happy to be meeting with Cal in person.

Cal stood up and walked around the desk to her. He shook her hand and said, "Forgive my lack of manners, Etta. Welcome to Bisbee, Arizona, the copper capital of the world." Cal gestured toward the visitor chair and Etta sat down. "How was your trip, your drive?"

Etta took a hankie out of her clutch and dabbed at her forehead and cheeks. "It was fast, hot, and dusty, Cal. But I must admit it was more fun than I've had in a very long time."

"Henry didn't lie, not one bit."

"Well, based on my brief meeting with him, I suspect that Mr. Henry Carter always tells the truth." Looking around the office she asked, "Where is the famous writer?"

"He's due in on the late train tonight. I'll pick him up around ten and we'll get together first thing tomorrow." He set the pencil down and asked if she'd made accommodations yet. "I think that the Bisbee Grand Hotel will be sufficient for the weekend. That way you'll be close to the office and if our discussions go well, we can find a less expensive, more comfortable place on Monday."

For just a moment they stared at each other, becoming, it seemed, instant friends. A sense of comfort and familiarity hovered over the desk. A keen observer might have described the scene as the pinnacle of professional relationships. Two hard-working smart people glad to be working together without any of the distractions of an intimate relationship.

"If you'll point me in the direction of the hotel," said Etta, "I'll get checked in and spend some time ridding myself of the dust I accumulated on the road."

"Let me call the hotel and get one of their front rooms. You'll want to get a sense of the Bisbee energy, plus all of the rooms on the backside of the hotel look out at the rocky face of the hill." He picked up the phone, talked to the desk clerk and made the arrangement for Etta.

Early that evening, Cal and Etta had dinner at the Copper Queen Hotel. Cal wanted Etta to be seen by the locals. Her appearance and presence would stir up discussion that he hoped would distract the mine managers. He needn't have worried, since several of them were present in the dining room with their wives.

During the meal, one of the *Review* pressmen walked into the dining room, glanced around the large room until he spotted Cal, then walked over and handed him a telegram. Cal scanned the words, thanked the man and said to Etta, "It seems that there's been a delay and Henry's train is running three hours late."

"Damn," whispered Etta.

Cal chuckled, pleased rather than shocked by Etta's quiet outburst. "So, we'll meet tomorrow morning. Since Henry will need to get some sleep and wash the train dust out of his hair, let's say nine o'clock at my house." He spent a moment writing down his address and directions to the house, then handed it to her.

Etta put the note in her clutch bag and said,

"I suppose that's what the life of a real reporter is like. When I was writing about Phoenix society, I never had to take a train to find out what kind of underwear rich and famous socialites wore."

Etta and Cal laughed and continued with their meal. They talked more about their personal experiences for another hour and then Cal walked her up the street to the hotel.

"Etta, the job is yours if you want it."

"Oh, I want it, Cal."

They shook hands inside the lobby and said good night. It seemed, even at this late hour, that the town was already buzzing with the news of her arrival. As he walked away, he thought, *I like this young woman.*

* * *

The train pulled into the depot at a quarter to one and Cal met Henry on the platform.

"Hi, Cal," said a worn-out looking Henry.

"It's good to see you, Henry. Go on up to your place and get some rest. Meet me at my house at nine."

Henry looked directly into Cal's eyes. "Well? Did she get here?"

"She did. We'll see her at nine, so *go home* and get some sleep. That should be easy now that you have something to dream about."

"Aren't you worried that someone would see me?"

"No one is even thinking about you. All of the talk on the street is about the new girl in town."

Cal laughed and led Henry out of the depot. He walked him to the foot of Brewery Gulch and nudged him in the direction of his cabin.

Chapter 11

Henry looked out of the window of Cal's home a few blocks from the high school. He hadn't slept well after his late arrival in Bisbee and decided to walk off his fatigue at dawn. He'd rested on the editor's front porch until seven o'clock and then tapped on the door when he heard Cal scuffling across the floor.

"You know that you're two hours early, don't you?"

After he was invited in and Cal left to get dressed, Henry paced around the room from bookshelf to window and back again.

Henry let the curtain drop and turned toward Cal's voice, making a guttural sound, something like a frog's croak.

"Would you like some coffee, or would you rather go to sleep on the sofa?"

Pulling the curtain aside again, Henry asked, "When is she coming?"

"She'll be here by nine." Cal paused. "Why are you so nervous?" he asked.

"I don't know, Cal," he growled. "Maybe it's just that she's here in Bisbee. It was different in Tucson. We were on… I don't know… neutral territory, I suppose."

"So what?"

"I guess I'm worried that whatever connection we made in that hotel may have changed. Maybe she doesn't want to work with me. I sure can't take her up to my place even to show her where I live."

"Why not? She's here because she wants to work. Besides, other than last night, you've been away from Bisbee for weeks." Cal moved in front of the young man, ending his pacing. "Settle down, Henry. You need to get your head cleared out before the three of us talk this morning. You have to find the journalist inside you and forget about the infatuated boy you are right now."

"But..."

"But nothing. Sit down. Have a cup of coffee and take off your cap, newsboy, you're inside my house, not on an assignment."

Henry tugged the cap from his head, slumped onto the sofa, and sighed.

"Did you finish your Kelly Field story?"

"I did. I left it at home. I'll bring it to the office later."

"Well, then go back home and get it! Besides, the walk will do you good, maybe clear the cobwebs out of your head."

When Henry hadn't moved toward the door, Cal asked, "Is it good?"

"I think so, but you'll have to decide if it's worthy of printing." Cal could see he was sulking.

"Damn it, Henry, snap out of it. What we have to discuss today is important. It concerns all three of us, so stop worrying about the girl and remember who and what you are."

Henry sighed loudly and looked at Cal. "You're right, boss. I think I'm just tired." He walked past Cal and out the door.

Henry returned but still couldn't settle down as Cal looked over his Kelly Field story. He paced the room, pausing to look at the clock after every circuit. When the wall clock chimed at nine, Henry moved to the window and pulled the curtain aside just as Etta stopped her roadster at the edge of Cal's yard.

"Cal, look at this. She's driving a car!"

"She sure is, isn't that something?"

Henry watched as she checked her face in a compact mirror.

"Just calm down and get away from the window."

"I'm not..."

"I know, I know, I'm teasing you." Cal moved to the door and opened it just as Etta reached for the brass knocker.

"Good morning, Etta. Come on in." He swung the door all the way open and stepped back to give her room.

"Good morning, boss," she said and turned to see Henry. "Good morning to you, too, Henry." They locked eyes for a moment, each, it seemed, feeling awkward in the different atmosphere.

"Good to see you, Etta," Henry said, a smile spread across his face. He walked up to her and reached out his hand. She shook it and returned his smile.

Turning toward Cal, Etta asked if he had any coffee brewing.

"I do," he said. "I'm very capable in the kitchen." He pointed her toward the stove and the steaming pot. "I'll go get my notes and we can get started. You two get settled in here and I'll be right back."

Cal walked down the hall toward the back of the house. Henry and Etta went into the kitchen. He poured a cup of coffee for Etta, and they returned to the living room. The two reporters glanced at each other and then sat down, Etta in one of the soft chairs and Henry on the couch.

"I wondered if I'd ever see you here in Bisbee," Henry said. "How was the road trip?"

Before she responded, Etta stared at Henry, sensing his awkwardness. "You must be tired after your trip from Texas."

He shook his head briefly and said, "You're right, I am very tired. But, I'm glad you're here, Etta. It's really good to see you again."

"That's more like it, Henry. I'm glad to be here and excited about discussing Cal's plans."

"Then let's discuss," said Cal as he walked back into

the room. "If either of you wants to take notes, go ahead, but the plan itself is simple. Carrying it out will likely prove to be difficult but not impossible."

Cal sat in the other chair and looked, in turn, at each of his reporters.

"So that we're all starting from the same place Etta, I need to give you some background." He spent the next half hour telling her about the relationship between the mining company and the newspaper. He told her about the influence that the people in business and politics had over the town and its citizens. Referring to Henry's story, he outlined why he chose to not publish it in the *Review* and to send it to New York instead.

"You have connections in New York?"

"I do, Etta." He smiled and continued, "I haven't always lived in the barren desert. Before I moved here I worked in St. Louis and Omaha, and reporters I worked with there actually got jobs in the big city."

Impressed with this news, Etta was speechless.

"With all of that in mind," Cal continued, "I want to tell you how I think we can keep the management and community happy and distracted from whatever impact came from the story. My plan has two elements. The first is to get Henry out of town and out of the thoughts of the folks at the mine. I think that they'll be working on their defense so they can be ready if this lawsuit ever comes to trial." He looked at Henry and added, "If they don't see you, son, they'll forget about you and your story."

"What about me, Cal? If Henry is going out of town, what will I be doing?"

"You'll be going with him, Etta. This is where the second element comes into play. There's a big story brewing over in El Paso, a good one that includes murder, conspiracy, and greed. There'll be a big trial and lots of newspapers covering it." He paused to sip from his cup and said, "but as interesting as a murder trial might be for our readers, there's another, much better and far more interesting story in New Mexico. One about greed, jealousy, and conspiracy *related* to the murder of a rich cattle rancher. And I want *my* team of intrepid reporters to be there, in Silver City, New Mexico."

Henry got up, walked quickly into the kitchen, and returned with the coffee pot, then filled the others' cups.

"You know how much people like to be in the know, how things like murder and greed get them thinking and talking about nothing else. You have the opportunity to distract them from thinking about you," Cal said.

"Yeah, maybe, but won't our names be on the by-line? How will that help?"

"It'll help because of the quality of the writing you two will produce and the way you'll feed the hungry minds of the citizens of Bisbee. Remember, these are the folks who work for the mine and the others who sell their supplies, and services."

"I need to give you some background. You'll probably want to make some notes because there's a lot of information and it's all important."

The young reporters grabbed their notebooks and pencils like eager students, the looks on their faces showed interest, excitement, and a bit of intensity.

"The murdered rancher's name was Tom Lyons. He was very, very rich and played a prominent role in the cattle industry in southwest New Mexico. The killer is a man named Felix Jones. What we know from other papers' stories is that he has a criminal background and made several trips to Lyons' ranch and enticed him to go to El Paso—where the murder occurred. It's pretty clear that Jones killed Lyons and he'll be convicted and get life in prison. From the articles I've read, there seems to be little doubt that Jones was a *paid* killer.

"Who hired him?" Henry and Etta asked at the same time, then shared a look.

"Well, that's the thing, the court doesn't seem inclined to find that out. So, I want both of you to go to Silver City and find out who did pay Jones, why they wanted him out of the way, and what was the true impact on the family and community."

"Okay," said Etta, "so Henry and I will go to New Mexico, to Silver City and start nosing around, building a story by gathering information from who?"

"Before we get to that, I need to tell you about the place where all the trouble that led to the murder started."

Cal picked up a Rand McNally road map of New Mexico from the table by the front door. "I got this at the service station on the highway. There's not much detail, but the map is good enough to give you an idea of the scope of the problem." He spread the map across the table that rested in front of the sofa.

Cal had drawn some lines on the map that essentially isolated the southwest quarter of New Mexico.

"This," he said as he pointed at the perimeter he'd drawn, "is about a million acres. It doesn't look like ranch land. There are lots of mountains, arroyos, and a great deal of desert. But it does have grasslands and water. These lines mark the boundary of the LC Ranch."

"The dead rancher, Lyons, owned a million acres?" asked Etta.

"No, Etta, he didn't own them, but he controlled them. Most of the control came from government water leases and land leases. Lyons and his late partner, Angus Campbell, had gained control of the scarce water resources through *some* land purchases, as well as the leases and contracts with the government."

Henry said, "That's a big ranch."

"It is. They typically have 100,000 head of cattle and need seventy-five cowboys and four hundred horses to manage the herd," said Cal.

"So, Lyons controlled the land and water, had a lot of cattle, and, I suppose, a lot of money."

"That's right, and you can imagine how the other ranchers in the region felt about it. Most of them were blocked from growing as large as the LC."

"Cal," interjected Henry, "you mentioned greed, jealousy, and conspiracy earlier. I can see where these two factors come into the picture: Lyons becomes richer than his neighbors, doesn't let them share in his access to water, which causes them to envy his wealth and in the process they grow angry."

"Plus," said Etta, "that can lead to a conspiracy of disgruntled ranchers pooling their limited funds to pay for someone to eliminate their enemy—the greedy, rich, Tom Lyons."

"Here's something else to consider," said Cal. "Both Lyons and Campbell became powerful influences in the politics and economy of Silver City and most of the county. Maybe twenty years ago, Campbell died and when Lyons' wife ran off, he married Campbell's widow Ida."

"How did Campbell die?" asked Etta.

"I don't know for sure," said Cal. "But that's the kind of thing you'll have to find out."

"Why did Lyons' wife leave?"

Cal smiled and said, "Good question, Henry, very good question. When Lyons shot and killed his wife's lover, she disappeared. The papers don't say much about her, but you two should be able to find out enough to enrichen the story."

"What a tangled web of deceit," Etta said as she scooted to the edge of her chair wanting to hear more. "But we sure don't want this to be some sordid coverage about infidelity. That may sell newspapers, but it's not what I want to be remembered for."

"The same goes for me, Cal," said Henry.

"Listen, you two, I'm giving you background, not content. If I wasn't convinced that your objective is genuine, I'd have never put you on this project." He looked at them and asked, "Got it?"

"Yes, sir," they said, their responses overlapping. This generated a round of laughter from the three of them.

"Anyway," Cal continued, "Lyons and Ida continued to build a very successful business. They incorporated, sold stock, set up their headquarters in New York City, and sales offices in California. For most of the last twenty years, they'd ship a third of their 100,000 head of cattle to market every year."

A low whistle slipped out of Henry's lips.

"Tom and Ida entertained lots of famous, important, and wealthy people at the huge ranch house they built in the upper Gila. There's a lot more details in these papers that I'll let you have, but I'll want you to verify everything. Remember these articles and stories were written by other, less cautious and less truthful reporters than the two of you."

Looking at her notes, Etta said, "You said that Lyons killed his first wife's lover, is that the murder?"

"It's *one* of the murders. It's been suggested that in the twenty or so years that the two men built the LC, that Lyons killed or had killed other ranchers in his effort to create this, what, this dynasty."

Henry looked at Etta and then turned to Cal. "So, we need to go to Silver City and find out who, among the dozens of *nearly* wealthy ranchers in southwest New Mexico, might have conspired to kill Tom Lyons." And we'll do this by talking to the residents of Silver City, and the ranchers who may or may not have conspired, the sheriff, the judges, the merchants who grew wealthy supplying Lyons and those who didn't."

"Also, the people in the town who may have encountered Mr. and Mrs. Lyons at restaurants, parties, church, or just walking along the streets," Etta said, carrying his thought further.

Cal smiled and looked at his reporters. Each was furiously writing notes, and he could see that they were now invested in the plan.

Cal shoved his hands into the pockets of his pants and walked toward the door. He opened it and turned back to them.

"So, get out there and get to work. Bring me a story if you can. If not, bring me another one."

"If we're missing something, how do we go about finding it?"

"It's probably too early to tell if we have enough information for a story," Henry said to Etta, then paused, looked up at Cal and added, "and *way* too early to tell if we'll have *all* of the information we'll need to finish."

"You know, folks, this is all speculation," Cal said, "and we want the truth. If I wanted to find out the answers to these questions, it wouldn't take me long to realize that I'd not find them here, in Bisbee." They each looked at Cal. "I believe that I'd be making arrangements to go to the city where the murder was arranged."

If Cal hadn't escorted them out of his house, Etta and Henry likely would have kept on working through the weekend. But since it was his day off, Cal suggested that they find another place to work. *Besides,* he thought, *if our objective is to cause a distraction, there's no better way than to get the two of them walking down Main Street on a sunny day.*

As they stepped off the porch, Henry said, "I really need to go home and get out of these clothes. I haven't changed since yesterday morning, and I need a bath. Maybe we can meet for lunch in an hour or so."

"Of course," said Etta. "Let me drive you home then I'll go back to the hotel."

"Uh, that's okay, Etta. I can walk from here. You don't need to do that."

"It's not a problem, Henry. Besides, I want to see where you live."

Outside, Henry stood next to the passenger door but didn't make a move to get in the car.

"You're not afraid of riding in a car with a woman driver are you," Etta laughed.

"No, it's just..."

Etta folded her arms across her chest and looked at Henry. "Will you quit being silly and get in the car?"

"You're right," Henry said as he leaned into the passenger seat. "Show me how a woman drives a Runabout."

Etta laughed again, opened the driver-side door and got in the car. She pushed the starter button, and the engine began to hum. "Alright, Mr. Carter, point me in the direction of your home," she said as she shifted into first gear and pushed on the gas pedal.

Henry directed her down the hill to Main Street and told her to turn left. As if the presence of a roadster in Bisbee wasn't enough, the fact that a woman was driving caused pedestrians on both sides of Main to gawk. Etta noticed the attention they were getting, and it added to her enjoyment of the ride. Henry hardly paid attention to the folks on the sidewalk. He was watching Etta.

"Turn left at the next corner," he said. "That's Brewery Gulch."

"That's the name of the street, Brewery Gulch?"

"It is. You'll have to drive a little slow, the road's all uphill from here." Henry looked at Etta. "I think Cal was right," he said.

"Right about what?"

"He said you would be a distraction. I'd say that by this evening everyone in Bisbee will know about the new girl in town."

Etta looked over at the smile on Henry's face. "Maybe we should put the top down and you can wave at them, Henry. Wouldn't that be fun?"

"Keep your eyes on the road," he laughed.

The foot traffic on Brewery Gulch thinned out after a few blocks and was nearly nonexistent by the time Henry pointed to the left.

"That's it over there."

"What a beautiful place to live," she said, as she got out of the car. "This is amazing. It's almost like I can reach out and touch the sky." Then she raised her arms in the air and turned a full circle in the yard, smiling all the while.

Henry breathed a sigh of relief, glad that she wasn't bothered by the shabbiness of his home. He also gained an insight into her character as well when she said, "When we have some time, I'll expect to be invited for dinner. But, right now, I'm going back to the hotel."

"Thanks for the ride, Partner. I'll get cleaned up and meet you in the lobby of the Grand in an hour." He pulled the watch—a graduation gift from Cal—from his vest pocket, looked at it briefly, and said, "See you at one."

Before she got in the car, Etta walked over to Henry, reached out and shook his hand. "Thanks for calling me partner, Partner." Then she returned to the roadster and drove back down Brewery Gulch. Just before she reached the first curve, she honked the horn and waved her hand out the window.

Henry waved back, smiled, and shook his head as he headed into the cabin.

Promptly at one, Henry walked into the lobby of the Grand Hotel and met Etta as she arrived at the foot of the stairs. Since she'd had dinner the night before at the Copper Queen, Etta asked Henry to take her to a less pretentious place, one where they could stay at the table awhile and discuss their plans.

"I don't mind being an attraction to the citizens of your city, Henry, but in addition to eating, we should find a quieter place, where we can talk without having to deal with inquisitive citizens."

"That sounds good to me." Thinking quickly and hoping that his choice would be acceptable, he said, "I know a place that's close, small, and has simple food. In fact, it's Cal's favorite establishment in Bisbee. St. Elmo's."

"Then let's go have lunch at St. Elmo's," said Etta.

They walked down Main Street, passing the *Review* building, the bank and the post office and turned up

Brewery Gulch.

When Etta realized that they were walking up Henry's street, she said, "You don't call your cabin, St. Elmo's, do you?" A sly grin spread across her face.

Henry wrinkled his brow and then caught the joke. "No," he said, chuckling, "in fact the St. Elmo is just up there on the left. It used to be across the street from the paper, but after the big fire back in 1908, they moved over here. Back then, before the state enacted prohibition, it was a quiet, busy bar. Now it's a quiet, not so busy, café. Someday I'll tell you more about the fire."

They entered the narrow building and found a table in the back corner. The waitress came to the table and Henry ordered cold water and Etta asked for a Coca-Cola. They looked at the menu, decided on beef sandwiches and relaxed as the young woman walked toward the small kitchen. The two reporters simultaneously reached for their notebooks and pencils, which caused them to laugh at one another. But it seemed that the gestures also signaled a sort of camaraderie, of teamwork and a common energy.

Henry remained quiet himself as he stared at his partner. As attracted as he was to this intelligent, independent woman, he was convinced that she was more interested in their joint objective than anything else. He was determined that he wouldn't let anything get in the way of their reporting; and that meant it was okay to *like* Etta, to *respect* her, and even to *struggle* alongside her as they reported the truth. But getting caught up in a romance wouldn't work and he sure didn't want to be the one to start that kind of drama.

He asked, "Do you think we are ready for such a large job?" Then he added, "It doesn't really matter, though, does it? We'll be talking to people, and we'll write what we see and hear, because we *are* reporters."

Etta smiled at him. "We sure are, Henry."

Chapter 12

After lunch, they walked to the *Review* office and began making plans for getting to New Mexico.

"There's one thing I need to do before we can go to Silver City, Henry."

"What's that?"

"I need to quit my job at the *Republican*."

"Of course."

"But I can't just leave a message with Mr. Sidney's secretary. I have to do it in person." She looked around the office and then turned to Henry. "It'll only take a few days to take care of that and get my things from the apartment. Once we finish in Silver City, I can think about moving here. Lyons is dead, his killer is in jail, and if there was a conspiracy, the people involved will probably still be in town when we get there. A few days won't make that much difference."

"I suppose," said Henry, "we can go there as soon as you get back."

"I need to talk to Cal right away and call my father, too."

Etta sat in the chair at Cal's desk and after a few false starts, finally made all the connections for the long-distance call to her parent's home. As usual, it only rang a few times before being picked up by the maid.

"Pearce residence."

"Hi, Marisol, this is Etta. Is my favorite father available?" Etta had always treated her parents' staff as friends of the family and refused to follow her mother's more formal approach.

"He is, dear. You father is in his study."

"Is my mother around?"

"No, she's spending the evening with her lady friends from the charity foundation."

Etta sighed and said, "Could you please tell him that I need to talk to him?"

Marisol set the phone down and Etta looked around the quiet office while she waited.

"Is this my runaway daughter?"

"It is your daughter, but I haven't run away, Dad, I'm in Bisbee."

He laughed and said, "What can I do for you young lady?"

She told him about her trip to Bisbee, her new job, and briefly about the next assignment.

"Daddy, it's the kind of job I've always wanted. The editor, Calvin Langley, is smart and kind and believes in me."

"Don't you think that you're moving too quickly?"

"Maybe I am, but I can do this job and it's clear that Mr. Langley doesn't care if I'm a woman. The other reporter, a young man named Henry Carter, is smart, insightful and a talented writer." She slowed down and continued. "Daddy, I'm going to Phoenix tomorrow morning to quit my job there and pick up some things from my apartment."

Mr. Pearce was quiet for a number of minutes and Etta wondered if he was still there.

"Daddy?"

"I'm here, Etta, and I can tell you that your mother is not going to like this one bit. She especially won't want me to help you. She'll accuse me of letting you ruin your life and her reputation."

"I know that she doesn't like who I've become, but I'm still her daughter."

"That's it exactly. You *are* her daughter and what you do reflects on *her*."

Etta only had to ponder the dilemma for a moment.

She sat back in Cal's chair and took a deep breath. "Okay, Daddy, I understand."

"You're welcome, Etta. Call me at my office after you get here. We can have lunch or something before you head back to the mining camp."

"I will," she said with a giggle.

After she ended the call, Etta sat quietly. She glanced around the empty room until her momentary disappointment dissolved and then rose from the chair and left the office. Walking down the stairs, she waved at Bert and strode out of the pressroom into the cool Arizona night.

Before dawn on Monday morning, Etta was already half-way to Tombstone. The sky above the canyon and the surrounding mountains was a muted blue, but it was streaked with copper-hued clouds. The wind blowing in the Ford's side windows was cool and refreshing. Etta thought she'd have enough gas in the roadster to get her to Benson, at least, but planned to stop at the first available service station. *I sure don't want to run out of gas.*

By the time Etta reached Benson, the town was busy and ready for travelers. She filled up the tank and had a quick breakfast at a diner. She really liked her new car and driving it was exciting as well as convenient. The road beyond Benson was somewhat better than the one from Bisbee, but she still had to keep an eye out for holes and other hazards, including creatures not yet used to a young woman driving a fast car. She had lunch in Tucson and got into Phoenix by late afternoon. Etta went directly to her apartment and started packing her clothes into a suitcase.

She showed up at the *Republican* offices first thing Tuesday. Mr. Sidney was, as she'd expected him to be, appalled at her "lack of professionalism" and said he was convinced that she'd soon come crawling back to Phoenix.

Etta said goodbye to her friends and then walked out

of the building and got into her car.

The return trip to Bisbee started well, and Etta made good time. She stopped to refill the car's tank and refresh herself every hour or so. The weather hadn't changed much. It was cool in the morning and only got hotter as the miles piled up behind her. Driving south from Benson, she spotted a car parked along the side of the road and came to a stop. Cautiously, she got out of the Ford and walked up to the sedan, a Dodge, then looked up the road and off to both sides and saw nothing but mesquite bushes, cactus, and lots of sand. She called out a "hello," but got no response.

"Hmm," she mumbled aloud as she circled around the car, then noticed a puddle of oil that spread out from under the vehicle. *That explains why the car's here,* she thought. *But where's the driver?*

Peeking through the side window of the Dodge, she noticed an open road map on the seat but there was nothing else visible. Etta called out once more and scanned the desert in all four directions but learned nothing new. *Well, I guess there's no one here.* She returned to the roadster and drove on toward Bisbee.

As she crested a short rise, she saw a tall man lugging a heavy-looking suitcase along the side of the road. He'd removed his coat and carried it in his free hand. When Etta tapped the horn button, he turned in her direction. Etta slowed down and stopped just short of where he stood.

"Do you need some help?" she said as he leaned down to look in the passenger window.

"I'll say," he said, "I sure hadn't counted on breaking down in the middle of the desert."

Even though his clothes were dusty and his face had a sheen of sweat, Etta could clearly see that he was good looking and relatively young.

"Then it's a good thing that I was going this way."

"More than just good, I think," he smiled.

"My name's Etta Pearce," she said extending her hand.

Taking it and shaking gently, he said, "Daniel... Daniel Foster."

"Well, Mr. Foster, I suppose we'll have to find a spot on my already loaded car for your bag. Etta turned off the engine and got out of the roadster. She knew that the small space behind the seats was already full and the trunk, too, had a pretty good load in it." I've got a coil of rope in the bottom of the trunk, maybe we can tie your bag on top."

"I don't want to put you to any trouble, Miss Pearce. Perhaps I could hide it behind that short tree over there and you could take me into the next town."

"You're not from around here, are you. I mean not from Arizona.?"

"No, I'm not. I came from Washington D.C."

Etta chuckled and said, "If we left your bag behind that tree, then drove to Tombstone to wait for someone to drive back and tow your car, the bag would have disappeared or become home to a family of rattlesnakes."

"Then I guess I should help you find that coil of rope," Foster said.

They tied the large leather case down on the trunk of the Ford. With the side windows open and the wind blowing in, it was difficult to carry on a conversation. She let Foster drink from her canteen of water and when they entered the old town, she stopped at the first service station garage they encountered. While he went to talk to the mechanic, Etta got out and stretched her legs.

Walking out of the garage, Foster said, "The mechanic says he can tow my car in this afternoon. Until he sees it, though, he won't know how long it'll take to repair it."

"Lucky for you there's a hotel and café across the street, Mr. Foster. Tell you what, I'll treat you to lunch, and you can tell me why a gentleman from Washington D.C. is wandering around our hot little corner of the world."

Foster smiled and replied, "Alright, Miss Pearce, I'll

join you for lunch, but I'm paying. And please, call me Daniel."

"Good enough, Daniel. You pay for lunch, but you still have to tell me your story."

They took the suitcase off of Etta's car and stored it in the garage. While Foster walked across the street to the café, Etta started her car and made a U-turn, then parked right in front of the café's window. He waited by the door and opened it for her, then followed her in.

"Let's sit by the window so I can keep an eye on all of my worldly goods," Etta said.

Etta ordered coffee, Daniel wanted water, and they each found something on the menu to eat.

"Just so you know," Etta said, "I'm a reporter for the *Bisbee Daily Review*. As I said, I'm interested in why someone from Washington is here, but I don't plan to tell the world any of your secrets."

A serious expression appeared on Foster's face, but his response was still friendly. "Miss Pearce..."

"Etta," she said. "Please just call me Etta."

"Alright, Etta, I actually am here on official business." He paused, almost as if he was thinking about what or how much to say. "I'm an investigator for President Wilson. He's asked me to come down here and look at the facts behind the recent deportation of miners out of Bisbee."

"So, I guess the events in our town have struck a chord in the national capital."

"They have, somewhat. I'm not here to convince anyone to do anything. In fact, I'd like to keep my official duties confidential. What Mr. Wilson wants to know has to do with a rumor that there might be some lawsuits initiated by the unions against the mines, lawsuits that might disrupt the production of copper. He's concerned about anything that will slow down the manufacture of war materials."

"I think that the lawsuits are more than a rumor. In

fact, my partner, Henry Carter, knows quite a bit about the deportation and my boss, Cal Langley, is up to date on the lawsuit issues. If you want current information, they would be good sources."

"Thanks, Etta, that helps me direct my inquiries better."

Their meals arrived and they spent the rest of their time together talking of more mundane things—the heat, Etta's move to Bisbee, and the differences between the east coast and the southwest desert. After Daniel paid the bill, they stood, and he escorted her out to her car.

"I hope your move and your new home work out, Etta."

"I'm sure they will, Daniel. I'm excited to be living in a community where I can be doing what I've always wanted." She shook his hand firmly and added, "I hope your travels improve from this point and that you can report back to the President that all is well."

"Before you go, Etta, I want to give you my card. I've learned that those of us in politics always need trusted contacts in the press and that the reverse is often true as well. If you ever need to bounce a story or an idea off me to get a government perspective, all you have to do is send a wire to my office. My assistant will always know where I am."

Etta took the card and said, "Well, Daniel, you already know how to find me," she smiled, "just have a breakdown on a desert highway."

"Perhaps we'll meet again," she said as she got into the Ford and drove away. "Perhaps we will," he whispered.

In less than an hour, Etta drove into Bisbee and parked near the newspaper office. She walked up the stairs and found her boss and colleague having a discussion at Cal's desk. "Good afternoon, gentlemen," she said.

Cal and Henry both rose from their seats and greeted her.

"Welcome back," said the editor. "How was the drive?"

"Interesting and informative," said Etta. "Did you miss me?"

"I sure did," said Henry, signaling for her to take his seat.

Cal laughed and then asked what she meant by "informative."

"We can talk about that later," Etta said. "I'm going to check into the Grand for one more night, take a bath and get some rest."

It took the rest of the day for Daniel Foster's car to be towed to Tombstone and repaired. Fortunately, all it needed was a new oil pan gasket. Nevertheless, it was dark by the time he'd paid the mechanic, so he spent the night in the historic town. Just before lunch the next morning, he checked out of the hotel and drove to Bisbee. He expected the city to be much like the one he'd just left but was surprised to find a somewhat urban setting. The brick buildings, the streetcars, and the heavy pedestrian traffic on the streets suggested industry and commerce, rather than gunfights and cowboys.

The afternoon sun's desert heat was already reminding him that he should have left his coat in the room. Expecting some mail from the White House, he checked with the postal clerk, but nothing had arrived for him. Back on the street, he turned left and walked past the *Review* building, which sent his thoughts immediately to Miss Etta Pearce. *What a fascinating young woman,* he thought. The way she dressed and spoke reminded him of some of the suffragettes he'd encountered picketing the White House. He sensed, somehow, that she probably shared their political interests. Shaking his head slightly to get her out of his mind, he continued up the sidewalk.

Foster was the son of a New Jersey congressman. His father, a close friend of the president's, had gotten the young Princeton graduate a job the day after he graduated three years ago. Daniel had earned degrees in history and commerce, and his early assignments for the administration involved mostly research. The quality of his work impressed some of the president's staff and soon he was sent out to do his research in the field, rather than the library.

Politically connected, and financially secure, he'd decided, much to his mother's disappointment, to avoid any serious relationships with women. He was nice looking, strongly built, and culturally literate. In other words, good husband material, but he didn't want to be a husband. The world of politics and finance was just too interesting and time consuming. But Etta Pearce had caught his attention.

The notes and files he'd collected in Washington were only part of the resources he'd need to determine the situation in Bisbee. The mining company management, the union leaders, and the miners each had an interest. But, so did the community—its banks, shops, and the vast number of service businesses. He would need to talk with all of them at some point. Then, he reminded himself, there was the Great War. In order for President Wilson to make the right decisions and lead the nation to support the Allies in Europe, he must have good information, timely information. *And that's why I'm here,* Daniel thought as he followed the street as it curved up the hill past the Elks Club.

Chapter 13

About the same time Daniel Foster arrived in Bisbee, the two reporters left town in Etta's car. Their drive took them east to the town of Douglas—another small mining town on the border with Mexico—and then northeast, through the edge of the Sonoran desert toward the New Mexico state line. The roads were rough and narrow, so the trip took a bit longer than they'd estimated it would. They finally arrived in Lordsburg just before dark.

"The fella at the gas station said that it's a good two-hour drive to Silver City and because the road goes through the mountains, he suggested that we wait until tomorrow."

"Then I guess we'd better find a place to spend the night, Henry."

"He said that the Hidalgo hotel just down the road is cheap and usually has a lot of vacancies."

The Hidalgo lived up to the reputation and they were able to get two rooms for the night.

Before leaving Lordsburg on Thursday morning, they filled the gas tank, topped off the radiator with water, checked the air in the tires (including the spare) and drove east and north on another rough road. The trip took nearly two hours, but as they coasted down into Silver City, they discovered that the town was somewhat larger than Bisbee and a great deal smaller than Phoenix. Etta steered the car to the side of the paved street and turned off the motor.

From the sidewalk on the corner, under a bank's hanging clock, they saw three or four hotels. The nearest was Schutz Palace, but a block farther to the west, a sign for the Hotel Broadway seemed to beckon to them.

Carrying their bags, they entered the hotel, paid the clerk behind the counter for two rooms for a week in advance, and followed the bellboy up to the third floor. Their rooms were just like others they'd seen in their travels: a bed, a chair, a writing table, a standing sink and an open transom above the door. They decided to meet in the lobby in half an hour, agreeing that taking a few minutes to freshen up would be a good idea.

During the ride from Lordsburg, Henry had concluded that *if* Lyons' murder had been random, the most they could expect from discussions with any of the victim's friends, neighbors, or business associates would likely just be speculation on their parts. Henry wondered who in the community liked Lyons, saw him as a contributing citizen, a philanthropist, a friend; or considered him a greedy landgrabber, tyrant, or thief? Henry expected that, as strangers, he and Etta might face obstacles and perhaps even threats; but if they hoped to create a picture of the *real* Tom Lyons and determine if the man was the victim of a paid killer, they would have to ask some very specific questions. *That's what reporters do,* he mused. *How else can we get the truth?*

When he woke up Friday morning, Henry decided to take a walk before meeting Etta for breakfast. Just across the street was a bakery, Schadel's, and through its open door, Henry could smell baking bread and a faint hint of donuts. Although he'd already had a cup of coffee, he thought that a fresh donut would be a wonderful way to start the day.

After waiting for a few cars to pass, he crossed the street and walked into the store. Not only were the aromas enticing, the glass-front cabinets displayed a delirious variety of cakes, pies, and donuts. Henry's mouth began to salivate.

"Mornin', mister. What can I get for you?"

Henry smiled. "Do you have hot coffee to go with those great looking donuts?"

"I sure do. I even have icy cold milk right there in the first and only *re-frigerator* in Silver City."

"Coffee will do," he said, "and two of those donuts with the pink frosting."

"Comin' right up."

The baker reached into the display case, pulled out Henry's donuts and placed them on a paper napkin. He poured coffee into a ceramic mug and set the items on the glass top.

"That'll be twenty-five cents."

Henry handed the aproned man a quarter and asked him if he was Mr. Schadel.

"I sure am," he said. "You must be a visitor to our town. Everyone knows who I am."

"I *am* a visitor. My name is Henry Carter. I'm from Bisbee."

"Welcome to Silver City, Mister Carter. Why don't you have a seat by the window there, and I'll join you for a minute or two. Even bakers get to take a break once in a while."

Henry carried his cup and pastries to the small table and sat in one of the wooden chairs. Schadel came from behind the cabinet, a full cup of coffee in his hand, and sat across from him.

"What brings you to our town?"

Cautiously, Henry began his first effort at investigating the possible existence of a conspiracy to murder the wealthy rancher.

"Well, Mister Schadel, I'm a reporter for the *Bisbee Daily Review.* My partner and I have been following the reports from the trial over in El Paso, and we wanted to get some background on Tom Lyons. We figured that the folks here in Grant County would know him well enough to give our readers a picture of what he was like."

Schadel stared at Henry for a moment before he

spoke. His face didn't change, but his eyes seemed to bore into Henry's own. The baker took a sip of his coffee and set the cup down on the table.

"From what I've read in the paper," Schadel said, "the folks over in Texas are payin' more attention to the killer, Jones, than to Mr. Lyons. I see and know a lot of people in town. Some were very jealous of his wealth and control of pastures and water rights which would limit their herd sizes. Still others talk kindly of him." He continued to focus on Henry's eyes. "Why are you interested in Lyons?"

"It seems to us, Mr. Schadel, that if people could know what Lyons was really like they might understand why he was killed." Henry didn't look down, didn't drink from his cup, or bite into one of the donuts.

"I suppose you're right, young man."

Henry didn't interrupt Schadel.

"Other ranchers, the banks, the fellas up at the courthouse knew about his business of course. But other than his poor wife, I'm not aware of anyone who was close enough to really know the man."

"What did you think of him?"

Schadel shrugged and sipped his coffee. "For a very rich man, he was always friendly—not warm or anything like that, but nice... friendly."

Henry bit into his donut, smiled at the first taste of sugar, and asked another question, this one very carefully.

"Do you think that Jones killed Lyons in order to rob him?"

"Well, if he did, he's found himself in deep trouble for the fifty dollars he took from Lyons' pocket."

Henry could tell that Schadel was avoiding a direct answer.

"But do you think that was his purpose, his reason to beat the man to death?"

"What else could it be?"

"This may just be speculation on my part, but I think the murder could have been paid for. Do you think anyone in the county would be pleased that Lyons was killed?"

"I don't know. Could be, I suppose. But robbery certainly seems to be the motive. Or at least the circumstances might show that the murder was carefully planned."

"Could you tell me," Henry asked, "who some of the bigger ranchers in the county are?"

"Look son, I can give you a few names, but that don't mean they had anything to do with a murder."

"I understand, Mr. Schadel, but it's possible isn't it, that they might have an opinion or experience with Mr. Lyons?"

For a while, Henry focused on his donuts and coffee, then he changed the subject. "Mr. Schadel, you sure make fine donuts. It's been a pleasure talking to you. I'll be back again."

"I'll be glad to see you when you come back. I was just thinkin' that you could talk to the Sheriff or someone up at the courthouse. They might know more, but I'm not sure they'll be much interested in helping."

"Why is that?"

Schadel paused while he finished his coffee then rose from the table. "Tom Lyons had a great deal of influence on the law and business folks in our town. Even though he's dead, his wife still holds some of that influence."

Henry finished eating and stood as well.

"Thanks again, Mister Schadel. I'm glad I followed my nose to your shop."

Wiping his hand on the napkin, Henry extended it to the baker, and they shook hands.

With the taste of Schadel's pink frosting still on his tongue, Henry went back across the street to the hotel. He spotted Etta as she walked from the front desk toward the dining room.

"Good morning, Henry."

"And a good morning to you, Miss Pearce," he replied

with a wide smile spreading across his face.

Picking up a bit of his good humor, she asked "Where have you been, *sir*?"

"I woke up early and decided to get to work. There's a bakery just across the street, and the owner, a Mr. Schadel, makes the finest donuts I've ever tasted."

Etta chuckled as she reached her hand toward his face and used her finger to flick a speck of pink frosting off the corner of his mouth. "Pink-frosted, were they?"

Henry smiled as he nodded. "They were, and Mr. Schadel was also kind enough to share his thoughts about Lyons." He glanced around the lobby, which was beginning to get busy as other visitors to the town started their workdays.

"Have you eaten, yet?" he asked.

"Uh huh, and I'm ready to work."

Henry put his hand on her shoulder and guided her toward the front door and out onto the boardwalk.

As busy as the hotel lobby had seemed, the corner of Broadway and Bullard on this morning was even more so. The noise from the several cars and trucks moving in the streets masked their conversation.

"I think that this is when we split up, Partner. I've got some ideas in mind and if I know you as well as I think I do, so do you."

"You're right. I made a mental list last night before I fell asleep, and the list woke me up this morning."

They spent a few minutes discussing their plans and discovered they each had done an excellent job of identifying different possibilities and opportunities to gain information from different sources.

"Looks like we won't be getting in one another's way. Let's meet for lunch at the café over there," Etta said, pointing across Broadway.

"Alright," said Henry. "See you at noon." He almost leaned toward her to kiss her on the cheek but stopped quickly and blinked as if confused.

Etta wasn't fazed by the change in his face. She simply smiled, nodded, and said, "Okay." Then she crossed Broadway and walked north on Bullard Street.

When she'd started her mental list, Etta's thoughts had quickly gone to her experience in Jerome. She recalled her meeting with the women at the church there and thought that something similar might occur in Silver City. The imposing, cathedral-like Catholic church a few blocks away was one possibility, but she was drawn instead toward a millenary store just up the street. Something in the store's window had drawn a small crowd of women and Etta decided that even if churches were first on her list, an active group of women at a shop was worth investigating.

She arrived at the back of the group and was surprised to find that they were enthralled with the clothes on the mannequin behind the glass display window.

"I love that short skirt!" said one woman who appeared to Etta to be about her own age.

"It is cute," said a lady a few years older, "but what would your mother think, Mary?"

Another, even older woman added, "or your father! Bless my soul, that skirt is almost obscene!"

The first girl, Mary, said, "But it's so modern, so exciting. I think it's beautiful."

Then, the half-dozen or so ladies began a civilized debate about fashion and Etta moved up toward the window—a real living example of the fashion on display.

The older woman gasped, but Mary and the other young women crowded around Etta.

"Oh, my goodness," said one.

"It is beautiful, isn't it," said Etta, "and it looks so comfortable."

Mary, evidently the boldest of the crowd, said, "It *is* beautiful." She paused only a moment, and asked, "Where did you get your hair cut? And did your mother and father approve?"

Etta smiled when Mary caught herself and began to

apologize.

"Well," said Etta, glancing around at the faces now filled with curiosity, "My mother hated it, but my father simply accepted it. He knew my mother was upset, even a little ashamed, but he also knew that I was the one person who was pleased with the change and that was enough for him to accept it."

A few more women had joined the group, some of them a little older than Mary, and added to the growing buzz of conversation about the clothing in the window and Etta, the living model.

"Are you new in Silver City?" asked Mary.

"No, I'm just a visitor. I'm a newspaper reporter here on an assignment."

"My word, a female reporter," stage-whispered the elderly woman. "What's the world coming to?" Shaking her head, she marched away from the crowd, never once looking back over her shoulder.

Several of the women went into the shop while Mary and those of her age clustered around Etta.

Mary asked, "What paper do you work for and what is your assignment?" There was excitement in her voice, as well as what seemed to Etta, genuine interest.

Etta replied in a matter-of-fact tone, "I work for the *Bisbee Daily Review* and I'm here to learn about the Lyons family. Our readers have been following the murder trial in El Paso and are interested more in how Mr. Lyons' death affected his family and his community."

This started another buzzing conversation that forced Etta to gently interrupt. "Ladies, please, I'd like to discuss this with all of you and each of you. It's important that our readers hear what friends and neighbors of the Lyons family think about not just the murder, or the killer, but more about the victims."

She waited until the conversation softened, then asked, "Is there someplace where we can sit and talk about this?"

A woman, perhaps just a few years older than Etta, standing at the perimeter of the gathering, said, "We could meet in my house."

Etta moved toward her and watched as the faces of the mostly young women turned toward the speaker.

"I mean, my husband is working in his office and won't be home until dinner."

"Are you certain we won't be a bother, missus..."

"Mrs. Acton, Emily Acton."

Etta glanced quickly at the rest of the group and inquired, "All of us?"

"Certainly," said Emily. "My home is just up the hill off Market Street. It's only a few blocks."

Etta said, "Then, let's go. I have lots of questions."

Within ten minutes, the group of eleven females walked through the waist-high gate into the Acton yard. Etta noticed a sign mounted on the wall by the home's front door which read, "Thomas Acton-Attorney at Law."

Once inside the home, Mrs. Acton made coffee and tea and even set out a plate of fresh cookies.

"These were supposed to be for a church social this weekend, but I'll just bake some more later."

Shortly, the group settled into the stuffed chairs in the living room and on those carried in from the dining room.

Over the next hour, Etta's questions, both general and specific, were answered by the few outspoken women. Most of the younger women's answers reflected things they'd heard from their parents, while those who were either married or had contact with the business community shared what they knew.

Etta diligently kept notes, ensuring that significant responses were verified by more than the respondent. Much of what she learned was similar to what she and Henry had learned from Cal and other conversations. There were a few interesting items that came up related to the murder, and Etta tried to steer the discussion away from the killing itself and toward the motive.

It seemed that a rather large number of the women thought that there could have been disgruntled competitors who might have used their combined assets to eliminate Lyons.

Other than Mrs. Acton, who made specific reference to something her husband had told her, the other responses, at least to Etta, were hearsay. Even so, she thought, the idea of a conspiracy was floating in the air of the community.

"Tell me about Mrs. Lyons… Ida Lyons," said Etta.

The ladies' response to the shift in topics was vivid. Etta noticed that the younger women seemed caught off guard, as if they knew very little about her. Yet, Emily's features brightened considerably.

"Ida Lyons is a wonderful woman," she said. "She's kind and generous."

Mary added, "My mother says she's so caring and that she frequently gives money to some of the poor families, especially those with lots of children."

Etta asked, "How well do you know her? I mean, have you spent time with her?"

"Not a lot," said, Emily, "but last fall she asked the lawyers' wives group to help her hand out some boxes of food to the families in the south part of town."

"Is that where some of the poor families live?"

"Yes, Etta," said, Emily. "Most of the families there are Mexican."

A red-headed woman whom Etta recalled had mostly listened during the discussion, said in a muted voice, "The Lyons may be respected, but they're not perfect."

Etta thought she'd like to speak with the woman alone, but went on with her planned questions,

"I wonder," said Etta, "does Ida Lyons have a best friend, one who is closer to her than anyone else?"

Mary interjected, "I asked my mother that same question right after Mr. Lyons was killed and her reply was something like, "Rich people don't have any real friends."

"Ladies, please, we shouldn't wear our envy like a peddler's sign," said Emily, "besides, Ida Lyons doesn't parade around showing off her wealth. She's so modest and congenial." She turned to Etta and added, "Although I wouldn't want to suggest that she doesn't have a best friend, I know that she's very close to her daughter and, I've heard, that she is good friends with the Johnsons, the foreman and his wife."

Etta said, "I have to ask this next question, Emily, "because as a reporter, if I use a name in a story, I must be able to prove what I write." She looked at her notebook, then said, "Emily, do you know this because you've seen them talking or overheard them talking?"

"Miss Pearce—Etta—I know this because of the charity activity last year. Mrs. Lyons and Mrs. Johnson were laughing and chatting while we all filled boxes with canned goods. I overheard them mention how together they encouraged their husbands to fund the effort. It seemed to me that this reflected a friendship... a genuine friendship, despite their different roles in society."

Etta saw and felt the presence of a lawyer's wife in Emily's phrasing and posture. She also thought that Emily presented herself as a qualified witness.

Etta looked at her wristwatch and said, "I hope we haven't overstayed our welcome, Emily. But I'd like to thank all of you for helping me do my job. And as an aside, I hope your town will happily approve of your change to short hair and short skirts."

This got laughs from nearly all of them and made it easy to stand and leave the Acton home.

Etta waited until the women were walking away and then said, "Emily, thank you again for letting me use your lovely home and for the information you shared."

"It was my pleasure, Etta. I do hope your story helps people understand how this tragedy occurred, and that its impact on our community won't be forgotten."

Etta turned left out of the gate and headed down the hill, hoping Henry had already acquired a table at the cafe. She noticed that the red-headed woman was waiting on the sidewalk a few houses down the street.

"Miss Pearce," said the woman, "from what was said this morning, you might get the impression that the Lyons were angels."

"Call me Etta. What's your name, miss?"

"Hilda, Hilda Farnsworth."

"In your experience then, your interaction with Mrs. Lyons, you have a different opinion?"

"I do, but you might consider it hearsay. My father worked for Tom Lyons for years. He used to tell us stories at the dinner table about some of the things Mr. Lyons would do to keep his ranch going. My father once said that there were several other ranchers, friends of Mr. Lyons, who asked him one time if he'd be willing to give them access to some of the water sources and that Mr. Lyons told his friends that he was sorry, but couldn't do that." Hilda paused for just a moment and added, "My daddy said that didn't seem friendly. That's why I remember the event."

"Hilda, I want to thank you for sharing this information. You've given me a picture of a man with many sides to his character." Etta hesitated and then asked, "Do you remember the names of the friends?"

"Daddy never told us who they were."

When they got to Bullard Street, Hilda said goodbye to Etta, headed down to the next corner and turned left. Etta, hurried to the café to meet Henry.

Chapter 14

While Etta was involved with the women she had met at the millinery, Henry went to visit the Sheriff.

At the Sheriff's Office, Henry was told that the sheriff was out of town. Henry asked the clerk if a deputy was available.

"Most of 'em are out on the county roads," said the middle-aged woman. "Why do you need a deputy?"

"I'm from Bisbee, and I wanted some information," he said.

"Well, no one's here right now."

Henry thanked the woman and turned to leave. Before he reached the door, she said, "There *is* a deputy in town, but he ain't working today. He might be able to answer your questions though."

"Where could I find him?"

"Well, he's likely up at his place on the hill behind the courthouse. You know where that is?"

"I do," he said. "Thanks a lot."

As he walked up the long street, Henry realized it was much wider than any street in Bisbee. The cars and trucks moving on Broadway were close to the curb, and those parked were in the middle of the street.

When Henry got to the courthouse, he walked around behind the building and saw a cabin maybe fifty yards up the slope of the hill. It wasn't much larger than his own home on Brewery Gulch. A framed and partially walled-in structure, maybe forty feet wide and twenty feet deep, was under construction.

Henry didn't see anyone in the front, but as he walked around the south side, he saw a man coming across the sloped yard pushing a wheelbarrow filled with rocks. The man pulled up short when he saw Henry.

"Help you mister?"

"I hope so," said Henry, "are you a deputy sheriff?"

"I am—Deputy Williams—what is it you need?"

Henry approached the tall, broad chested man and stuck out his hand. "My name is Henry Carter. I'm a reporter for the newspaper in Bisbee."

Williams shook Henry's hand but remained silent behind the wheelbarrow.

"I'm working on the Lyons murder story, trying to make sure that the victim and his family aren't ignored, that they get the justice they deserve while the court in El Paso focuses on the killer."

"How do you think I can help you do that?"

"Well deputy, I had hoped to speak with the various authorities in the community about Mister Lyons. My partner and I believe that Mr. Lyons' story rests with the people who knew him here in Silver City."

Henry removed his cap and continued.

"The clerk in your office told me that you were off-duty and were the only deputy in town today. I was hoping you could answer just a few questions."

"I *could* answer some questions," he replied, "but whether I *will* depends on your answer to a few questions of mine."

"Certainly, Deputy," ask your questions."

Williams stepped around from behind the wheelbarrow and stood directly in front of Henry. He looked into Henry's eyes and said, "Do you intend, Mister Carter, to write a story that will embarrass the Lyons family? Do you intend to disturb the citizens of our community?"

Henry didn't flinch nor did the calm look on his face fade.

"Deputy Williams, my only intention is to tell a story that describes the life of a man who has been part of this community, who has served it, who has enriched it, and who was brutally murdered." He paused briefly and continued. "But rest assured that I won't put anything in my story that isn't the truth. I won't make anything up. I won't investigate anything that isn't directly related to the man's life and brutal death. I will always respect his family, his home, and his life. But I must tell it truthfully."

Williams listened intently and then quietly backed away, giving Henry some space.

"Let's go sit on my nearly finished front porch. I'll give you ten minutes and then I need to get back to building."

They walked around to the front of the cabin and sat on a row of boards laid across a foundation of rocks. Despite being anxious to learn something about Lyons, he also knew it was important to take his time and gain Williams' trust.

"Your home here is not much different than mine in Bisbee—built on the side of a mountain with a great view toward the rising sun."

"Your place is small like this?"

"It is. Bisbee isn't much different than Silver City. Your valley is bigger and the streets are wider, but they are pretty much the same."

"Hmm," Williams sighed. "What do you want to know?"

Once again, Henry quickly gathered his thoughts and asked Williams how well he personally knew Tom Lyons.

"Mr. Lyons was very rich, very powerful, and very respected in the county. I'm not rich or powerful, and if I'm respected at all it's because I wear a star. All I *really* know about Lyons comes from what I read in our newspaper or what I hear on the street."

"And what is it that you hear on the street?"

"Tom Lyons was smart, some think he's a genius because he's worked closely with the federal and state governments to control so much of the grazing and water rights in this part of the state. I know that he's rich but he's also generous. He and his wife donate lots of money to various charities and they employ a lot of people on their ranch and various depots and stores around the county."

"Thanks. Let me ask you about the murder. I know it didn't happen here and that your office didn't participate in the investigation."

Williams interrupted Henry. "Actually, we did try to find out what actually happened when Jones was in the county just a few days before he killed Lyons."

"What did you learn?"

"Actually, nothing much. Jones was here, stayed in one of our hotels, and then he left."

"But as far as what happened in El Paso, you've not had a role."

"That's right."

"Do you think the killer's motive was to rob Lyons?"

"I've been a deputy for nearly ten years, Mr. Carter, and I know that greed frequently leads to violence." He paused, pondering Henry's question. "So, do I think robbery was the motive?"

Henry nodded.

"*Maybe* it was," Williams emphasized, "but any other motive would be hard to prove since Jones was caught so quickly and no evidence I've seen or heard about supporting any other possible reason exists so far."

Henry nodded as he made entries in his notebook.

"Do you think it's even remotely possible that someone paid Jones to kill the rancher?"

"I suppose it's possible, but where's the evidence?" Williams scratched his chin and looked at Henry.

"That's what I'm trying to find out," said Henry.

"There are a lot of medium and small size ranchers who are probably jealous of Lyons' success. There are probably others who want access to his water reserves and grazing lands. But could they afford to hire a killer, and would they even do that? I don't know, Mister Carter. I get no sense of that even now, months after the murder."

Williams thought a moment, and said, "Here's another thing, Mr. Carter. Tom Lyons was a strong man, he was liked by most folks and feared, at least in business, by a few others."

Henry's gaze wandered past the backside of the courthouse. He looked at the hills across the valley to the north and the scarred mine-blasted land to the south, then addressed Williams.

"So, a conspiracy is possible, but unlikely given what you know about Lyons' competitors, the people you are sworn to protect, the people you see daily while you carry out your duties?"

Williams nodded his ascent.

"Let me ask you one more question. Would you be able to comment on the relationship between Mr. Lyons and the Sheriff?"

"Officially, no I won't. Unofficially, though, I believe the Sheriff and Mr. Lyons were good friends."

"Well, deputy, I thank you for your time and I suppose you'd like to get back to hauling rocks, sawing boards, and pounding nails."

Williams smiled and shook hands with Henry.

"I'll be in town maybe another day or so. If we run into each other, I'll buy you a drink... when you're off duty of course."

"Of course," Williams chuckled.

After leaving Williams' cabin, Henry hurried down to the cafe. He wanted to bring Etta up to date on what he'd learned and decide what they'd do for the rest of the day.

"I thought," Etta said as she and Henry sat across a table drinking coffee in the cafe, "that I'd get a better reception if I asked my questions in the stores and businesses that cater to women. You know that I'm not avoiding asking questions of men out of fear, but rather that women would be more likely, perhaps more open, to talking with another woman."

When Henry summarized the discussion he'd had with Williams, Etta nodded her head and said, "Had I been talking to him, I'm not sure he would've been as forthcoming as he was with you." Then she paused, and added, "I also got a hint on Mrs. Lyons' best friend."

"Really?"

"Yes, Emily Acton, the lawyer's wife I met, said that Ida's best friend was the wife of the ranch foreman, John Johnson."

"That's interesting, very interesting. Maybe when we take the trip out to the ranch, you can talk to her while I spend my time with the foreman."

"That's exactly what I was thinking," she said.

"Tonight, after we have a chance to go over all of what we learn today, we need to sit down and write something for Cal. We'll need to get it onto the morning train to Bisbee, either tomorrow or Sunday." Henry stopped and wrote a note on his pad. "I'll have to check at the depot to get the departure time so we don't miss it."

"Alright, then, I'll spend the time until dinner asking my questions at the female oriented businesses."

"And I'll do the same at the saloons, hardware stores, the courthouse, and the county clerk... maybe the banks as well."

"We should have enough to send to Cal about our initial discoveries in Silver City that will be a good preliminary background for our conspiracy theory." Etta stood up, slipped the strap of her purse over her shoulder and said, "See you at dinner, Henry."

She was out the door before he could even rise from the table. He called the waitress over and paid the bill, then he left to start on his own investigation.

At the top of Broadway, the courthouse almost called to him—clerks, judges, records. He glanced down Bullard and saw the shops that could give him information of a different nature. Henry thought of flipping a coin but decided to turn left and head to the courthouse. His first stop was the County Clerk's office. He entered a reception area and approached a counter, behind which stood a man wearing round glasses perched on his nose.

The man looked up as Henry walked toward him. "May I help you, sir?"

"Yes, thank you. My name is Henry Carter, I'm a reporter with the *Bisbee Daily Review*." When he didn't get the typical negative response to his introduction, he continued. "I'm working on doing a background story on Tom Lyons. As you can imagine, there is a lot of interest in him because of his death and the trial that is presently going on in El Paso. We at the *Review* believe that despite what may come up in that trial, people would like to know more about the victim than the killer." Henry paused, trying to read the man's face, to gain an insight into what his response might be. "Would you be willing, if you are allowed to, answer some questions regarding the already public knowledge related to Mr. Lyons and his place in Silver City society?"

"As an acquaintance of the late Mr. Lyons, sir, I am willing to answer *some* questions. I cannot, however, discuss any of the details related to his known assets, contracts, liabilities, or special agreements with state, national, or local governments."

Noticing the name plate on the counter in front of the man—Lester Phillips, Clerk—Henry said, "Mr. Phillips, it seems that we have something in common. I too am interested more in Mr. Lyons' life as a citizen of your community than his position in the business world."

Phillips' response revealed a few facts that Henry was surprised to hear given the clerk's earlier comment.

"Yes, you see, Mr. Lyons was quite active in our county and state. He owned large parcels of land, had control through many leases and other forms of acquisition, land that was quite functional for his chosen industry. Mr. Lyons was a wealthy cattleman in a state that has a large number of struggling cattlemen."

"I see," said Henry, not wanting to interrupt the flow of Phillips' comments.

"But, as a man, as my friend, Tom Lyons was a generous contributor to our community. He and his lovely wife made more positive contributions than any of the spitefully advanced negatives that some of his competitors suggest that he did."

"Would you, Mr. Phillips, be willing to share the names of his major competitors?"

Phillips' scowl quickly disappeared and he said, "The list of competitors is long, of course, but those who would misspeak, would denigrate a fine man is much shorter. Rather than say them out loud, I'd prefer to write them down and let you do your own investigation. These men are well known in the community and others in our town could have given you the same list." He took a slip of paper from a shelf below the counter and wrote down several names quickly, then slid the paper over to Henry.

"Thank, you, Mr. Phillips. I'll remember your discretion in handling this when I compose my story. You've been very helpful. Good day, sir."

Henry slipped the note into his coat pocket and walked out onto the steps of the courthouse.

Henry found it interesting that a town the size of this one had, in addition to the office of the County Sheriff, a police department, and a marshal's office. He hoped by calling on the latter two, to learn something new. At present, he had a fairly good picture of Lyons from his earlier discussion with Deputy Williams.

Henry went to the Marshall's small office and learned very little from the Marshal who indicated that he "didn't know nothin'." Then he met with the Chief of Police who refused to answer any questions regarding the killing.

Realizing that law enforcement in Silver City was somewhat weak, Henry decided to make a call on the local newspaper office. He found the Silver City Times and met with the publisher. This last interaction was very brief since the man agreed to meet Henry simply to tell him that there was "no damn way" he was going to talk to another reporter. *We'll see about that,* thought Henry.

Henry had another impulse and decided to re-visit Mr. Phillips at the courthouse and ask him one more question. Although a bit reluctant, Phillips took off his glasses and said, "Alright, ask your question."

"Thank you. Has anyone been in here asking about the water rights or leases at the LC Ranch?"

"Well, there have been inquiries, but I'm not at liberty to answer that, sir. That information has been forwarded to Mrs. Lyons' attorney."

Etta visited shops on the numbered streets intersecting with Bullard. Most of these were small; a seamstress who repaired tears and worn clothing; another which sold herbs and ointments for various ailments; a small lunch counter where a person wouldn't have to wait long if they were in a hurry for a quick meal.

She went into the lunchroom and was greeted quickly.

"Good afternoon, miss, can I help you?"

Even though she wasn't thirsty, Etta asked, "Could I have a cup of coffee?"

"Of course. Please have a seat and I'll bring one over." The woman returned quickly and set the cup in front of Etta.

"You have a nice little shop here," she said as she lifted the cup to her lips.

"Thank you. Are you new in Silver City?"

"Actually, I'm a visitor. My name is Etta Pearce. I'm a reporter from over in Bisbee."

"I'm Mildred, the owner and only employee of this place." She smiled. "Why is a reporter from Arizona in our little town in New Mexico?"

"My partner and I are gathering information for an article we're writing about the Lyons family and the effects of Mr. Lyons' murder on his poor wife."

"Shouldn't you be in El Paso, following the trial?"

"Perhaps, but we thought our readers would rather learn how such a tragedy affects the family of a victim."

"It's terrible, actually." Mildred's smile disappeared and her face paled.

"I'm sorry," said Etta, "have I said something wrong?"

"No, it's alright. I just..." Mildred pulled a hankie from her apron pocket and dabbed at the tears leaking from her eyes. She sighed and looked at Etta. "I just lost my own husband last year."

"I'm sorry, Mildred, I didn't mean to upset you."

"It's not your fault. Even after all these months since... the accident, I still get weepy." Mildred forced a smile back onto her face. "There weren't many people doing articles about my husband after he was killed over in the copper mine in Santa Clara. I guess a rich rancher gets more notice than a man who digs dirt."

"Did you ever meet the Lyons?"

"In here? No, never."

"When you first heard about Mr. Lyons' murder, what did you think?"

"I'm not sure I thought about it at all. Although once the newspapers started sharing pictures of the man they said killed him, I was surprised."

"Surprised?"

"Yes. Because I'd seen that man before."

"Here? In Silver City?"

"Yes. I know it might seem strange that I'd remember seeing him, but the picture looked so much like my cousin that it reminded me that the man had been here, in my diner."

"So, Felix Jones was in your diner?"

"Or his twin, Miss Pearce. I remember how odd it was that someone looking like my cousin was actually sitting at one of my tables. At the time, that was strange enough.

But when they said he was a murderer, I was, I don't know, shaken up."

"Are you certain that the pictures you saw were of the man who was here?"

"Yes, because of the face that matched my cousin's. Seeing the picture, I remembered how odd it had been when he was in here, drinking coffee with a man I'd seen before around town, a rich man, and I never get those folks in my little shop."

"So, the man who looked like your cousin was sitting at a table in your shop with another man whose presence here was strange?"

"Yes, and to learn that the killer was talking to the local man frightened me a little. I mean, this was just before the murder."

"Did you ever talk to anyone about this?"

"No, I started to have doubts about my memory and then figured it wouldn't matter, since they had the killer in jail."

"If it ever *did* matter, Mildred, would you have been sure enough that it was Felix Jones who had been in your shop talking to a man you had seen around town?"

"Oh, yes."

Henry stopped at every store or shop on Bullard and at any likely places on the various side streets. He asked questions about both of the Lyons. He even made it a point to find out about any of their employees. Henry also sought information about Jones—had anybody noticed the stranger in town in the days before Lyons was killed. He spoke to the barbers, bartenders, bank tellers and proprietors. All of them praised Mr. and Mrs. Lyons for their great support to the town. Most of the responses he received about Lyons from people he encountered on the street were similar—ranging from a rich, compassionate, civic-minded man to repeating the rumors and street-talk about the murder of Lyons' first wife's lover. Even this diligence resulted in no information supporting his conspiracy idea. He had a hunch and stopped in one of the hotels and spoke to the clerk.

"Excuse me, sir, my name is Henry Carter. I'm a reporter from Bisbee and I'm working on an article about the Lyons family."

"Yes, sir, how can I be of service?"

"I was wondering if the alleged killer of Mr. Lyons stayed in your hotel in the days leading up to the killing?"

"No sir, he did not. I told the Sheriff and the investigator from Texas as much a few days after it happened."

Henry thanked the man and repeated his question to three more clerks on Bullard Street. Thinking the hunch wasn't going to produce anything, he stopped at the last hotel on the block and tried once more.

"Well, yes sir, that Jones fella did spend a night in our hotel."

Surprised and pleased that his hunch had paid off, Henry said, "Was the man, Jones, alone or did he spend time with anyone else?"

"He was alone. I never saw him with anyone."

"Did he ever use the telephone?"

"Well, he never *called* anyone, but he did *get* one call."

Henry took a quick breath and asked, "Were you able to hear the conversation?"

"No sir, it was a local call, but I couldn't hear what they discussed. Mr. Jones seemed to be having a very private conversation."

Henry could feel his heart pumping faster. *So, Jones, supposedly an Oklahoma rancher, had some sort of contact in Silver City. This doesn't prove any conspiracy existed,* Henry thought, *but it certainly could if it's true.*

The clerk couldn't recall anything else, so Henry thanked him and walked out onto the street.

As the afternoon wore on, Henry knew he still didn't know enough about Lyons. Deciding to take another chance that the local newspaper might be willing to let him have access to their records, he walked back to the office of the *Silver City Times* and entered the building.

"Can I help you, sir?"

Henry showed the young man his press credentials and said, "If it wouldn't be much trouble, do you think I could look into some old issues of your paper to get some background on Tom Lyons?"

"We usually don't share that information, mister... uh, Carter. Especially with a competitor."

"That's our policy as well, sir. But occasionally we do grant access if the competitor is willing to allow us to review the results of their investigation."

"I should ask the publisher, but I don't think he'd object to your looking at copies of our fine product." The man turned away from the counter, walked over to one of the offices at the rear of the room, and tapped on the door. He entered the office and closed the door behind him. Henry could only imagine what the person the clerk was talking to might be telling him, but he was still hopeful that he'd get a chance to look at old issues of the paper.

"Mr. Walton, the archive manager, has agreed to let you have until we close the office," he pulled a steel watch from his vest, "in about two hours. He also agreed to grant you access as long as he could see a draft of what you gather."

"That's great," Henry said, trying to contain his enthusiasm.

"Then follow me, Mr. Carter, and roll up your sleeves. The old editions are in the warehouse behind the pressroom, and that's one place that never gets dusted."

Left alone with the stacks of newspapers that, thankfully, had been tagged by date of issue, Henry began scanning through them. Looking for any mention of Lyons. He kept on the task, sweating and sneezing and didn't stop until the clerk came up behind him in the back of the warehouse.

"Time's up, Mr. Carter. We need to close up."

"Okay, sir, just give me a minute to make sure I have all of my notes."

The clerk escorted Henry out of the warehouse, locked the door behind him. Out on the sidewalk, Henry wiped his face with a handkerchief and turned toward the hotel, looking forward to hearing about Etta's day.

While Henry was gathering information from around town, Etta had been equally active. After lunch, Etta considered making a visit to the city library or to the newspaper office. Thinking that Henry would be more likely to go the newspaper than to the library, that's where she headed, but she quickly learned after asking a police officer she encountered that there was no public library in the town. He suggested she visit the one at the college and gave her these directions, "you go up Twelfth street about eight or ten blocks. When you've done that, you are on university property. Someone there can direct you to the library."

Etta trekked up to the school and asked the first person she met where the library was. Getting directions, she followed them to a building that contained the library and a number of classrooms.

The college library was spacious and most of the tables set between the bookshelves were occupied by young people. Some were clearly studying, others, it appeared to Etta, were chatting with friends. She approached the checkout desk and spoke to the elderly woman standing there.

"Excuse me, ma'am," said Etta.

The frown on the woman's face spoke volumes to Etta. Another old person who isn't ready for change, she thought.

"May I help you?" The woman's tone was dismissive, brusque.

"Yes, thank you. I'm wondering if your library keeps copies of local or regional newspapers."

"We do," she paused, "for students' research."

"I see. I'm not a student, I'm a reporter from Arizona, and I'm doing research on Silver City for an article." Etta paused, working on a way to get the woman to at least point out where the papers were. "I was hoping that you'd allow me to spend some time looking at your collection."

Seeming disinterested in Etta's request, the woman tried unsuccessfully to make her uncomfortable.

"I would certainly like to give your college and its library staff some positive publicity in my article."

This seemed to get the woman's attention. She still wasn't smiling, but she did say, "If you'll come with me, I'll see if we can accommodate you."

She led Etta to a door at the back of the room, opened it and said, "Here's where we store our newspaper collections. They're filed alphabetically by title and by date of issue."

Then looking sternly at Etta, she added, "You may look at any of these you deem necessary for your article, but those you do take from a shelf must be stacked on this table." She pointed at the one by the door. "We don't want them returned to the racks or shelves, since you might put something in the wrong spot."

"Thank you, ma'am, I'll be sure to do just that. I appreciate your assistance."

Etta spent the rest of the afternoon searching through the newspapers, at least those published in the past ten years or so, looking for any articles that mentioned the Lyons' ranch. In the process she spotted stories about the cattle market, and about other ranchers. She did find a short entry buried in the back pages of the Silver City paper from four years earlier, about the challenges faced by some small herd ranchers.

She also found a single column entry in the back of the paper near the want ads, about a bartender at one of the saloons who had called the Sheriff's office and reported a situation that occurred in his establishment. The article said that "several local ranchers had come into the saloon and interrupted a conversation between Tom Lyons and John Johnson, his foreman." According to the bartender, the group of ranchers spoke harshly to Lyons and Johnson, about "something" and Mr. Lyons ignored them. His refusal to respond to their tirade seemed to anger the group. The bartender said that when the ranchers began to yell at Mr. Lyons, he called the sheriff and then told the noisy group that the deputy was on the way. When the deputy arrived the group of ranchers was not present, so when he asked Lyons what they'd said, Lyons replied, "They were just some folks who'd asked me to do something, and I said, 'no.'" The deputy reported that Lyons refused to identify the men and the bartender followed suit, telling the deputy he wasn't sure who the men were."

Etta copied this article word for word in her notebook, closed it and put it in her bag and left the library.

On her way back to the hotel, she saw a Baptist Church, and walked up the steps to the door, but found it locked, so she turned away, disappointed, and continued toward Bullard. When she saw the spires of the Catholic church a few blocks to the south, she decided to see if she could gather any information there.

St. Vincent de Paul Catholic Church was huge. She took a chance and entered through the large double doors of the sanctuary where she met a man mopping the floor. The fellow, a Mexican, said that the priest was in his office.

"Do you think I could meet with him?" she asked.

"I don't know, but I will take you to him."

Etta followed the man back out of the church and across the street to what appeared to be a house.

"This is his office?"

"Yes, it is," the man answered and gently knocked on the door.

After a moment, the door opened and Etta faced the priest, a man probably her father's age.

"Oh, hello," he said, "how may I help you?"

"I'm sorry for bothering you at home, sir. My name is Etta Pearce, I'm a reporter for the *Bisbee Daily Review*. I'm in Silver City to write a story, and I wonder if you have some time to answer a few questions."

"Unfortunately, I don't have the time today, Miss Pearce. I'm in the midst of counseling with one of my parishioners. Could you possibly come back tomorrow morning?"

Not being familiar with the Catholic church, and not sure what to call the priest, she remembered a story she'd read in college in which the priest was referred to as 'Father O'Malley'.

"Thank you, Father..."

"I'm Father Carrasco, the minister here at St. Vincent's."

"Father Carrasco, would nine o'clock tomorrow work for you?"

"Of course, Miss Pearce. I'll see you at nine tomorrow."

Etta sat on the edge of her bed while Henry relaxed in the straight back chair. They'd spent the last half-hour going over what they'd learned.

"So, Dusty, what did you learn digging around in the newspaper archives?"

"What I learned by looking at old news stories is that Cal's information was correct. Lyons was powerful and controversial. Back in the 90s he and his partner, Campbell, had a lot of trouble with cattle rustlers. Lyons had a *great* deal of difficulty in his marriage. His first wife, Emma Noyes, had an affair with a local cowboy some thirty years ago. Lyons found out about it and invited the man to come to the ranch. Lyons shot and killed him in front of Emma and she ran out of the house. This was in May of 1890. She eventually moved to California and they divorced."

"That's some background, Henry. Was there any legal

action taken against Lyons?"

"No, a short trial determined that Lyons' action was justifiable homicide, but there's more. Lyons' partner in the cattle business, Angus Campbell was married to Ida Runyan in 1890, but he died in the spring of '92."

"So, Cal was right about that too."

"He was. She and Lyons were married in 1898. According to the stories I read, the two of them have been working hard on building an empire in this part of the state ever since. They are always graciously presented in the paper as 'contributors to society,' and 'great benefactors to the city and state.'"

"That's good information, Henry. Did you find anything that would lead us to a conspiracy?"

"I still think, although I can't yet prove it, that there was a conspiracy to kill Lyons, and it was probably led by some of his competitors. I did get a lead at one of the other hotels in the city, though. Jones received a call from someone in Silver City on the night he stayed here. But the clerk had no name and heard none of the conversation. It's an interesting element, but the only thing left for us to do is to go out to the ranch and speak with the foreman."

"That sounds reasonable."

Henry said, "Most of the people I spoke with today believe that robbery was the motive. There was some support for our theory, but no evidence."

"Well, at least we'll have another chance to pursue that line of thinking at the ranch tomorrow."

"Right, but tonight we have to keep writing Part I of our article so we can get it on the train for Cal."

Henry asked Etta about her afternoon, and she filled him in on what she'd discovered at the college library, her discussion with Mildred, and the appointment she'd made with the priest of the catholic church. Henry agreed that the article would be something they could discuss with the foreman at the ranch.

* * *

On Saturday morning, after having breakfast with Henry, Etta hurried over to the priest's house.

Father Carrasco opened the door as she walked onto the porch, invited her into the office and offered her a seat.

Etta thanked Carrasco, and said, "My partner and I are reporters for the *Bisbee Daily Review*. We've come from Arizona to do a story about the Tom Lyons family."

Carrasco nodded, and said, "Mr. and Mrs. Lyons are people I *know*. What sort of questions do you have?"

"I'm sure you are aware," she said, "of the murder trial going on in Texas. We have been asked to do a story about the death of Mr. Lyons, but unlike most other newspapers, we have decided to not focus on the trial of the murderer, but rather on the victim. Our objective is to ensure that Mr. Lyons is remembered as a man and not just a dead body. We hope to learn why he was killed and focus on that rather than how he was killed."

"I see," said the priest. "How can I help?"

"You said you know the Lyons."

"Yes.

"Do you know, or can you tell me if there are any people in this part of New Mexico who'd be, I don't know... be pleased that Mr. Lyons is no longer a wealthy cattleman?"

"I am just a simple priest, Miss Pearce. Most of the people I know are neither wealthy nor are they 'cattlemen.'"

"I understand, Father..."

"However," he interrupted, "If I was allowed to speculate, I'd guess that there would be a number of local men who, because of the Lyons' control of land and water rights prevents them from accessing that land or that water, these people might be pleased that he's no longer around. I couldn't give you any names, of course, but certainly those interested in gaining access to these assets would likely be inquiring their availability from the state and county authorities or even the Lyons' lawyers, wouldn't they?"

"Of course you're right, Father, so forgive me if I'm putting you on the spot." Etta decided to ask one more question.

"Since you encounter many people in your daily life, I wonder if you would be willing to speculate that there might be a small group of previously disappointed people—people who might have desired access to Lyons' assets—who would join with others to remove the impediment to their future growth."

"In other words, Miss Pearce, would I know if there are people who'd pay to get rid of Mr. Lyons?"

Etta remained silent.

"I can tell you that I know of no such group of people or any conspiracy. But as an educated thinking man, I would speculate that it is certainly a possibility."

Carrasco stood and said, "I hope I have been helpful, Miss Pearce, but if you'll excuse me, I have other duties that need my attention."

"Thank you, Father Carrasco, I do appreciate your help."

"I don't think," Henry said, "that we'll actually get finished with part one tonight even if we write until dawn. Besides, we need to rest up for the trip out to the ranch in Gila tomorrow."

"You're right. Besides, the last few days have been busy and I know I'll need to rest before tackling the writing."

Henry said, "We may even learn something tomorrow that'll enhance part one, so let's call Cal and tell him we'll finish part one tomorrow and put it on the train the next morning."

Etta yawned and said, "Besides, we haven't eaten dinner yet."

"Are you hungry?"

"I'm not starving, but I could eat something."

"Okay, I'll go call Cal and you can powder your nose and think about where you want to go." He was quiet for just a moment, then said, "But we need to each outline part one as we see it now and then put our ideas together tomorrow when we get back from the ranch."

Henry went down to the lobby and placed the call to Bisbee.

"Daily Review, this is Cal Langley."

"Cal, it's Henry."

"Hello, son. I figured you'd be calling tonight. Can you give me a summary of what you've learned and your current plans?"

"Well, we have been busy."

Henry brought him up to date on the various interviews and then said, "Tomorrow we're driving out to the Lyons' home—the ranch—in Gila to meet with the foreman. Then we'll come back here and write the full part one of our article. We plan to say that at this point we don't have enough information to name suspects, but we do believe that a conspiracy was possible and that Jones was paid to kill Tom Lyons. We'll put part one on the train to you not later than the day after tomorrow."

"Okay, Henry."

Henry was on the telephone at the front desk when Etta arrived in the lobby.

"Yes, thank you, Mr. Johnson. We'll see you before noon at the ranch."

Henry turned toward Etta, then took her by the arm and led her across the lobby. He glanced quickly around the room and said, "Mr. Johnson has agreed to meet with us tomorrow. When I asked if it would be possible for you to talk to his wife, he said that would work better for him, since he'd be quite busy and didn't want to sit around for a 'gabfest.' Those were his words."

"Well, I hope Mrs. Johnson and I talk a lot about Ida Lyons."

Chapter 15

On Sunday morning, Etta and Henry drove out of Silver City up Market Street to the highway and turned left onto the macadam road. The route to the town of Gila—the nearest community to the ranch—wound through the desert, up and down gentle hills through a shaded glen and took a couple of hours.

Rounding a curve on the highway, they saw the sign indicating that Gila was to the right. Henry backed off on the accelerator pedal as they approached the turn.

"I'm thirsty, Henry. Let's look for a place to get a drink before we head to the ranch."

"Good idea, my mouth feels as dry as this highway," he said as he made the turn onto the narrower side-road. It wasn't long until the first sign of civilization appeared—a small general store, one that provided a shaded outdoor bench and a chance to rest.

Henry parked the car next to the store and turned off the engine.

Etta got out of the car and walked toward an outhouse behind the building.

"Be right back," she said.

Henry walked up the two steps onto the veranda of the little store, then went inside. He glanced around and finally asked the storekeeper if he could have two Coca-Colas.

The man reached into a large, ice-filled chest and lifted out two bottles. Putting them on the counter in front of Henry, he said, "Here ya go."

"Henry thanked him, put a dime on the counter, and carried the bottles outside. He sat down on a bench, rested his back against the wall and stretched out his legs.

Etta walked onto the porch and gladly accepted the cold, bubbly offering from Henry.

"You have the map, Henry?"

"Yeah," he said and unfolded the hand-drawn directions provided by the hotel clerk in Silver City.

The storekeeper, a portly, cigar-smoking man, glanced at the map when Henry asked him if the directions to the ranch were accurate.

The man nodded and asked, "Whatcha doin' out at the ranch?"

Henry looked up at him and was about to respond when Etta said, "We're going to meet with the foreman."

"You two strangers here?"

"No stranger than most, I suppose." Henry thought a little humor would deflect any snooping.

"Ever been out there?"

"Nope, first time."

"You know Mr. Lyons is kilt, right?"

"Uh huh."

Etta said, "Can I ask you a question?"

"Nah, I ain't much for talkin', nor messin' around in other folks' business."

Surprised by the hypocrisy in his statement, Etta said, "You're not?"

"Nope. Nosiree, not me." The man turned and walked into the store.

Henry drove away from the little town and found the ranch just as the clerk at the hotel in Silver City had described it. He drove through a wide gap in the fence, parked the car next to a black sedan and as they got out of the vehicle, a tall man wearing denim pants, boots, and a cowboy hat stopped in front of them.

"Are you folks lost?"

"Not if we're at the LC Ranch, we're not." Henry walked toward the man and added, "we're looking for Mr.

Johnson. I'm Henry Carter and this is Etta Pearce, we're reporters with the *Bisbee Daily Review*, we spoke last night about talking with him about an article we're doing on Mr. Tom Lyons. Are you Mr. Johnson?"

"I am John Johnson, the foreman and I don't have a *whole* lot of time to spend with reporters. but I did agree to speak with you purely on the basis of your description of the article. Besides, I'm not sure Mrs. Lyons would appreciate me speaking about her ranch since she's got enough trouble goin' on in her life," The man wasn't rude, Henry thought, just busy. So, he decided to be brief and to the point.

"It seems to be a foregone conclusion that Jones murdered Mr. Lyons and will be convicted. But our story is not going to focus on the killer or the trial in Texas. We were hoping to get some information on Mr. Lyons' background."

"Why?"

Etta spoke up, "Mr. Johnson, while most papers are following the trial, concerned with the details of the murder by Felix Jones, we intend to focus instead on the victims—Mr. and Mrs. Lyons. We are trying to learn *why* Jones killed Tom Lyons. We also want to be sure that people don't forget the victim and his poor wife."

Etta's comment was interrupted by the arrival of a rather strong looking woman who said, "I can assure you that Mrs. Lyons is doing as well as might be expected. After all, it's been six months since that bastard killed her husband."

"Mrs. Johnson?" asked Etta. She got a nod in response. "If it's not inconvenient, I'd like to speak with you about Mrs. Lyons. I believe our readers would be encouraged by her life and ability to recover—however much that is—from such a tragedy. Is there someplace we can talk while your husband and Mr. Carter discuss the ranch and how it's been affected by Mr. Lyons' death?"

Mrs. Johnson seemed to calm a bit, Etta's words

somehow giving her a sense of comfort. "Let's go into the kitchen. Would you like some coffee?"

"I certainly would."

"Most people," said Henry, "believe that Mr. Lyons was killed in a robbery, that Jones murdered him for money. Do you think that's possible?"

"Possible? Yes."

"Do you believe it's true?"

"No, I don't. I saw that man, Jones, here just before the murder. He was a strange sort, and I remember that Mrs. Lyons didn't like him."

"Why do you think Jones killed Mr. Lyons?"

"I don't have a clue, but Jones was strange enough when I saw him here that he could have done it for any number of reasons."

"Let me put it this way, sir. It's well known that the LC Ranch is huge, has land leases and water rights that cover much of southwestern New Mexico. It's also known that this property is coveted or desired by other cattlemen with herds of varying size who all wanted access to his water."

"Okay, and why wouldn't they? Look, Mr. Carter, it's no surprise that some people were jealous of Mr. Lyons. I know most of the ranchers in this part of the state, but my time is spent managing the ranch, dealing with small herds that wander onto the pastures, and occasional squatters. I don't know, at least yet, if Mrs. Lyons is selling land or cattle, or giving up water leases."

Henry listened, choosing to remember the man's comments rather than take notes.

"Mr. Johnson, when I was in Silver City, I spoke to a number of people, men who were familiar with Mr. Lyons and his role in the civic life of the county. Many of them thought very favorably of the Lyons family. One person, a county official, even gave me a list of ranchers that he thought might have been most interested in the meadows and water rights controlled by Mr. Lyons."

Henry slipped the list from his coat pocket but didn't unfold it.

"Mr. Carter, I believe that most of the ranchers and businessmen in Silver City and throughout the county could give you a list that would include a dozen or so ranchers who wanted what Tom Lyons had." He paused, glancing at the paper in Henry's hand. "Picking the top five or ten wouldn't be a difficult task."

Johnson seemed to be carefully choosing what he'd say next, so Henry maintained his silence.

"Of those dozen ranchers, several were good friends of Tom Lyons, and had accepted that he was who he was, and that he had no intention of sharing what took him more than twenty years to acquire."

"But..."

"But," said Johnson, "the rest of the list would include some men, ranchers, who at one point or another offered to pay Mr. Lyons a fee for access and who became upset, sometimes *angrily* upset when he refused their offers."

"Did any of them make any threats against Mr. Lyons?"

"A few did, some of them right here at the ranch and in a saloon in Silver City, but I will not tell you which ones did. I will tell you, though, that Mr. Lyons made certain that they understood that there would be a high—very high—cost if they acted overtly."

"Mr. Johnson, I appreciate your candor and your reservations as well. You still have to live in this county, and pointing out the remaining ranch owners as possibly being involved in threatening Mr. Lyons would not be healthy for you."

"True enough, Mr. Carter, and thank you for understanding."

Henry paused, wanting to be certain how to proceed. "If I show you my list, the one provided by the county official, would you tell me if any of the names fit into the list you would recognize as those, umm, *difficult* ranchers?"

"I'll tell you what, Mr. Carter, I'll look at your list and then decide if or what I'll say regarding your question."

In the modest kitchen of the Johnson's quarters at the LC Ranch, Etta and the foreman's wife sat at a table drinking their coffee. Etta's notebook was open to a blank page, but her pencil rested, unused, next to it. Etta had chosen, once again, to listen rather than to write. She'd only asked one question of Mrs. Johnson, and it took the strong, loyal woman several long moments to ponder her response.

"You asked, Miss Pearce, what type of woman Ida Lyons really is."

Etta remained quiet, simply nodding.

"As the spouse of a trusted employee, I've known Ida for over fifteen years." She was quiet for a bit, seemingly reflecting on those years. "In all that time, she treated me kindly. Not, perhaps as you might imagine, as an underling, or someone less than herself. We both knew our places, but she set that aside more and more through the years. She seemed to progressively trust me, trust my judgment, trust my advice. She would often make a comment about how I kept my house... this one," she said referring to the room in which they sat, "and reflect on how similar our ideas about decorating and furnishing were."

When Etta didn't respond, Mrs. Johnson continued.

"But those discussions changed over time. We talked about more personal things, more important topics, the longer we knew one another. The thing that I'll remember most about Ida is that she never looked down on me, never once. My husband and I worked hard for the Lyons and they paid us fairly. But money never seemed important to Ida."

Etta was ready with her second question. "Mrs. Johnson, what would you say has allowed Ida Lyons to survive, to get through these last six months? What character trait do you believe keeps her from despair?"

"You know, Etta, I asked myself that very same question and the only thing that makes any sense is not truly an answer to the question. Ida Lyons is a woman of integrity. She is always honest in her evaluation of events and situations. She never expects to be treated any differently because of the position she has in society. She sees herself as a woman—period. When that man, Jones, was here, she knew he was trouble, she told her husband so. When she was told who had killed Mr. Lyons, she felt responsible. She chastened herself for not insisting that Mr. Lyons refuse to deal with him."

Etta thought of asking another question, but Mrs. Johnson said, "She told me to not weep for her, ever, that she would be fine even as much as she misses her husband. That's the woman your readers need to remember."

Etta rose from her chair and left the woman at the table, thanked her for her time, and rejoined Henry and Mr. Johnson. She found them on the porch and heard Johnson say, "If any ranchers wanted to do something to Tom Lyons, some of them are on this list."

He handed the note back to Henry and said, "unless you two have any more questions, I'm busy."

"We appreciate you talking to us, sir," said Etta, "but I did have one final question. What did *you* think of Mr. Lyons, as a boss and as a man?"

"I liked and respected him, Miss Pearce. Have a good trip back to Arizona."

With that, he turned and walked away.

Still full of questions, Henry and Etta walked over to the car and got in. Etta started the engine and drove out of the yard. They didn't stop at the general store in Gila, choosing to avoid the fat man, and drove non-stop back to Silver City.

Unable to discuss the meeting with Johnson because of the wind and noise, and unwilling even more so as they pondered their situation, the two reporters didn't say much as they rode to Silver City. When they reached the town, she parked in front of the hotel and they walked into the lobby.

Standing at the foot of the stairs that led to the second floor, Henry sighed deeply and looked at Etta.

She spoke first. "We have lots to do and limited time in which to finish the job." Etta kept her eyes on Henry's face. "So, let's go wash up, get the dust out of our brains and start working with *what we have*."

Henry caught the emphasis on her last three words. "You're right, Etta. Let's get to work."

As Etta unlocked her door, she said, "Meet me here in fifteen minutes so we can start writing."

Half an hour later, sitting in Etta's room, they worked separately, composing their ideas into a story. They sat, as before, Etta on the bed and Henry in the chair.

An invisible observer would have heard the rustling of note paper, and the grunts and sighs from the reporters. This ghostly presence would have seen the frowns on their faces and heard the occasional expressions of discovery.

Though individually they seemed unaware of the specter's role in their efforts, they dug deep into their gut-level skills and ground out of the raw material of notes, memories, and a clear objective, the first rough drafts of part one of their article.

When Etta finished her draft, she stood and went to the window. Pulling the curtain open, she gazed out at the afternoon traffic of downtown Silver City. *Those people,* she thought, *aren't thinking about a murder or a trial. They're planning dinner or closing a deal or wondering what their children are up to.*

Henry looked at Etta, not wanting to interrupt her. He set his pad on the desk and closed his eyes, going back over in his mind what he'd recorded over the past few hours. Despite his desire to rest, his need to finish the task urged him to speak.

"We need to keep working, Etta."

She turned toward her partner and handed her draft to Henry. "Take a look at this and be brutal."

Henry nodded, gave his notes to her and said, "Likewise."

The invisible observer would have smiled, inspired by the genuine dedication expressed by the reporters.

Murder for Hire: The Conspiracy to Kill Tom Lyons—Part I

Reported by Henrietta Pearce and Henry Carter

The shocking murder last year of Tom Lyons, the well-known citizen of Silver City and Grant County, New Mexico, has generated much interest and increased news coverage with the start of the trial of his murderer, Felix Jones in El Paso Texas. That trial began in the past few weeks and has been narrowly focused on the killer, with authorities seemingly driven to convict Jones without regard for discovering the motive, that element which might comfort the other victims of the murder—Tom Lyons' wife, Ida, and the rest of his family.

We at the *Bisbee Daily Review* have chosen to ignore the trial and instead to provide for our readers the most important element of the case—motive. *Why* did Felix Jones, a known criminal in Texas, and Oklahoma, lure Lyons from New Mexico to El Paso and then beat him to death with a steel pipe on the side of a road? Many of the citizens of Silver City whom we interviewed thought that the motive was robbery. But, luring a man a hundred miles to a city simply for fifty dollars makes no sense. There has been no evidence presented to indicate Jones even knew Lyons or had ever encountered him in his years of criminal activity in Texas and Oklahoma. In fact, Mrs. Lyons and the LC Ranch foreman, John Johnson, have each confirmed that Jones was completely unknown to Tom Lyons.

We have spent considerable time and effort in trying to determine the motive of the killer. We asked ourselves and scores of others—primarily the citizens of Silver City, New Mexico—the people who knew Tom Lyons, the people who had experienced his largess and his influence, why someone might want to kill him. We have discovered, as our readers might expect, that not everyone believed Lyons to be a saint. Some feared him, others envied him, but no one in this part of the country has publicly said he deserved to die.
Yet, Mr. Lyons *is* dead, and while judges and lawyers consider points of law and release individuals who were likely complicit in the murder, such as the two Coggins brothers who, though initially indicted along with Jones, have been released in order to testify against him. Should not the authorities be prosecuting anyone complicit in Mr. Lyons' death even if they might not have wielded the murder weapon?

While the judges and lawyers are rushing through the trial, they openly disregard the impact of Lyons' death on his wife. In addition to loneliness and despair, she is now faced with managing a million-acre ranch and dealing with the scores of ranchers who want what belongs to her and who are willing to pester the widow in order to gain control of the numerous land parcels, the government issued water rights, and the profits they would otherwise generate for her. People working closely with Mrs. Lyons attorney, have indicated that they are frequently contacted, either by lawyers representing local ranchers, or the local ranchers themselves seeking to acquire Mrs. Lyons' property, or ownership of the various leases and grants. Officials in the County Clerk's Office report similar levels of activity regarding the same assets. We have learned that the family, their attorney, and the county authorities are, almost daily. being asked about the assets and their availability. It appears that even six months after her husband's death, there are people whose pecuniary interests are so important that they care little for the woman's losses—peace, comfort, and the presence of a loved one.

Where is the justice for Ida Lyons, a woman who is revered by those in the community, such as the largely poor citizens in the southern part of the city with whom she shares some of her wealth, and the widow of the late Baptist preacher, whom she continues to support? Certainly, she will see the killer, Felix Jones be convicted for murdering her husband. Perhaps she will even see him executed. But will she ever learn why her husband died?

When asked about public interest in the assets, a county official indicated that there is considerable interest in the assets. Without

> naming any of the citizens seeking Lyons' property, he indicated that he is regularly questioned by them as to their availability. One of Mr. Lyons' trusted employees described for us meetings between Lyons and ranchers before the murder who sought to entice him to share the assets. He said that his employer always refused and sent them away. We have asked ourselves, is it not possible that avarice and greed could entice some of these ranchers to band together, to pool their resources, to seek out a person willing to kill for money and then hire him to kill Tom Lyons?
>
> We have confirmed, in a discussion with an employee of the Plaza Hotel, that while Jones was a guest at the hotel, he received a call from an unnamed person using a local telephone number. Furthermore, we learned from an employee of a café that she witnessed a discussion between a known resident of the county and Jones a few days prior to the murder. Could the call and the meeting be, as some have suggested, merely efforts to sell cattle to Jones? Perhaps. Could they not also be about murder for hire?

Etta reread this first page and placed it on top of the other five which made up Part I of the article. She slipped the pages into a large envelope and addressed it to Calvin Langley. After sealing the package, she handed it to Henry as he walked out of her room on his way to the depot down the street from the hotel.

When Henry got back from the depot, he asked a question that led to a lengthy discussion. "When we name the conspirators in Part II, what affect will our article have on the trial in El Paso? Will it generate another criminal case, one charging the four or five or six conspirators for murder? The court in Texas may not have an interest in a crime committed in New Mexico."

Chapter 16

Henry and Etta had each made detailed lists of questions that needed provable, logical answers to support their speculation that a conspiracy was carried out to kill Tom Lyons. The ultimate question that each believed was most important was *why kill Tom Lyons*? In order to determine the motive, the why, they'd need to discover who wanted him dead. That meant digging deeply into the backgrounds of the six ranchers on Phillips' list.

On Friday morning, as they sat in Etta's room, they discussed possible answers to their questions, such as, what did the ranchers want?

"We know, or believe we know, that they wanted access to the grazing lands and water resources that were controlled by Lyons. This answer is supported by the discussions with the Sheriff's deputy, with Mr. Phillips, and with Johnson, the foreman."

"What else, besides these things could they have wanted?" asked Henry, not wanting to possibly miss anything important simply because their first conclusion seemed so obvious and was supported by the input from reliable sources.

Etta flipped through the pages of her notebook, then asked, "Having been rejected regularly by Lyons, according to Johnson, they might have been angry enough at Lyons for his demeaning treatment of them."

"Possibly," mumbled Henry.

"We have no witnesses yet to suggest what was actually said at any gathering of Lyons and the ranchers, so we can't say what was said by whom, nor how it was said."

"We do know," said Henry, "that according to Johnson,

the ranchers had met with Lyons and that he, Lyons, had adamantly refused to deal with them."

"So, we need to ask around and determine if any of these discussions were held in town, or at least in a public place that might have had witnesses."

"Like bars or saloons."

"Right," said Etta.

Henry added, "Anger and embarrassment could lead to violence, but murder by a third party? I'm not so sure."

"Something else, Henry. They wanted the land and water in order to increase their herds in size and quality so that their profits would improve substantially. So, more than anger or embarrassment, they'd want profit growth."

"Otherwise, if we believe that some of them arranged a substantial payment to Jones, they must have believed that they could recoup the money through herd growth. That also assumes," said Henry, "that they believed with Lyons out of the picture, they alone would have access to the land and water."

A few minutes ticked by as they considered this.

"How can we narrow down the list? How do we determine which of the six were involved?"

Henry said, "Johnson told me that some of the names on the list were in the group likely to threaten Lyons."

"Then we need to work this list with a goal of determining which of the six are likely co-conspirators. It's possible, isn't it Henry, that some of these ranchers could have been asked to join the effort to get rid of Lyons, but decided against doing so, because of any number of reasons—they didn't want to murder Lyons, or they feared him..."

"Or they didn't like the ranchers who were asking them to help."

Neither of them was hungry, so after a cup of coffee in the dining room, they left the hotel and headed in different directions. Etta planned to meet with Emily Acton and find out what she might know about any of the six ranchers. She and Henry felt that such a discussion with her bore little risk and might show the lawyer's wife that Etta trusted her. Henry was on his way up Broadway to the courthouse. He planned on meeting with Phillips, to thank him for the list, to let him know that it was validated by Johnson, and especially to find out more about each of the ranchers. The reporters knew that the six men were cattle ranchers. Each of them had sizable herds, though not as large as Lyons managed. Furthermore, they hoped to prove that the ranchers had access to an amount of cash that when added together would reach an amount that would entice someone like Jones to carry out a murder. Henry was hopeful that Phillips would be willing and able to provide him with answers.

Etta stopped at the drug store and called the Acton home.

"Acton residence, this is Emily."

"Hello, Emily, this is Etta Pearce. How are you this morning?"

"Oh, good morning, Miss Pearce. How nice of you to call."

"I wanted to thank you again for allowing me to use your home the other day and to ask you another favor."

"You're welcome, of course. I thought the gathering was pleasant and very informative. I hope you acquired enough information for your article."

"I gained much from the discussion and the ladies' responses greatly enhanced our work." Etta paused and added, "Henry and I are in the midst of preparation for the second part of the article, and I wondered if you had time today for me to drop by with a few more questions."

"Of course, Etta, I've no other meaningful plans for the day. Why don't you join me for lunch at say twelve-thirty. That will allow me time to spruce up the place."

"That time will work, of course, but there's no need to

clean up for me."

"It's no bother, I usually clean house on Friday anyway."

"Alright," said Etta, "I'll be there at half past noon."

"Okay, bye."

With a few hours to spare, Etta decided to try the Baptist church again.

When Henry entered the County Clerk's office at the courthouse, he asked to see Mr. Phillips.

"I'm sorry, sir," said the woman behind the counter, "Mr. Phillips is in a meeting this morning. I believe he'll return around eleven o'clock. Would you like to make an appointment?"

"If it would be convenient, I could return shortly after eleven."

"Alright then, and who should I say will call for Mr. Phillips?"

"Henry Carter."

"Okay, Mr. Carter, I'll give him the message when he returns to the office."

Henry left the courthouse and walked down Broadway to the Plaza Hotel, where he'd spoken to the clerk who remembered Felix Jones and the local telephone call.

When he entered the Plaza, the same man was behind the desk, and surprised Henry by remembering his name.

"Hello, Mr. Carter."

"Good morning to you as well. I wonder if you have some time to spare. I have a few follow-up questions for you."

"Well, we're not very busy at the moment. Let's get some coffee and sit down by the window."

The desk clerk walked into an office behind the counter and returned with two cups of coffee. He placed the cups on a table which rested in front of a sofa, then sat down next to Henry.

"So, follow-up questions, huh? Still trying to find out

who in town might have spoken to the killer?"

"Actually, yes," said Henry. He pulled his notebook from a coat pocket and flipped the pages until he found a blank one. "Since we last spoke, I've done some research which led me to wonder who Jones's local caller might have been. Since he had claimed to be in town to buy cattle, I thought he might be talking to a rancher, someone from whom he could buy cattle."

"That makes sense, but I never heard the caller's name and without that, how do we determine who Jones was actually speaking with?"

"You're right, without that name, the existence of the call itself isn't much help." Henry flipped a few pages back toward the front of his notebook. He stopped at the page which had the list of names from Phillips.

"I have a few names here of ranchers who may or may not have spoken to Jones. But the ranchers I've identified might have been interested in selling some of their stock. What I'm interested in specifically this morning is, do you know any of these ranchers and if you do, could you tell me about them."

Taking a sip of his coffee, the clerk said, "Why don't you let me see your list."

Henry placed his notebook in front of the desk clerk.

"Are you familiar with any of these gentlemen?"

The clerk glanced quickly at the list, then read it again more slowly.

"Okay, Mr. Carter, you've shown me a list of some pretty powerful men, at least powerful now that Tom Lyons is dead." He slid the notebook back to Henry.

"What can you tell me about them? What kind of reputations do they have in Silver City and Grant County?"

"If you're asking me to identify a murderer, I'd be foolish to do that, wouldn't I?"

"Of course you would. But if you could anonymously pick three or four who you thought might be capable of such a thing, and your name would never be connected to the list, could you do that?"

"By never, you mean never?"

"Absolutely, first of all, I don't know your name, and second, I'm not doing anything more than reducing the number of... people I have to interview." Henry waited for a response while the clerk turned once again to the notebook and pulled it back in front of him.

"Of the six, I could eliminate two of them very quickly."

"Why?"

"Because I know them and know that they'd never do something as heinous as get someone murdered."

"How do you know them?"

The clerk didn't respond.

"Sir?"

"Mr. Carter, I just *know* that Block and Cardell aren't that kind of person."

He pushed the notebook back toward Henry and rose from the sofa.

"I have to get back to work, and I'd appreciate it if you didn't come back around."

When Etta walked by the Baptist church, she tried the door again, but it was still locked. As she turned back toward the street, she met an older lady coming up the walk.

"Excuse me, dear, can I help you?"

"Perhaps you can." Etta had to bend down to face the very short woman. Despite her being already of limited height, the woman's back was curved so much that she could barely keep her head erect. "I was actually looking to speak with the pastor or his wife. I'm a reporter for the Bisbee Arizona paper, and I'm looking for some information on the Lyons family. I hoped that some of your members might be familiar with them."

"I'm sorry young lady, but since our pastor died, we've not been able to hold services."

"I'm so sorry ma'am."

"Oh, you needn't be sorry, the old coot was nearly a hundred, but I loved him anyway."

"I'm not sure I understand," said Etta.

"Well, you see, I was married to Charles Vincent for seventy years and for fifty of those years he preached right here, in this building."

"Oh my."

"But, I'm still here if you want to talk about the Lyons."

"Did you know them?"

"Goodness me, yes. In fact, Ida Lyons has been helping me since Charles died. If it wasn't for her, we'd have starved years ago."

"Did she attend your church?"

"No, but she tended to us. Still does actually, even after she lost her husband. But since I'm the woman of the church, you'll have to take my word on Ida Lyons."

Mrs. Vincent walked slowly up the walk, then turned toward Etta.

"Have a wonderful day, dear."

A stunned Etta watched her slowly climb the steps and sit in a chair on the porch.

While Etta walked the few blocks to Emily's house, she pondered the things the woman had said. Though there wasn't anything that would lead to the motive in the death of Tom Lyons, Etta learned a lot more about Ida. *I wish I'd heard this before we sent off Part I,* she thought.

When Etta arrived at the Acton home, Emily was sweeping off the porch.

"Hello, Emily," she said.

"Etta! Come on in, I've just finished my Friday chores and I'm ready for some company."

Emily leaned the broom into a corner of the porch and met Etta as she reached the top step. She gave Etta a slight hug and led the reporter into the house.

"Have a seat, Etta. Can I get you something to drink?"

"A glass of water sounds wonderful."

"Coming right up." She disappeared into the kitchen

and reappeared just as quickly.

Setting the glass on a table next to Etta's chair, Emily said, "So tell me about your article."

"Well, we finished the first part and are sending it to Bisbee on the morning train. It'll likely be published sometime next week."

"If you can, could you get some copies of your paper sent here? I know the article will be of interest and those ladies who spent time with you will enjoy reading an article partially written by a woman—a young, intelligent, daring woman."

"I'll send a telegram to the editor, and I know he'd be pleased to send some copies."

"Thanks, Etta." Emily took a sip from her own glass of water, then said, "What would you like to talk about today?"

"In a way, the first part of the article was the easiest. Our objective, you recall, was to point out that the victims of the murder are more important than the killer and his trial, that his shameful act had an impact on the family and the community. We were able to show Ida Lyons' strength of character and how it shines when compared to the killer's lack of character. We also tried to show how Silver City is facing the loss of a valued citizen."

"We are so fortunate that you and Mr. Carter came to our town."

"Thank you, Emily. But as I said, the first part was easy when compared to the rest of the article. The theme for part two is that since the court in Texas seems to focus only on the killer without regard to defining a motive—one that might give some peace to the surviving victim—Ida Lyons."

"Might she get some peace when the killer is convicted?" Emily asked.

"Perhaps, but she still won't know *why* her husband was murdered. Henry and I believe that a conspiracy was elemental in Tom Lyons' death.

"Wasn't he murdered for the money in his pocket? That's what I read in the El Paso paper."

"A number of your fellow citizens are of that opinion. But we strongly believe that some people here in New Mexico paid Felix Jones to murder Tom Lyons, yet, as of today, we don't have sufficient evidence to name the killers, the active members of the conspiracy."

"You think someone, or some people, planned and carried out hiring Jones? Someone from our community?"

"Yes, Emily, we do."

"Oh, my."

"And that's why I needed to talk to you today."

"But, Etta, I'm not sure how I can help. I know very little of the cattle ranching crowd, or how they do their business. I'm a town girl, born and raised in Silver City, totally blessed to be married to a hard-working attorney."

"I know it must seem odd that I'd be asking your help regarding such a sordid thing like a conspiracy to murder someone. However, I believe that you can help. I have just one key question to ask you. If you can answer it, that is provide additional information, then that will help us identify the troublemakers. If you can't, then we've still done our jobs by asking."

"I guess I won't know if I can help until you ask the question."

"That's right, and because I respect you and trust you—even only knowing you for a few days—I won't ask you to put yourself at risk."

Emily hadn't taken her eyes off Etta's face throughout the discussion. When Etta finished her last statement, Emily closed her eyes for a moment, took a very deep breath and said, "Go ahead Etta. Ask your question."

"Alright." Etta took her notebook out of her clutch bag and opened it to Mr. Phillip's list. She looked at it quickly, then passed it to Emily. "I want you to look at these names and then, if you can, I'd like you to tell me what you think of the character of these men. That's all."

"Okay," said Emily as she looked at the page, almost holding her breath, her hands shaking a bit as she held the notebook.

After a minute or two, Emily handed the notebook to Etta and said, "I've heard all of these names at some time in my years as an adult. Two or three of them seem more notorious than the others—things I read about in our newspaper, or things I've overheard my husband mention on occasion."

"If you had to divide the list between sound character and questionable character, could you, would you be able to do it?"

Emily finally exhaled and nodded.

"You won't tell anyone that I helped, will you?"

"Not by name or any specific reference."

"Okay, then. In my opinion, the names I'd put in the 'sound character' group would be Mullen and Ryder."

"Thank you, Emily. I truly appreciate your assistance. Now, let's forget about the article and you can tell me about growing up in Silver City, okay?"

Emily sighed loudly and said, "Good, let's have lunch."

When Henry arrived at the courthouse a few minutes before eleven o'clock, he entered the County Clerk's office and approached the counter.

"Mr. Carter," said the woman behind the counter, "Mr. Phillips is waiting for you."

She led him into the office and closed the door behind her when she left.

"Still full of questions, Mr. Carter?"

"That's one of the hazards of being a reporter, Mr. Phillips."

"Yes, I suppose it is." He moved some papers from one corner of his desk to the other. *Either bored or nervous,* thought Henry.

"Thank you for making time to see me this morning, sir. I actually do have some more questions that I hope you can help me with."

Phillips sat back in his chair and stared at Henry before responding.

"The same rules still apply, you know. I'll respond to your questions with truthful answers, but I'm not allowed to violate any confidences nor any of the regulations that I'm governed by."

Henry sat in the single chair across from Phillips. As he thought again how to broach the new topic—conspiracy—he took his notebook from a coat pocket. He opened it to the list, glanced at it casually, and said, "Although we've completed the first part of our article, thanks to information we obtained from a number of citizens and officials such as yourself, we've made some conclusions and are moving forward with our investigation in order to complete the article."

"Go on, Carter."

"One of the most helpful bits of information we received was the list you provided the last time we met."

A slight frown appeared on Phillips' face. "You did honor our agreement, of course, and did *not* credit me as the source?"

"Just as I promised you, Mr. Phillips. We did pursue our interest in other cattle ranchers with some of the individuals in the community that we felt would have knowledge of these men and their character."

Phillips leaned forward and put his elbows on the desk. "What do you mean by 'character'?"

"We have come to believe that there was a conspiracy here in your county to hire someone to kill Tom Lyons. As I mentioned when we first met, it is our primary objective to determine a motive for the murder, so that we can help the surviving victim—Mrs. Lyons—deal more thoroughly with the tragedy that changed her life. Additionally, we wanted to make the focus of the crime the victims rather than the perpetrators." Henry paused only a moment. "In discussing the character of the men on your list, with these concerned and knowledgeable citizens, it appears that there is a consensus."

"What do you mean?"

"Of the six names you gave me, two or three of them were consistently identified as having 'questionable' character. We believe that these three men conspired to hire Felix Jones to murder Mr. Lyons. We cannot prove it yet, so I will not reveal which of the men on your list are—or could have been involved in the conspiracy."

"Suppose your theory is valid," said Phillips, "why would they have wanted Tom Lyons killed? What was their motive, their objective?"

"These men, we believe, had tried on numerous occasions to negotiate with Lyons in order to gain access to his pastures and water resources. One of our contacts indicated that Mr. Lyons was adamant in his refusal to grant that access. We believe that being blocked from expanding their own cattle empires, and being relegated to a secondary position in the cattle industry enraged them. Furthermore, their ability to substantially increase their profits, and thus their income, was essentially blocked by Lyons."

"If what you say is true, or at least possible, why hasn't it come up at the trial in El Paso?"

"It's our conclusion that the court in Texas is focused on convicting the killer. Period."

"But, by extrapolation, your conspirators would also be guilty, would they not?"

"Yes, guilty of conspiring to have Lyons killed, and that crime would have occurred in New Mexico."

"Yes, so?"

"The Texas courts would have no jurisdiction in a crime committed in New Mexico—no jurisdiction, no interest, no excessive cost to pursue justice."

"Mr. Carter, are you prepared to publish the names of these supposed conspirators?"

"No, sir, not at this time. We still have a lot of work to

do to collect sufficient proof. Obviously, we cannot accuse them without proof."

"Then, why have you come to see me today?

"I hoped you would first consider a few things, and then do what we've asked our other contacts to do. First, consider why you chose these six ranchers, and second, which of the six are of questionable character." Henry leaned toward the desk and looked directly at Phillips' face. "If there is a correlation between your evaluation and those of our other contacts, then we will pursue our search for proof. If there is no correlation, then we'll have to reconsider our theory."

"Hmm."

"Mr. Phillips, will you look once more at your list and, based on your experience and knowledge alone, identify any of the ranchers as being of questionable character?"

Likely deep in thought and consideration of any number of potential consequences, the County Clerk didn't speak or move for several minutes.

"Let me see the list."

That Monday evening, Etta and Henry didn't even want to take a break for dinner, but hunger finally got the best of them, and they went downstairs to the dining room. There were no empty tables, but they found room at one of the nearby cafes.

"So," said Etta, "our theory seems to make sense."

"At least to our limited number of reliable citizens and officials, it does."

"What do we do next, Henry?"

"One thing we *don't* do is confront the three ranchers."

"Or give their names to the sheriff."

"Or say their names in public… like in this café."

Henry signaled to a waitress, and she brought a menu for them to peruse. He passed it to Etta; she made a quick choice and handed it back. He also chose quickly and they ordered their dinner. Knowing they needed to be careful about what they might say, they automatically sat quietly until their food arrived. Despite the crowd and the noise in the café, they managed to eat slowly and to relax.

"You want dessert?"

"I'd rather have a drink," said Etta.

"Me, too. Let's go next door, have a quick one, and get back to the hotel."

They were quick. At the Clubhouse, they stepped up to the bar, Etta ordered two shots of Bourbon and when the bartender set them in front of the reporters, they each avoided the sip-method and drank the whiskey in one gulp. Henry left a few dollars on the bar and they went out the door.

Back in Etta's room once again, Henry said, "We need to call Cal."

Etta nodded in agreement, then added, "and we need to stay here another week unless he has a better plan."

Henry made some quick entries in his notebook. While Etta let him finish his thoughts, she, too, considered their situation.

"We can't confront the ranchers, at least not yet. Even though our sources are reliable, they're too few."

"Maybe we won't have to, Henry."

"What do you mean?"

"What if we leave them anonymous, noting that in the article that naming them would put innocents at risk... ourselves at risk. Or, we can say that we've shared our discoveries with the local authorities and are leaving the next steps or actions to their discretion."

"We really need to discuss this with Cal, but we can't use the hotel telephone or any one of the public ones."

"Right, too much risk of being overheard."

"Tomorrow is Saturday, maybe I can ask Emily for one more favor. If she and her lawyer husband would let us use their telephone, we could keep it private."

"Do you think they would allow us to use their telephone?"

"Maybe, with our promise to continue to keep their names out of the article."

"Can you contact her?"

"I'll try in the morning."

"Let's send a telegram tonight and tell Cal we'll call him before noon tomorrow. If you can use their telephone, we'll be in a good position to talk freely. If you can't, we will have to guard our words and be brief."

At eight o'clock Tuesday morning, Etta called the Acton house. Emily answered, and, after hearing Etta's situation, told her that her husband was on a hunting trip and she would help. "I'll even leave the house while you make your call," she said. "That way you'll be free to speak openly to your boss."

"Okay, then," said Etta, "we'll be on your front porch at ten o'clock."

Etta knocked on the door, and immediately Emily appeared.

"Good morning," she said and stretched her hand toward Henry. "You must be the remarkable Henry Carter."

"Well, not necessarily remarkable," replied Henry, shaking her hand.

"Henry, this is Emily Acton, one of the bravest women I've ever met."

"Thank you, Emily for accommodating us on the weekend."

"You're welcome, Henry, and you, Etta, are stretching the truth."

"No, I'm not," she said with a broad smile on her face.

"You two come in. The telephone is in the living room. All you have to do is dial zero and give the girl the number. She'll place the call for you."

"We'll gladly pay any extra charge for long distance."

"No, you won't, Mr. Carter," she said and reached back into the house for her hat and purse. "I'll be back at noon, but you take all the time you need."

With that, Emily walked to the curb and turned toward Bullard Street.

After just a few minutes, the operator called and connected Henry to Cal.

"Cal Langley."

"It's Henry, boss. Etta's right here as well."

"Good, I'm glad you were able to arrange a secure telephone."

"As secure as possible, anyway. We've had some pretty good luck the past few days, but we wanted to clear our next steps with you without giving too much information in a telegram."

"That's smart, Henry. Why don't you bring me up to date first, then we can talk about what's next."

Henry gave a thorough summary, and Cal interrupted him just a few times, asking for clarification.

Etta asked Henry for the phone. "I need to cover something else. Cal, one favor you can do for me is send ten copies of the *Review*, those with Part One, to Silver City care of Emily Acton." She gave him Emily's address. "Okay, good. I'll tell her to look for them this week."

She handed the phone back to Henry. He listened to Cal for another five minutes, then handed the receiver to Etta. "He wants to tell you what he just told me."

"Okay, Cal," said Etta when the editor had finished his statement. "I don't see anything being troublesome as long as you'll cover things on your end. Hold on a second." She handed the telephone to Henry. He listened to Cal for just a moment, then said, "Alright, if we have any more questions, we'll send you a telegram or call you again."

Henry hung up the telephone and turned to Etta.

"I'm glad we called him," she said. "We could have put

ourselves in danger or at least at risk if we'd gone through with some of the things we discussed this morning."

"I think I know what he wants us to say about not naming the conspirators."

"He was pretty clear on that. But we can each draft something and check to see if we both heard the same caution"

"So, we don't name any of the ranchers, especially the ones we believe are conspirators."

"And after we've communicated with the Sheriff's Office, we're free to state in the article that we've turned over our suppositions to the local authorities so that they can conclude an investigation and, how did he put it, 'prevent any retribution against witnesses by the alleged co-conspirators.'"

Etta glanced at her wristwatch and said, "It's nearly noon. We should wait for Emily so we can thank her again and I can tell her that copies of the Lyons article are on the way."

Henry looked around the floor near the telephone to confirm he hadn't left anything, then they stepped out onto the porch.

By the end of the day Tuesday, after they'd paid a visit to the Sheriff's Office, both Etta and Henry had finished their individual drafts of Part Two and subsequently blended the two separate versions into a finished product. They packaged all five pages of Part Two as they had done with the earlier article, and Henry took it to the depot.

Murder for Hire: The Conspiracy to Kill Tom Lyons—Part II

Reported by Henrietta Pearce and Henry Carter

The motive for the brutal murder of Tom

Lyons by Felix Jones has finally been determined—not in an El Paso, Texas court of law, but, rather on the streets and in the public houses of Silver City, New Mexico. We have, through diligent and thorough investigation, identified a group of men, some of whom we believe are the real killers of the late New Mexico rancher. Although none of these individuals wielded the pipe that crushed Mr. Lyons' skull, their greed led them to pay the perpetrator, Felix Jones, to kill Tom Lyons. These two or three men had tried frequently to use their funds to encourage Lyons to sub-lease some of his fringe area properties, or to share at a premium price, access to water. When these oft-repeated efforts failed to convince Lyons, the ranchers decided that their only option was to have Lyons eliminated. Their solution was to hire a killer, the known criminal from Texas.

As instructed by the publisher and management of the *Bisbee Daily Review*, we have arranged with the local authorities in Silver City, New Mexico, to turn over to them all of our collected notes and instead of publishing the names of the conspirators, allow the Sheriff's Office to take appropriate action, thus protecting our sources and ourselves from any retribution by those involved in the conspiracy…

Chapter 17

The Daily Review reporters didn't have to stay in Silver City another week. They checked out of the hotel on Wednesday morning, having decided that an early start back toward Bisbee was a good idea.

On Saturday, Etta had told Emily that the *Review* copies would arrive in a week or so. She'd also contacted Father Carrasco and the Baptist preacher's widow to thank them for their help.

Henry had made only one farewell visit. He bought a dozen pink frosted donuts at Schadel's Bakery before they left town. He'd considered going up the hill to see Deputy Williams but decided that the officer would know soon enough that the reporter had left town.

At daybreak, Henry and Etta drove south and west out of Silver City. The view to the west was, in Etta's words, gorgeous, as the rising sun behind them spread its glow over the flat landscape ahead in the distance.

Since the ride was mostly downhill, the trip was shorter than they expected. They arrived in Lordsburg too early for lunch but still managed to find an open café that had some breakfast leftovers.

A few miles out of Lordsburg, they turned south toward Douglas, crossing into Arizona and drawing ever closer to Bisbee and home. Even with the rough roads and the blowing sand, they arrived in Bisbee well before dusk and went up Brewery Gulch first to drop off Henry, then Etta drove to her place, ready to live in her new home.

On Friday morning, a beautiful day greeted Henry as he stood on his front porch. Well-rested, having slept in his own bed, and energized with a fresh cup of his own hot coffee, he was anxious to go to work.

A few blocks away, Etta saw the new day through her own front window. Familiar with her bed, but not yet with the obstacles in the new home, she'd bumped her knee once already and limped a bit. She'd started to make coffee, then remembered she hadn't shopped before leaving Bisbee. A shot of Bourbon sounded good to her, but she figured that Cal would have coffee going by the time she and Henry arrived at the agreed upon eight o'clock. Etta managed to squeeze in a quick bath before driving to the office.

I wonder, she thought, *if Cal has another small unused closet that can be made into an office.*

When Etta parked her car in front of the *Review* Building, Henry was standing at the curb, dressed in a suit. He waited while she turned off the engine and pulled on the parking brake. She got out of the car, smoothed her skirt, put her bag strap over her shoulder and walked up to the door.

"Good morning, Miss Pearce," said Henry, a very wide and genuine smile on his face.

"Good morning, Mr. Carter. What a fine morning it is."

Henry pushed open the tall door, gestured for Etta to precede him and followed her in and up the stairs. When they reached the crest in front of Cal's desk, he handed each of them a ceramic cup filled with his version of coffee—hot, strong, and black.

"Thanks, boss," said Henry.

Etta added, "Thanks, Cal, I needed this."

The three journalists glanced at one another, then they all broke out into huge, genuinely happy laughter. The realization that they *were* the *Bisbee Daily Review*, they *were* a team, a well-oiled machine. And this brought all three of them great pleasure.

It was up to Cal, though, as the boss to put things back

in order, or at least to provide guidance.

"Well," he said, "here we are, the journalists of southwest Arizona, ready to gather and produce all the news that's fit to print."

The two reporters smiled in agreement.

"Did you bring a copy of the part-two article you put on the train?"

"We did, although it's a rough copy."

"Thanks, Henry. I think Bert can still set it as it is. I know he'll catch any strange construction and ask you about it. Is it good?"

"Yes, Cal," said Etta, "it's good and is likely to stir things up in El Paso and in Silver City when they receive their complimentary copies."

"Then give me the rough copy and I'll give it a quick mark-up and get it ready for tomorrow's paper."

"That soon?" asked Henry.

"Yes, Henry," said Cal. "I want certain people to see what kind of work their two reporters are producing. It's good timing anyway, they seem to have forgotten about your story in the *New York Monthly*."

"I guess I get to stay in town, huh?"

"For now, anyway." Cal was quiet for a moment. He was anxious to edit the second article and he was also anxious to sit down with his reporters and discuss the future. "I'll start work on this for Bert. You two see if there's enough room in that closet, err, that office for two chairs. If there isn't, then we'll create a real modern, newsroom in the open space by the stairwell." Cal chuckled and then turned to the article.

Etta and Henry, still holding their coffee cups, wandered over to the closet office in the corner.

"Put another chair in that room and no one's getting out," said Etta.

"Or in."

They turned around to look at the space available around or near Cal's desk.

"If we can arrange something like a partner's desk, we might make it work."

"What's a partner's desk," asked Henry.

"It's really just a larger desk, but with entry space on opposite sides," Etta responded. "They work too, as long as the partners get along with one another."

"Then," said Henry, "let's find one or make one."

"In the meantime, we'll do what we can, right?"

"Right."

Cal said, "This is great, every bit as good as you did on your roundup story, Henry." Then, turning to Etta, he said, "and your parts, Etta, are solid, well-written and structured."

With a quizzical look on her face Etta said, "you can tell who wrote which parts?"

"Yes, I can, Etta. Although your styles are similar, they sound, or taste, or smell different to my… reading of the words." Shaking his head slowly back and forth, he added, "I must be the luckiest editor in the world, to have two nearly-rookie reporters who write as well as the masters." Cal looked into their faces, focused on their eyes and asked, "How can I be expected to teach geniuses?"

Looking at them again with a more practical mind, he said, "So, get to work, *rookies*," with a smile on his face.

"Where can I find the last ten issues of the paper, Cal."

"In the small cupboard next to Henry's corner office. We keep four weeks in there and make a change every week."

"Thanks."

Henry watched as she peeked into the cupboard and grabbed a week's worth of the papers. She took them over to the wide bench that sat at the head of the stairs and set them down. Etta took out her notebook and pencil, and picked up the oldest of the ten issues.

* * *

While Etta studied the past week's news, Henry went into his office and looked at the mail on his desk—two envelopes, one an advertisement about the new show at the Lyric Theater, and the other a letter from a reader of his deportation story that praised his effort at describing the perfect method for dealing with traitors. He threw both of them in the waste basket.

The letter about his story reminded him to ask Cal about his earlier comment on the local reactions to the same story. He picked up his notebook and, noticing that Etta was no longer on the bench, he approached Cal.

"Have you got a minute?"

"Sure, Henry."

Cal put his pencil behind his ear and waited for Henry to speak.

"Where's Etta?"

"She said she was going to walk around her new hometown and find out what her neighbors wanted to read in the paper."

"Huh." Henry then remembered why he wanted to talk to Cal.

"Earlier you said that they seem to have forgotten about my story. Forgive my direct question, Cal, but what's your proof?"

"It's a good question, so no forgiveness is necessary. While you were gone, I was invited to attend two management meetings. One was about the increased productivity which they credited to 'our loyal and patriotic American laborers.' The other was more specific. As a group, they wanted me to let you know that, based on your articles about the military training—especially your airplane adventure—they were no longer concerned about any possible problems with your deportation story. They referred to the 'vast amount of supportive correspondence' they received after that story was published."

"So, no more problem?"

"No more problem."

"Okay, then. What do you want me to work on now?"

"As I read your Lyons article, I wondered about its impact on the Texas trial. Unless I send a copy of the paper directly to the judge and the District Attorney, we're not likely to get any feedback on it. If I did send it directly, they would almost have to act on it or at least reply to it. Which they'd likely not want to do, knowing I could publish something about 'ignoring significant details'."

"You're probably right."

"So, Henry, while Etta spends some time getting to know Bisbee, I want you to go to El Paso and nose around. Spend a day or two to listen and look, especially after they've had a chance to stumble onto a copy of tomorrow's edition the one you will conveniently leave at their office doorsteps."

"This sounds a lot more fun than trying to not get attacked by angry ranchers."

"It sure does. So, get a ticket for a train ride to El Paso and we'll see you in a few days. I'll make sure she understands that I want her here. I like what she's doing today, and I think it will have more value in cementing her future in Bisbee journalism than keeping you safe in El Paso."

On Tuesday morning, Henry woke early and was ready for his trip an hour before sunrise. He walked down Brewery Gulch and went into the *Review* Building through the back door into the pressroom. He found Bert and his crew in the process of making the various bundles of newspapers and loading them on the truck.

"Morning, Bert," said Henry.

"What're you doin' up so early, Henry?"

"I need to take a trip to El Paso. Can I have three or four of today's edition?"

"Yep, got 'em right here. Cal said you'd be comin' by sometime this mornin' for 'em. Only I didn't expect it to be this early." He walked to one of the tables and picked up the copies. "Here ya go, Henry."

Henry thanked Bert, waved at the other men and rushed back out into the alley. From there it was a short walk to the depot and the train.

He boarded the single passenger car attached to the mine's train heading east to the refineries in Douglas and El Paso. It was mid-afternoon when he arrived at Union Station. Rather than wasting time checking into a hotel, he decided to make his deliveries first. He'd asked the clerk at the ticket counter for directions to the courthouse and got into a taxicab as soon as he left the depot.

At about the time Henry sat in the train car, Etta was getting ready for her day. She'd rested well again, satisfied with her new home and her new town. Having done some grocery shopping after leaving the office and feeling relaxed after sharing a grownup drink with Cal, she'd had a relaxing evening in her living room.

She drove to the office early and parked again in front of the *Review* Building. The front door was still locked, so she walked around the block to the alley and went into the pressroom.

"Well," said Bert, "two reporters in the pressroom before the day has even started."

"Did I miss Henry?"

"Yep, by an hour or so. He's probably half-way to El Paso by now. I thought you'd be lookin' for a copy of the paper, too." Bert smiled at Etta. "That was some article you two wrote."

"Thanks, Bert. I'm glad you liked it."

"It was well writ," he said as he handed her a copy. "You can get into the office by goin' up them stairs."

"Thanks, Bert," she said as she walked away.

Carrying his small suitcase, Henry walked up the steps of the nearly new courthouse, a grand structure that dominated the area. Once inside, he went up the stairs to the floor that housed the various offices. He found Judge Howe's office without any trouble and simply slipped the newspaper under the gap between the bottom of the door and the floor. Walking away quickly, he went back downstairs and asked one of the police officers for directions to the District Attorney's office.

"Mr. Clark's office is on the third floor sir. You can take the same stairway you just came down."

"Thanks, officer. I appreciate your help."

Henry went back upstairs and continued to the third floor landing. He followed the convenient signs which pointed the direction and went through the door under a sign which read, "District Attorney Offices." He walked toward a reception desk, behind which sat a middle-aged woman who seemed annoyed at his presence.

"May I help you sir?"

"Yes ma'am and thank you. I have something I'm supposed to deliver to Mr. Clark."

"If you'll leave your "something" with me, I'll see that the District Attorney gets it."

"Okay," he said and placed the newspaper in front of the woman. She picked it up, glanced at the banner at the top and looked back at Henry, but he was already going out the door.

Henry went back to the main floor and found the same officer who'd helped him earlier. "I'm not familiar with El Paso, officer. I have some information that is needed by the defense attorney in the murder trial that's being held here, and I don't even know the lawyer's name or where he might have his office.

"The offices of Bridges, Vowell and Harrington are just a few blocks from here." He gave Henry directions and returned to his position just inside the door.

Back on the street, Henry followed the officer's directions, found the building and walked into the lavishly decorated office of the defense team.

"I'm not sure which of the attorneys in the firm are

defending a," he paused, as if confused, "a Mr. Felix Jones for murder, but I have something that he'd be interested in seeing."

"If you'll give it to me," said the clerk behind the desk, "I'll see that it is delivered to the right person."

"Oh, thank you sir," said Henry as he gave the man the newspaper, trying to appear unsure of himself. He turned quickly and rushed out the door.

Pretty good acting, he thought. *Three deliveries made and no one will even remember the delivery boy.*

Outside, on the street, Henry looked and felt more like himself. He took a taxi back to the depot, then walked across the street and checked into the Hotel Bristol.

"Good day, sir. Do you have a reservation?"

"I don't, but I'll need a room for, perhaps, two days."

"We do have some rooms available. If you'll sign our register, I'll get a bellboy to carry your luggage."

Henry looked at the single, modest bag next to him on the floor and said, "I'll carry my bag, if it's okay."

"Of course, sir. Will you be paying cash?"

Refreshed by Cal's strong coffee, and very pleased with the way the Lyons article was presented in the paper, Etta made one more trip to the pressroom and had Bert send a bundle of ten copies of the latest edition to Emily Acton in Silver City. She wrote a note to her and made sure it went with the bundle.

Then, she glanced out the window overlooking Main Street and saw that the town was waking up. Her car was no longer the lone parked vehicle, and Main Street was getting busy.

As she let the tall front door close behind her, Etta turned left and began her canvassing, still hoping to learn something from readers or potential readers of the *Review* what they wanted but weren't getting in their newspaper.

There was a café several blocks west of the paper that

Etta hadn't yet been into.

The early crowd had evidently headed to work, since the café had just a few customers. Etta wandered in and sat next to a woman dressed like herself and about her age seated at the counter.

"Good morning," she said to the woman, who replied by nodding. "I'm sorry for interrupting your coffee break." She stuck her hand out toward the woman. "I'm Etta Pearce, a reporter for the *Review*."

The woman nodded again.

"Would you be willing to answer a few questions? I'm doing a survey of residents, trying to determine if we, the *Review*, as a source of news, are providing the stories that citizens want."

The woman set her cup on the counter and took Etta's hand.

"Catherine Smithson."

"Nice to meet you, Catherine. Have you lived in Bisbee long?"

"I was born here. I've never lived any place else."

Etta smiled and said, "That would make you a native, and fully qualified to represent the town."

"But I'm just a woman, what would *I* know?"

"I suspect you know a lot more than you are given credit for."

"I think, Miss Pearce, that you and I probably have some similar experiences."

"Such as?"

"I'd guess that, judging by your attire and that you are gainfully employed, you've had to overcome a lot of grief on your way to being yourself, the woman *you* want to be."

"I have."

"Well so have I."

"Then, as a female, working resident of Bisbee, I could assume that you'd have little interest in reading about women's fashions—the old style—or society news, or anything along that line."

"You assume correctly. Can I ask you a question?"

"Of course."

"What do you think about women voting?"

"Our right to vote is long overdue."

"How about our right to sign contracts, file for divorce, and to be credited for our contributions to society?"

"I believe that these, too, have been delayed too long. Although some progress is being made, it's just too long in coming to fruition." Etta glanced at the woman and asked, "Catherine, which of your four topics—voting, signing contracts, filing for divorce, or getting credit for contributions is most important to you, and is something you'd like our paper to address?"

"You *are* a reporter." She chuckled and said, "Your question requires two answers. First, and most important, this equal rights issue must be settled. We have to be able to vote."

Etta nodded, "Go on."

"And second, since I have seen progress in the contracting area, I believe it's the fact that women do not often get credit for their contribution—at least those that don't include raising children, caring for the poor, and things like that."

"Miss Smithson—"

"That would be Mrs. Smithson, at least for now," said Catherine as she stared into her nearly empty cup of cold coffee dregs."

"Then, Catherine, I have learned a great deal in our short conversation. Thank you for your frankness." Etta paused and added, "And I hope you find a solution to the 'Missus' issue."

In El Paso, Henry was also having lunch. But he was in a saloon, a noisy one, filled with people who stormed out of the courthouse, evidently tired of the hard bench seats and their dry mouths. He'd found a small table, just off the bar and sat by himself. That lasted for just a minute or so until another group, again likely from the courthouse, invaded the saloon. A man near his age also wearing a suit and carrying a small notebook asked Henry if he and his colleague could share the table.

"Okay," said Henry.

"Thanks," said the man. His colleague, a larger, older man, grunted some deep sound from his throat and sat in the other chair.

They ordered two beers each, drank one quickly and began sipping the second.

"You been at the trial," they asked Henry.

"Nah. What trial?"

"What trial? Why the murder trial, the one where a man from New Mexico was killed here in El Paso."

Henry shook his head and sipped his beer. "You fellas lawyers?"

The young one in the suit chuckled, the big man grunted.

"We're not lawyers or reporters, are we?"

Another grunt from the big man.

"Then why ya watchin' a trial?"

Henry wasn't sure they were buying his dumb guy responses. *Go slow on the questions, let them bring it up.*

"Do you know anything about cattle ranches?"

"Know what they are, but don't know anythin' about horses, and roundups, nothin' like that."

The big man finally spoke, his voice a deep rumbling sound from his chest, "What do you do?"

"Nothin' as interestin' as that," he said, his mind trying to chase down an idea.

"Must be doin' somethin', yer wearin' a suit."

"Tryin' to get a job. Friend of mine said suits make ya look smarter." He paused and said, "ain't worked yet."

"Still haven't answered my question," grumbled the big man.

Henry sat up straight, slid his beer over to the side away from the grumbler. In as strong a voice as he could come up with and not be loud, he asked, "You a cop or somethin'?'

The young man smiled, the grumbler was silent, for just a moment.

"Would it bother you if we were cops?"

"No, why should it. I'm just a guy lookin' for a job."

"Uh huh."

As Henry reached into the inside breast pocket of his coat, they both sat back and flinched, the grumbler actually pulled what looked like a gun butt partially from his pocket.

When Henry brought his wallet out and found enough money to cover the cost of the two beers he had, he put it on the table and stood up.

"This is one strange town. I'm pretty sure I don't wanna work here."

He started away, a step or two, then turned around. "You two gentlemen have a good day," and never looked back as he walked out of the saloon.

Wandering in a direction that was not toward the courthouse or his hotel, he crossed a few streets, turned down a few others and never felt once that he was being followed.

I guess they weren't cops, but they did have guns and thought that I did. Were they following me or was I just a chance encounter?

Henry eventually made his way back to the Hotel Bristol and the relative safety of his rented room.

While enjoying her lunch at the Copper Queen, Etta was tempted frequently to pick up her notebook and write down the things that jumped in and out of her thoughts. Each time that the urge occurred though, she was able to push it down. She ultimately decided that the work could wait to be done in the workplace *and* after dessert, which she was ready for right now.

By three o'clock, Etta was back in the office. She sat in one of the chairs across from Cal and filled him in on the discoveries she'd made, about an article related to what she'd learned from Catherine, and her plan to keep walking and asking what people want to read in their newspaper.

At six o'clock, Etta was ready to go home. Still not hungry after her lunch, she decided she'd skip supper and perhaps have a grown-up drink. After driving slowly home, Etta parked the car and walked up to the porch then unlocked the door, tossed her hat and coat onto the sofa and headed to her kitchen. She opened a cabinet and took a bottle of whiskey out, setting it on the counter. She poured a double shot of Kentucky Bourbon in a glass and carried it into the living room. She spent the next half hour sipping the whiskey and pondering the discussion with Catherine Smithson.

When she finished her drinking and pondering, she headed for the bathroom and took a long hot bath. When that too reached a quitting point, she wandered into her bedroom and turned on the light next to her bed.

Cal spent another hour or so clearing his desk of unfinished business and occasionally thinking about his reporters. What seemed to stand out—at least in his mind, in his estimation, was that he'd been somehow gifted with two enthusiastic, intelligent, *committed* young people. As he signed off on another invoice, he wondered, *why me*?

He shook his head at the thought, tossed the invoice into his out box, and reached for another document in his in box when the telephone rang.

"Cal Langley."

"Mr. Langley, this is Bill Pearce, Etta's father."

"Yes sir. How can I help you?"

"Mr. Langley, I need to get in touch with Etta. I'm not sure if she's acquired a telephone of her own yet, so I thought you could get a message to her for me."

"Of course, Mr. Pearce. I'll do it right away." Cal took the pencil from behind his ear and reached for a blank piece of paper. "What is the message?"

"Please tell her that her mother has become very sick and is in the hospital here in Phoenix and that I really need her here. I realize that she's just getting started with her new job, but it's vitally important that she be here."

"Of course, sir. You shouldn't concern yourself about Etta's position here. We'll make do. I will head up to her house right now and then bring her back here so she can call you."

"Thank you, Mr. Langley. Just tell her that, well, tell her that it's not an emergency, but I need her here very much."

Cal hung up the telephone, put on his coat, and left the office. It took him less than fifteen minutes to reach Etta's house. At least she's still awake, he thought, noticing a light on in one of the rooms to the left of the porch. He knocked on the door and waited.

Etta had wrapped a robe around her tired body and gone into the living room. She picked up her coat and hat and had just turned to go back down the hall when someone knocked on her front door.

She went to the front window, pulled the curtain aside and saw Cal.

Making sure her robe was closed properly, she opened the door.

"Cal, what is it?"

"Etta, I'm sorry, but I have some bad news."

"Please come in, Cal." Etta pulled the door wide open and stepped aside as Cal removed his hat and walked in.

"What's the bad news, Boss?"

Cal cleared his throat, and said, trying to keep the drama out of his tone, "Your father just called me. He says that your mother is very sick and is in the hospital."

"Mother is sick? What's wrong... did he say?"

Cal put his hand on Etta's shoulder. "He didn't give me any specific information, just that she's ill and he needs you to come to Phoenix."

Etta began to walk back and forth in her small living room.

"Mother has always been a bit weak physically, but in the *hospital*?"

Trying to settle her down, Cal said, "Look, it won't help to speculate on what's wrong with your mother when you should be getting ready to go to her, right?"

Etta stopped her pacing and looked at Cal. "You're right. I need to pack the car and get going."

"Wait a minute, Etta. I don't think you should drive, especially tonight. Your father said it wasn't an emergency, so why don't you let me get you a ticket on the morning westbound train. It may not be as quick as driving, but at least it'll give you time to rest and still get there to help your father."

"But..."

"But nothing, Etta. I'll call Henry and have him head back here. He should be finished in El Paso and could take your car to you. Besides, you're both in between assignments, so you can focus on the situation in Phoenix."

"Maybe," she said. "I need to call my father."

"Alright, then. I'll wait while you get dressed and we'll go back to the office, and you can call him from there."

When Etta left a half-hour later, Cal called his friend who ran the train depot and arranged for Etta's transit to Phoenix. Then he called Henry.

"Henry? This is Cal."

"Hi, Cal, what's going on?"

"There's been some bad news about Etta's mother."

"What kind of bad news, boss?"

Cal told him about Mr. Pearce's telephone call and then his conversation with Etta. "There's something I need you to do now."

"But if she's going to Phoenix, I need to get there too."

"I know, son, but you need to come to Bisbee first. Etta's car is here, and she may need it while she's home. If you come here and drive the car to Phoenix, then she will also have you there to help her."

Henry was silent for only a moment. "I have a ticket for the morning train to Bisbee. I'll be there tomorrow. Mr. Pearce said it wasn't an emergency, but I'd like to be on the road to Phoenix tomorrow afternoon. I hope my being there is going to be helpful and not a distraction."

"Henry, I know there will be things you can do for her and the family. They may need someone to run errands, make calls, or..."

"Cal, I need to finish getting ready for the trip," Henry interrupted, "so I'll see you tomorrow."

"Okay, Henry. Get going, be safe, and I'll see you soon."

Chapter 18

THE BRIGHT SUNLIGHT OF a Phoenix morning seeped in through the gap in the closed drapes of the hospital room. There were lights on, but they did little to dispel the gloom of sickness and despair.

"When did she start getting sick, Daddy?"

"A week ago." Mr. Pearce stood near the head of his wife's hospital bed. His face was drawn. Sunken cheeks and a wrinkled brow gave him a ghost-like look. "She came home from her club meeting and started coughing... not much at first, but it didn't let up."

He continued to gaze at his wife, barely looking at Etta.

"She just kept coughing," he said, "and, even when that would let up for a bit, she'd cry or whimper."

Etta watched her mother's pale face wrinkle as a stab of pain worked its way up her body. Etta reached toward her hand but withdrew it quickly when she recalled the doctor's orders: "Don't touch her, dear. Don't kiss or hug her even if she asks you to." The doctor had said they were trying to keep her as comfortable as they could, then added, "But be sure you keep your own face—nose and mouth—covered to protect yourself and her."

Mr. Pearce continued, even though he'd stood unspeaking for several long minutes. "When the cough didn't go away, she began to complain about a pain in her back. Then it was her legs that started to hurt. Finally, when she started quivering and shaking uncontrollably, I brought her here." Pearce slumped into the chair behind him. "I just didn't know what else to do."

"You did the right thing, Daddy." Etta looked at her father, holding back a choked feeling of compassion for him. "Do the doctors know what made her sick?" She watched tears leak from the corners of his eyes.

Several long minutes passed before he spoke. "They're not saying, but I think they've got an idea that it's this influenza that's going around."

"But they're not sure?"

Pearce nodded slowly. "Right, mostly because the fatigue and listlessness is more pronounced and that it came on so quickly."

Etta's thoughts went to what she'd read about an epidemic in Europe, but the thought disappeared when her mother began to cough weakly and groan as she tried to take a deep breath.

"What about medicine?"

Pearce looked across the bed at his daughter and shook his head. "There's no magic elixir, Sweetheart. Apparently, the medical community was caught off guard."

"What can we do, Daddy?"

"I wish I knew."

Etta's mother slept a lot all day—uncomfortably, fidgety, groaning and moaning at each cramp, each sharp pain in her chest. Etta knew she had to be here with her mother. She knew she couldn't do anything for her, but it was clear that her father needed her as well. He hadn't left the hospital and had barely eaten or slept since bringing his wife here. But, these things paled in comparison to his changed presence. Etta wondered where the commanding businessman was. The worn-out, often speechless figure that sat in the chair across from her had no resemblance to the virile, happy, strong man who'd taught her so much.

Etta tugged at her mask, even thought of pulling it off so she could kiss her father's tired cheeks and eyes. But she didn't. She had to be strong for him, and for herself as well. She turned as she heard the door open quietly behind her, and waited as the doctor, and a nurse, walked in.

"My nurse needs to bathe Mrs. Pearce with cool, damp cloths in order to reduce her fever. This is best done in private. We three can take a break while I bring you up to date on her situation."

They walked to the end of the long hallway into a waiting room and sat on a wooden bench. The doctor set a chair facing them.

For the moment, they were the only people in the room. Even masked they were able to hear each other's muffled voices but with only their eyes to interpret the words, concentrating was critical.

"Mr. Pearce, young lady, we're certain now that Mrs. Pearce has influenza. We needed to run some tests to be sure."

The doctor looked at each of them closely, sighed deeply and continued.

"In Europe and our own large cities, this influenza is spreading rapidly. There are at least two different strains. Each is deadly and difficult to treat. The government is pushing scientists to develop effective vaccines, but unfortunately that takes time. Those large cities—New York, Philadelphia, Chicago, San Francisco—are requiring everyone to wear masks in public. They are forbidding large gatherings of people, so no school and no church. They are limiting the number of passengers on trains and streetcars. There are even strange new laws appearing, such as making kissing and spitting in public a crime."

"This epidemic, doctor, how..." Etta groped for the right words, "how bad is it here?"

"The best answer I can give you is that those people exposed to the virus have a good chance of surviving if they are young, generally healthy, and realize early that they have influenza symptoms. This, of course, is not the case with your mother. Her symptoms are clearly troublesome, and she is neither young nor healthy. We are, however, doing everything we can to help her."

Etta and her father looked past the doctor when his

nurse rushed from Mrs. Pearce's room.

"Doctor, we need you in here now!"

Etta screeched, "What's going on?"

With a calming gesture, the doctor said, "You folks stay here. I'll let you know soon." He quickly rose from his chair and followed the nurse into the room, closing the door behind him.

Bill Pearce stood up and moved toward the room.

"Wait for me, Daddy."

Pearce stopped and turned toward his daughter.

"I've got to..."

The door was opened again, and the doctor stuck his head out, saying, "Please come inside, quickly."

Anxious and a bit frightened, Etta followed her father through the open door. He, too, appeared frightened.

While the doctor bent over Mrs. Pearce, the nurse whispered, "Mrs. Pearce is struggling at the moment. It's a very serious situation, and the doctor knows you'd want to be here." She looked at the father and daughter and added, "We must stay calm and quiet in order to avoid upsetting her any further."

Etta could only speculate that her mother's life was in danger. Her father seemed to *know* that it was.

The doctor gently wiped his patient's forehead with a damp cloth, said something to her that neither her husband nor her daughter could hear, then turned to look at them.

"Mrs. Pearce is quickly losing whatever strength has kept her alive these past few days. I'm sorry to say that other than keeping her comfortable, there's nothing else we can do to save her life. Her breathing is becoming increasingly difficult, and her heart is beginning to fail. I'm sorry we can't do more."

He looked at the two sad people and said, "The nurse and I will step out and let you spend whatever time you want with her. If you want us, we'll be just outside."

Bill Pearce pulled his daughter against his chest and

hugged her while she wept. He struggled to keep his own tears from flowing down his cheeks. He pulled his mask down below his chin and kissed Etta on the forehead then walked around to the far side of the bed and gently clasped his wife's hand.

Etta moved up to the side of the bed and took her mother's other hand. Disregarding the doctor's earlier instructions, Etta removed her mask, leaned over the still face of her mother and kissed her softly on the cheek.

"I'm sorry I was not the daughter you wanted, Mommy. I love you," she whispered.

Her father also kissed his wife on her cheek then whispered something, but Etta never learned what he said.

When it was clear that her mother was no longer breathing, Etta looked at her father and when he nodded, she went to the door and told the doctor.

The next day, Henry arrived in Phoenix and called the Pearce residence right away. At first, the maid was reluctant to give him any information about the family, but when Henry explained he'd brought Etta's car to Phoenix, the woman told him that Etta and her father were at the mortuary planning for tomorrow's funeral. Henry hadn't expected to hear this news. He knew Etta's mother was ill. *But dead?* he thought. *At least Etta's with her father.*

"If you hear from Miss Pearce, ma'am, would you please ask her to call me? I'm staying at the 6th Avenue Hotel."

Henry waited impatiently in the hotel lobby, pacing across the room which earned him nervous glances from the hotel clerk. Finally, after what felt like days to Henry, the clerk called Henry over and told him that he had a telephone call. Henry picked up the phone on the desk.

"Etta?"

"Yes, Henry, it's me."

"Oh, Etta. I am so sorry to hear about your mother's

passing."

"Thank you. It happened so quickly, it still hasn't really set in that she's gone, you know?"

Henry agreed, then Etta said, "why don't you come over to the house so we can talk about tomorrow?

"You mean now?"

"Of course." She gave him the address and directions. "I'll see you when you get here.

The Pearce home was a large, two-story home on a big lot in one of the nicer areas of Phoenix. He rang the doorbell and was invited in by the maid. He removed his cap and walked through the entryway into a large parlor. Etta sat on a sofa and there were two other men in the room. Etta stood up from a sofa when she saw him.

"Henry."

Seeing his partner, he said, "Etta, I'm so..." he started, but she pulled him into a tight hug and said, "I'm so glad you're here, Henry."

She moved slowly out of the embrace and looked into his eyes. "My mother *died*, Henry. It happened so quickly."

Henry pulled her close to him and kissed her on the forehead. "I know." They stood silently for a moment. Tears filled their eyes as she hugged him again and turned toward the others in the room.

"Henry, I want you to meet my father." She gestured at a tall, distinguished man.

"Daddy, this is my partner, Henry Carter."

Mr. Pearce approached them and reached out to shake hands.

"Sir, I just want to say how sorry I am for your loss."

"Thank you, young man. I appreciate it. I know Etta is glad you've finally arrived."

Standing in Etta's father's grand home, in a big city, Henry was struck with the differences between his and Etta's backgrounds. But he was learning to set those thoughts aside as their friendship had progressed.

Etta said, "Henry, this is my father's best friend for as long as I remember, Mr. Stewart Bradley."

Henry shook hands with Bradley, then Mr. Pearce said, "Etta, could you and Mr. Carter excuse us for a while? Stewart and I have some things to discuss."

"Of course, Daddy."

"Oh," Pearce said, "I think it would be a good idea, Henry, if you check out of the hotel tomorrow and move in here at the house. We have plenty of room and it would be far more convenient for you two to get back to doing what you do."

"Thank you, Mr. Pearce."

"It's Bill, Henry. Okay?"

"Yes, sir. I mean, yes, Bill."

As the two older men walked out of the parlor, Etta led Henry back to the sofa. They sat down, and gently clasping Henry's hand, Etta said, "How did you do it, Henry? How did you find a way to survive your mother's death?"

Unprepared for *that* question, Henry was truly at a loss for words, and he—a reporter, a user of words, a clarifier of thought—couldn't find the right ones. So, he took a deep breath and returned her direct look.

"When my mother died, Etta, I was frightened but I didn't want anyone to know I was just a scared sixteen-year-old boy." He paused, dredging up the memory. "I wanted to cry. I wanted to hit someone, anyone. I wanted to run away. She'd been sick, very sick for weeks so I should have been prepared, but all along I just didn't *believe* she'd die, simply because I didn't *want* her to die. I... I thought I was going to be left alone with no family, no one who really cared for me until I felt Cal's arms surround me in a bear hug." Henry's red eyes showed a mixture of grief and the warmth of salvation. "He saved my life, Etta. That one gesture made me realize that we don't have to be related by blood to be family."

Etta looked at her partner, her eyes red, silver-edged,

and said, "Henry, I loved my mother, and I know in my heart that she loved me. I never appreciated her grace in allowing me to become who and what I am. Yet, she trusted my father's wisdom and his trust in me." Then, with a pure, gentle smile on her face, Etta said, "My greatest concern, though, is how Daddy's coping? How will he survive?"

Sitting alone in the large room, they spoke softly when they had something to say and then not at all as they thought about their mothers.

At one point, Henry said, "Tell me about your father and Stewart Bradley."

"He and my father met while standing in a line on their first day of school in Kansas City. They were five years old."

"That's a long time to maintain a friendship."

Etta nodded. "According to the stories I've heard, they were always together—playing or working—at school or around the neighborhood. Along the way, they were never rivals for attention, or for girlfriends, or, well, anything. They each stood up for the other, even at their weddings. According to my mother, and confirmed by Gloria Bradley, Daddy saved Stewart's life when they went to Cuba with the Rough Riders. When they got back, they decided to migrate to Arizona. Both couples moved to Phoenix with everything they owned. Daddy began his own commodity trading firm and Mr. Bradley worked for a Territorial representative."

"Do Stewart and Gloria have any children?"

"Gloria lost her only child when it was just a few weeks old. My mother cared for her while she recovered both physically and emotionally." Etta was quiet for a while, then said, "And I'm pretty sure that Daddy helped Stewart through his own grief." Etta continued staring out the window.

Patiently, Henry waited.

"Gloria and Stewart always treated me like their own

lost daughter. Always. So, they became Uncle Stewart and Aunt Gloria."

"Does Mr. Bradley still work in politics?"

"He does. Daddy said that Stewart is probably going to run for the U.S. House of Representatives, but no formal announcement has been made."

They sat quietly for a few more minutes, then Etta finally spoke, "The funeral is tomorrow at ten o'clock." She picked up a note pad and pen from the table in front of the sofa and wrote the name and address of the cemetery. "Why don't you go back to the hotel, get some rest and I'll see you in the morning."

"Alright, Etta."

They stood together and shared a gentle hug.

"I'll see you at the cemetery," Henry said. They walked back toward the front door, hugged once more and Henry left.

When Henry got to the Pearce residence on the morning of the funeral, he learned that Etta and her father had already left. The maid, Marisol, told him she was aware he'd be staying in the home with the family.

"If you'll leave your bag here, Mr. Carter, I'll put it in your room."

Henry arrived early at the Cemetery and found Etta, her father, and their friends sitting quietly in a private room. He shook hands with the men and then Etta introduced him to Stewart's wife.

"Henry, this is Gloria Bradley."

They shook hands, then Henry took Etta's arm and led her out onto the porch of the funeral home.

"I've been thinking," he said "and I know you're concerned about your father, and he's concerned about you. I've only just met him, but I believe that with the help of his friend Stewart, he will survive. If, and I mean this, if you do as well. Listen, Etta, we've only been working together a few weeks, but I know that you are strong—tough even—and smart. You have passion and aren't silly like so many other women." He smiled at her and said, "And you have Cal and me as your friends. One a boss who trusts and cares about you and the other a brother who'd give his life for you."

A few minutes before the service was to begin, the funeral director entered the room.

With a great deal of deference, the man approached them and said softly, "We are ready to begin the service. If you'll follow me, I'll take you to the sanctuary and your guests."

Etta put her hand on her father's arm and let him lead her out of the room. The Bradleys followed and Henry trailed behind them.

The peacefully furnished room was filled with a large number of people. Henry was a little surprised when he recalled that there were less than a dozen at his mother's funeral. Compared to the nearly fifty friends, co-workers, and associates in this room, his mother's guests had included Cal, the madam of the brothel where his mother did laundry, three or four of the prostitutes, and the young black boy Henry considered his best friend. *Quite a difference, but just as meaningful*, he thought.

Etta, her father, Stewart and Gloria were seated in the first row of chairs Henry sat in the second row behind them. The other people moved quietly to fill the empty chairs. As soon as the last guests were seated, the funeral director approached the pulpit-like fixture behind the open casket and faced the gathered guests, then spoke in a clear bass voice.

"We are here today to celebrate the life of Wilma Pearce, dear wife of William and mother of Henrietta."

The service was relatively short, much shorter than Henry had expected. When the director had finished, he addressed the people in the room and told them that the burial service would begin in ten minutes.

When the family and friends arrived at the grave, the director spoke quietly to Bill and led him to a spot behind the casket which was now closed.

Bill stood quietly, his head bowed. He gently cleared his throat and said, "Etta and I appreciate each one of you for sharing this time with us. Most of you know how precious Wilma was to us. And we know how much you all cared for her." He stopped, seemingly unable to continue. Then he glanced at Etta and smiled gently. "Please remember her, remember what she meant to you, and cherish her memory."

Then Bill went to Etta, took her arm and led her to the casket. Each of them put a hand on the casket and bowed their heads, then turned toward one another. Etta hugged her father and kissed his cheek.

The guests began to gather around the two family members. Hugs and handshakes were abundant. Henry stood next to Etta, his eyes watching her interaction with her friends and acquaintances. His ears focused on their kind words.

The service ended when the family walked away. The people quietly dispersed and after Etta hugged Bill and Gloria, she walked over to Henry.

"Daddy's going to Bill's house for a while. I told him we'd see him at home later. I thought we, you and I, could go find some lunch."

When they got to the car, Henry said, "You're the local citizen, where do you want to go?"

Etta drove them to a small, but elegant restaurant a few miles away from the cemetery. Once they were seated at the table, a waiter arrived and they ordered. Then Etta spoke.

"Henry, I've been thinking about something, and I want to know your thoughts about it."

"Sure, what is it?"

"Well, in general, it's about this Spanish Flu. I know that my mother isn't the only victim. Right before she died, her doctor said that it was becoming a problem because so many people were sick, and the medical solutions were still unclear." Etta leaned across the table and said, "I've not read anything about the flu except that there have been lots of cases at military bases on the east coast."

"I read that too, and there *hasn't* been much written about it. At least not out here."

"Exactly," she replied. "Henry, I want to find out more about this influenza. I want to see how bad it is here, in Phoenix and in Tucson as well. I want to know about where it comes from, how people get it, what doctors do to care for the sick, and how they can keep them from dying. I want to know what a son or daughter or spouse can do to keep their loved-one from getting sick. I want to find out how survivors cope with what comes after the flu." She looked at her partner and said, "Henry, I want to write about all of this. I want to do this for my mother."

"You know what Cal would say, don't you?"

"I think so. I believe he'd say, 'then get writing,' and point me to a desk with a typewriter sitting on it."

"Yes, Etta, that's what he would do." He paused and watched her eyes, then asked, "What are you waiting for?"

While Etta and Henry had been in Phoenix, Cal had continued to run the *Review.* There wasn't much going on locally other than the frequently delayed lawsuit between the mine and its former workers. That left Cal searching for news to fill his pages. At least he could fill empty columns with war news stories from other papers and add others about the ongoing revolution in Mexico.

He needed his reporters back. Henry's call a week earlier about Etta's interest in the epidemic would help a lot, but it seemed to Cal that her research and investigation would take weeks, if not a month or two, to produce a story. He had concluded that he wanted Henry to finish the Lyons conspiracy article before people no longer cared. *And,* he thought, *the only way that will work is to have Henry return to Bisbee.* But Cal needed to be sure that Etta had regained her confidence and skills since the death of her mother. *I need to hear it from Henry, and I need to hear it face-to-face.*

Cal took a blank telegram form from the stack on his desk and wrote out a message to Henry. *Better to keep it simple for now,* he thought. When he finished, he asked Bert to send up one of the boys to run it over to the telegraph office.

Chapter 19

In Phoenix, in a building that provided space for a dozen or so law offices, a meeting was taking place. In an office on the third floor, two men sat by a large window. They could see the shimmering heat coming from the street below, and hear the normal sounds of the cars, trucks and pedestrians as well. But their discussion was anything but normal.

Julius Parker, a well-known politician, relaxed in a high-backed padded chair. His tie was loose in his collar and trailed across his large belly. He held a glass of rye in his hand and frequently lifted it to his large, puffy lips. Most of the whiskey made it past those lips into his mouth, but some managed to drip on his tie and the shirt beneath.

The other man, Lou Riggs, was drinking rye too, but he did so in an almost dignified manner. Riggs was tall, trim, well-dressed and a gangster. Lou Riggs ran the vice rackets in Phoenix. Bootleg alcohol, extortion, gambling, and prostitution were his business. Riggs controlled nearly all aspects of this activity in the city. He had a large staff of enforcers, collectors, thugs, and, when necessary, gunmen to aid him in his "business."

"So, Julius, what's on your mind?"

"Oh, yes." Parker cleared his throat and ran his pudgy hand down the front of his tie, smoothing out a wrinkle and smearing some dribbled whiskey at the same time. "I found out recently, Lou, that some upstart has been *talking about* challenging me for the House seat." He tried unsuccessfully to sit erect in the chair as he added, "In fact, I don't believe he's ever held elective office."

"If this person is an 'upstart,' Julius, why are you worried?"

"Well, I need to win the election, unopposed, to show the state and the crowd in Washington D.C. that I'm a power to be reckoned with. They need to see that no one can stand up against Julius Parker." He reached for the whiskey bottle sitting on the low table between himself and Riggs, pulled the cork and poured two fingers worth into his glass.

"If you *are* that person, why the concern?"

"I'm not really concerned. At least not yet. I just wanted you to know about this. If I lose, then I'd not be able to pay back all of the money you've loaned me. Suffice it to say that I need your financial support, your loans, to keep my position and you need me to stay in office so I can repay you... with cash, with connections, and with information. We may have to get rid of this new candidate... permanently, but I can't be linked to a bloody murder or anything like that. It'll have to be done some other way."

Riggs was growing weary of the fat man's worries. He had other things on his mind and needed to send some of his boys out to take care of a few trouble spots.

"Listen, Julius, you just keep me posted on your upstart challenger. And keep those payments coming in. You don't want to fall behind. In the meantime, I'll check with this fella I know who might help solve your problem if needed."

Life for Albert Willoughby M.D. had not turned out quite as he expected. Even though he'd graduated from the University of Chicago Medical School and had once had a very successful private practice in that city, he'd made some bad choices. Having an affair with a patient had cost him his state license and his family. He'd moved west to Arizona to practice, hoping his history would remain unknown. During his first years in Phoenix, things had settled down, and he'd treated his patients as... patients, leading an exemplary public life. His private life, however, was problematic. Willoughby had turned from infidelity to gambling, but even that didn't keep him out of trouble. He was either very unlucky or just a bad gambler. His problems seemed to have been resolved when he met Lou Riggs. The man willingly loaned him money—at a high interest rate—to pay off his debts, but as the luck ran out, the debts grew, and the doctor found himself owing Riggs *more* than money.

When Riggs telephoned him earlier, Willoughby had felt a chill on the back of his neck. Riggs usually sent one of his men with instructions or a message telling him what he wanted. But today, Riggs had personally instructed him to 'drop by the office at his convenience.' The doctor interpreted this invitation to mean 'get over here right now.' Immediately after he put the phone's earpiece in the cradle, he told his nurse to either cancel or reschedule his appointments since he had an emergency which required his attention.

"Sit down, Doc." Riggs was standing at the small bar near the window. "Do you want a drink?"

"Do I *need* one, Mr. Riggs?"

Riggs turned toward him and smiled. "Rye or bourbon, Doctor. It's just a drink."

"Bourbon, please."

"Good choice, Willoughby." He handed one of the two glasses he held to the doctor and sat in a chair opposite his guest. After he took a sip of the whiskey, he looked at Willoughby for a few seconds longer than the doctor liked. "I have a theoretical question for you, Doc." He kept his eyes on Willoughby. "You are in the business of saving lives, aren't you?"

Willoughby waited, thinking there was more on Riggs's mind.

When the gangster didn't continue, the doctor said, "I am... of course, I am."

"Good," said Riggs, "then you'll know how to *end* someone's life?"

Willoughby was quite stunned. Struggling with the directness of Riggs's question, he said, "I would know how, yes. But my oath as a doctor is to *not* end someone's life."

"Right, but now your oath is to me. You do know how to..."

"Yes, yes, I do know how to end a life." The doctor didn't want Riggs to say what was on his mind. The mere image of purposely ending a human life gave Willoughby a deep, bone-freezing chill. He began to shiver and yet beads of sweat formed on his brow.

"Take it easy, doctor. I'm not asking you to pull a trigger or push someone off a cliff." Riggs secretly liked seeing the doctor uncomfortable.

"Then what is it you want?"

"I want to know," Riggs said, "how we could kill someone but make it look like they died from natural causes. And I want you to give me some ideas."

Willoughby was suddenly very frightened. Riggs was asking him to come up with a way to kill people. The doctor wanted to leave the office. He wanted to unhear what he'd just been asked. But he knew that Riggs wouldn't just let him go. Neither would he let him live if he didn't comply with his request.

"Can I..." He tried to swallow, but his mouth was dry. "Can I have a day or so to think about your request?"

Riggs smiled and said, "You can take all the time you want, Doc. But I want some ideas by four o'clock tomorrow afternoon.

Willoughby didn't return to his office but went straight to his rented house and tried to think about a way out of his problem. He wasted a few hours planning an escape but eventually realized that running was futile. By midnight, he came up with a solution... an evil one at that... and then spent the next six hours working it over in his head. He never did fall asleep.

Later that afternoon, Doctor Willoughby drove over to Riggs' office. *But maybe today,* he thought as he walked into the gangster's building, *I can get clear of Riggs.* He'd been following the influenza crisis in various medical journals and personal discussion with doctors who would still speak with him—in Chicago and New York. Willoughby was convinced that the epidemic would get worse and the influenza would provide an opportunity to help Riggs in a big way. *Big enough,* he thought, *to clear my debt permanently.*

"Doctor Willoughby," said Riggs when Albert walked into his office. "Would you like a drink?"

"Not yet, Lou. Maybe later."

"So, do you have anything to share with me?"

Willoughby sat down across from Riggs, looking at the gangster's gray eyes, hoping the man would like his idea. He coughed lightly and said, "Lou, I know you're aware of this sickness, this influenza, that's going around."

Riggs nodded and said, "Yeah, so what?"

"So, you've seen lots of people wearing masks, which, by the way, is a good way to keep from getting sick. Just these past two weeks here in Phoenix, the number of cases is rising. There is no known *cure,* but there are things people can do to *prevent* it. But, Lou, it's going to get worse over the next several months or so. There will be a lot of sick people crowding the hospitals, many of them will die because there won't be enough doctors and nurses to care for all of them."

"What does that have to do with what I asked you for? Just get to the point!"

"Lou, in your... business... I suspect that periodically you need to get rid of... nuisances... or competitors or other people problems. When you use conventional methods, you could find yourself at risk." He waited for some acknowledgement from Riggs. When there was none, the doctor went on. "I've found a way for you to rid yourself of problems without the risk." He swallowed hard and said,

"By passing their deaths off as Spanish Flu."

Willoughby noticed the frown on Riggs's face and decided to go on.

"Look," he said, "with all of these people dying—you know... can't breathe, lungs filling with fluid—anyone who is weak, confused and short of breath will fit in. This will work because patients will die rapidly, and the physicians will be so busy trying to save struggling sick people they won't have time to..." He paused, dealing with some internal struggle. "They'll just quickly tag them as flu deaths."

"Are you sure, doc?"

"No, I'm not sure, Lou, but this method is the best chance we have to get rid of your enemies."

"C'mon, doc..."

"No, listen!" He took a deep breath and calmed himself as he stared into the face of his violent acquaintance. "I have a lot of thallium in my office from when I was treating the whores for syphilis. It's colorless, odorless, and tasteless and if we use greater amounts, a *busy* doctor wouldn't recognize that what he's dealing with is not influenza."

Riggs nodded and listened, willing to hear what the man had to say.

"As long as we don't pull this stunt too often or set a pattern by picking on your well-known enemies, no one will be the wiser." Willoughby was getting wound up, his eyes shuttling left and right, his hands actively involved in the conversation. "This will work," he continued, "but I sure as hell don't want to get caught or go to prison because you're holding a money debt over my head."

"Calm down, doc. If I let you help me get rid of these problems and the cover works, I'll call it even."

"How many... *problems*?"

Lou frowned and said, "As many as I want."

Chapter 20

Henry heard the Pearce's doorbell ring but thought nothing of it. until he heard it again after a few minutes had gone by. He went to the front door and opened it.

"Western Union, sir. I have a telegram for a Mr. Henry Carter."

"I'm Carter."

"Sir, we'd like to apologize for the late delivery of this wire. It actually arrived the night before last but somehow went missing."

"Missing?"

"Yes, sir. We found it this morning under the Out Basket. Please accept our apologies, sir. We hope the delay didn't result in any difficulties for you or the sender."

With that, the boy rushed down the walk and took off running.

Henry went to the telephone and dialed the *Review* office.

"This is Cal Langley."

"Good morning, Boss, I just got your wire."

"Just now? I sent it the day before yesterday."

"Apparently it got misplaced or something and they finally got around to delivering it." Henry could tell that Cal was a little angry. "I know you want me to come to Bisbee, and I can do that if you really need me. But, Etta and I planned to work on wrapping up the Part III of the Lyons article today."

"That's good," said Cal, "but I *would* like to see you—both of you if possible." He didn't speak for a moment while he considered the question he wanted to ask.

"Cal?"

"I'm here. Listen, Henry, this may sound strange, but I need to know how Etta's doing. Is she alright? Do you think she's ready to go back to work?"

"Oh, she's ready, Cal. She spent most of yesterday outlining a plan for her investigation of the flu. I read her notes this morning and it sounds like it will work."

"Okay, but how is she *feeling*, Henry?"

"I think that she's more like her old self."

"You're sure?"

"I am, boss."

Cal asked Henry what work they planned to do on Part III of the conspiracy article.

"We know that you need an update on what has occurred in New Mexico since we turned all of our evidence over to the authorities in Grant County, and that we need to get it to you soon. So, we plan to meet today and share our notes and create a detailed outline. We've learned a lot more since we last spoke. The sheriff told us on the telephone just two days ago that they have considered acting based on the evidence but have decided not to rush the process. I have a feeling, Cal, that despite the quality of the information, they are being cautious because of the potential risk to particular citizens in Silver City and the county. We'll also mention that the evidence could be used in El Paso, but that the Texas court, having already convicted Jones, will ignore the role of New Mexico conspirators because of the jurisdiction factor."

Henry paused to see if Cal had any questions. "It'll only take me a couple of hours to write the first draft. I can put it in the mail this afternoon."

"Alright, Henry," said Cal, wanting to trust his friend's promise and his judgment. "After you two meet, if you don't think you'll be able to get me a story by next week, then call me. If I don't hear from you, I'll assume that you'll be here by Monday."

"Okay, Cal," said Henry. They spoke for a few more

minutes and Cal hung up.

Etta walked into the parlor just as Henry got off the phone.

"Who were you talking to?"

"It was Cal. He's anxious to see Part III *and* he wanted to know how you were doing."

"You told him I was good, right?"

"I did. I also told him we were going to discuss the article today."

"Then let's get some coffee and get to work."

Marisol carried a tray with fresh coffee into the parlor. She had to step around and over the stacks of notes on the floor.

"Thank you," said Etta. "We really need that coffee." She saw the strange look on the maid's face and added, "But don't worry about this mess. We'll clean it up and be out of your way by dinner."

Marisol looked doubtful.

Henry watched her leave and said, "So we agree that a conspiracy—a murder for hire—was possible and likely did occur. But our supportive evidence has now been turned over to the authorities in New Mexico."

Etta nodded.

"We also agree that since the case has already been tried and the killer convicted, we probably couldn't get the authorities in El Paso to do any further investigation since they have no jurisdiction in New Mexico."

"Right, Henry. But the court's unwillingness to no longer pursue the truth will be part of our story."

"Then," Henry said, "our key points are: first that there was a conspiracy carried out by currently unnamed New Mexico residents. Second, we turned over all of the evidence we collected to the authorities in Grant County New Mexico."

"And third," said Etta, "in El Paso during the investigation and the trial, the District Attorney and the Judge made separate and joint decisions that affected the case but did not make these decisions public. What we have, Henry, is the truth as we believe it to be, but the authorities in Texas were unwilling to pursue the facts once they had a conviction."

"That's how I'll write it, Etta. I sure hope it's enough for Cal."

"It will be. You're sure you can read my scribbles, Henry?"

"I can and I think I'll have a draft for you to look at in the morning."

"Great." Etta sipped cold coffee from her cup and headed for the hallway. "I'm going to see if I can get an appointment with my mother's doctor."

"Are you sick?" asked Henry, suddenly worried.

"No, but I think he can give me some detailed information about the Spanish flu."

Later that afternoon, Mr. Pearce walked into the parlor and glanced at Henry. The reporter was sitting at the large table writing in a notebook.

"What are you working on, young man?"

Henry looked back over his shoulder and then quickly stood.

"Oh, Mr. Pearce. I'm writing our story on the conspiracy article."

Pearce smiled at Henry and said, "I guess it takes a lot of paper to finish a story." He indicated the stacks of notes and the crumpled rejects spread around the room.

"You're right, sir, it does." He glanced at the mess on the floor and then at Pearce. "Did you ever have a project where you worked and worked and then discovered you couldn't go on?"

Pearce nodded. "I suppose that's happened to me a number of times."

"Well, this story is a bit like that. Etta and I have worked hard, trying to... well, complete a story that doesn't have a good conclusion. We'd hoped to learn enough about the victim and the handling of the trial that would prove something different than the lawyers did. We did find a few people with good information that will help us do that."

Henry sat down hard in the chair.

Pearce looked at the young man, saw defeat on his face. "Did you really try? Did you each work hard and do everything you could to achieve your goal?"

"Everything we *could*." He shook his head. "But the authorities worked against us."

"Then maybe you just need to think about it some more, or you could ask your boss, Mr. Langley, for some help."

At the mention of Cal's name, a memory flashed in Henry's mind.

"You know sir, Cal once told me that sometimes a story, a search for the truth, can't be finished. Sometimes leads don't lead anywhere. Sometimes stories die before they can be told."

Pearce watched as Henry seemed to dig back in his memories for more.

"He said that it hurts to give up. It's not in our blood to quit, but sometimes that's what we have to do."

"Where's my daughter?" Pearce asked.

"Working on her own story. She promised to be home by five."

Pearce nodded and said, "Good. We've been invited to have dinner with Stewart and Gloria tonight at seven. That includes you, too, Henry."

"Thank you, sir..."

Pearce held up his hand. "Call me Bill, please, Henry."

"Alright, Bill. I'll clean this up and be out of your way in five minutes."

True to her promise, Etta walked into the parlor at five o'clock expecting to find Henry working on his article.

The room was in order and her father stood at the bar.

"Hello, Daddy," she said. "Have you seen Henry?"

"I have. He's getting ready to join us for dinner with Stewart and Gloria."

"Tonight? What time?"

"Gloria said seven o'clock, so I told Stewart we'd all be there a bit early."

"Then I'd better get ready as well."

"Did you learn anything new today?"

"I did, but there's so much more I need to know." Then Etta walked over to her father and hugged him. Pearce gently patted her on the back. Etta kissed him on the cheek and said, "Gotta go, Daddy. I'm hungry and ready for a family gathering."

As Henry, Etta, and her father walked up the steps to the Bradley home, Henry noticed that it was as large and as nice as the Pearce residence.

The maid opened the door and invited them into the entry hall. Pearce thanked her and led the two reporters to the large dining room beyond the parlor. The table was set for at least a dozen people.

"Looks like we aren't the only guests, Daddy," said Etta.

"Stewart said he might invite a few others because..."

Before he could finish his comment, Gloria Bradley walked into the room and hugged Pearce.

"How are you doing, Bill?"

"I'm doing fine." He put his arm around Etta's shoulders and smiled. "*We're* doing fine aren't we Sweetheart?"

"We are," she said as she kissed Gloria on the cheek. Then she looked at Henry and grinned. "My partner, there, is very skilled in helping lost souls re-discover themselves."

Gloria greeted Henry warmly, then asked if anyone wanted a drink. Like most residents of Arizona, they honored the state's prohibition law in public places but had no such rules in their home. Henry followed the ladies past the table to an alcove that had a small bar. Gloria set down two short glasses and poured them half-full of whiskey.

"Would you like ice, Henry?"

"Yes, please."

Gloria added a cube to her own glass.

"Not for me, Gloria. I still like mine neat," said Etta.

Smiling broadly, she said, "You're still like your father, I see." She handed the reporters their drinks and said, "To family."

Stewart Bradley walked into the room straight back to the bar. "I see everyone has had a head start on me." He filled his short glass from the same decanter and took a healthy swallow.

"Good evening, Mr. Carter," he said, lifting his glass to Henry. "And how's my favorite newspaper woman, Etta?"

"I'm fine, Uncle Stewart. You are looking very dapper this evening."

"It's a special night, Etta."

The maid entered the room and gestured to Bradley. He walked over to her, listened for a moment and sent her to Gloria. Then he left the room, taking Pearce with him.

"What is it, Clarisse," asked Gloria.

"Mr. Bradley's other guests have arrived. They asked to meet with him before coming in to join the rest of your company."

In a few moments, Bradley and Pearce returned, leading the other guests into the dining room.

"Let's go meet Uncle Stewart's friends, Henry."

Henry and Etta were introduced to Arizona's leading Republican legislators and their wives as investigative journalists. Bradley spent the few minutes after the introductions making sure that those who wanted a drink had one while Gloria kept up the conversation with the guests.

Etta leaned toward Henry and whispered in his ear. "This is going to be a special night for Stewart." She still had her arm locked in Henry's as they stood among the guests, Henry suspected the dinner event had something to do with what Etta had said a few days ago. But he decided not to speculate and simply enjoy the evening.

Henry watched as Stewart waited until the conversations began to wind down before he tapped his whiskey glass with a spoon. The tiny bell-like sound turned all eyes in his direction.

"First, I'd like to thank my distinguished guests from the legislature and their lovely wives for visiting our home. I'm also pleased that my favorite young lady and her partner in journalism had time to steal from their worthy endeavors to spend it with us. Next, I'm proud and pleased to have my life-long friend and trusted advisor at my side. Of course, my beautiful wife to whom I owe everything joins me in welcoming you all here tonight."

There were a few murmured comments and then he continued.

"Tonight is very special in another way as well. I have decided to accept the offer of the Republican leadership of Arizona to seek the open Congressional seat in the U.S. House of Representatives."

A round of applause interrupted his announcement, and Bradley bowed slightly, smiling all the while. He evidently had more to say because he raised his hand. This led the gathering to listen again.

"Of course, we know that this will be a tough battle. My opponent has been campaigning for months while we are just beginning. He has assumed for most of the time that he would win since he was unopposed," Stewart paused. "But that is no longer the case."

"Tomorrow morning, across the state, most of the loyal newspapers will announce that Mr. Julius Parker now faces a tough contest with a candidate who has the full support—thanks to you gentlemen here tonight—of the Republicans of Arizona. Starting tomorrow, I'm going to speak at Republican sponsored lunches and dinners and outline my position on the many issues facing the state and the country. I'm going to counter the points that have been published and stated by Julius Parker."

There was more applause, but sensing that Bradley was still not finished speaking, they quieted down quickly.

"When the election is over, we'll have time to celebrate in earnest and look forward to many more of these wonderful social gatherings. But, all that being said, I am truly ready to sit down at the table with you, my supporters, my friends, and my family." He looked around the room and added, "Let's eat."

Throughout the dinner, the conversations among those around the table varied. The men, with Henry quietly listening, spoke about politics and business. The women, with Etta listening more to the men's discussion, talked about the life of a politician's wife.

"Ladies, gentlemen," said Stewart, as they gathered near the front door, "Gloria and I appreciate your visit."

Henry watched as the group shared handshakes and cheek-kisses and then left the Bradley's home. By the time the other guests departed, he felt confident that in just those few hours he had learned something. He'd also noted Etta's efforts at listening in on conversations, so he was anxious to talk with her about her insights.

"Gloria, why don't you send Clarisse home. I'd like the five of us to have a talk about something before we forget about what we've learned tonight and what lies ahead."

"Alright, Stewart." She turned to the others and said, "Let's sit in Stewart's office."

She left to deal with Clarisse, and Bradley fixed drinks for the others before he led them to his office. Walking into the room, Henry's first impression was that it was exactly like Bill's office. Then he noticed the difference. The bookshelves were filled primarily with law books and histories, unlike Pearce's business and economic works.

"I'm glad that event is over. It was essential that it occur, but I need to start on the real work."

"Stewart, can I say something first?"

"Sure, Bill."

"I think you are the only person who can beat Parker, and the one man in our state who has the support of the legislature and who can win the support of the citizens. I say this not because we are friends, but because it's true."

"Thanks, Bill."

"But," Pearce continued, "for the benefit of Etta and Henry, we need to discuss your opponent—who he is, what he's like, what are his strengths and weaknesses."

Bradley rested his hands on his knees and leaned forward across the table set between the two sofas. "Etta, Henry, I'd like you to help me fill in some blanks—blanks in my knowledge about Julius Parker."

Henry turned to Etta, but she kept her eyes directed toward Bradley. "How can we help, Uncle Stewart?"

Bradley glanced at Pearce then addressed the two reporters.

"I suspect that Parker is not the man he presents to the public. In fact, I'm fairly certain he's not without some faults and friendships of dubious nature. But, and here's where you two come in, I need to *know*, to have *facts* that can *prove* his corruption, and expose his dishonesty."

Henry's focus was entirely on Bradley, questions and plans already racing across his mind. Once again, Etta spoke first.

"So, you'd like us to use our investigative skills to confirm or deny your beliefs, your suspicions, right?"

Henry was amazed, though not surprised, that Etta had arrived at the same conclusion he had.

"We don't have a lot of time, though, do we?" asked Henry.

"No, we don't." Bradley sat straight in his seat. "We have less than a month to not only discover the truth, but to find ways to get it out on the street so that those Arizonans thinking about supporting him will have a chance to change their minds *before* election day."

Over the next hour or so, the five friends discussed Bradley's concerns. He mentioned the rumors about Parker and some crime boss, about his opponent's suspected involvement in gambling and bootlegging. Etta and Henry took turns asking questions and clarifying concerns.

All the while, Gloria remained quiet. She didn't take notes, she didn't interrupt. But as the clock approached midnight, she said, "If you four are going to have any success in achieving your goal—our goal—of getting my husband elected, you will need rest. Tired friends, investigators, and candidates will not succeed as well as rested ones."

But when they finished their discussion and headed home, Henry remembered his promise to Cal. Once he got to his room, he didn't follow Gloria's advice. He stayed awake and finished Part III a few hours before dawn. Then he wrote a short note for Mr. Pearce to put the article in the mail for Cal, clipped it to the draft and set it in the hallway just outside the bedroom door. That task finished, Henry lay down on the bed, still fully clothed, and fell asleep.

Chapter 21

THE NEXT MORNING, JUST two weeks before the election Julius Parker sat at the table in his kitchen. While the coffee pot heated up on the stove, he opened the morning edition of the *Arizona Republican* and read the headline.

Stewart Bradley Seeks House Seat
Will Oppose Julius Parker

Parker read the headline again, not believing what he was seeing. At first he was stunned, the words hitting him like a blow to the chest. *I need to calm down and do it now.* He rose quickly and walked down the hall to his study. At his desk, he picked up the telephone and called Lou Riggs. After a half-dozen rings and no response, he returned to the kitchen. *Now it's official,* he thought, *so now it's time to do something about it.*

He poured himself a cup of coffee and returned to his seat at the table and read the entire article. He discovered that not only was Bradley seeking the position, but he also had the full support of the Republicans in the Arizona Legislature. *That can't be. Some of those men have already committed to me.* Parker's anger rose as he continued reading. In just a few sentences the leaders of the party stated that not only was Bradley going to win the election, but that he would "soundly defeat the opposition's tainted candidate." *That's slander,* he thought, *they can't get away with this!*

Parker dialed Riggs again, hoping that this time the gangster would pick up the phone. But even after a dozen rings there was no response. Parker shouted, "Answer the phone, Riggs!" Slamming the telephone down with a thud, he paced in front of his desk, grumbling and clenching his fists. In an effort to control his anger he took a deep breath, walked slowly to the sofa by the window and sat down. He sat motionless for ten minutes, then stood and returned to the telephone.

"Okay! You'd better answer the damned phone this time, you crook." He dialed the number and looked out the window at the clouds turning a pale coral shade as the sun rose.

"I'm not hanging up 'til you answer this time, Riggs," Parker mumbled just as the gangster picked up the phone.

Lou's voice was loud, ferocious even, "Who the hell is this?"

"It's me, Parker."

"And why are you calling me so damned early in the morning?" he shouted.

"Lou, have you read this morning's paper?"

"What? You just woke me up, you idiot. How could I have read the paper? Now hang up and call me this afternoon!" Riggs started to end the call when he heard Parker yell.

"No! Don't you hang up on me. We need to talk now!" Parker spoke as if he was addressing a child.

For a moment, Riggs did not reply. When he did, his words came quietly and slowly from his lips. "Listen to me you lousy wind-bag politician. You are just one word away from becoming coyote food. *You* don't order *me* around, *you* don't tell *me* what to do." He waited to see if Parker had a reply. "That's a good *boy*, Julius. Here's what I want you to do. After you hang up the telephone, you will think really hard about what a mess you've just put yourself in. Then, you will come to my office this afternoon at one o'clock—not a minute earlier or later. *Then* we will discuss whatever disaster you read about in the paper. Is there any of this that you don't understand?"

Parker remained silent.

Lou Riggs quietly hung up the telephone and went looking for his copy of the *Republican*.

Precisely at one, Parker stood in front of Riggs's desk. He had hoped to speak to the gangster as an equal, or at least with some dignity, but his outburst had eliminated any chance of that. Sounding more like a supplicant than a politician, Parker asked if Riggs had seen the paper.

"I have. So what?"

"Lou, Stewart Bradley is running for *my* House seat."

"It's not yours yet."

"Exactly, but I... we need it to be my seat."

Riggs enjoyed watching Parker beg. He said, "What are you going to do about your opponent?"

"What do you mean, Lou. What am *I* going to do? I thought we agreed *you'd* find a way to eliminate him?" Parker calmed himself a bit, not wanting to upset Riggs more than he already had. "Did you find a way to have him killed that won't link back to... you?"

"I did, but you need to remember that no matter what happens or how it happens, you are the responsible party. If there's even a hint that I'm linked to anything, *you... are... dead*. Do you understand me?

"Yes, yes of course, Lou. I understand. But it has to happen soon. I don't want him to get a chance to influence any of the voters. If he gets elected, you know, all of the advantages I'd provide you will disappear—no more influence, no more advanced knowledge of opportunities, no more protection against prosecution."

"Are you threatening me, Julius?" Riggs was angry, his words strong, but controlled.

"It's just that..."

"Shut up and listen. You need to give me all of the information on him that you can get. I need everything. Where does he live, is he married, does he have children, where does he work, and who are his friends?"

"Why do you need all of that?"

"You don't need to know why. But I hope my plan works. If it does, I won't need to hurt his family."

"What is your plan? Did you find a way to keep me... us out of trouble?"

"Listen to me, Parker. You get me this information by tomorrow morning." Parker started to argue, to challenge Lou's demand, then stopped when Riggs said, "I'm done," and stood up.

"Sorry, Lou."

Riggs turned to Parker, pointed his finger at him and said, "I will take care of this for you. But you will *owe* me, Parker, owe me a big favor. It will take a day or so, but I'll make the arrangements to get him out of the way... permanently. If all goes the way I plan it, you can read about his untimely death in the newspaper."

Parker said, "I'll have the information not later than noon tomorrow." Then, when Riggs didn't respond, Parker turned and walked out of the office. He headed straight for the campaign office.

"Winston," he said, "my office now!"

The campaign manager rushed to his desk, grabbed a pencil and pad, and scurried into Parker's office.

"Yes, sir?"

"Have you seen this morning's paper?" Not waiting for Winston's reply, he said, "I want you to get all of the information that exists on Stewart Bradley. That means family, friends, where does he go, what does he do, who he's worked for, what kind of man is he, does he drink, cheat on his wife, that sort of thing."

Winston hurriedly jotted down notes.

"That means now, Winston, I want this information now!"

Winston delivered his report to Parker before the end of the day. "From what I was able to discover, Mr. Parker, This man Bradley is squeaky clean. No vices, no girlfriends, no criminal record. He's married, no children, and has been a hard worker for the Republican Party for many years."

"How come we've never heard of him?"

"Evidently he's always worked behind the scenes, writing speeches, creating policy statements, that sort of thing."

Parker asked, "Do you have all of this written down?"

Winston handed Parker a thin stack of typed pages.

Parker put them in his briefcase, put on his coat and hat and quickly headed out to see Riggs

By the next evening, Riggs had some of his men following Bradley. They knew where he was staying and where he worked. They knew the people he worked with and those who were his friends. Bradley was so busy, so focused, that his habits varied little. The men Riggs had chosen to carry out the job were thorough and clearly knew that their methods were approved by him.

Riggs had one of his "men" contact Willoughby and advise the doctor to be ready for his first 'patient' not later than tomorrow night.

"Who is it?" asked Willoughby.

"You don't need to know that Doc. You just need to do the job like Mr. Riggs said."

One night, ten days after he'd begun the campaign, Stewart Bradley walked out of his Headquarters in downtown Phoenix and walked up the street. The sky was dark, but the few streetlights aided him in walking the block or so to where the car was parked. As he approached the vehicle, he reached into his coat pocket for the key.

"Excuse me, sir."

Stewart turned and faced a tall man wearing a white mask who grabbed him by his tie. The man hit him hard on the left temple with a sap, knocking him out cold, blood flowed freely down his face. The tall man took the key from Stewart's hand just as another man, also wearing a mask, appeared and helped carry the unconscious candidate through a breezeway to a lot behind the building where they put him into the back seat of a car. The tall man got in the driver's seat while the other ran back to Bradley's car. They drove a few miles and pulled up in the alley behind the office of Albert Willoughby, MD.

The man who'd used the sap banged on the back door. It was immediately opened by Willoughby, and he led them to a table, indicating they should put the body on it, face up on the sheet.

The doctor avoided looking at the unconscious man's face. He didn't want to know whose life he was taking. He took an empty syringe, filled it with 20cc of thallium, and inserted the needle quickly into the vein in Bradley's arm.

Stewart was still alive, and the poison began to affect him quickly. His temperature rose, and his body began to thrash about. Willoughby recognized the reactions as stomach cramps, and spasms in the legs and abdomen. Bradley immediately vomited whatever had accumulated in his stomach. Willoughby would have preferred clearing the man's airway, but followed Riggs's orders and did not touch any of the fluids. In his unconscious state, it didn't take long for Stewart to begin choking. Convulsions soon took over and his body bucked as it tried vainly to fight against death. The process didn't take long. When the doctor was certain that the man was dead, he wrapped the sheet around his body and told the men that they could take him away.

The two men carried the shrouded body back out to the car. They drove both vehicles to the nearest hospital, stopping a half block short of the service entrance. Looking up and down the dark street, assuring themselves that there were no witnesses, they placed Bradley face down, his head resting on the curb near the front of his car. Leaving the driver-side door open, the first assailant ran up to the hospital, entered the service door and yelled, "Hey!

There's a man who just fell on the street at the corner. He looks pretty sick."

A nurse looked up toward the door, but the man had turned away. She rushed to the exit and saw him point left down the street. She looked back into the hospital and shouted for help. Two orderlies came up the hall carrying a litter and she waved them on. When she turned back toward the street, she saw a car driving away to the right. Then she turned her attention to the left and ran toward the corner. She found the injured man on the street, then quickly checked his pulse, but couldn't tell for sure if he was still alive.

"Get him on the litter and back to the hospital," she said to the orderlies. "Hurry."

She didn't wait for them but hurried back to the entrance and called for a doctor as soon as she reached the desk. Then, following the orderlies as they raced past the desk, they entered a small room and placed the body on a table.

This time when she checked his pulse, it was clear that the man was dead. It appeared to the nurse that he had been sick—he was covered with vomit—and must have passed out, hitting his head on the street or curb in the process.

Looks like another case of Spanish flu, she thought.

The nurse turned away just as a tired looking doctor entered the room. She said, "No hurry now, Dr. Lane, he's gone.'

"What happened?"

"Someone came to the service door and shouted that a man had passed out in the street. I took two orderlies to where he fell and found him unconscious. I took his pulse and..."

The doctor took a deep breath and quickly examined the body, stepped back, and said, "Looks like Spanish flu." The nurse nodded. "Listen, leave him here and we'll get to him later. Right now, I need your help in the waiting room.

I've got nine new *living* patients who are also vomiting and fainting. I'd like to keep *them* alive.

Three hours later, the same nurse and doctor found a few minutes to return to the room where the man's body was. They searched his pocket and found his wallet. They quickly determined that he was Stewart Bradley. Neither of them recognized the name as the newest candidate in the coming election. The nurse wrote down the details and told the doctor she'd get the information to the administrator as soon as he showed up for the day shift.

A little after eight o'clock, the hospital's duty nurse reported to the Chief Surgeon that around midnight a person had died as a result of a fall following a seizure from Spanish flu. The doctor and nurse who'd found him were tied up all night with patients and reported the incident just before they went home.

"So, who is the deceased?"

"A Mr. Stewart Bradley, doctor."

"The politician?"

"I don't know, doctor."

"Is he in the morgue?"

"Not yet. He's still in the room by the service door."

"Mrs. Young, I want you to do three things for me. First, get the doctor and nurse who were on duty last night back here immediately. Second, don't let anyone near the deceased until I tell you it's okay. Third, get me the telephone number for the Republican Campaign office here in the city."

The nurse acknowledged the assignment with a nod and walked out. The surgeon went to the room where Bradley's body was and noticed that the two staff members had at least covered the dead man. Pulling the sheet away, the doctor saw the dried vomit, and the now dried blood on a head wound. The man's wallet was open and placed on the litter next to his body. Normally, the doctor would contact the next of kin, but since the deceased was a high-profile politician, he decided to let the campaign take care of that task.

Gloria Bradley rested quietly on the sofa in her parlor. Etta sat next to her, with a comforting arm around the somber woman's shoulders. Henry was on her other side, watching Bill Pearce pace the width of the room. The older man was troubled, worried about his friend who'd been missing since late yesterday. He barely heard Gloria when she spoke.

"Where is he, Bill? We've called everyone we know in Phoenix—the campaign workers, the legislators, even his office." She stopped and wiped her eyes with a handkerchief. "This is not like him. He would have called if he'd been going to a meeting or a rally."

Pearce stopped and leaned across the table in front of the sofa. "We'll find him, Gloria. I've called the police and the hospitals, and they have no word on him."

"Daddy," said Etta, "Maybe we could call the hospital again." She looked at her wristwatch. "It's after eight now, the hospital day shifts must be working. It's possible that whatever may have happened hasn't been reported yet."

Gloria looked at Bill and then Etta. "Do you think that could help?"

"I think it's a good idea," he said.

In just those few minutes, Gloria began to cry. Etta hugged her gently and patted her back, softly whispering to her, seeking to comfort her.

Bill glanced at the two young people and then said to Gloria, "Let's do this. Etta, you and Henry drive to the campaign headquarters. I'll start calling the hospitals and police right away. Whether I learn anything or not, I'll leave a message for you with whoever is in charge." Pearce looked directly at Gloria. "I'll stay here with you, dear. I won't leave you alone."

Etta looked up at her father with tear-filled eyes. "We'll find him, Daddy. We have to."

After they left, Bill asked Clarisse to sit with Gloria while he started making telephone calls.

In the hour or so he was on the phone, Bill never once put the telephone down. The Police and Sheriff's departments had no word on the missing candidate. He called two hospitals and had no luck. Then he tried the third one.

"St. Joseph's Hospital, how may I help you?"

"My name is William Pearce. I'm looking for a friend of mine who's been missing since yesterday evening. Could you please check your records to see if he's in your facility?"

"Of course, Mr. Pearce. What is your friend's name?"

"His name is Stewart Bradley."

Hesitating for a moment, the woman said, "Please hold on, Mr. Pearce, I'll get someone to help you."

Bill held the phone to his ear and glanced across the room to where Gloria rested. *This isn't good,* he thought. Although he felt like yelling, he couldn't. He had to remain calm for her sake. Yet, his heart was pounding, sweat trickled down his back.

The hospital woman pushed a button on her desk that buzzed in the Chief Surgeon's office.

"What is it, Miss Reitz?"

"Mr. William Pearce is calling about the man... Mr. Bradley."

"Okay, I'll be right there."

"Mr. Pearce? This is Doctor Gilliam. I'm the Chief Surgeon of St. Joseph's."

"Yes, doctor."

"We do have information regarding Mr. Bradley, but I'll need more from you before I can share what I have."

"What's happened to him?"

"Sir, please, can you tell me how you are related to him?"

"We are life-long friends, doctor." Bill paused and said, "and I'm trying to find him for his very worried, very distraught wife."

"Thank you, sir. I'm sorry to have to tell you this, but late last night Mr. Bradley passed away."

"He died? How? What happened?"

"He was found on the street near the hospital. It appeared that he'd driven himself here because he was ill. As much as we know at present, the indication is that he had symptoms of Spanish flu—vomiting and seizures—and fell from his car, sustaining a fatal head wound."

"You're sure it's him? Stewart Bradley?"

"Yes sir, his identification was found on his person. Our medical staff got to him as quickly as they could, but it was too late."

Bill quietly ended the call and sighed. *There's no easy way to do this,* he thought. *But it's better coming from me than from a stranger*. He left the parlor and headed slowly toward the back of the house, to Gloria's bedroom where she rested with Clarisse.

He tapped lightly on the door, opened it and stepped into the room. Gloria looked up at Bill and must have seen something in his eyes, because she screamed, "No!" and began sobbing.

Henry drove as quickly as he dared to the Stewart Campaign Headquarters. He turned left onto a broad avenue and screeched to a stop in front of the building. Hung along the brick wall above the large glass windows was a red, white, and blue banner proclaiming, "Stewart Bradley for Congress."

He'd barely pulled the brake handle when Etta got out of her seat and marched into the building. Right behind her, Henry caught the door before it closed. They had expected to find a crowded, busy, energized room. Instead, it was quiet. People stood in small groups, none speaking above a whisper. *This is not good,* Henry thought.

The arrival of the two young people caught the attention of a refined looking, middle-aged man. He walked up to Etta and said, "Are you Miss Pearce?"

"I am."

"My name is Alvin Monroe. I'm the campaign manager. Your father called and he wants you to contact him right away."

"May I use your telephone, Mr. Monroe?"

He led Etta across the room and into a separate office, followed by dozens of pairs of eyes. *What's going on,* Etta wondered.

As she walked away, Henry turned toward the nearest cluster of people. The three men and two young women continued to watch Etta and Monroe until Henry cleared his throat.

"Excuse me," he said. "What's going on?"

"Who are you?" asked the tallest of the men.

"My name's Henry Carter. My partner and I," he gestured to where Etta had gone, "are close friends of the Bradley family."

The tall man considered Henry's statement and was about to continue when he was interrupted by one of the women.

"Mr. Bradley is dead," she blurted, and then began to cry. The other woman put a comforting arm around her. The tall man, who seemed annoyed by the woman's outburst, spoke to Henry.

"We've just learned that Mr. Bradley passed away last night. My name is Walter Adams." He shook hands with Henry and introduced the others. "We're not sure what will happen now."

At that moment, Etta walked up behind Henry and said his name softly. He turned and stared at her face. He saw pain and sadness on the surface, but there was no sense of fear. He took her hand and turned back to the others.

"This is my partner, Etta Pearce." The others nodded,

but Etta was silent. "If you'll excuse us for a moment, we need to talk."

Henry took Etta's arm and walked her toward the windows at the front of the room. He was attentive and gentle, and even though he already knew what Etta was going to say, he listened to her.

"Henry, Uncle Stewart is dead. Daddy spoke to a doctor at St. Joseph's hospital. We need to go there and do a positive identification for them. Daddy and Gloria want me to make sure it's him."

"We'll do it together, Etta."

"Thank you." Etta seemed calm, but Henry knew she was having trouble processing the news.

"Henry, I need to be with Gloria and my father. They are both struggling with this and, well, I need them too."

"I'm so sorry, Etta." He took a quick glance around the room and added, "Give me a moment, okay. I want to talk to some of these campaign workers before we go."

"Whatever you think is best, Henry."

Henry got Etta a glass of water, then left her just long enough to set up a meeting with Bradley's campaign staff. Adams agreed to meet him at seven o'clock at the restaurant just across the street from the headquarters.

On the drive to the hospital, Etta spoke little.

"Etta, I know you've been working on the flu story, and I know why it's important to you." She didn't look at him, but he saw her give a slight nod. "But Stewart's death is a tragedy for Gloria, your father, *and* you. It might be a good idea to let the story simmer for a while and spend whatever time it takes to help Gloria through the next few days."

"You need to turn right at that traffic signal." Etta's voice was soft.

Henry made the turn and spotted the hospital a few blocks ahead on the right.

"We should call your father as soon as we can. He and

Gloria will want to know for sure *if* the dead man is Stewart."

When he parked at the curb, Henry expected Etta to hurry away from the car like she'd done earlier. This time, however, she remained still, her hands folded in her lap and gazed into the distance beyond the hospital. To Henry, she looked numb, in shock.

"I'm frightened, Henry." She brought her hands to her lips. "I'm worried that it's him and we'll have to look at a man I've known all my life and remember how his dead body looks. I'm also worried because Gloria will want to know everything even if it's sad, or if it's painful."

She finally looked over at Henry.

"But," she continued, "I can't *not* do this for her and my father." Etta reached for the handle and pushed the door open.

Henry got out of the car and moved around to meet Etta. They walked through the entrance and found the information desk.

"We're here to see Dr. Gilliam," said Henry. The woman at the desk dialed a number on the telephone and whispered a few words into the mouthpiece. She nodded once and hung up.

"Dr. Gilliam will be right with you."

Henry led Etta away from the desk toward some chairs along a wall. Before they could sit, a doctor approached them.

"Miss Pearce, I'm Dr. Gilliam. All of us here at St. Joseph's are saddened by your loss. Before we do an identification, I want to relate to you everything we know and what we speculate might have caused his death. I will answer *all* of your questions." He looked directly at Etta. "These things—the identification—are always sad but are vitally important for your sake and for ours."

Over the next hour, the doctor narrated the events of the previous night. He identified the nurse who first encountered the man, the doctor who attempted to treat him, and even the orderlies. He described how they found Mr. Bradley near his car, and then how they determined that the Spanish flu was a factor in his death.

Henry asked, "Are you certain that he had Spanish flu? Mr. Bradley has not shown any symptoms of influenza in the past week or so."

"Mr. Carter, the symptoms as described by the nurse and doctor are consistent with some cases of Spanish flu." He glanced at Etta, seeing only the top of her cloche hat. "But am I *certain*," he continued, "that the flu is what caused him to faint and then to fall where he did, injuring himself fatally?"

Henry nodded.

"Then, no sir, I am not certain. It's possible and very likely true. But I cannot say without performing an autopsy that it is *absolutely* how he died."

Neither Henry nor Etta had considered the need for an autopsy. They also knew that a decision to proceed in that direction would have to come from Gloria.

"How long can you keep him here? How soon *could* an autopsy be performed if such a decision is made by Mrs. Bradley?"

"Once we have approval from his wife, we'd need no more than 24 hours to complete the exam. By then we should be able to release the body to the family and arrangements with a funeral home can then be made."

"Doctor, I have another question," said Etta. "In your experience with this form of influenza, have you seen other sudden deaths like this one?"

"That's a good question, Miss Pearce. We are certain that the flu probably didn't kill him. An autopsy will show us whether he died from the head trauma or influenza. Perhaps it might show some other cause. But it's possible that the flu caused the nausea and vomiting and the fainting." He considered something for a moment and said, "We've treated over a hundred cases of the flu in the hospital and have had some deaths. This one is enough like them to *possibly* be caused by the flu. Because Mr. Bradley is a highly visible person, I recommend an autopsy."

"Thank you," Etta said. She looked at Henry. "Let's get this over with."

Dr. Gilliam led them down to the morgue in the hospital's basement. He spoke to an orderly who'd quickly appeared and then led them to a door on the far wall. The room was bright and the sheet-covered body on the elevated table left little to the imagination.

The doctor had described the head wound to both of them earlier and how, that despite the process of cleansing it might yet be frightening. As Henry stood next to Etta, he nodded at the doctor. Gilliam took one corner of the sheet and lifted it away from the head of the table.

Etta's body collapsed when she saw that the dead person *was* Stewart. Henry kept his arm around her waist. When she finally spoke, it was with a gentle firmness.

"This is my uncle, Stewart Bradley, doctor."

Replacing the sheet, he said, "Thank you, Miss Pearce."

Before going back to the house, Henry called the Bradley residence and then put Etta on the telephone.

"Daddy, it's me."

"Etta, I..."

"Daddy, it's him. Uncle Stewart is dead"

"I'm so sorry you had to go through that process, Sweetheart." He looked across the room at Gloria.

"Daddy, I need to be home with you and Gloria."

"I understand that, dear, but I think... no, I *know* I want you and Henry to do something for Gloria and me."

"Do what, Daddy?"

"Let me talk to Henry if he's close by."

Etta's brow wrinkled as she turned toward Henry and handed the telephone to him.

"Yes, Bill?"

"I want you and Etta working on something, anything,

that will keep her busy. Two deaths so close together may be too much for her to handle."

"We're meeting with some people in Stewart's campaign who *may* know some of Parker's staff. I'm not sure where it might lead, but I'm setting up a meeting with some of the people in the campaign and then we want to interview Parker himself. Also, the doctor here wants to perform an autopsy. He said that's the only way to be certain that Stewart's fall, his fainting was caused by the flu."

"I'll call him right away and arrange that. I just want you and Etta to keep checking on this man Parker. Be as circumspect as you think necessary but learn something about him. I think that Stewart knew more about Parker than he let on that night we were with the Republican leadership and Stewart's last request of you was about Parker as well."

"We'll do everything we can, Bill."

"Now put Etta back on."

"Yes, Daddy?"

"Gloria and I need some time to fully absorb what we now know, Sweetheart. So, we want you to stay busy. Work with Henry to find out all you can about Parker. Can you do that?"

"Are you sure you don't need me, Daddy?"

"Yes, Etta, we are sure. Don't worry about us. You just keep being strong for us."

"Alright, Daddy. Bye."

Henry took the telephone and set it down.

Before he and Etta left the restaurant, Henry used the telephone to call Parker's headquarters. He spoke to a man who identified himself as the campaign manager.

"Sir, first let me apologize for calling so late. My name is Henry Carter. I'm a reporter with the *Bisbee Daily Review*."

"How can I help you, Mr. Carter?"

"My partner and I are in town for a few days and were

wondering if it would be possible to set up an appointment with Mr. Parker. We'd like to have some comments from him regarding his campaign for our readers in the southeast part of the state."

"I can arrange that for you. Mr. Parker is quite busy, as you can imagine, and his time is short." He looked at a calendar on his desk and said, "Would the day after tomorrow work for you?"

"We could be there at ten o'clock."

"Very good. We'll see you in then."

On their way back to the house, Etta said, "I've been thinking about something else we could do."

"What?"

"Remember the government agent I told you about?"

"The one whose car broke down near Tombstone?"

"Right, the one who works for President Wilson. He told me that if I ever needed something for a story, I could contact him, and he would help if he could."

"So?"

"Since he said if I ever needed to get in touch with him all I had to do was contact his assistant in the capitol and the assistant could relay a message." She paused and continued, "I think that he might be able to give us some information on Parker. Daniel is close to the President, and thus likely in the know about Democratic Party topics and concerns. He's probably aware of party problems. And even if he can't or won't share something about the President's interests, he surely might be willing to talk about a troublesome member of the party."

"It can't hurt to try, Etta, and it may prove valuable."

"I'm gonna do it as soon as we get to the house."

Bill Pearce called Etta from the Bradley house. When she answered, he said, "Etta, I've heard from Dr. Gilliam."

"What did he say, Daddy?"

"The autopsy showed that Stewart did *not* have the Spanish flu as they originally suspected."

"I'm confused, Daddy. If that's true, then why did he drive to the hospital?"

"No one knows why or how he could have driven."

"What do you mean?"

"Gilliam said that there was significant evidence that Stewart had been poisoned with something called thallium or some other poison."

"Oh God, no! Who would want to poison him, Daddy, and why?" Etta's eyes began to flood with tears.

Pearce thought for a moment about what words he wanted to use. Then he said, "The only person I can think of who'd want Stewart out of the way is Julius Parker."

"The opposing candidate."

"Right, Sweetheart. The other night Stewart said he suspected the man was dishonest. That was why you and Henry were going to see what you could learn about him."

"Henry and I already have an appointment with him for the day after tomorrow—that's the soonest he is available. We want to interview him, to see him, listen to him, try to find out what kind of man he is." An idea flashed in her mind. "We could probably even ask how he feels about the death of his opponent."

"That kind of questioning could bring out his real feelings. But, you two will, or at least *may be* talking to a man capable of murder, so you'll have to be cautious."

"We'll be careful, Daddy. I'll call you when we're finished."

Early on the morning that she and Henry were scheduled to interview Parker, she was walking out of the kitchen when she heard the telephone ring.

"Hello, Pearce residence. This is Etta."

"Etta, this is Daniel Foster I'm sorry for the delay in getting back to you."

"That's okay, Daniel, thanks for calling back. I guess

you were telling the truth in Tombstone when you said your assistant would always know where you are."

"He does perform well at all times."

"Were you able to learn anything about Parker."

"Yes, I was. According to a few of my contacts in the party, Mr. Parker does not have a very good reputation. He's considered by much of the party leadership as *untrustworthy*."

"Interesting."

"Yes, it is. Especially when you consider that *that* word typically means he associates with the wrong crowd and his motives are not always in the people's best interests."

"Daniel, I really appreciate this. When we finish this business, we'll all have to get together and have a more sociable meeting. If we learn anything of value at our interview, I'll call you."

"Good, I would *really* like that, Etta."

Chapter 22

Henry and Etta worked non-stop preparing for their meeting with Julius Parker. They walked into the kitchen almost simultaneously, but they didn't react as they'd done before when their similar thoughts and actions seemed synchronous. They were serious, focused, essentially ready to plan a brutal attack on a hated enemy.

The first thing Etta did was spend a moment with Marisol. "We're going to need lots of your strong coffee. We might get hungry later, Marisol, but I'll let you know."

"Alright, Etta. I'll make plenty of coffee and keep it fresh and hot. Will it bother you if I keep filling the cups."

"Oh no, we'll be so focused, we won't notice your presence."

"Very well, I'll be right back."

"I think," said Henry, "we should prepare for two things. First, we need a plan, one we can stick to, one that will help us set him up for a killing blow."

"How would you design that plan?"

"It seems to me that we'll almost want to lull him to sleep, make him feel comfortable with his superiority over us. We can play on his pride, probably. We're going to have to ask all of those silly, dumb, unimportant questions that lazy reporters ask."

"I know, and it makes me sick to even think about it," she said.

"Me too, but we have to do it.

"Henry, I think we have to make him believe we're on his side, that we'll write down everything he says." She paused, chewing on an idea. "If he has an ego, we need to feed it."

"Right," said Henry. "So, I suggest that we introduce ourselves first and paint a picture for him of two rookie, inexperienced reporters excited to be on their first important assignment. We should give him our resumes. You are a college graduate with a degree in English and Civics. But, and this will hook him I think, I'm just a high school graduate who wrote about school sports in the local newspaper."

"We'll ask him questions about himself, ones to get him bragging."

"Like, how long have you been in public service, or where did you study, or how long have you lived in Arizona?"

Etta smiled and nodded. "Then, since he'll likely ignore me as a woman reporter, I'll have to work on his vanity. I can ask, 'are you married?' If he says yes, I can ask who the lucky woman is. If he says no, I can reply, 'how sad for the women of Arizona,' then give him a little smile."

"If he gets fussy because of our pace, we can start on another level of questions, addressing his campaign plans and promises, his long-range plans, perhaps for higher office."

While they spoke, they each were jotting down notes, possible questions, even things to be cautious of saying.

"When we get to the next level, we could ask something like, what qualifications do you have for the U.S. House of Representatives?" said Etta.

"I thought of some things we need to watch out for," said Henry. "Like asking questions too quickly, although doing things that way might make him see our youthful exuberance and measure it against his mature strengths."

Etta's response was given coldly. "We need him to trust us, and to think he's smarter and wiser than we are."

"Without getting overconfident, we should wait for some mystical sign that it's time to hit him with the tough questions," said Henry.

"The ones about Uncle Stewart," he repeated.

"Right. This is where he might balk or even refuse to answer. When that happens, we can't quit. He'll have built up a trust in us and might even be confused or thrown off guard."

When they next reached for a sip of coffee, they each noticed that their cups were full and steaming and they hadn't even noticed Marisol's presence. The coffee was refreshing and their energy moved up a notch in intensity.

"When we get to that point, Etta, a point we both recognize as time to act or attack, we need a signal."

"What do you mean, Henry?"

"Something slight, simple, a signal."

"Like scratching your nose or," she paused, and a huge, face-wide grin appeared on her face. "Or you do what Cal does when he's getting serious."

"I put a pencil behind my ear."

"And if I think the time is right, I'll give you a nod."

For the next hour they separately organized their notes, sorting and rewriting, making sure the plan looked solid. Then Marisol appeared as if summoned and carried in a tray of sandwiches and another serving of coffee. The reporters stopped to fuel up then went to work, blending their two draft plans into a final version of how they would deal with Julius Parker. They took turns picking the questions and statements they wished to address. Most of their decisions seemed to settle naturally, while a few others took some discussion, some debate. But, by the time Marisol announced that Mr. Pearce had returned home and dinner was on the table. Etta and Henry were ready to quit for the day.

At a quarter to ten the next morning, the two rookie reporters, anxious in their youth and excited to be on their first real assignment, showed up early for the appointment at the Parker campaign headquarters. When they entered the large room they seemed in awe, but in reality, they were ready for war, one they knew they had to win.

He looked at Etta, and she gave a youthful nod. The reporters were met at the door by a young woman.

"Good morning," said Henry to the woman, "we, uh, have an appointment with Mr. Winston to, uh, talk to Mr. Parker."

The girl asked for their names, they responded boldly, hoping the change in tone would signal their lack of experience.

The girl checked her list of appointments and confirmed that Henry and Etta were expected. She asked them to follow her down a short hall. She opened a door and ushered them into a plush office—pictures of the candidate on the wall, carpeted floor, leather covered chairs and a massive desk.

"Mr. Parker and Mr. Winston are on a call to Washington, D.C. at the moment, but they'll be right with you." She asked them to take a seat and returned to the front of the office.

They thanked her and sat down. While they waited, the reporters looked through a large wall-to-wall window and watched the activity in the vast room, paying attention to the faces and attitudes of the young campaigners. Individually, Etta and Henry noted the stress and eagerness, the excitement and dread, wondering why those with negative states of mind continued to carry out their tasks. This observation, though probably not note-worthy or even significant, meant something to Etta and to Henry.

Perhaps ten minutes later, Parker led Winston into the room. Immediately, Henry stood up, Etta was right behind him.

"Ah," said Parker, "these must be our reporters. Good morning to you. I'm Julius Parker, and this is Mr. Winston, my campaign manager."

"I'm Henry Carter, sir. It's good to meet you." He looked at Winston and added, "Mr. Winston and I spoke on the telephone a few days ago."

Etta said, "I'm Etta Pearce."

While they shook hands, Parker seemed aloof, but ready to start talking. Winston watched them more closely, likely protecting himself, wanting to be sure the interview would go smoothly and his boss, the candidate, would be in a good mood when they finished.

"Well, we're glad you're here too, aren't we Winston?"

Still staring at the reporters, Winston remained silent, simply nodding in response to the question.

Seemingly embarrassed, Henry quickly covered his short experience as a reporter, then said to Parker, "we are thankful for your willingness to see us on short notice."

"Mr. Carter, I appreciate having the opportunity to address your questions. I've not yet been able to call on constituents in the southeast part of the state. Perhaps what we cover here today will end up in your article."

"I can assure you sir, that our readers will get a thorough report of today's meeting."

Winston moved behind Parker, so he'd have the same view of the reporters as his boss.

Parker turned toward Etta. "And you, Miss Pearce, are the first female reporter I've had the opportunity to meet."

Etta smiled, feigning embarrassment and looked down at her pad while she made a note.

Henry began by directing his questions, the ones they'd crafted and practiced the previous afternoon. Occasionally, Etta would interject one of her own as they worked their tactics, almost encouraging Parker to speak about himself, to paint a picture of civic duty, of patriotism, and virtue.

Feeling ready to move forward, Henry asked, "How long have you been in public service, Mr. Parker?"

"Most of my adult life, I think, Henry." Etta noticed the shift to his use of a first name and thought that they'd succeeded in letting him feel superior, in control.

Then, Etta asked him if he was married.

Parker's face automatically shifted to a sad look, almost as if he'd practiced it. "Well, Etta, I was married, once." He looked at her and added, "but my poor wife died in childbirth. It was a very trying time for me."

"How sad," she said. "But you're so young."

Parker's shift back to the interview was quick and well executed.

Henry realized that they'd reached the next level, so he asked, "What qualifications do you have for the U.S. House of Representatives?"

Parker moved quickly into his repertoire of well-rehearsed responses, so both Henry and Etta fed him similar questions for another quarter hour. They took notes, watched Parker's and Winston's expressions, and sensed that the politician was ready to end the interview. Henry looked up from his pad and put his pencil behind his ear. Out of the corner of his eye, he saw Etta nod.

"Mr. Parker, we came prepared to hear about your plans and get your position on the various issues and topics of concern. But the incident involving your opponent, or, rather, your late opponent leads us to ask a few related questions."

Winston started to say something, but Parker held up his hand. "Of course," he said, "go ahead."

"Now that you are running unopposed, are there any of Mr. Bradley's ideas or plans that you could—or would—adopt in order to win over his supporters?"

Parker sat back in his chair and seemed to be considering the question. "Mr. Bradley and I didn't see things in the same light, but I am disappointed that we didn't get to complete our competition. Did you have any particular issue, any position in mind?"

Etta spoke up, her voice calm, professional. "Certainly, Mr. Parker. In one of Mr. Bradley's recent speeches, he stated that he believed the country, and especially Arizona, needed to take a harder position on the illegal traffic in alcohol." She paused and looked at her notes. "He said just last week that we 'need to deal more harshly with the criminals who bring liquor into our cities. Bootleggers deserve the maximum punishment.' Do you agree with this?"

"Well, Miss Pearce, it has always been my position that the federal laws are strong enough. I most certainly won't spend time pushing legislation for laws that already exist."

Etta wanted to say, *"Will you enforce them?"* but she kept quiet.

Henry had another question. "Mr. Parker, Stewart Bradley also had proposed stronger punishment for gambling and prostitution."

"My answer would be the same on those issues. Again, we have federal laws and our state will uphold and enforce them."

Henry could see that Winston was growing nervous, and though he covered it well, so was Parker. He shifted to another topic.

"Sir, the death of anyone is often difficult to discuss. Certainly, now that our country is dealing with this flu epidemic there are still likely to be more deaths as a result."

Parker nodded.

"But for those who knew and supported Mr. Bradley, would you have any words of consolation? How, for instance, did his sudden death affect you.?"

"Of course I was saddened by his passing. As wonderful as running unopposed may seem, no one likes a good political fight any more than I do. I expected that our battle for the House seat would be well and fairly fought. I do feel sorry for his wife and have already tendered my condolences to her." He looked over his shoulder at Winston, who nodded his head.

Both Henry and Etta realized they were running out of time, so Etta said to Parker, "I have heard from some sources that there is discontent among your staff."

Winston spoke before Parker even opened his mouth. "That's absurd, Miss Pearce. We have a large group of people who are united in working to get Mr. Parker elected.

Any rumor otherwise is simply not true."

Parker added, "I think, Miss Pearce, that perhaps your sources are misinformed." He looked at his watch and then at Winston. "I do have another appointment in just a few minutes, so I want to thank you for dropping by. Perhaps we can meet again after the election."

Winston moved back around to where they sat and waited for the reporters to stand. Henry looked at Etta and they both rose from their chairs, shook hands with the men and walked out of the building.

As soon as the door closed, Winston turned to Parker and said, "There's something about their questions that makes me suspicious about their motives. I think I'll do some inquiries."

"Good idea, Winston."

After they'd watched the reporters drive away, Parker said, "I want you to get everyone together right now!"

"Charlie Nelson is in Tucson."

"I forgot," said Parker, "Just get him up here as soon as you can." Winston hurried out of the office.

"We better not have a spy in our group," Parker growled to himself.

In less than ten minutes, Winston had gathered the workers in the center of the vast room. Parker marched out of his office, clearly upset and definitely prepared to hurt someone. Absolutely all eyes were on him. Other than Winston, no one knew what the purpose of the meeting was. Yet not one of them—young or old, male or female—doubted that there was some kind of trouble.

Parker had left his genial politician self in his office and said to the gathering, "Someone in this group is talking too much to the wrong people. One of you is a traitor to the cause of my winning the election. One of you has broken the faith." He looked across the gathered workers, watching facial reactions to his accusation. "When I find out who you are, and I will find out, you will lose more than your job. The two reporters who were in here earlier described a campaign organization in disarray, a campaign organization that is... how did she say it, Winston... ahh, yes, *discontented*,"

A heavy blanket of fear seemed to cloak the room. No one moved, yet there was a feeling, almost a vibration evident.

"If you are the traitor to our quest, when I catch you, you will wish you'd never..." He stopped and glared at them, his face reddening. "You'll have nothing worth wishing for." Parker turned away from them, strode back to his office and slammed the door. Even his departure brought no relief to the gathering.

"Let's get back to work," said Winston. "We've still got an election to win."

"Not me!" growled one of the volunteers. "No one threatens me." He walked toward the exit with several others in his wake.

When the reporters drove away from Parker's office, they didn't speak. But they'd gone only a few blocks when Etta pulled over to the curb and turned off the engine. Still gripping the steering wheel, she took a deep breath and said, "That man murdered Stewart."

"Hold on, Etta. I agree with you that he is a despicable man, but we don't *know* that."

"He did it, Henry... or had it done." She turned and looked at him. "Henry, who had the most to gain from Stewart Bradley's death? Who had the power or the desire to actually get rid of him?"

"But, Etta, we can't just accuse him of something like that without proof." He looked at her and said, "It's like any story we write, Partner, we have to prove it."

"I'll prove it, Henry. I will. And I'm going to make sure everyone knows it."

Henry kept his eyes on her, he could feel her anger, but he also sensed the determination it bred.

"Alright, but you won't do this alone. Rushing into this won't bring Stewart back. We'll do it, but we'll do it right."

That afternoon, Parker called Riggs. The first two times, there was no response. He waited another hour and tried again.

"Who's this?"

Parker didn't recognize the voice. "I want to talk with Lou Riggs," he said.

"Ain't here."

"Well, if he *ain't* there, when will he be?"

At first, the silence was annoying, but when it dragged on for at least a minute, it began to frighten Parker.

"Do you know when Riggs will return?"

"*Mister* Riggs will be here tomorrow." The telephone went silent.

Around seven, Charlie Nelson, Winston's assistant, walked in the front door and looked around quickly for either Winston or Parker.

"Over here, Charlie."

Nelson spotted the campaign manager off to the left, sitting at one of the desks, gazing out at the street.

Charlie pulled his fedora off and hung it on a hook next to the coat rack. Still looking around for Parker, he pulled a chair up next to Winston and sat down.

"What's going on? Why did you need me to drop what I was doing in Tucson to get back here?"

"The boss is as mad as I've ever seen him."

"Mad about what?"

Winston filled him in on Parker's tirade about a spy. Then, having thought about the wisdom of keeping things to himself, decided to tell his one ally in the organization what he thought Parker was really upset about.

"Two reporters scheduled an interview for today. When they showed up, they seemed legitimate at first—

asked simple questions and took notes. But it didn't take long before they focused on the Bradley situation." He described the questions, Parker's responses and his own fears that they might suspect Parker was at fault for his opponent's death.

"Did they actually accuse him?"

"No, and there wasn't even a direct implication that he did anything."

"But Mr. Parker took it that way."

Winston nodded at Charlie's statement just as Parker came through the front door.

"Nelson," he said. "I'm glad you're here. Come into my office, we need to talk." He turned to his campaign manager and said, "Let's call it a night, Winston. You and the others can go home."

Nelson followed the candidate into the office and watched as Parker removed his coat, loosened his tie, and sat behind the desk.

"Winston fill you in?"

"Yes, sir, he did."

"Charlie, I'm going to need you to spend some time getting to know these two reporters. In a way, I'm glad you weren't here earlier, because they won't know you or anything about your part in the campaign."

"So, who are these reporters?"

Parker leaned forward. "Henry Carter, and get this, a woman reporter called Etta Pearce."

"Etta Pearce? Can you describe her?"

"She's tall and nice looking. She acts and dresses like those women they call flappers. You've seen a few of them around—short hair, short skirts. Why, when they left, *she* was driving the car."

"You said Etta Pearce."

Parker nodded.

"I know her, boss. Her father is William Pearce, a commodities broker here in Phoenix. He's a good friend of Stewart Bradley."

Stunned, Parker said, "I knew something was off about those reporters. So did Winston." Then he asked, "How well do you know her?"

"We went to college at the same time, and we hung out with the same crowd. Maybe a dozen of us, men and women. We found ways to have fun and not get in trouble with the professors or the administrators."

"So, you were just acquainted with her."

"Yes sir." He mused on this for a moment. "Never close, but always friendly."

"Tell me about her, Charlie, and I don't mean about her looks."

"Etta Pearce, at least the one I knew then, was smart, very smart. She was well-read on subjects most girls either didn't care about or were afraid of—politics, history, even philosophy." He scratched his chin and continued, "She was persistent, like a bulldog. She never quit." Charlie thought for a moment. "She was cold-blooded, boss."

Parker sat back in his chair. "What do you mean?"

"When she believed in something, she always fought for that belief and was willing to face-down anyone who disagreed with her."

Parker stood up and paced around the room for a bit.

"Charlie, I want you to set aside the job I had you working on in Tucson. I'll give it to Winston. I want you to follow Miss Pearce and Mr. Carter. See where they go, what they do. I'll have Winston find out where they're staying. They work for a Bisbee newspaper, so I assume they'll be at a lower priced hotel."

"I can do that, Boss. They may even be staying at the Pearce residence."

"Alright, but don't let her see you just yet. Keep out of sight but watch them. I'll be working on a way to deal with the two reporters. I know a man who can make this all go away."

The next day, Parker waited until early afternoon and

called Riggs. They made an appointment for four o'clock.

Precisely at four, Parker stood in front of Riggs.

"How's your worthy opponent these days?"

"You know how he is, Lou. And thank you for seeing that he is no longer a problem of ours."

Riggs took a moment to sip from a glass of caramel colored whiskey. A quick frown creased his brow. "So, what is it you want to talk about this afternoon?"

"I had an interview yesterday with two reporters from Bisbee. They asked a few of the usual questions but spent an inordinate amount of time focusing on Stewart Bradley and his death."

"Then, last night I learned that one of my staff is an old acquaintance of one of the reporters—a woman! He knew her in college and described her as smart, persistent, focused—in a word, nosy."

"So, what do you expect me to do?"

"I want—I would like for you to do to them what you did to Bradley."

"That won't happen, Parker. This time you will handle your own problem, and you will ensure that it doesn't ever become my problem. Never. Do you understand? Because if it does become something I need to deal with, you'll be spending a long, long time commiserating with your friend Stewart Bradley."

He picked up some papers from his desk, but Parker didn't move.

"Why are you still here?"

Chapter 23

CHARLIE NELSON WAS IN his rented room, relaxing with a glass of bootleg whiskey when someone tapped on the door. He set the glass behind a stack of old books and opened the door.

"Charlie," said the land lady, "there's a call for you."

"Okay," he said and followed her to the living room.

"This is Charlie."

"Parker here."

"Yes sir," he said, thinking it was strange that Parker would call him at home.

"Meet me at the office as soon as you can get here. We need to talk."

"I'll be there in fifteen minutes."

Nelson parked in the alley behind the building, then unlocked and entered through the back door. The only light in the building was coming from Parker's office.

Julius sat at his desk; a half-filled bottle of whiskey on the blotter. His vest was unbuttoned, his tie undone, and a well-chewed cigar hung from the corner of his mouth. He looked up at Charlie and pointed to the empty chair.

"What can I do for you, sir?" Parker refilled his empty glass and poured some in another glass. He slid it across the desk toward Nelson.

"Charlie, there's been a change of plans. Or perhaps, an enhancement to the original plans."

"Alright."

"What I'm going to tell you will be known only by the two of us. Absolutely no one must ever know of this. What we talk about, plan and do is exclusively ours to know."

"Absolutely, sir."

Parker had planned a small speech, chosen the right words he'd say to Nelson, but the anxiety and the whiskey had eliminated much of the smooth talk of a practiced politician.

"I told you to follow those reporters."

Nelson nodded. "Yes, sir, I will."

"Good." Parker looked at Charlie, all hesitation now gone and said, "We need to eliminate the problem."

"Sir?" Charlie heard Parker's words but wanted clarification on their meaning.

"These reporters, especially the woman are a serious problem and need to be eliminated."

"Eliminated, as in..." Charlie didn't want to say the word until he heard it from his boss.

"Let me put it this way, Charlie. I need to be elected and these two may have a way to stop that from happening. If I do get the House seat, I'll need someone here, in Arizona, to be my representative, my voice to the people. Understand?"

"I do."

"That person can be you if you help me get rid of the problem."

"I understand," he said.

"This also needs to happen in the next week, no later. I think getting rid of Pearce will keep Carter out of the way for a while. But she needs to be gone first and soon."

"I'll do it, Mr. Parker, you can count on me."

The bright sun was leaking through a gap in the curtain when a knock on her bedroom door woke Etta.

"Just a minute," she said as she rose from the bed and slipped a robe tightly around her. "Who is it?"

"It's me, Etta."

She opened the door, recognized Henry's warm face and invited him in.

"What time is it?"

"It's nearly nine, Partner." Henry felt odd standing in Etta's room.

"I didn't sleep well last night. Too much on my mind, I guess."

"It *has* been a couple of rough weeks for you."

"I think it's more about the last few days, really. What you said last night—about not rushing into anything—makes sense. But it took me a long time to convince myself to calm down."

"I understand your need for resolution, Etta."

That's one word for it, she thought, *revenge is more like it.*

"Have you eaten?" she asked.

"Hours ago. I've been on the telephone to your father. He's still with Gloria. I filled him in on yesterday and I called Adams."

"Why Adams?"

"I wanted to learn more about campaigns and how they work."

"Okay."

Henry moved toward the door. "I need to get over there now. I'll be back by lunch. So, I'll see you here around one o'clock."

Etta put the keys to her car in Henry's outstretched hand and closed the door behind him.

She washed up, got dressed, *like a real reporter,* she thought, and walked into the kitchen.

Charlie Nelson had seen the reporter, Carter, drive away nearly an hour before. He'd decided to keep watching for Etta from his car parked a half-block away. His patience paid off when she walked out of the house and waited at the curb until a cab pulled up. She got in the taxi, and he followed it until the driver pulled over in front of the *Sunshine Diner.*

Here we go, he thought. He waited a few minutes then went inside and sat at the counter.

* * *

Etta picked an empty table and sat down. The waitress came over with a pot of coffee and a cup. Etta looked up, said, "Please," and smiled when she poured the cup full.

"Menu?"

Etta nodded, looked quickly at the offerings and pointed at the "One Egg Breakfast."

While she waited for her meal, Etta wrote a few things in her notebook. She sensed people moving around her, some leaving their tables, others arriving and being seated.

She barely touched the meal—picked at the scrambled egg and nibbled on the toast—but drank three cups of coffee. When the waitress picked up the plate, a man appeared behind her. She recognized his face as he started to walk past her. Then he stopped, looked at her and smiled.

"Well, if it isn't Etta Pearce."

"Charlie? Charlie Nelson?"

Still smiling, he said, "What a surprise. Etta Pearce… I haven't seen you since, what? graduation?"

"I guess so." Nelson looked awkward standing next to the table, so she pointed to the empty chair. He sat down and took off his hat.

"Three years at least. What are you doing in Phoenix? I figured, no, we all figured you'd be in New York, telling those folks how to run the country by now."

"You and who else," she asked, a smile breaking out on her face.

"Every one of the Dining Hall Rangers, of course."

"You haven't changed much, Charlie," she said, realizing it was true. He hadn't. Nelson was still a handsome man and still thought a lot of himself.

They spent a few minutes discussing other members of the Rangers, then Nelson asked, "So Etta, why aren't you in New York? What are you doing these days?"

"I'm a reporter for the *Bisbee Daily Review*."

"A reporter, hmmm." He smiled and continued, "and I bet you're not reporting on fashions and weddings." The smile never left his face.

Etta wondered how much to tell him, then decided that he was likely harmless, the same as he'd been in school.

"I just finished working on an article about the murder of a rancher in New Mexico and I started looking into the Spanish Flu epidemic here in Phoenix. What do you do, Charlie?"

"Well, I'm currently managing a haberdashery, but I *was* working in politics."

"Politics?"

"Uh huh. I was one of the campaign staff for Julius Parker. He's running for the House in the coming election."

Etta's heart skipped, her mouth felt instantly desert dry. "Really? Politics?"

"Yeah, it's hard trying to convince someone to vote for a candidate you don't trust." He forced a frown on his face, letting his lips turn downward.

Etta leaned forward. "You said Parker?" He nodded, maintaining his stolid posture. "What's wrong with him that you don't trust him?"

He quickly glanced at his watch and said, "Oops, I'm late for an appointment and need to get going." He stood and put his hat on. "Tell you what. Where can I get in touch with you? I'd like to see you later and talk about Parker."

She gave him her telephone number and added, "Call me and let me know where we can meet, okay?"

Charlie Nelson smiled. *Hooked the big one,* he thought, and walked out of the diner.

When Henry got back to the house, Etta was waiting in the parlor. She told him about meeting Charlie Nelson but set his mind at ease when she finished. "I told him I wanted to talk some more about Parker. He seemed neutral about it; there was nothing about the conversation that was strange. When he calls, I'll set up an appointment for us to see him."

Henry told her that Adams said one of his workers had told him she had an acquaintance who worked for Parker's campaign. He said the girl's friend called and told her that Parker was pretty upset and even threatened them. Her friend almost quit."

"I think we rattled his cage," said, Etta.

"Yep," he said. "Oh, and Dr. Gilliam had left a message for me here."

"Why'd he call?"

"Apparently a Detective Malone wants to talk to me about Stewart Bradley."

"Are you going to see him?"

"This evening after six. He's still finishing up his report on another case."

"I'll go with you, Henry. That is, unless I hear from Nelson."

Henry didn't like the idea of her seeing him alone but knew that each of the leads had value. "Let's see how things fall, okay?"

At half past five, Henry drove Etta's car to the Phoenix Police Headquarters. Before he left, they'd agreed that Etta would try to hold off any meeting with her former classmate until Henry could participate. Etta agreed to go along with his concern.

But when Henry hadn't returned by eight o'clock, and Charlie Nelson called her, Etta had to take a chance.

"Alright, Charlie. Tomorrow would be better, but if this is the only time that works for you, I'll see you at the *J. Gaines Haberdashery* at nine tonight."

Etta asked Marisol to call for a taxi. While she was on the telephone, Etta wrote a note to Henry, giving the time, the address where she was going, and a short apology for leaving before he'd returned from seeing the police. She handed the note to the maid and said, "Be sure you watch for Mr. Carter and give this to him as soon as he arrives."

Since Nelson had asked her to meet late at night and in a less busy part of the city, Etta planned to be vigilant, watchful, and careful. She wasn't particularly worried about him—he seemed just like the nice guy she remembered from college. *But,* she thought as her taxi pulled up to the curb next to the haberdashery, *that doesn't mean I should be stupid*. After she paid the driver, she pulled her pistol out of her bag and slipped it into her coat pocket, then watched the cab move down the street.

When Henry came through the front door, Marisol said, "Excuse me, Mr. Carter. Miss Pearce asked me to give you this note as soon as you arrived."

Henry glanced quickly at the words and asked when she'd left.

"Not more than twenty minutes ago."

Henry asked her for a phone directory, found the listing for the shop and asked Marisol if she knew the directions. She thought about it for a moment, wrote something on a piece of paper and said, "That's about a ten-minute drive if you don't make any stops."

Henry ran out the door and got in the car. He tried to drive quickly and read the directions at the same time. The dark sky and distant streetlamps made it difficult to hurry. All the while, he grew angry at Etta for not waiting for him and, because he was afraid for her. The racing thoughts only slowed him down.

There was a light on in the men's store and a dim streetlamp on the corner a half-block away. Etta stepped up to the display window and peered between the brown-suited mannequin and a rack of hats, hoping to spot Charlie. Hearing someone walking up the sidewalk from the dark end of the street, she turned quickly.

"Etta, it's me," Nelson said, his voice a loud stage-whisper. "Sorry I'm late, I missed the streetcar."

Her heart pounding a bit, but her voice under control, she said, "That's okay, Charlie, I'm glad you're here."

He pulled a key from his vest pocket, unlocked the door and led Etta into the shop. They walked past a row of shelves stacked with folded dress shirts. When they reached the end of the room, Charlie opened a door and they entered what appeared to Etta, to be his office. A modest sized desk was set in front of a row of tall filing cabinets lining the wall. On the left was a table that served as a bar—a tray of short glasses sat in front of several bottles of high-priced whiskey.

"Would you like a drink before we talk," Nelson asked as he locked the door.

"Not yet," Etta said, "maybe after we've finished. But I'd prefer you unlocked the door."

Nelson ignored her, took off his fedora, and tossed it onto the desktop. Then he poured himself a drink. He gestured to a chair in front of the desk, asking Etta to take a seat.

"I'd rather stand," she said, "I've been sitting all day."

Etta *was* anxious to ask her questions; she needed the information Charlie claimed to have. *I guess reminiscing about old friends and experiences is a small price to pay,* she thought. but she didn't relax—the locked door bothered her. She chatted with him for the next few minutes, then reached into her bag for the notebook and pencil.

"I guess story time is over," Charlie chuckled. He rose from the chair and walked to the table, then poured another drink and added, "What is it you want to know about our representative?"

Just as Etta looked down at her notebook, Nelson grabbed her by the shoulders from behind and pulled her backwards, letting his whiskey glass fall to the floor.

Etta cried out, dropping the notebook and pencil as she extended her hands to break the fall. But Nelson didn't let go of her. Instead, he threw his left hand around her body and pulled her back against his chest. He slapped his right hand across Etta's face and clutched her jaw hoping to keep her from calling out. Even as she struggled, trying to break his hold on her, Etta remembered her gun.

Henry slowed down briefly as he turned onto the street where the shop was supposed to be. He looked at signs on the buildings, finally spotting the one that said *J. Gaines*. He parked the car, got out and rushed up to the door. The shop appeared to be closed, since the interior lights were off and the door rattled, locked tight. He moved back and forth across the front windows, trying to see if anyone was inside, but it was too dark. He did notice a thin bar of light beneath what must have been another door at the back of the shop.

Speaking into her left ear, Nelson growled, his teeth clenched, "You've been asking too many questions, Etta, and some very important, very angry people want you to stop."

As much as she wanted to break his hold on her, Etta decided to relax her body, just a bit, hoping to convince him she'd given up.

"That's much better," he said. "Now I have some questions for you." He kept a strong hold on her but relaxed his grip on her face. As he let his hand drop from her mouth, Etta quickly brought her right hand up and drove her long, sharp, crimson-polished nails into his face. She felt something pop and heard his scream. She broke free and spun around, Nelson was on the floor, covering the left side of his face. Blood streamed between his fingers.

"My eye," he howled. He reached around for the gun he'd put in his waistband. and struggled, trying to pull it free, but the hammer got hooked. "I'm gonna kill you."

Etta's heart pounded in her chest as she looked down

at the supine man. Without stopping to think, she pulled the small revolver from her pocket, pointed it at him and pulled the trigger. The gunshot was loud in the small room.

When the crack of the gunshot sounded, Henry moved quickly. He stood back from the front door and drove his foot, with all the strength he could muster, at the wood frame by the knob. The door now hung freely by its hinges, so he pushed his way in, calling out for Etta. He moved toward the second door, then broke through that door with another well-placed kick.

The room was still, as Etta stared at Nelson. But the momentary silence was quickly filled with the wailing screech that roared out of Nelson's mouth.

Henry rushed into the room, the pungent smell of both gunpowder and blood filled his nose. He glanced quickly around, searching for threats and spotted the pistol in Nelson's waist band. *He was going to kill Etta!* He reached down quickly, pulled the gun out, and slid it across the floor, out of Nelson's reach. Etta hadn't moved, her eyes focused on Nelson and the blood spreading out beneath him.

Henry stepped between Etta and the wounded man. He lifted her face up with his hand. A flood of tears ran down Etta's cheeks as she began to weep, deep churning sobs rose from her chest. He gently removed the gun from her hand and hugged her.

"It's okay, Etta. It's okay. Everything will be alright." Even though she probably couldn't hear him through her sobbing, and Nelson's howling, he kept it up until the cries became whimpers.

"What have I done?" she whispered, looking around the room. Her notebook and pencil and the empty whiskey glass all lay on the floor next to the wounded, groaning man.

"You did what you had to do, Etta. You stayed alive.

You did nothing wrong."

"But..."

"But nothing, Etta. He was going to kill you."

"Yes, but..." she whispered as she gasped, this time really seeing the blood on Nelson's face, even more of it pooling under his shoulder.

"He can't hurt you, Etta. He wanted to, he meant to, but he didn't."

Still holding on to Etta, Henry reached for the telephone on the desk and told the operator who answered to connect him with the police department.

"Police Department, Sergeant Collins."

"Sergeant, this is Henry Carter. I was with Detective Malone this afternoon, I need to talk to him immediately, this is an emergency."

"Hold one, let me connect you."

"Malone."

"Detective, this is Henry Carter. I need your help. My partner was just attacked by a man. She shot and wounded him."

Although it seemed like a long time to Henry, in less than three minutes two police officers came through the broken door. The younger one leaned down, checking Nelson's bloody shoulder. "Just wounded," he said to his partner. "But his face is a mess and it looks like he's gonna lose his eye."

The other cop had nudged the two reporters a few feet away from Nelson. "Did you make the call sir?"

"I did. My name is Henry Carter."

Nelson continued to groan and cry while the young policeman attended to his bleeding wounds.

"So, what happened here?" asked the older cop.

Henry saw that Etta's shock was wearing off. "Can my partner sit down, please?"

The policeman made a quick note about the overturned chair and then moved it over to the file cabinets.

Henry led Etta to the chair, sat her down and turned back to the officer. Henry spent a few minutes telling him about their investigation and why Etta had met with Nelson.

"Is Detective Malone coming?"

"He's on his way." The cop paused as he glanced around the room, noticing a gun on the desk and another on the floor.

"How'd he get shot?"

"This guy," Henry pointed at Nelson, "grabbed and held Miss Pearce. She tried to get away and scratched at his face. She said that made him fall. He threatened to kill her with his gun, then she pulled out her own gun and shot him. That's when I got here and tossed his gun over there."

While the officer wrote notes, Henry kept his eyes on Etta. She sat, slumped in the chair, her eyes on the bloody floor.

Nelson continued to groan and cry out. "It's not my fault… he made me do it… Parker made me do it."

Just then, two white-coated orderlies entered the room followed by Detective Malone. He acknowledged the uniformed officers and spoke to them as Henry walked over to Etta. She looked up at him, her eyes seemingly filled with questions.

"Don't worry, Etta," he said, resting his hand on her shoulder. "Just remember, he was going to kill you."

Malone leaned over Nelson and asked him, "Why'd you try to kill this woman?"

"I didn't want to," Nelson wailed. "Parker made me…."

Accompanied by the young policeman, the orderlies carried Nelson on a stretcher out of the room. The other cop continued writing notes, and Malone walked Henry and Etta out into the shop. He found some chairs near the counter and told them to sit down.

"So, here's where we stand, Miss Pearce."

Etta remained silent but looked directly at Malone.

"It's clear to me from what we've discovered here that Mr. Nelson intended to do you bodily harm. Based on the things he said while the orderlies worked on his wound, he was ordered to kill you by Mr. Julius Parker."

Henry watched as Etta nodded, still not speaking.

"Miss Pearce, I'll speak to the District Attorney, but I will recommend to him that you not be charged with any crime for defending yourself. Mr. Nelson will be charged with attempted murder. If and when we find Mr. Parker, he'll be held in jail and questioned as an accessory. Do you understand?"

"Yes," she whispered, "I do."

Turning to Henry, he said, "Mr. Carter, although there's nothing here to indicate that either Nelson or Parker had anything to do with poisoning Mr. Bradley, I think there's enough for us to investigate their probable roles in that murder." The detective looked at the two young reporters and said, "What you've experienced here was dangerous and nearly deadly. But it also led to finding the truth about one crime and gives us sufficient information that will likely lead to the truth about another."

Henry reached for Etta's hand and helped her rise from the chair. Then she shook hands with Malone.

"Miss Pearce, although you'll need to stay in Phoenix for a while, you are free to go." The detective escorted them to the door of the shop as the officers continued to document the scene. Henry helped Etta into the car and drove them to her father's house. As they walked up the steps, Pearce came out onto the porch and met them.

"Henry, a Detective Malone just phoned and asked that you call him."

"Thanks, Bill, did he say what it was about?"

Bill had put his arm around Etta and guided her into the house. Marisol was standing just inside the door and slowly led Etta toward her bedroom.

"Why would a detective be calling you, Henry?"

"One of Julius Parker's employees tried to kill Etta

tonight." Henry went on to describe the events of the evening and what he discovered when he kicked in the door at the back of the shop. "Etta did all she could to protect herself. She shot the man but didn't kill him." Henry ran his fingers through his hair and watched Etta disappear behind the bedroom door. "We had suspected Parker's role in Stewart's death and since Nelson—that's the guy that took Etta—worked for Parker we were convinced he did it or had it done."

"Henry, why don't you call the detective and see what he wants. I left the number by the telephone."

"Okay."

"And, Henry, thanks for saving my daughter's life tonight."

Henry looked at Bill and said, "Sir, she saved her own life. I was too late to do anything but console her."

When he reached Malone, the detective said that he had spoken with the District Attorney and that he wanted to meet all of them at the courthouse in the morning. Henry agreed and they set a time for the appointment.

At ten o'clock the next morning, Etta and Henry were ushered into the District Attorney's office. Detective Malone and the uniformed officer who had first showed up in the back of the men's shop were seated at a large conference table. The District Attorney took a seat at the head of the table and indicated that the two reporters should sit opposite of the policemen.

"Well, Miss Pearce, it seems that in protecting yourself, you have given us a very talkative witness to some highly criminal activities. Although the injuries you inflicted on Mr. Nelson are bad enough, and will result in much trouble for him, he has begun to give us some very interesting information."

Speaking to Henry, but looking at Etta, he said, "He's identified several prominent men in Phoenix who, according to him, are likely involved in the murder of Mr. Stewart

Bradley and perhaps other serious crimes.

Henry started to interrupt him, but the D.A. said, "We can't make any of this public yet, but... Miss Pearce you are still free to go, we just need you to stay in Phoenix for a few days while we sort this out."

Although Etta's voice was soft and a bit shaky, she managed to respond like a reporter. "Sir, do you think that as you learn more about this criminal activity in your investigation, given my role in this event you could grant *our* paper an exclusive on the story once you've put it all together? We'd certainly appreciate it."

"Of course, I'll have to clear it with the State's Attorney, but I'm sure they will try to accommodate you." He smiled and added, "after all, you, Mr. Carter, saved our brave citizen, and you, Miss Pearce encouraged our key witness to reveal plenty of damning information that should lead to some very evil people spending a long time in prison. Even more important, the citizens of Phoenix and the state of Arizona won't likely have a criminal representing them in Congress."

He gave them some additional instructions along with his card.

"You can reach me any time at this number if you remember anything else."

Out on the sidewalk next to Etta's car, he said, "Etta, I want you to know that I am proud of you. You were brave and didn't hesitate to do what your father taught you to do. Don't think for a moment that you did anything wrong.

"I didn't mean to shoot him..."

"I know you didn't, but you also did what you had to do to protect yourself. If you hadn't done it, we wouldn't be having this conversation."

Etta gave a tentative smile. "Well then, I think you should get me a cup of coffee to celebrate that fact."

Two days later, the Review reporters got the details of the event before any other newspapers. They learned that based on Charlie Nelson's testimony, Parker ordered him to kill Etta, so the candidate would be facing attempted murder charges alongside Nelson. When Parker was interrogated, he gave up the gangster. Riggs, in turn, identified the doctor, Willoughby, who had poisoned Stewart Bradley. When the police went to the doctor's office, they discovered he had taken his own life.

Chapter 24

A FEW WEEKS LATER, the news of Parker's arrest for his role in the attack on Etta and the murder of Stewart Bradley became public knowledge. The downfall of a politician was big news. The Phoenix police made sure that the credit for ridding society of violent criminals went to "the two intrepid reporters, Henry Carter and Etta Pearce of the *Bisbee Daily Review*."

The *Review* staff—Cal, Henry, and Etta—were sitting at the editor's desk, each reading articles from some of the big-city papers. Dallas, Chicago, and even Washington, D.C. had described the end of Parker's campaign. Perhaps reluctantly, they had included the *Review* reporters in their articles and gave praise as well to "news reporters everywhere."

"Well," Cal gloated, "you two have put our paper in the limelight. The mine manager has decided you both deserve raises—modest, of course, and I've been patted on the back for my brilliance in hiring good people."

"A raise," Etta chuckled, "anything they give me is a raise since I'm paying my own way."

Henry laughed with them, but his thoughts were elsewhere.

Langley was about to reply when a messenger from Western Union delivered a telegram. Cal opened the envelope, glanced at the wire, and handed it to Etta.

"Me?"

"It's addressed to you and Henry, but I think you should read it first."

Etta read it out loud.

"Please consider this wire as a formal offer of full-time employment for each of you at the *Arizona Republican*. Although pay is negotiable, we are offering two times whatever you are currently earning. Having now read your previous articles regarding the past year's deportations, the murder conspiracy in New Mexico, and of course, the whole Parker affair, I'm convinced that we need your expertise and diligence on our team. Please advise soonest."

Etta added, "It's signed by my old boss, Frederick Sidney. "Well, I can say that I'm *not* interested, Cal. That crowd, especially Mr. Sidney, wouldn't let us have free reign to follow stories." She paused, looking directly at Henry. "They'd pick the stories *and* tell us what to write. No thank you."

Henry simply shook his head, slowly, back and forth. He looked at his friends and said, "Where else would we be able to follow leads, investigate what we believe is important, and follow the trail to the end? Why would we want a big paycheck if we aren't free to find the truth?"

He stood up and began pacing. "Isn't it our duty to always report the whole story, the truth no matter the cost?"

"It is, Henry," said Etta. "That's what we do. Even if other newspapers ignore the truth, or push it aside for convenience or selfishness, or even to protect themselves, we don't have to. In fact, we can't."

Cal's dumbfounded look turned quickly into pride. These two young people embodied, in his judgment, the perfect example of what writing news is all about—truth over self, truth over wealth. *Henry was right,* he thought, *truth no matter the cost.*

"So?" he asked.

Etta looked at Henry through silver-lined eyes. His response was, "Well, Partner, we'd better get out and start looking for another story."

"Wait a minute, Henry. I... *we* already have another story." Etta cast a quick glance at Cal, then stared at Henry.

"The Spanish Flu."

The words hung in the air for a moment.

Etta said, "There's a lot more to discover before we can write this story."

"Let's get out of here for a while and get some lunch," Cal said.

The three journalists walked down the stairs and out the door. When it had closed behind them, they stood still on the sidewalk. This was their town, their home, and it felt good to be here.

Etta had her new house, Cal had his friends, his reporters back where he could see them work. Henry had his family.

"Let's really have lunch, "Cal said. "I'm treating at the Copper Queen!"

The two reporters immediately agreed, and the group headed across the street in the direction of the hotel.

They sat at a table in a quiet corner of the vast dining room. While they perused the menus, Cal chuckled softly.

"Something funny, Boss?" asked Henry.

"I suppose 'funny' describes it. Do you realize, Henry, that this menu hasn't changed much in the twenty years I've lived here?"

Henry looked at his menu and nodded in agreement. "You're right, although I haven't dined here as frequently as you have."

"Then," said Etta, "making a decision about what to have shouldn't be a challenge, even for the three best journalists in Bisbee."

"Excuse me, Etta, but that would be the *only* journalists in Bisbee."

"Yet, still the best," said Cal.

The waiter took their orders and provided cold water from an ice-filled pitcher.

Throughout their meal, they talked about interesting, though not necessarily important things. Perhaps it had been an unspoken plan to avoid shoptalk, to save that for the office. In any case, when they finished lunch and Cal paid the bill, they headed back to the *Review* building.

When they reached the second floor, Henry and Etta headed toward their tiny office.

"I still think we need to get a partners desk, Henry."

"I don't think we'll find one here in Bisbee, though."

"You're right. Maybe we ought to check the *Sears Catalogue*. They seem to have everything else."

"Alright, you two. Let's get to work."

Bert came up the stairs from the pressroom and dropped the day's mail into Cal's in-box. He pointed to the envelope on the top of the pile. Cal picked it up and glanced toward the closet office. The letter Bert had indicated was addressed to Henry.

Cal rose from his chair and carried the letter to the small office. Henry sat behind the desk and Etta was seated just inside the door.

"This just came for you, Henry," Cal said as he handed the envelope to him.

Henry glanced at the piece of mail quickly, then more slowly as he looked at the sender.

"It's from the Selective Service Department."

Cal didn't reply.

Etta looked at him and then focused on Henry.

"Should I open it?"

"Probably," said Cal.

"It's okay, Henry, you won't know what it says until you read it." Etta's voice was calm, almost comforting.

Henry took the penknife from his vest pocket and slowly slit the envelope open. Pinching the folded letter, he pulled it out and unfolded it, then laid it on the desk, face-up and smoothed out the folds.

Henry swallowed, and read aloud, "Greetings, you are hereby ordered for induction into the Armed Forces of the United States and to report for forwarding to the Armed Forces Induction Station at..."

Henry stopped reading and looked at Etta, then at Cal.

"I've been drafted."

"When do you have to report?" asked Cal.

"In a few weeks—Monday November 11th.

"Well, Henry," said Etta, "you don't have to pack tonight and rush to the depot, so let's take a while to consider how this change will affect what we need to do for our jobs." She looked at Cal and said, "I could sure use a grown-up drink."

"Me too," said Henry.

Cal returned to his desk and pulled the bottle of whiskey from his deep desk drawer. He found two glasses and an empty coffee cup, poured healthy shots into each of them and called out to the reporters.

"Why don't you two come out of that closet. We'll need some elbow room to deal with this untimely news."

Etta and Henry stood next to Cal's desk and took the whiskey he offered to them.

"I'm not sure who needs the cup more; me or you, Henry."

Etta said, "I'll take it."

That generated a weak laugh from the men.

Cal said, "Then I propose a toast to Henry Carter, my best friend, May the war end soon, thereby making this order to report for duty ineffective."

"And," added Etta quickly, "may he be safeguarded by God even if the war continues."

Henry looked at his friends. "And may I toast to the two best friends *any* man could *ever* have."

When they'd drained their glasses, no one spoke, no one moved, it seemed as though no one even breathed. The only motion was in their eyes, and that created no noise.

Almost in unison, all three of them seemed to come out of their shock and began to speak, their voices overlapping. This time, however, there was no laughter. An attitude of determination was evident on each face and in each voice.

Etta said, "Whoa, whoa, whoa. One at a time, please, and I'll take notes."

Henry spoke first. "Whatever ideas we come up with, whatever plans we make, I want it understood that I *will* report for induction. It's my duty as an American and I will not shirk that duty." He waited for a response, then getting none, he added, "Understood?"

Cal and Etta each nodded, then Cal suggested that they sit down and discuss their thoughts and ideas.

"You first, Cal," said Etta.

"Okay, some of these ideas may not work, or seem strange, but they're only ideas that came to me since I saw the letter." He sat in the chair behind his desk and took the pencil from behind his ear.

"I think I should talk to Thad Samson. He's the chairman of the Draft Board as well as president of the bank. I want to find out if he could get the Draft Board to grant Henry a thirty-day delay. This might give us more time to construct a strong plan for the rest of the year."

"Makes sense," said Henry, "But how likely is it to succeed?"

"We won't know until we ask?"

Finishing her note, Etta said, "I like it, even if it's only temporary."

"Next, I want to talk to the Mine management team. They are currently feeling pretty pleased with both of you. Your actions in Phoenix got national press and the various articles by other papers all mentioned mine ownership of the *Review*. Their role in providing copper for the war effort might add some weight to a request for a delay in Henry's induction."

"Anything else, Cal?"

"Not at the moment, Etta. What have you got?"

"I'm thinking that we might shoot for more than just a delay. If we could get the order for induction cancelled *for the good of the nation* or, if not cancelled, at least delayed for six months or more it would be better than a temporary delay. Of course, the cancellation shouldn't void Henry's position of honoring his duty, which I totally support."

Henry asked, "How could we get a delay of that magnitude?"

"I was thinking I could call Daniel Foster again and see if he'd be willing to go to his boss—President Wilson—and suggest that what Henry did for the country in helping catch a murderer, and preventing that murderer from being elected to Congress, could make a good talking point for Wilson."

"Any other ideas, Etta?"

"I have a few more, Cal. I'm sure my father would be willing to get his and Uncle Stewart's contacts in Phoenix to endorse a delay. Also, I think Gloria would be willing to stand up for Henry."

"Hold on a minute," said Henry. "Etta, I didn't do any of these things alone. You were involved in all of them."

"That's true, but my involvement shouldn't dilute any credit *you* earned."

While Etta finished summarizing her notes, Cal watched Henry, noting the young man's determination not to lose his integrity.

When Etta looked up, Cal said, "Alright, I'll go see Thad now and call the mine president when I get back."

"And I will probably have to send Daniel Foster a wire to set up a call. But I can telephone my father and Aunt Gloria and bounce some ideas off them yet this afternoon."

"I see no issues of concern in the plans right now," said Henry. "But please, we need to be honest, we need to be true in what we do and in what we ask. Okay?"

"Okay," said Etta.

"Yes, okay," added Cal.

For the next ten days, Cal and Etta kept up with their contacts by wire and telephone. By election day, November 5th, it was clear that the President wasn't going to say anything about the arrest of a member of his own party. He did indicate to Foster, though, that he thought Henry was a brave man and would make a fine soldier. Thad Samson was told that it would take the Selective Service department at least thirty days just to consider a delay and it was, even then, unlikely to be approved.

The mine management team happily forwarded the request for a delay to Selective Service, as did the friends of Bill Pearce and Gloria Bradley, but the response they received from the government was the same as what Thad had received.

On November tenth, Henry boarded the train for his trip to Fort Bliss. He'd provided documents to both Cal and Etta that gave them authority to deal with any issues related to his limited personal property. As the three of them stood on the platform in Bisbee next to the chugging engine of the train they disregarded the noise.

Cal shook Henry's hand and gave him a hug. "Be strong and true, son and we'll see you when you get back." Cal couldn't hide the tears in his eyes and those that ran down his cheeks and he didn't try to hide them either.

"I will, Cal. You can count on it."

Henry turned to Etta and stuck out his hand as if to shake hers. She ignored the hand and wrapped her arms around Henry. She couldn't hide her tears either.

Henry whispered in her ear, unable to break the hug. "I really like you, Etta. I care about you."

Etta released Henry but put her hands on his shoulders and looked deep into his eyes."

"You come back to me, Henry Carter. Promise me."

"I promise, Etta."

"Good, because I love you."

Henry gently kissed Etta on the forehead and whispered, "I love you, too."

At eight the next morning, Henry reported to the induction center at Fort Bliss, Texas. As he handed his letter to the soldier behind the counter, he was advised that earlier this morning, at three o'clock Texas time, which, he said was eleven o'clock in France, the Allies and the Central Powers had announced an armistice.

"You're lucky Mr. Carter. The war is over and there's a thirty-day delay in inductions until further notice."

Epilogue

CAL CALLED HENRY AND Etta into a meeting with the Mine management about a week after Henry returned from Texas. They didn't have a clue why they were there, and Henry wondered if he was finally going to be punished for his pursuit of the truth about the deportation of the miners that had happened what seemed like so long ago. Mr. Greenway, the President of Calumet Mining, the owner of the mine in Bisbee and, of course the owner of the *Bisbee Daily Review* called the meeting to order.

"This special meeting has been called to deal with some changes in one of our departments. A gentleman who has been part of our organization for nearly twenty years has decided to retire. His contributions to our success and notoriety led, without question, to Calumet's and Bisbee's quality of life and place in this wonderful country in which we reside and do our business.

"Calvin Langley was hired as a part-time reporter and began to show his skills in the newspaper business within days of his being hired. Throughout his career as a reporter, editor and ultimately managing editor of the Review, he has been ever loyal to the organization and to his trade. In the last month or so, he has elevated the reputation of the review to a national level, in large part because of the people he hired to report the news. These folks are with us today."

Greenway gestured toward Etta and Henry.

"Henry Carter and Henrietta Pearce were working on a story of national importance in Phoenix last month that ultimately, as a result of their investigation, solved the murder of a candidate for the House of Representatives of the United States and prevented the man who conspired in that murder from being elected to that high office. We supported Mr. Bradley, and the diligence of Miss Pearce and Mr. Carter showed that they understood the power of the press and the value of telling the truth.

"Therefore, with the eminent retirement of Mr. Langley, I am hereby promoting both of these fine employees and great reporters to Co-Editors of the *Bisbee Daily Review*. Would you all stand and give these three folks a round of applause."

Now, in the upstairs office of the *Bisbee Daily Review*, Henry Carter and Etta Pearce, Co-Editors of the newspaper, sat on each side of the elegant partners desk that had been recently donated to the newspaper by Mr. William Pearce of Phoenix. He thought it only proper that the paper's excellent reporters' role in solving the murder of his friend and in identifying his killers be rewarded.

Henry and Etta glanced at one another across the desk, saddened by Cal's retirement, but happy for him. Ever doubtful of their capabilities as editors, they struggled with coming to terms with the changes in their lives.

On the day he left town, Cal said to them, "Each of you represents the best of American journalism, hard work, and loyalty. I'm proud to have worked with you and will always, *always* consider you my family. So, to use Old Testament terms, go ye therefore and always tell the truth. I love you both."

Then he got on the train and left for Chicago or New York or Philadelphia and said he'd let them know where he ended up.

"I sure hope we never let him down, Henry."

"I'd die before I let Cal down, Etta."

Etta smiled and said, "I guess we'd better get to work."

"Yep," said Henry as he put a pencil behind his ear.

Author's Notes

Just as my previous novel, *No Place That Far,* was a spin-off of its predecessor, *Death in the Black Patch,* this work is also a spin-off rather than a sequel. In the course of my writing career, I've realized that there are some characters I've created that I just can't release to the nothingness in the world.

For all of their assistance in providing background for *Muckrakers 1917,* I'd like to thank Jerry Lebdill, author of *Last Train to El Paso,* and Ida Foster Campbell and Alice Foster Hill, co-authors of *Triumph and Tragedy A History of Thomas Lyons and the LCs,* for information on the Thomas Lyons murder.

For the fantastic cover art, all of the credit goes to my friend, Fred Barraza of Silver City, New Mexico.

For her continued devotion to my desire for writing, my life-long thanks go to my wife Mary. Her diligence, her sometimes ardent, but always deeply felt convictions and suggestions have made me a better writer. But, mostly, I am grateful for her love.

About the Author

Bruce Wilson is an adjunct Assistant Professor of History at Western New Mexico University. He earned a BA in Business Administration at Cal-State Fullerton in 1968 and his Master's Degree in English and History in 2010 at WNMU. A life-long student of American History, once he retired from corporate America, he melded his interest in history with his skills as a wordsmith and created three historical fiction novels. The first two (*Death in the Blackpatch* and *No Place That Far)* won several literary awards upon their publication. Recently, he joined his two younger brothers in publishing an anthology of their short stories (*Brotherhood: Stories by the Wilson Boys*).